All characters in this book are figments of my imagination and any similarity to persons, living or deceased, is purely coincidental.

No portion of this book may be copied, reproduced, or transmitted, in any form without permission from the author; except by a reviewer who may quote brief passages in a review to be printed in a newspaper, magazine, or journal.

First Printing

© 2015 by J. Cherbonneau

****

To Kathy,

My Sunshine from Florida!

Dedication

This story is dedicated to those who are lost and missing; dead or alive.

These individuals, who no one searched for, their reports were not splashed across avenues of the media. The people who achieved this coverage were

'Only The Pretty Ones'

Jane Charbonneau

****

PROLOGUE

"You have no fucking idea who I am, do you?" ZenJa asked the man who had already wet himself.

"No, ZenJa...who are you?" the man screamed while he looked down the barrel of one serious weapon.

"My name is FBI Agent ZenJa Beckwith, ass hole and I'm going to blow your fucking brains out of your head!"

"Let me explain! We never meant to kill all those girls!" he cried.

"What do you mean...we and all those girls? You never meant to kill those girls?" ZenJa asked; shocked at the statement that was spewing from the lips of a one time keeper of the peace.

"Please ZenJa...let me explain! Please don't kill me! If I tell you what happened, will you let me live?"

"Of course. I'm not about to become a murderer myself!" she declared, training her Glock on the intended target.

"Are you talking about Constance and Morgan?" ZenJa asked; confused by the instant developments that were unfolding; the man obviously under the impression ZenJa knew more than she did.

"Those were the two murders that were investigated, ZenJa. No one investigated the disappearances of the other girls from the area; one being your sister, Zippy. The ones that the we had to solve; we sought answers for were Constance and Morgan because their families had money, the heat was coming down, and they were the pretty ones."

"An innocent man sits in prison, you bastard, for these crimes you and God only knows who else committed the kidnaping, rapes, and murders of these girls and God only knows how many others!" she screamed in a fearless rage.

"Just get the fuck out of the car! I don't want to muss the interior of your fancy Dodge Viper by splattering your brains all over the dash. It'll reduce its resale value," she said forcing the man from the sports car but before she pulled the trigger, a man appeared and told her it wasn't worth it *and to leave the man on a lonesome road in the back woods of New Hampshire and he would take care of it. Moments after ZenJa left the scene, and a single shot rang out on that deserted back road.*

"What in the fucking hell! Shit! That asshole wasn't the only one responsible and involved in the Longberry murders," the lovely young lady exclaimed, ever so sadly, and steered her Dodge Charger toward her home at Sanders Bay, on Lake Winnipesaukee and opened her cell phone to make a call.

ZenJa Beckwith woke in a cold sweat, reliving a nightmare *similar* to the one she had already lived.

Chapter 1

"Thanks for the ride, Chief Connors," Zippy Beckwith and Olive, *Pickles,* Pickering said and waved goodbye to Longberry, New Hampshire's distinguished police chief, after he left them off at Molly's Market Place; the only local convenience store, café, and gas station in the small town; with a population of slightly over twenty-five hundred residents.

"You girls be careful, now," Chief Connors yelled after the girls and clicked on the siren inside the silver Ford Crown Victoria and waved while the two best friends ran up the steps and entered Molly's Market Place for an ice cream sundae.

"Why did you accept a ride with Chief Connors?" Zippy asked her twelve year old friend, once the girls settled onto two metal stools at the end of the café's counter. "He gives me the creeps."

"Oh, come on, Zip. It beats walking in this heat," Pickles continued, wiping the dust and dirt off her face, glasses, and shirt.

"Who gives you the creeps?" Molly, the proprietor/waitress asked the young ladies at her counter.

"Oh, nothing, Molly; Zippy's just spouting off about Chief Connors. She thinks he's creepy."

"Good Lord, girls. I've known Bob since we went to high school together, a hundred years ago. He may act a little weird, at times, but he's harmless."

"Now, what can I get you, young ladies, besides big glasses of iced water. You look pathetic."

"Thanks, Molly. We love to come here to this fine establishment to be insulted. We have little enough self-confidence as it is so we don't need you knocking us down even more," Zippy commented with a smirk on her face.

"You know I'm only kidding with you girls, but you do look thirsty."

"We'll have two Banana Splits and yes, we'll take the iced water, please and because we won't need to pay for soda, we can leave you a tip, Molly." Zippy continued.

"We're not leaving her any tip!" Pickles whispered.

"No, of course we're not! She doesn't deserve one after that comment she made, but we can mix some sugar in the salt shaker; just for fun," Zippy said while unscrewing the caps of each container and continuing to complete her innocent prank.

"Here you go, ladies," Molly said while setting down their dishes of ice cream and glasses of water on the counter. "Enjoy!" she continued and walked to the other end of the counter to wait on another customer.

"Who's that?" Pickles asked her friend; eyeing the stranger who had entered the café; the stranger Molly was handing a simple lunch menu to and neatly arranged a place-mat with napkin and silverware.

"I don't know," Zippy answered sipping some of her iced water. "But he sure has a nice new red Mustang."

"I wonder how fast it goes and maybe he'd give us a ride." Pickles murmured.

"Are you crazy? We don't know shit about him. You can ask him for a ride if you want, but I'll walk, thank you. Didn't your mama tell you not to take rides from strangers?"

"We rode with Chief Connors," Pickles reminded her friend and continued to eat her ice cream.

"Yeah! And that freaked me out enough."

"You gotta live a little, Zippy. Do you plan on staying in this Godforsaken town forever?"

"If I leave this town, I don't want it to leave in a wooden box."

"Oh, you're so immature, Zippy' I'm looking for adventure."

A few moments later, after the girls discussed their plans for summer vacation that was about to start in a week and other trivial gossip, Zippy kicked her friend, and said, "Come on, Olive, I'm going to walk you home and then I'm heading home, too. We have homework to do, you know."

"Molly, can we have our bill please?" the teen asked while standing at the register, beside the Mustang driving stranger.

"Be right there, Pickles," Molly hollered from the kitchen.

Before Molly brought the pre-teens their bill another tall, dark stranger, wearing blue jeans, a black tee shirt, wearing a Boston Red Sox baseball cap and sun glasses entered the establishment and seated himself in a booth, accessing a view of the front parking lot by the bay window. His loaded weapon, a 9mm Glock was safely hidden in a shoulder holster, beneath his leather jacket.

"Molly! You have another customer," Zippy yelled toward the kitchen.

"Okay! Okay! Goodness gracious, this is a busy place today," she hollered while scurrying around the kitchen.

The newer arrival, reached out and helped himself to a menu; his eyes quickly glancing over the interior of the small café; not missing anything.

"Hello ladies," said the Mustang driving, tall, dark haired twenty-something year old stranger. Before either girl responded, the man left his perch on a stool near the cash register, nodded, and asked, "I gather your name is Pickles?"

Without shame, this stranger looked at the long legged, mousy brown-haired, awkward twelve year old, who continued to adjust her eye glasses and hide the braces she had on her teeth.

"Yes, I'm Pickles and this is my friend..."

"You'll be a real looker when you get matured; if you know what I mean," he said cupping his hands in front of his shirt to assimilate a woman's breasts. "And when you loose the glasses, and get a nose job. You two aren't really ugly, but you both could use some improvement," the man continued and snickered.

"Her name isn't Pickles and what my name is none of your business, Mister and no one gives a rat's ass if you think we're pretty or not," Zippy spat and threw down three one dollar bills and dragged her friend from the café.

"I can take your order now, mister," Molly began and paused. "Where did the girls go?" Molly asked the first stranger.

"Oh, they left you this ten dollar bill and *Pickles* told you to keep the change," the man said; closed his wallet; eyeing the newcomer suspiciously; and left the café without placing an order.

"Well, thank you, mister. That was mighty nice of *them* ," she said, tucking the bill into her bra and putting the remaining singles into the cash register. "You come on back, now," she hollered when the screen door slammed shut behind the man.

"Come on you idiot!" Zippy yelled to her friend. "Look! He's coming outside. Don't even think about taking a ride with him."

"I'm not going to! You think I'm that stupid?" she spewed in disgust. "I haven't forgotten about those two young girls, Ashley and Rose-Ann, who disappeared a few years ago from up north," Olive replied.

"Okay! Just so you know...we're walking home."

The bright red Ford Mustang peeled out from Molly's Market Place and headed down the highway; in the opposite direction in which the young girls were walking.

The second male stranger exited the booth he occupied and left the Café, also without placing an order. He quickly entered his brand new black Chevy Camaro and sped off after stranger, number one.

"What the hell?" Molly exclaimed. "Is there a sign out front that says, get a free glass of water at Molly's and then leave'?" she asked the cook who chuckled into his apron, hoping not to raise Molly's ire any further.

The girls walked toward their homes and their conversation was directed toward a certain boy at school who had been flirting with them, in recent weeks, before school ended for the summer.

"What do you think of Ivan Sweeney?" Olive asked her friend. "He seems to like us," she added.

"I think his last name should be Swiney. He gives me the creeps and reminds me of a pig."

"Why do you say that?" Olive asked while the girls continued down the road to their houses.

"Oh, I don't know. He's a Senior in high school, this year, and I think he smokes and drinks and I just think he's a perv," Zippy explained.

"Yes, I agree, but it doesn't hurt to do some innocent flirting, Zippy. You don't want to grow up to be a spinster do you?"

"Why do you think he picked us to flirt with?" Olive asked.

"I don't know. There certainly are prettier girls than us at school."

"Maybe he wants to date girls who have brains," Olive offered. "Some people aren't focused on looks, all the time."

"Yeah, right!" Zippy replied sarcastically and laughed. "You know that isn't true and make sure you ignore Ivan and don't tell anyone he's been flirting with us; I'd die of embarrassment if someone found out about that jerk."

"Oh shut up and go home," Olive replied when they neared their first destination.

Three miles from the café, Zippy left her friend at her home and walked another quarter mile to her own home to finish her homework.

Olive, *Pickles,* Pickering was never seen again; from that day on June 1st.

Chapter 2

"Can you give me a description of the stranger that was here at the café, yesterday afternoon, Molly?" Chief Connors asked the proprietor of the small market complex in Longberry, New Hampshire, on the 2nd of June.

"Oh, this is terrible! Do you really think *Pickles* is missing, Chief? Maybe she just stayed overnight at a friend's house," Molly blabbered, wishing against all odds that this was a simple misunderstanding.

"Molly, we don't know anything at this point. We're just trying to find the girl and someone mentioned a stranger was here in the café yesterday."

"That would be Zippy. She and Pickles were here having ice cream sundaes and this guy came in to get some lunch, but now to think of it, he never did order anything and he left right after the girls left, Chief."

"I know that, Molly. What can you tell me about the guy. Give me a description."

"Actually, Chief, there were two strangers who came into the Café yesterday. Both were similar in appearance; tall, wore blue jeans, tee shirts and one wore a Boston Red Sox baseball cap and sunglasses.

"Okay, Molly, start with the first stranger."

"He drove a bright red Mustang. It looked pretty new. I didn't notice what license plate he had on it, whether it was from New Hampshire or not."

"What did he look like?" Chief Connors asked in an effort to hide his frustration with this witness and her vague responses.

"He was about six feet, three inches tall. He had a full head of jet black hair, nice blue eyes and a slim build. I would say he was about twenty five years old and wore blue jeans and clean white t-shirt...short sleeved. He also was carrying a black leather jacket and wore boots."

"You noticed a lot about him, Molly," Connors replied, complimenting the sixty year old woman on her observation skills.

"Well, Bob, we don't get many good looking, young guys in here and it was nice to rest these weary eyes on this handsome dude, if you must know."

"Okay, now describe the second man."

"He came inside a while after the first guy. He was about the same age as the first guy. He had on blue jeans, a black tee shirt, and wore the sunglasses and baseball cap. He also had on a black leather jacket. I didn't really notice what vehicle he drove, but I think it was black," Molly replied, struggling to jog her memory of the facts as she remembered them.

"You didn't notice what the license plate was or what state it was from, did you?"

"No, Bob, I didn't," she replied sadly.

"Thanks for your help, Molly and if you think of anything else, give me a call."

"I will Bob and I pray they find this little urchin soon."

"Me, too! Bob Connors replied before driving off in his squad car, heading toward River View Middle School.

"Is there anything else you can tell me, Zippy, about the time you spent with Olive, yesterday?" Chief Connors asked the visibly upset pre-teen who sat in the Principal's office, surrounded by her parents, home room teacher and Assistant Principal Jackson Miller.

"I told you all I know this morning. We went to school, as always, and then after school we started walking toward Molly's Café and you gave us a ride the rest of the way. We had ice cream sundaes and water," she replied not hiding the fact that she despised the officer who was questioning her.

"Who was in the café when you got there?"

"Only Molly, the cook and some strangers walked in, after we got there," she continued with tears flowing down her cheeks into the Kleenex she held in her hands.

"Can you describe the strangers?" Assistant Principal Miller asked.

"I got this, Miller. Your brother's the cop, not you," Connors curtly responded.

"Sorry...I was just trying to help."

"So, Zippy...can you describe the strangers?"

"They were both older... must have been twenty five," she acknowledged, those questioning her realized she would have considered anyone more than fifteen, as being old. "They were both tall; had black hair; and one drove a red Mustang...and oh yeah...he heard Molly call Pickles by her nick name and he spoke to her. He was kinda flirting with her."

"The other guy wore jeans, like the first guy and he drove a spiffy black Camaro."

"So, they didn't come into the Café together?"

"No, they came in separate cars."

"Did they appear to know each other?"

"I don't think so. They didn't speak to each other."

"Anything else?"

"The guy with the red Mustang said he bet Pickles would be pretty without her glasses and once she got her braces off her teeth, got some boobs and a nose job. He was a pig and I told her so."

On the 2nd day of June, Zippy Beckwith was never seen or heard from, again.

Chapter 3

Molly and several of the café's regular patrons scanned copies of the Daily Reporter; what Longberry's residents jokingly referred to as their version of the Boston Globe; the following morning after the disappearances of Olive Pickering and Zippy Beckwith.

"My God! This is horrible. Wasn't it only a few years ago two other girls went missing from the area? What in hell...do we have a serial killer here in the state?" Molly asked; the local folks nodding in agreement.

"Molly, no one has said Olive or Zippy are dead, you know," Chief Connors cautioned the owner.

"I know, that Bob, but if I may be so bold to ask, why in hell are you sitting here eating your pancakes, sausages and drinking your third cup of coffee while those two girls are missing? Haven't you got anything better to do than stuff your face...like find them?" Molly asked sarcastically.

"Yeah, Bob, this isn't a joke, you know. Our kids aren't safe in this God forsaken town. Get your ass off that stool and get outside to search for the girls!" a local mother screeched at the law enforcement officer. "All our friends and neighbors out scouring the area for them and I just stopped by to get some coffee, but I'm going right back out looking." How about you, Chief?"

"I just so happen to be waiting here for Officer Miller and the state police are on their way. We decided to hook up here before we head over to the school to set up a staging area," Connors replied indignantly.

"Miller and I have been going for the last twenty four hours, looking high and low for those kids. They probably just ran off. God only knows they most likely had a fight with their parents and took off or ran away with some boyfriend or something."

"What time did you say the state police are showing up?" a local man asked?

"They should be here any minute."

"You two clowns couldn't find those other two girls that were missing a few years ago, so I'm sure you won't have any luck this time, either," another man retorted.

"The other two girls were missing from up north, Jim. That was out of our jurisdiction, but just so you know, Miller and I did help in that search, too," Connors replied, finishing his coffee, paying his bill and storming off toward his cruiser to wait for his officer and the state police units to arrive.

"Connors's a jerk," Molly said and once again, the patrons continued to read their copies of the Reporter.

"It says here, Olive was last seen here at the café," Jim Bacon said.

"Well, she and Zippy were here, yes, but then they left to walk home," Molly clarified.

"There were two strangers in the café while she and Zippy were here, but when they left, in separate cars, they both headed off in the opposite direction the girls were walking."

"Doesn't mean they didn't double back and pick them up, Molly," another man added realistically.

"There are some descriptions of the guys in the paper," Molly added. "What is written is what I told Connors and I guess they must have interviewed Zippy, too, before she went missing."

"We'll keep an eye out for those two cars and come on folks, we gotta get out of here and start looking for the girls. This makes four of our young girls missing from this area in only a few short years. We have to do something to find them and bring whoever the bastard is, who's doing this, to justice," Jim Bacon added while herding the informal search team from the small restaurant.

"Your meals are on the house and will be, you guys, until the girls are found."

"Thanks a lot, Molly," the townsfolk replied in unison before they entered their vehicles and drove off toward the staging area at the school.

Chapter 4

"ZenJa's on her way home from college, Tony," ZenJa and Zippy's mother informed her husband while they waited for any news or calls they might receive in reference to their youngest daughter's disappearance.

"How could this happen? First Olive went missing and now our beloved Zippy," the distraught woman tried to reason; in shock of the events that had unfolded in the sleepy town of Longberry, New Hampshire, in the last two short days.

"I don't know, Ann. This doesn't make any sense. I know they didn't run off together. We know Zippy wouldn't ever do that and she wouldn't have any reason to run away," Mr. Beckwith continued and sank into his favorite recliner and stared out the window in hopes of seeing his youngest daughter run into the house, slamming the door like she always did, for which he continually scolded her. More than anything, he wanted to hear the door slam, now, he realized while tears flooded his eyes.

"Has Chief Connors stopped by or called this afternoon?" Ann asked her husband, gently setting a cup of tea on the end table, beside Tony's chair. "I thought he might have come by while I was trying to rest. The doctor gave me some awful medicine and it knocked me out for hours. I don't know why he did that," the broken mother wailed.

"He knows you need some rest. It's been two days and there's been no word. We've been running ragged, searching here and there with the volunteers, answering questions at the police station and we're getting nowhere."

"Exactly, Tony! That's why I don't need rest. We need to keep looking. I know she's hurt or something...somewhere out there and she needs us," she cried while rocking back and forth in her favorite love seat. The love seat she and her youngest daughter sat on and read books together, since her beloved daughter was a toddler.

Several neighbors came calling to the Beckwith home, after spending the day searching their neighborhoods, their own garages, basements, sheds and surrounding acreage. Followed by streams, river banks, through thick forests, cemeteries, parking lots and trash receptacles with no sight or sound from either twelve year old, missing girl.

"We're not giving up, Mr. and Mrs. Beckwith," Lanny Williams said, speaking for the self appointed neighborhood search team who crowded into the family's living room, in their modest Tudor style home.

"I can't thank you enough for all you're doing," Ann said while walking toward the kitchen, dazed and numb from the shock of the last few days events.

"Can I help you, Ann?" Carol Williams asked. "I brought some sandwiches and I'll make coffee, if you'd like."

"That would be so nice, Carol. I don't even think I can find the coffee, cream, or sugar, at this point," she added while sitting at the breakfast bar.

"We won't stop looking for Olive or Zippy until we bring them home, Ann," their neighbor assured her friend.

"I'll never be able to thank you enough, Carol," Ann replied and laid her head in her arms and began to cry, once more.

"ZenJa's here, Ann," her husband called from the living room, while opening the door for his college aged daughter.

"Mom...Dad, what in hell is going on?" ZenJa cried while hugging her parents in her arms. "What in hell are the cops doing to find the girls?" she screamed.

"It doesn't appear there's much activity at the police station, ZenJa," Lanny Williams quietly replied. "I just drove by Molly's Café and both Longsberry's police cars are parked outside. At least the state police are taking this seriously and seem to have taken the investigation out of the Chief's hands."

"That's a good thing. It appears all the local cops can do is fill their damn faces with a nice big lunch while my sister and her friend are missing! The FBI needs to be called in!" the strawberry blond haired beauty, ZenJa Beckwith, exclaimed and marched out the door toward her older model silver Subaru station wagon and sped away.

ZenJa Beckwith entered Longberry Middle School gymnasium, the staging area, the local and state police were utilizing for the search efforts to find the two missing girls.

"What area do you want me to search today?" the young lady asked Trooper Alton, of the New Hampshire State Police.

"Hi, ZenJa. Why don't you take a break today. You've been out there in the field ever since you got back from college. Your mom and dad need you," Trooper Daniel Alton expressed with honest sincerity.

"Thanks Trooper, but I need to find my sister and her friend and nothing or no one's going to stop me."

"I appreciate and admire your efforts, but you're exhausted and I don't want you to get lost or fall and hurt yourself. You can barely stand up," he added.

"Come on, Trooper. Just give me an area you haven't checked yet. I'm going to be partnering up with Jim Bacon, his wife and some others, today. We want to check the quarry area."

"You can't go into the quarry, ZenJa. We're going to send experienced divers there tomorrow."

"We're just going to check the wooded area around there," ZenJa replied and left to meet with her neighbors in their vehicles.

"She sure is a stubborn one."

"Well, Connors, if your daughter or sister or any other family member were missing, you'd be as determined as she is, wouldn't you?" Trooper Alton replied with disgust at the insincere attitude this townie appeared to show regarding two missing children.

"Oh, yeah, definitely," he replied and headed toward his police cruiser parked in the lot.

Chapter 5

"I still can't believe it," Molly exclaimed after several local residents, regular customers of her café, continued to discuss the fact that two more young girls who attended River View Middle School were gone without a trace, only a few months after Pickles and Zippy went missing.

"Who are the girls?" she asked in alarm.

"They're Constance O'Leary and Morgan Childress," Officer Brian Miller responded sadly.

"What the heck is going on in your brother's school?" Molly asked as the shock of other disappearances in their small community began to sink into her brain.

"My brother is only the Assistant Principal, Molly, but I don't the school could be the link between the missing girls."

"What makes you say that?" ZenJa Beckwith asked, upon entering the small restaurant. "What evidence do *you* have concerning my missing sister, her friend and now these two other girls, that *our* families don't have, Officer Miller? We haven't heard squat from anyone or gotten any updates about the disappearances of Zippy or Pickles in months and now there are two more poor missing girls who will simply disappear from the face of the earth and never be found?" she asked and sat down on the same metal stool her sister occupied the last time she was at Molly's...eating her ice cream sundae.

"ZenJa, I know you're upset and know you don't feel we're doing everything we can, but I assure you, we're looking into details we can't disclose. We have few and limited resources in our small town, as you're aware and we can only be in so many places at one time," the officer added callously. "We now have Miss O'Leary and Miss Childress who are missing and because this is a fresh case, we have to focus on this now."

"There appears to be a serial kidnapper or murderer in our midst?" Molly questioned.

"You can't assume anything, Molly. We don't want our citizens to become more alarmed than they already are," Officer Martin explained.

"Excuse me, Officer. Am I to understand you consider my sister and her friend's cases, as cold?" she asked; her authoritative voice raising another decibel. "It's only been two months, Officer Miller.

"ZenJa, please have this coffee," Molly offered to break the tension that was escalating inside her establishment.

"Thank you, Molly, but I just lost my appetite," ZenJa said and left.

"Mom...Dad, I'm going out, again and heading up toward the lake and see if I can find any evidence of...," ZenJa began and quickly fell silent after she noticed the expressions on her parents faces.

"You don't think Zippy or Olive will ever be found alive, do you, ZenJa?" Ann asked her daughter.

"No, Mom, I don't, but if it takes me the rest of my life, I'll move heaven and earth to find their bodies."

"The police really seem to be focused on finding Constance and Morgan, of which I have no problem," ZenJa began. "I pray they find them alive and well, don't get me wrong, but I wish they had exerted a little more effort in finding whoever kidnaped Zippy and Olive. They didn't simply disappear off the face of the earth and maybe if they had spent more time looking for the perpetrator or perpetrators who took them from our lives, they may not have two more girls to look for," she added angrily.

"I really don't want you going to the lake by yourself," ZenJa's father said. "There's still a very dangerous person lurking around out there and until they find him, or them, you need to let the officials do the searching. I know the local folks have more or less forgotten about Zippy and Olive and I understand they have their lives to get on with, but I don't think it's wise for you to continue this search on your own. Your mother and I are simply not up to trudging through the woods; up and down mountainsides; or over hill and dale and frankly I can only have hope, as long as no one finds a body. If and when their bodies are found, ZenJa, that will be the end. It'll mean there's no hope. I'm not ready to give up...to give up the hope that my daughter is still alive," Tony Beckwith said and walked away, to the seclusion of his bedroom.

"ZenJa, you really need to go back to college," ZenJa's mother said in an effort to comfort her surviving daughter. "You need to get on with your life. We beg you to go back to school. Be a success in your sister's memory."

"I've already considered that and as a matter of fact I've decided to change my major from Business Management to Criminal Justice and Law Enforcement. I'm going to apply to become an FBI agent. Maybe I can save someone else's family from going through what we've all been through. Maybe I can make a difference," she whispered. "I can make a difference for Zippy and Olive and now Constance and Morgan."

"I know you can and will make a difference, dear," Mrs. Beckwith said. The two women hugged each other, like their lives depended on it.

"You do know the application to become an FBI agent is at least a hundred pages long and the government will give us a colonoscopy and our neighbors, too, to check us out, Mom, so if we have any deep, dark family secrets, you better tell me now," ZenJa said; cried and laughed at the same time.

While the Beckwith family sat down for supper, in their dinning room that evening, their phone rang and ZenJa went to the kitchen to answer it.

"Oh! I'm sorry to hear that, Chief Connors. Sorry that there wasn't a better outcome for the O'Leary and Childress families, but thankfully they have been found and they can be laid to rest. I know that will be a small comfort for their loved ones," she said and returned the phone to the receiver before walking into the dinning room.

"Constance and Morgan's bodies were found in the woods at Devils Point. It appears they were shot," ZenJa said and left the table.

Chapter 6

ZenJa stopped by Molly's Café for a cup of coffee before returning to Claybourne College in Boston, Massachusetts.

"Hi ZenJa," Molly said. "What can I get you?"

"I'll take a black coffee and blueberry muffin, if you have any."

"Coming right up."

Once the elderly owner placed ZenJa's order on the counter, she came and sat down beside her on one of the metal stools near the front window.

"Oh! Wait, ZenJa. That man, just driving in the parking lot; the guy with the fancy black Camaro is the guy who was here the last day Olive and Zippy were here. Play it cool," Molly advised. "He may be the guy responsible for the girls disappearances," she continued and left the stool to wait on the tall, blue-eyed stranger, who entered her establishment.

"Well, hello, stranger," Molly greeted the man after he sat down in the same booth he occupied several months before "Nice to see you came back to our little town," she continued, handing the man a menu and once again set his place-mat and silverware on the counter in front of him; while eyeing him suspiciously.

"It's nice to be back, but I'm afraid I'm only passing through, again."

"Where ya heading?" Molly asked, loud enough for ZenJa to listen to the unfolding conversation.

"I'm heading back to school where I'm taking some advanced classes at Claybourne College, in Boston."

ZenJa's interest was peaked and she continued to listen to this man's conversation.

"You don't look like a college boy."

"Oh, I've already graduated, but want to take some refresher courses. You know, all this new technology that's out today, a guy has to keep up with where the action is."

"Hmm! If you say so," Molly muttered, keeping her eye on the stranger.

"What can I get you?"

"I'd like a BLT, onion rings, and a large diet Coke, if you please. Extra mayo on the sandwich, too," the man said, looking intently at ZenJa, after removing his sunglasses.

"It'll be right up," she said, made eye contact with ZenJa and entered the kitchen.

ZenJa and the stranger stared at each other without comment, and ZenJa continued to sip her coffee.

"I'll have another cup of coffee, Molly," ZenJa shouted to the proprietor who remained in the kitchen.

"Be right there, sweetie," she hollered and quickly brought out another steaming cup and saucer filled with fresh coffee.

"See if you can find out what his name is," ZenJa whispered when Molly added more cream to the beverage.

"Okay! Will do," she whispered in return.

ZenJa wrote down the make, model and license plate number of the powerful sports car that was parked directly in front of her field of vision.

"Oh! Jesus, you scared the shit out of me!" ZenJa yelled at the stranger who crept up next to her without her realizing it."

"If you want to know what my name is and what my license plate number is, Miss...all you have to do is ask me," the tall, muscular man advised her and smiled.

"Shit!" ZenJa blurted out in embarrassment and crinkled the piece of paper she had written down, concerning the powerful sports car.

"What in hell are you doing, sneaking up on me like that and why are you eavesdropping on my conversations?"

"Sorry, Miss?...but I don't particularly appreciate people talking about me behind my back."

"It wasn't behind your back, Mister..., in fact it was right in front of you," she barked.

"I have all the information I need about you, buddy, so you can go and sit back down where you were and eat your BLT. It's ready," ZenJa replied, motioning with her head toward where he had initially come from.

"No, Miss...you don't have all the information you need. My name is *Mr.* Levi Harris," he snickered and returned to his stool and meal.

"ZenJa, what was that all about?"

"Oh, nothing, Molly. He's just another asshole who's passing through," the young lady replied; loudly, for Levi's benefit.

Levi looked up, smiled and said, "Great BLT, Molly. Thanks," he continued and kept his eyes on ZenJa Beckwith.

"You're welcome, Mr. Harris," she responded with a wave of her hand.

"Okay! Where were we, ZenJa," Molly asked, once again seating herself beside her customer.

"Oh yeah, I wanted to tell you, before you leave town, that I'm sorry there have been no new developments in your missing sister's case or Olive's for that matter. However, I'm glad the Childress and O'Leary families will be able to find some closure, now that their daughters were found last week," Molly began. "I know that doesn't bring any comfort to you and your family, ZenJa. I still pray for Zippy and Olive to be found, safe and sound."

"I know, Molly. I'm also glad the families can at least bury their daughters, but they will never find closure until their murderer is found and brought to justice."

"I know I shouldn't say this, ZenJa, but I wonder why it seemed the police department didn't exert much of an effort to find Zippy or Olive, but left no stone unturned finding Morgan and Constance. I also noticed when there were television notices and reports about all the missing girls, all I heard was how Constance and Morgan were lively cheerleaders. Blond, young, petite, and *beauuuutiful*, over and over again; their appearances were described and it seemed as if they had been ugly or less attractive, their disappearances wouldn't have mattered that much. Even on the television cable channels; you know those talk shows that broadcast on the Liberal networks in the evenings; continued to mention Constance and Morgan as petite, tiny little cheerleaders, and so *beauuuuutiful*, over and over and over, again! I wanted to scream at the television and ask, 'What about the ugly ones?' I guess they don't matter?"

"Like Zippy and Olive, you mean. They were, let's be honest, less attractive than Constance and Morgan and of course our families don't have the money, connections or prestige the O'Leary and Childress families have. And I've also noticed there are many minority children missing and their disappearances are never mentioned in the news, local or otherwise. That's bullshit!"

"I shouldn't have mentioned that, ZenJa, but I couldn't help notice the media and what appeared to be their bias in reporting what few facts there were in these cases.

"I was so wrapped up in the events, searching high and low, Molly, I never noticed the reporting aspects of these *alleged* crimes, but now that you mention it, I think you're right."

"Be right back," Molly said and left her seat.

"Well, Molly, thanks for the free coffee and muffin," ZenJa said after leaving a ten dollar tip under her plate. "I gotta go," she said to the woman who was busy checking in some food supplies for the café.

"Good luck at school," Molly shouted in return.

ZenJa climbed into her silver Subaru, but not before Mr. Levi Harris walked up to her car window.

"Hey, Miss...I apologize for being an ass hole. I really am a nice guy. Can I at least get a name to go with your pretty face?" he asked; a handsome smile on his face that highlighted his brilliant blue eyes.

"The name is ZenJa," she replied and sped out of the parking lot, but not without noticing Mr. Harris was writing down her license plate number on a piece of paper.

"Serves me right," she admitted.

Chapter 7

"Thanks for taking care of my plants while I've been gone, Mrs. Martin," ZenJa said and escorted her landlady toward the door of the small, conventionally styled home she rented near the Clayborune College campus, in Boston, Massachusetts. "I had no idea I would be in New Hampshire so long and I can't tell you how grateful I am."

"That's the least I could do, ZenJa. I can't imagine what you and your family have been going through...with the loss of your sister and those other girls from your home town. I'm so sorry there has been no results in the searches and please convey my thoughts and prayers to your mother and father, if you will. If there's anything I can ever do, please feel free to ask me or Mr. Martin. There is nothing we won't do for you, my dear."

"I appreciate all you've done and your thoughts and prayers will never be forgotten. Please keep praying. Prayers are all we have now," ZenJa sadly replied and closed the door behind her landlady.

"How are you my little babies? I have missed you so much," ZenJa conveyed to her Swedish Ivy, African Violets, and pink Geraniums that adorned her comfortably decorated rental property before she flopped into her favorite brown leather recliner and promptly fell asleep.

Darkness had fallen upon the city of Boston before ZenJa woke, startled by a vivid dream she had. An illusion that involved a forceful abduction of a young girl, her cries for help and a sense of being thrown into a deep, dark muddy enclosure, far from any residential area, near a rushing waterway.

"Oh my God!" ZenJa yelled before she realized she was safely inside her own home. She wiped the tears from her eyes and sweat from her brow with a Kleenex. "That was Zippy! I know that was Zippy trying to call out to me!" she exclaimed. She quickly grabbed a pen and paper from the end table and jotted down what she felt, had seen, smelled, and heard in the dream before the bits and pieces would be forgotten.

After several hours of analyzing her notes she called her parents to assure them she had arrived safely in Massachusetts. There was no reason to mention her dream to her parents. They had enough to worry about and ZenJa didn't want to get their hopes up...false hopes that their daughter might be found alive.

The next morning brought sunshine cascading into ZenJa's modest and tastefully decorated second floor bedroom; one of two rooms that encompassed the entire floor; other than two full sized bathrooms. She stretched and gently slipped out from underneath the cool white sheets on her Queen-sized bed and turned off the air conditioner.

She noted her appearance in the hallway mirror. Her auburn-red hair had grown several inches and now hung past the middle of her back. Her once, pleasingly curvy body, had lost at least twenty pounds and the strain of the last few months had taken a toll on her beautiful face and complexion, but ZenJa Beckwith was still a stunning, young lady.

It took ZenJa three hours, after her awakening, to shower, water her upstairs plants, vacuum the thick, beige wall to wall carpeting, dust the oak furniture in both bedrooms, and hall stands. Soon after she straightened the abstract paintings, she purchased at several local art galleries, she dressed for the day and walked downstairs to make herself some breakfast.

"I think I'll have a key-lime pie yogurt, coffee and a chocolate fiber-nut bar," ZenJa said out loud, talking to the red Geranium that was in full bloom in her kitchen window. "On second thought, I guess I won't, damn it! I have no groceries in the house and everything in the frig is spoiled," she added, slung her Gucci purse over her shoulder and drove to the local grocery store three miles away.

Two hours later; ZenJa's car was filled with groceries and other essentials she needed at her house. When she left the parking lot, she spotted a bright red Mustang and a black Camaro closely behind, speeding down Boston's Storrow Drive, in the same direction she was heading. She followed the fancy sports cars as far as she was able, validating the fact that it was, indeed, the black car she had seen in New Hampshire at Molly's, by the fact that the license plate indicated it was registered in the state District of Columbia, that she had noted at the Café. She, again, marveled at the unique vanity plate that was displayed near the rear bumper.

"What message is Mr. Levi Harris trying to send?" she asked herself out loud. "I wonder how "LAWLESS" this guy really is?"she questioned herself; wondering why the man had those letters displayed on his plate.

Both sports cars continued to race down the highway after she took the next exit to bring her groceries to her house.

Chapter 8

"Miss Beckwith, on behalf of our professors and our entire staff, I wish to express our deep concern in the disappearance of your sister. You and your family have been in our thoughts and prayers since day one and will continue to be, until she is found and brought home safely," the Dean of Claybourne College said, while offering ZenJa a cup of freshly brewed coffee.

"I appreciate that, Dean Thompson. "It helps to know so many people care and have been so kind."

"You know if there's anything we can do, please let us know."

"Well, Dean Thompson, that's why I'm here. I want to change my major from business to Criminal Justice and Law Enforcement. If it takes me the rest of my life, I'm going to become an FBI agent," ZenJa stated in no uncertain terms.

"Actually, my secretary notified me of your plans and we have begun the process of changing your schedule to accommodate your request.

"ZenJa, I've no doubt you'll become one of Americas best and brightest stars. I'll personally see that your curriculum is adjusted and your existing credits applied to your change of venue."

"Thank you, Dean Thompson. I certainly appreciate it."

"As a matter of fact your first class is going to start in about ten minutes, if you wish to scoot over to the bookstore, get your books and start today. There's one other new student starting today, also, so you both can join the class together, if that suits you."

"That sounds great, Dean. Thanks again; I really appreciate this."

"Attention, students!" Professor Smith began. "It's time to settle down and get started," the forty five year old, Dartmouth graduate, dressed in jeans, sport coat, shirt, and bow tie said, addressing the auditorium that was filled to capacity with eager students. "We are fortunate to have two new members of our Legal Procedures and Ethics class join us today," he added. "Please welcome Miss Beckwith and Mr. Harris. I assume you have found seats? If not, please let me know," he rambled on.

"Well, Miss Beckwith, it's a pleasure to meet your acquaintance, once again," Levi whispered to the woman who had unknowingly seated herself directly in front of the driver of the mysterious black Camaro.

"Oh my God! It's you!" she hissed and turned her back on him, but not without noting how nice he smelled; wondering what kind of after-shave he wore.

"Yesterday, class, we were discussing a situation that involved a police pursuit and high speed chase. Will one of you ladies or gentlemen be kind enough to bring our new students up to date on what we discussed? Okay, Jeffrey, thank you."

"Well, there was a known heroin addict who had taken a used pickup truck, from a local dealership, for a test drive. He did not return the vehicle at the agreed time, so the owner of the dealership notified the city police department. The police spotted the vehicle at the man's residence and the officers staked out the property. A while later, the man and his girlfriend, who was also suspected of being an addict, left their apartment and entered the pickup and headed down the highway. The police then followed the vehicle and once the occupants of the pickup saw the police units and heard the sirens, the driver sped away, initiating a high speed pursuit. The result of that pursuit ended with the pickup crashing into a tree and the passenger, the girlfriend, was killed and the driver was subsequently arrested."

"Thank you Jeffrey; that pretty much sums up what we discussed yesterday," Professor Smith acknowledged. "Any questions or comments?"

"Yes, I have several observations and questions," ZenJa blurted out.

"Please, speak freely, Miss Beckwith," the professor said.

"You mentioned the man was a *known* heroin addict. Now, was he known as an addict only to the police or everyone in town, including the owner of the dealership? I mean, if he was a known addict, to the dealer, what business did he have trusting the pickup truck in the hands of this *addict*?"

"That's a good question," the professor agreed. "That is a question we don't know the answer to, at this time."

"Just to be clear, you're telling us this is an actual incident that happened?" ZenJa asked.

"Yes, it is. It happened and I can give you folks more interesting facts about the events that unfolded that unfortunate day; several years ago," Professor Smith continued.

"The incident began to unfold at approximately eleven thirty on a Monday in September...the year doesn't matter, but what does matter is that it was around noon; a weekday; after school had started. The pursuit started in one city, escalated and continued through three towns, down an interstate highway, and ended in another city, some thirty miles away."

"What elements of interest in this case need to be addressed?" he asked.

"Well, for God's sake; first of all; why didn't the officers arrest the man while he was in his apartment, for possessing stolen property? Why did they sit there and wait for him and what may have been an innocent victim, enter the vehicle before attempting to arrest him?" ZenJa again spoke up, more forcefully than she meant.

"Secondly," she continued in front of the class that was completely stunned by this newcomer's passion on this subject. "It was lunch time, on a school day. I'm assuming there were school buses in the area bringing kindergarten students to and from school at that time and there must have been students and other civilians walking around going for lunch breaks, during the hours this pursuit took place, through three towns and two cities, you said."

"Thirdly, was the damn *used* pickup worth risking any lives, including those in the vehicle? You said the woman was killed."

"Okay, these are great points," Professor Smith said. "Anyone want to answer or justify the reasons this incident began, continued, and ended as it did?"

"If I may?"

"Please, Mr. Harris; feel free to speak," Smith replied.

ZenJa snapped her head around and glared at the man who had somehow entered into her life without her consent.

"Miss Beckwith's observations are indeed admirable and I appreciate them, but it's easy to sit on the side-lines and Monday-night quarterback after the facts and incidents are over."

"Law enforcement officers vow to protect and serve all citizens and put their lives on the line every day for everyone. It's their obligation and duty to bring criminals to justice."

"Oh my God! An innocent woman was killed and just because she may have been a drug addict, does that make her life any less valuable than anyone else? If she was a victim and a pretty one, at that, would that have made a difference how they handled that situation? If she was some banker's wife or a senator's wife, or his girlfriend, would they have continued the pursuit or handled it in a different manner? You know damn well, they never would've allowed that man to leave the residence. It appears to me those in charge allowed this situation to escalate to the degree that it did. And of course, they called the pursuit off, immediately *before* the crash, right?" ZenJa exclaimed. "They always do!"

"Oh wow! This is going to be one interesting class," a student sitting several rows away commented, loud enough for everyone to hear.

"Yes, Miss Cameron. That's exactly what we want. Lively discussions and the fact that you people need to see both sides of any given situation and we must try to find the safest way to seek justice."

"Isn't *justice* supposed to take place in a court of law and not in the middle of a busy interstate?" ZenJa seethed with anger.

"Exactly, Miss Beckwith," Levi began. "But, it's a known fact, that those in law enforcement are trained, in situations when necessary and when appropriate, to shoot to kill and ask questions later."

"That's bullshit! If that's the case why didn't they just shoot the bastard before he got inside the vehicle?" ZenJa exclaimed.

"Oh my God! I'm not saying *that* incident justified shooting someone...," Levi continued.

"Exactly! And no one deserved to die, either!" ZenJa stated.

"Okay, class. Unfortunately we have run out of time for today and I must admit the statements we have expressed today, give us all cause to ponder and consider likely alternatives that may have been utilized. I would like to see papers, siting your theories of this case and how you would have handled it, if you were engaged in it, as an officer of the law. Thank you for your attendance today and we will see you next week."

"Mr. Harris and Miss Beckwith, before you leave, would please see me in my office." Smith said, pointing to a doorway next to the auditorium.

"Oh, Jesus! We have to stay after school, already," Levi chuckled while following his irritated classmate down the steps.

"Jesus, isn't going to help you, Harris. No one can," ZenJa stated in disgust.

"Well, you two certainly brought much needed life to my class, today. I can't thank you enough. It's obvious you both share a passion for law enforcement and those who protect and serve. If I may ask, what are your plans regarding your service in the area of the law; if either of you do plan to embark on that career."

"I'm going to become an FBI agent," ZenJa replied with forcefulness and determination. "I'm going to hunt down the person who stole my sister away from my family and all the other girls...," ZenJa began, halting mid sentence. "Sorry, I was just rambling on."

"Actually," ZenJa began again. "I'm really writing a mystery novel and I want to learn as much as I can about law enforcement so the book is realistic."

"I see." Professor Smith replied. "I'm sure your book will be both a thriller and riveting and I do hope I get an autographed copy when it's published."

"Indeed! And I'll be happy to autograph one for you, too, Harris, but you'll have to pay for your copy at a bookstore."

"It would be my pleasure, Miss Beckwith."

"So, Harris, why are you enrolled in this college and why have you selected to take criminal justice courses. Don't tell me you're writing a novel, as well."

"No, sir. My imagination is extremely limited. Combining fact and fiction to be logical and understood by intelligent readers is far beyond my mental capacity," Levi replied, eyeing his classmate with interest.

"I think anything intelligent or otherwise is beyond your mental capacity," ZenJa hissed and left the office.

Chapter 9

"Any sign of that red Mustang or the black Camaro, Chief?" Officer Brian Miller asked when the daily briefing was about to begin, for the benefit of the press, in front of the local police station.

"Molly said she saw the black Camaro and the same man the other day, at the café, but no one else has seen hide nor hair of the Mustang or its driver. It appears the Camaro and driver were just passing through, again. He said he was taking some college classes, or something."

"Did Molly mention if the guy said what college it is?" Miller asked. "We should check it out and see if his story jives with what actually he said."

"She didn't mention it, but you can ask her when you go back later."

"Did Molly at least get a plate number?" Miller continued.

"No, she said the car was parked at a rather odd angle, so she couldn't see it."

"Jesus! We're getting a lot of help, aren't we?"

"Well, you know, Miller, this is a small town and these people aren't the most intelligent creatures on earth."

"That's uncalled for, Bob," Miller stated, shaking his head in disgust.

"Yeah, yeah! Okay, the Troopers are here; we can begin the press conference," Connors said and approached the microphone.

"Once again, folks, we are gathered here to give you an update of what we know about the murder victims, Constance O'Leary and Morgan Childress. It isn't much more than we elaborated on before. Both girls were kidnaped, brutally raped, and shot, and as you know, their bodies were found in a secluded area near Devils Point on the northern edge of Lake Winnipesaukee."

"What about the other girls? The girls who are missing?" a reporter from the Boston Herald asked.

"We're handling those cases, Miss." Trooper Daniel Alton said. "We will address those questions after Chief Connors is done and the FBI will answer any questions you may have concerning the disappearances, from several years ago, of Ashley Winters and Rose-Ann Olsen."

"Thank you, Trooper Alton," Chief Connors replied, glaring at the law enforcement officer who rudely interrupted him.

"As I was saying, the State Medical Examiners office is in charge of the autopsies and other evidence has been sent to the FBI labs in Washington, DC. As you know, those tests take many weeks, so it will obviously be a while until we have any news to report on that front."

"Are any of you, in law enforcement, closer to making an arrest in any of these cases?" a reporter from the New England Telegraph asked.

"No, unfortunately, we aren't, but we are following up on some leads, but we can't disclose that information at this time.

"Wouldn't it be more beneficial for you to let the media know what leads you are following, like any vehicles or persons of interest you have in your sights, to spread the word. It's a well known fact that many cases are solved because of tips called in by the public. You have to admit how successful the television show, *'America's Most Wanted'* is in capturing criminals," a reporter from the Boston Herald mentioned.

"Actually, there's a segment that's already been taped and will air in two weeks," Chief Connors said proudly.

"Because our time is limited, I'll hand the podium over to Trooper Alton and the FBI," Connors said and handed the microphone to the trooper.

"Must be our beloved chief needs another coffee," Lanny Williams muttered with other citizens nodding in agreement.

While the press conference continued, Chief Connors had important items on his agenda, while the majority of the town's citizens and all investigating law enforcement personnel were attending the daily briefing.

Today, Connors was scheduled to meet a stranger, who drove a red Mustang, out in the middle of nowhere.

This was not the first time the two men had met; unfortunately for the young stranger, he had entered Molly's café on a prior visit and he and his bright red Mustang had been noticed; co-incidently on the fateful morning, only a few hours before Miss Pickering went missing,

Today, Longberry's police chief dialed an unlisted number into his cell phone and said, "To bad Alex Lyons didn't take orders very well. He had to show his fancy car off in town, on his last visit, and made a spectacle of himself. But, now that I think of it, this works out better than we could have planned," Connors said to an anonymous person on the other end of the phone.

"What have you got up your sleeve this time?"

"Just wait and see. This idea is brilliant!" he chuckled and disconnected the call.

He had to make an arrest in the murders of Constance O'Leary and Morgan Childress, even if that person wasn't the perpetrator of the crimes.

Chapter 10

"Thanks for meeting me here, Alex. I realize it's a little out of the way, but you never know who's watching, what, and where these days, with the Feds and State Troopers around."

"Jesus! I know. I heard a rumor they're all here because of some dead and missing chicks?"

"Yeah, it's a real shame," Chief Connors said. "Some of those girls were mighty pretty, too. It's a real shame."

"Well, anyway, here's the dope and weapons I promised you," the chief continued.

"Hey, thanks and here's the cash I owe ya," Alex said after handing over a wad of hundred dollar bills and reaching for the keys to his trunk.

"It's okay, guy. Stay put, I'll load this stuff in the trunk for you," Connors said.

"I wanna see the stuff."

"See, here's the stuff," Connors said holding the three rifles, two handguns, a satchel full of drugs, for his customer to see, while Alex remained behind the steering wheel. "I'll load 'em up for you," Connors assured the man.

"I'll help you, Alex insisted at the same time, Connors realized it was vital that Lyons actually handle the weapons, to insure his finger prints were on the *goods*. Chief Connors had been in law enforcement long enough to know to wear his leather gloves at all times.

"Okay, here ya go," Connors said handing each item to the man. After Alex Lyons loaded up the drugs and weapons and was walking toward the driver's side door, Connors added another small satchel to the inventory in the trunk. A package the stranger was not expecting.

"You can count the cash, Connors."

"I trust you, Alex. If you can't trust anyone, you have no faith," Connors expressed while yucking it up at his own sick sense of humor, closed the trunk lid, and handed the keys back to the owner and waved when the young man continued on his way.

Connors entered his squad car and made an urgent call on his police radio that was connected to the same radio frequency the State Police and FBI agents used, and unbeknownst to anyone else in Longberry, AFT agents, as well.

"I'm in pursuit of a new red Mustang; the vehicle we have an APB out on; Massachusetts plate number MHL 3559. This Mustang is leaving the scene of the O'Leary and Childress murders at Devils Point. He is approximately two miles out," he shouted, started the ignition of his car and sped toward the unsuspecting man.

Alex Lyons hadn't driven three miles down the dirt road, known as Devils Point, when Police Chief Connors turned his siren on and pulled the red Mustang over, for a traffic stop at the same time the local, state and federal authorities descended, like a tidal wave, on the bewildered driver.

"Get out of the car!" Connors yelled, with his weapon drawn, quickly approaching the operator of the red Mustang at the same time a battery of law enforcement vehicles; those from the town, state and federal agencies, surrounded the vehicle from all directions.

"What the fuck!" Alex Lyons cried when four law enforcement officers forced the man to the ground and immediately handcuffed the terrified soul.

"What the fuck is going on?"

"I've been keeping an eye on this area, where two of our lovely young girls were found murdered, in hopes the perpetrator might return to the scene of the crime. This red Mustang and the unknown suspect fits the description several of our residents noted as having been spotted in Longberry on the day of the disappearance of Miss Pickering, Upon my initial visual contact with the vehicle and owner, the trunk was open and using binoculars I spotted what I assumed to be several weapons inside. I swooped down on the man and vehicle and after I identified myself as an officer of the law, this young man jumped back into his idling vehicle and sped away from the former crime scene," Connors stressed for the benefit of the authorities who had arrived on the scene in record time.

"I'll just open this trunk and see what we've got!" Connors sneered with an overabundance of joy.

"Hold it! We're getting a search warrant so this arrest, if there is one, is all legal. You know about that sort of thing, don't you, Chief?" FBI Agent Edward Emerson suggested sarcastically and ATF Agent Wyman agreed.

"I have probable cause. I saw the weapons from my vantage point, with my binoculars."

"We're going to do this the right way, Chief," Trooper Alton agreed.

"Are we going to stand here all day?" Alex Lyons spat.

"You got any better place to be right now?" Agent Emerson asked.

"If you feel more comfortable, you may sit here in the shade and, hell, I'll even share my lunch with you. Molly packs a nice picnic lunch," Emerson said and smiled.

"Screw your lunch," Lyons sputtered.

"Well, if that's how you feel about it, may I see your license and registration?"

"Yeah, asshole, it's in the glove box and my license is up my ass."

"We'll have that checked out soon enough," Chief Connors replied once again sneering at the man he duped.

"The search warrant is on its way, Mr. Alex Lyons," Agent Emerson said as he examined the license and registration of the man who remained sitting under the shade trees.

Once the search warrant arrived by another FBI agent, Chief Connors eagerly approached the trunk of the car with the keys.

"Well, lookie here," Chief Connors said after he and Trooper Alton, along with the FBI agents, witnessed the opening of the trunk.

"We got ourselves a whole lot of illegal weapons, and well, what do you know, looks like some...what... marijuana, maybe some cocaine and ecstacy? And what the hell is in this little girl's back pack, Lyons?" Connors asked while unzipping the larger compartment of the pink bag.

"Holy shit!" Connors exclaimed while staring inside the bag, but not touching it's contents. "Get me some evidence bags," he hollered. "By the looks of the items I can see, these appear to be some of the clothes that Morgan Childress was last seen wearing," the chief noted.

"Don't touch any of that stuff," Officer Miller and ATF Agent Wyman demanded simultaneously.

"I know!" Chief Connors spat at the two gentlemen; "If I may remind you, I'm wearing gloves."

"You fucking son of a bitch! You set me up, Connors!" the man screamed, while trying to escape from the confines of the metal handcuffs.

"Okay, before we go any further, I'm going to place you under arrest and Mirandize you; read you your rights," Agent Emerson said to the stunned stranger.

"What the hell?" Connors interrupted.

"Excuse me, Chief, but while you were grandstanding, over here, I inspected the man's driver's license and called it in to see if there are any outstanding warrants. It appears this man, being a potential drug and weapons runner and/or murderer of two young ladies, is the least of his problems. This man is wanted on Federal warrants, including the cold blooded murders of two Drug Enforcement Administration agents and a Federal Judge in Boston, Massachusetts," the agent informed the eager police chief and stunned the remaining law enforcement officers of this dangerous man's recent activities. This man is under the jurisdiction of the FBI and ATF."

"I'm placing you under arrest, Mr. Lyons, and anything you say can and will be used against you, in a court of law. You are entitled to an attorney and if you cannot afford one, one will be appointed for you. Do you understand these rights?" Agent Emerson questioned.

"You son of a bitch, Connors! I'm going to kill you," the man yelled and continued to struggle with his hands bound at the same time he was forced into the FBI's Chevy Suburban.

"Once, again, Mr. Lyons. Do you understand your rights?" Mathews growled again.

"Yes! Damn it, I do!" he sputtered and continued to struggle in the back seat of the luxury vehicle.

Chapter 11

The next morning ZenJa and Levi made their way into the Auditorium to attend another of Professor Smith's lively Procedures and Ethics classes.

"Good morning, Miss Beckwith. Did you do your homework?"

Yes, Mr. Harris, I did and I assume you did likewise?"

"Of course, but if there's a time when you don't want to complete your assignment, let me know and I won't either and we can stay after school together," Harris suggested smugly. I bet it would be fun."

"You're impossible," ZenJa replied and took her seat, ignoring the man who once again seated himself behind her.

"Thank you, ladies and gentlemen for handing your assignments in on my desk. I know I'll be enthralled to read these works worthy of consideration by the Supreme Court," Professor Smith chuckled, along with the student body, before getting down to the business at hand.

"Today, students, I would like to discuss the pros and *cons*, if you will, considering the death penalty.

"Oh boy! Here we go," a student near the front of the class gleefully stated.

"That's what I love about this class and you, my beloved students. You're so eager to learn and debate. You're going to need all the debating skills you can muster in whatever field of law enforcement you embark."

"These debating skills will probably benefit us in dating or marriage, even more!"

"Well said, Mr. Harris," Professor agreed; all the class members snickering at the comment; all the students with the exception of Miss Beckwith.

"Who would like to start the debate about the death penalty issue?" Professor Smith began.

"Yes, Jonathan?"

"First of all, I believe the death penalty should either be constitutional in all states or not at all. I'm not saying I agree with it one way or another, but I don't think it's appropriate for someone to be found guilty of a crime in one state and another person found guilty of the exact crime and one receives a death sentence and the other doesn't."

"Interesting opinion," another student commented. "But unfortunately, states are entitled to determine what sentences their convicted citizens receive," another student declared.

"I simply think sentencing should be straight across the board," Jonathan replied.

"What crimes do you think deserve the death penalty?" the professor asked.

"Until recently," ZenJa began. "I didn't believe in the death penalty. I never thought another person should decide the fate of another. It appeared to me that sentencing someone to death was no better than the person who murdered someone else and I was brought up to believe that was God's job to sort that out, when the time came."

"So, what changed your mind about the death sentence," Miss Beckwith," Professor Smith asked.

"Oh...well no reason, really. I've changed my way of thinking about people who commit serious crimes, I guess."

"Another thing to consider is what's fair to the taxpayer, though most inmates sentenced to death remain in prison for fifteen or twenty years or more and cost the taxpayers millions of dollars for their housing and their appeals before they're executed. What's wrong with swift and absolute justice?" another student asked.

"Miss Lee, what would you like to add?" Smith asked.

"What about those people who've been wrongfully convicted of crimes and then executed? That's a travesty of justice."

"Absolutely!" the majority of the class agreed.

"I do believe over one hundred people have been wrongly convicted and sentenced to death, if my memory serves me right," Smith added.

"Thank God for the Innocence Project," another student mentioned. "They've saved lives, especially with today's technology and use of DNA that wasn't available in years past. I'm not sure how many lives have been saved, but each innocent person who's been in prison for a crime they haven't committed, is a crime in itself."

"I have a comment, before class is over," ZenJa voiced. "I don't believe a jury or judge has the right or authority to sentence anyone to death or not. I think it should be left up the victims and/or families of the victims. Some family members may not feel two wrongs make a right and others may. I think it should left to the people directly involved in the situation. There is no one on a jury or any judge who can fathom what it's like to have your life stolen away from you."

Levi Harris was speechless and for the first time looked upon his classmate with more compassion than he ever had of any human being in his lifetime.

"Great class, today, ladies and gentlemen. As you did yesterday, please write a report on the death penalty, but this time I would like it in the form of a debate. No matter how you feel about his issue, I would like the ladies to favor the death sentence and you gentlemen, explain why you disagree with it."

"This should be an easy assignment," ZenJa murmured on her way out of class.

"Would you like to continue this debate over dinner or coffee?" Levi asked. "I think we would make good study-buddies."

"What makes you think I want to spend any more time with you than I have to, as it is now?"

"I can tell you're becoming infatuated with me, Miss Beckwith."

"Oh my God! You're a dreamer, that's for sure."

"I think of you in my dreams, as a matter of fact," Levi continued and walked beside his fellow student.

"I could be your worst nightmare," ZenJa stated, her irritation more than evident.

"I think I'm up to the challenge and I rather appreciate something I have to work hard for."

"Exactly what do you think you're going to be working for?"

"Your respect, ZenJa. All I can hope for in my life is to have the respect of people I care about."

"Aren't you getting a little ahead of yourself, Mr. Harris?"

"I never told you, my mother was a fortune teller, did I?"

"No, but I bet you were brought up in the circus," ZenJa retorted; shocked at the hurtful expression that overshadowed Levi's face.

"I'm sorry; I didn't mean that. I simply haven't been myself lately. If your mother truly is a fortune teller, I would rather wish she be physic," ZenJa muttered, but not without Levi overhearing her.

"So let's have dinner," Levi asked one more time, to lighten up the intense situation, that was developing.

"I'm on a very tight budget," ZenJa expressed, but I'm willing to go 'Dutch'.

"Please, I'm rather old fashioned when it comes to the treatment of a lady. I was brought up to open doors for women and pay for dates I ask for. If

I can't afford a date, I don't ask. So, you can see, I wasn't raised in the circus!" Levi laughed.

"Okay, I guess it wouldn't hurt to have dinner with you, after all we should have a further discussion about the death penalty."

"I was rather hoping we could discuss something less intense than that, on our first date."

"You're insufferable!" ZenJa said and walked toward her car.

"What time and where can I pick you up?"

"Slow down cowboy! We can meet somewhere."

"Now, I'm a cowboy?"

"Well, it's better than being a clown, isn't it?" she asked and chuckled.

"I guess and oh, here's my cell phone number and please give me yours in case something comes up, okay?" Levi asked.

"That's interesting. You happen to have a business card, but it only has your first name and number on it?" ZenJa questioned.

"I haven't figured out what else to have printed on it, yet. Do you think I would impress anyone if I had Levi Harris, Private Eye or IRS agent or maybe even FBI or ATF engraved on it?"

"Actions speak louder than words," ZenJa replied.

"Indeed," he replied and his date handed him her cell phone number written on a piece of paper.

"You need to have some business cards printed up, ZenJa."

"What do you think my card would say?" she asked, not waiting around for his response.

I bet it would say, *I'm a beautiful young lady who needs help. Your help, Mr. Harris*, he thought.

Chapter 12

"I'll meet you at The Les Paris' at 7:30, tonight, if that's okay with you, ZenJa?" Harris asked after calling his date on her cell phone.

"My...my! I am impressed, Mr. Harris. That's a pretty swanky place, so I've heard."

"I have to let you in on a little secret...Fortune Tellers make a lot more money than the clowns!"

"You're not a clown, Mr. Harris. You're an ass!"

"And I've seen you checking it out, too!" Levi said and howled; a pleasant laughter, ZenJa couldn't deny; neither the fact that she found his voice most alluring and his ass pleasant to look at, as well.

"See you tonight at 7:30," Levi confirmed and smiled and closed this one cell phone and selected another phone to make other calls.

The black Camaro with the vanity license plate *LAWLESS* was parked one block away from The Les Paris' at 7:00 that evening. The driver was confident in what direction ZenJa would be arriving. This establishment being situated on a one way street, near Copley Square, off Boylston Street, in the heart of Boston. He wanted to arrive at the same time his date entered the valet parking area.

At precisely 7:30, ZenJa arrived and the black Camaro drove directly behind her and exited his vehicle before the lovely young lady was able to gather her purse.

"I'll get it, Mark," Levi said opening the door for the auburn haired lady and handed the valet both sets of keys and an unknown amount for a tip.

"Thank you, Mr. Harris. I'll personally see that these cars are taken care of," the young man announced and smiled at the big tipper.

"Well, Mr. Harris, you're on a first name basis with the valets here?"

"You know what they say, ZenJa. Keep your friends close and your enemies even closer," he replied, handing her a small bouquet of yellow roses and hugging her tightly. "Is this close enough?" Levi asked and smiled.

"It is if I'm your enemy," she began, but was obviously stunned with this gentleman's manners and gift of flowers. She had no idea how long it had been since she received any flowers, not to mention on a first date.

"These flowers truly are lovely," ZenJa admitted while the young couple entered the restaurant.

"Not as lovely as you," Levi commented while noting this slender young lady's attire that consisted of a lavender multi-tiered, layered short skirt and form fitting bodice and slender straps. To complete her ensemble she wore a multi colored matching cape, shoes and purse. To finish her outfit she wore and a shimmering necklace and earring set of small diamonds.

"You're rather handsome, yourself, Mr. Harris," ZenJa noticed and gazed upon the well tailored dark grey suit and black turtleneck he wore, complete with expensive looking black leather shoes.

"I feel like I'm going to the prom," Levi said; the young couple laughed; ZenJa thinking the same thing.

"Good evening, Mr. Harris. Your table is ready," the maitre d announced and showed the couple to a private table toward the rear of the distinguished establishment.

"Thank you, Robert," Levi replied and assisted seating his date across from himself.

"Good gracious! Is there anyone here you don't know?" ZenJa asked in amazement.

"I do believe they've hired a new dishwasher that I have yet to meet," he replied, smiling coyly.

"Is this employee a friend or enemy?" she teased.

"I don't know, I told you I haven't met this employee yet!"

"You're..."

"Handsome?"

"No, I was going to say incorrigible."

"I have taken the liberty of ordering a fine Chardonnay of the white Burgundies of France, if you like, but if you'd rather something else, please feel free to let me know," the Somelier said while pouring a special bottle of the white wine for his guests.

"ZenJa?" Would you rather have some other beverage?"

"No, thank you. This is delightful," she said and raised her glass, waiting for Levi to do the same; to toast their first date.

"Thank you, Jonathan," Levi said dismissing the wine server.

"This is such a glamourous restaurant. I've driven by here so many times, but of course never had an opportunity to indulge myself..."

"Oh, I don't frequent this fine restaurant on a regular basis, if that's what you're asking," the young man mentioned while sipping his wine, looking over his glass, admiring the beautiful woman who sat before him.

"What does bring you here?"

"Business, on occasion and of course tonight I couldn't think of a better place to bring a lovely woman on our first date."

"It's going to be difficult to continue to impress me, if you have raised the bar so highly to begin with," ZenJa commented, logically.

"I'm curious to note you said that I might continue to impress you. I gather you're willing to see me on other occasions?"

"What do you suggest?"

"I thought on our next date we might go to the Boston Aquarium or even see a Boston Red Sox-Yankee game and have hot dogs afterward."

"That would be wonderful, actually."

"You'll soon learn there are many dimensions to the man who sits across from you at this table, my dear. I'm not all about fine wine, fine restaurants, or baseball, for that matter."

"What are you all about?"

"I'm a Yankee's fan!" he replied and snickered into his glass of wine.

"Well, you see, we're off to a bad start, right off the '*bat*', if you will," ZenJa said and smiled into her own glass of wine. "I'm a die-hard Red Sox fan."

"May the best team win the Series and cross home plate in victory," Harris replied and offered another toast.

"Speaking of plates..."

"Yes?"

"Exactly what does your license plate represent or what kind of message are you trying to send?" ZenJa asked with eyebrows raised.

"LAWLESS certainly is an interesting choice."

Before Levi was able to respond or the couple order their meals, ZenJa's cell phone rang.

"Please excuse me," she offered while taking the call at her seat.

"Hi Dad," she began. "What did you say? Say that again," she continued, urgency in her quiet voice that Levi noted, while he watched his date intently.

"Oh my God! Thank God; is there any news concerning...?" she asked excitedly.

"Oh...I'm sorry to hear that. I'll call you in a few minutes, just as soon as I get home," the ashen faced woman replied while automatically closing her cell; in a trance-like state.

"What's wrong, ZenJa?" Levi compassionately asked; deep concern displayed on his face and his manner.

"I'm sorry, Levi. I have to go home," she replied as her date, who had already risen from his seat, helped her from her chair.

"Is everything all right?" the Maitre d asked, after scurrying over from his station at the door.

"There's a family emergency, Robert. Please..."

"It's all taken care of, Mr. Harris," the man replied and ushered the couple from the restaurant.

"Please get my car, Mark and make sure Miss Beckwith's car stays secure."

"Right, away, Mr. Harris," the valet said and rushed to get one of his best customers vehicle.

"I'll see that Miss Beckwith's car is parked in the underground parking lot," Mark said and handed the Black Camaro over to its owner and refused a tip.

"Thanks again, Mark," Levi said while the couple sped out of the parking lot.

"Are you okay, ZenJa?"

"No, Levi, I'm not. Please just take me home."

"What's the address?"

"Oh, I forgot. You don't know where I live," she wrongfully assumed. Levi was indeed aware of where Miss Beckwith made her residence, but under these circumstances this fact was to remain a secret.

"It's a little house on Isabella Street," she said holding her head in her hands and tears flowed from her eyes.

"Okay, ZenJa. I know where the street is," he assured her and raced to the address he already was aware of. "It'll be okay. I'm here for you," he assured the grief stricken woman.

The black Camaro screeched to a stop in front a comfortable two story dwelling, complete with wrought iron fencing that encompassed a lovely, bountiful flower garden and neatly trimmed hedges and a rose bush laden terrace.

"You can park in the driveway," ZenJa motioned, not realizing her date coincidently stopped directly in front of her home.

After turning off the ignition, Levi exited the car and ran around to open ZenJa's car door, locked the vehicle with his remote control device, and held her arm and walked up the three steps to her home.

"I'll get it," Levi said taking the key from the overwrought woman, and opening the door to her comfortable home.

"I have to call home," ZenJa said after throwing her purse on the couch. "Would you like some privacy? I can wait outside."

"No, have a seat!" she ordered callously and began to cry.

"ZenJa, let me help you," Levi said taking the cell phone from her hand and checking the contacts and selecting the name that was listed as Dad.

"Mr. Beckwith? This is Levi Harris, a friend of ZenJa's and she's here, at her house, and would like to talk to you."

"Mr. Harris, I don't know who you are, but if you're a friend of my daughter and are in fact in her home, I know you must be okay. My daughter and our family have been under extreme circumstances of late and I'd appreciate it if you'd please keep an eye on her."

"Absolutely, Mr. Beckwith. If there's anything else you need or that I can do, please feel free to let me know. This is my cell phone number, if you ever need it," he added while reading the number for the distraught father to write down.

"Thank you Mr. Harris. I appreciate it and if I could speak with my daughter..."

"ZenJa, here's your father," he said and handed the phone to the woman sitting, curled up on a love-seat.

"Hi Dad. I'm sorry I had to hang up, but I was at a restaurant and I knew by the tone of your voice, that was not the place to take the call. "Is there any news...?"

"They have arrested a man who they think murdered Constance and Morgan. He was the man everyone in town was talking about...the man in the red Mustang."

"Oh my God!" ZenJa cried like a wounded animal.

"What's that bastard's name?"

"It's Alex Lyons."

"Alex Lyons?"

The hair on Levi Harris's neck and arms stood on end, at the mention of the name Alex Lyons.

"Yes, he appears to have been dealing in weapons, drugs, and small children," Tony Beckwith snarled.

"I'll kill that son of a bitch!" ZenJa screamed into the phone.

"He's been arrested, ZenJa and I assure you he'll be prosecuted to the fullest extent of the law."

"Oh, he better hope he is, because if that fucker gets off, I promise you I'll kill him."

"The FBI and AFT have arrested him and I believe he's in custody in Boston."

"Well, that'll save me traveling to New Hampshire to cut his throat, now won't it! And why do the Feds have him under arrest?"

"Some Federal charges he's wanted on."

"What kind of Federal charges?" ZenJa asked out loud, while Levi Harris sighed in relief.

"I don't know ZenJa, but be assured the FBI and AFT will take care of it."

"Thanks Dad, but that doesn't help us find Zippy and Olive."

"Maybe that fucker will admit to the O'Leary-Childress murders and tell us where Zippy and Olive are."

"Dad, thanks for calling, but I think I'm going to vomit, so I'll call you later. I can't talk anymore," ZenJa said and dropped the phone while she ran into the bathroom.

"Mr. Beckwith? I couldn't help but overhear ZenJa's end of the conversation and not knowing any details of what you and your family have been going through, I can't begin to imagine, but if there is anything at all I can do, please let me know."

"Thank you...what is your name...Mr. Harris?"

"Yes, it is."

"Please keep an eye on my daughter and tell her I'll be coming down to Boston on the next flight. Tell her I'll rent a car and she won't need to meet me," he said hung up the phone.

ZenJa walked, unsteadily from the rear of the house and shuffled toward the settee, once again.

"Can I get you some tea or a drink?" her date asked.

"I could use a good stiff shot of something and a cold compress for my head."

"Coming right up!"

"How do you know where I keep my booze?" she asked without opening her eyes.

"I'll find it. Liquor and I go a long way back and I'm like a bloodhound when I go looking for something *or someone*," he added in a whisper.

A few moments later the owner of the black Camaro, entered the living room with two shot glasses and a fresh bottle of whiskey on a tray and arranged the contents on a coffee table in front of the love-seat.

"Napkins, even," ZenJa mentioned before she chugged the contents of her glass and placed a cold compress on her forehead.

"I pride myself on being a gracious host..."Levi began at the same time his own cell phone rang. His second cell phone.

"Excuse me, ZenJa," he said and noted the number of the person calling.

"Yo! What's up?"

After several minutes of listening to the person on the other end of the phone, Levi disconnected the call without having said one word. This contact knew when it was appropriate to speak and not expect any response. The salutation, "Yo! What's up?" Was just that signal.

"I'm sorry, ZenJa, it was just a telemarketer," he lied and he knew his friend realized that, also, but she was in no condition to question or care, for that matter.

"Are you feeling any better? Would you like another shot?" ZenJa's date asked after downing his own drink.

"Yes, please," she said and held out her glass for him to refill.

"Thank you. Well, I guess I owe you an explanation after ruining the entire evening," ZenJa began.

"Only if you feel like talking about it and trusting me, for that matter."

"I have no one else to trust, except my family, so I guess you're it."

"Oh, shit! I forgot to tell you, your father said he was taking the first flight to Boston and he'd rent a car so you wouldn't have to meet him at the airport. He doesn't want you to be alone."

"Okay...thanks."

"ZenJa, I know you don't know me or even think very much of me, but I stress again, if there's anything you want to talk about, I want you to know you can trust me."

"You know, Levi, nothing really matters anymore. You could be a serial killer, at this point, and I truly wouldn't care," she said and began to cry.

Levi sat down beside the woman and cradled her in his arms, like he would a wounded child.

Within moments, ZenJa cried herself to sleep and her date eased himself from the settee and removed her high heels and covered her with a blanket that had been neatly folded on an armchair.

Levi turned off the bright light nearby and opted for a small light near the piano and proceeded to return the tray, empty glasses, and bottle of booze to the kitchen.

With the water running in the sink, he eased his cell phone...his second cell phone, from his jacket pocket and made a call. "Is everything okay?" he asked the person who answered on the first ring.

"We got it all taken care of," the person responded. "Keep in touch,' the man continued and disconnected the call.

Levi Harris spent the night, with ZenJa Beckwith, not as any healthy male would have hoped, but sleeping at her home, in an recliner, was better than nothing, he surmised. It really is a nice home, he noted, admiring the various paintings, sheet music displayed on the piano, and plants that adorned her comfortable abode. He strolled over to the mantle, over the stone fireplace, and was transfixed by the family photos that graced the various family heirlooms and treasures.

Levi noticed a fairly recent photo of ZenJa surrounded by who appeared to be her mother and father and a much younger sister. The sister, appeared to be at the awkward age of twelve or thirteen. She had straight, sandy brown hair, glasses and from what he could see, she wore braces on her teeth. Several other photos, displayed, reflected the family as a close and bonded unit. Photos taken on vacations and baby pictures of each family member. The two pictures that peaked his interest most of all were one of ZenJa, approximately four years old, outfitted in a tiny cowgirl hat, red fringed vest and skirt, white western styled shirt and black cowboy boots. Slung on her hip was a holster and toy six-shooter. The second photo appeared to be ZenJa, at approximately sixteen years old, at an outdoor shooting range. She displayed a handsome Glock 9mm. weapon in one hand and a paper target with as many as twenty bullet holes, with nearly half of them hitting the center of the paper *victim*. "My kind of girl," Levi murmured. A nice wholesome family, Levi also correctly concluded.

Several hours later, as dawn was beginning to embrace the city of Boston, there was a knock at the front door of ZenJa's home. Leaping from his resting spot in a recliner, Levi Harris removed his own Glock 9mm. from his shoulder holster and approached the entryway with caution.

Chapter 13

"Well, if it isn't Chief Connors," Molly announced to the patrons who frequently dined at her establishment.

"Good evening, folks," the chief replied, sauntering toward his usual stool at the counter. "I know you've all heard by now that we've made an arrest in the O'Leary-Childress murders and we're hoping to connect this individual to the disappearances of Miss Beckwith, Miss Pickering and the Winters and Olsen girls. I hope and pray this man confesses or is at least found guilty of these crimes and this will lead us to their whereabouts in order to bring closure to the families," the chief continued, as proud as a peacock.

"All I hope is that the criminal justice system works," Lanny Williams, a local farmer and friend of the Beckwith family said. "There'll never be closure for any of those families."

"So, what's the scoop on this guy?" Jim Bacon, the owner of a local automotive repair shop asked.

"From what I know, he's from Massachusetts and has quite a long criminal record. We aren't even going to be able to bring him to trial here in New Hampshire, yet. The Feds have him in custody on more serious crimes he's committed prior to the murders," the chief explained.

"You mean, allegedly committed, right, Chief?" Molly asked while serving several regular customers their meat loaf dinners.

"Well, yes, of course...I mean allegedly."

"Am I to assume you and Miller, along with the FBI and state troopers are still looking for the other four girls?" Jim Bacon asked. "I mean we're all utilizing every spare moment we have to keep on looking."

"The federal and state authorities have scaled back their operation, somewhat, but of course Miller and I are doing the best we can. We can never give up hope and I always notify the families if there is anything new to report."

"There is nothing to report, is there?" Jim asked.

"No, unfortunately, there's not, but I've established a rapport with the cable channel networks and the legal analysts on board, to keep these stories in the headlines."

"And yourself in front of the cameras, aye," Lanny Williams scoffed.

"Think what you want, Williams, but as long as the story gets important attention, the end justifies the means, I always say."

"From what I've seen from the coverage, Connors, it appears the media has pretty much dried up on the Beckwith, Pickering and disappearances of the girls from three-four years ago, now that the O'Leary and Childress girls were found murdered and the alleged perp has been arrested. And as Molly has reminded us, over and over again, the news media continues to highlight the fact that Constance and Morgan were perky, gorgeous, lively cheerleaders who were *beautiful*. So much for the ugly girls, well I mean, less attractive girls, who go missing everyday in the country," Carol Williams added to the conversation, while she and her husband ate their dinners.

"Yeah, I keep saying, *only the pretty ones*, get the publicity," Molly confirmed.

"I'm sorry you folks feel that way," Chief Connors replied, finished his meal, and paid his tab before returning to the Longberry Police Station.

Once inside his cramped and musty office his personal cell phone rang and he answered it on the first ring.

"Hello?" he asked.

"Any news on that Alex Lyons situation?" the caller asked.

"No, the Fed's are keeping pretty closed lip about it. They're not even returning my phone calls."

"Well, just as long as that bastard stays in jail..." the caller said and drifted off.

"What about that Beckwith woman?"

"The *missing* one?" Chief asked.

"No, you fucking asshole, the sister."

"Oh, she's gone back to school, somewhere in Boston. It's a known fact that after a few months, people seem to loose interest in finding their loved ones. It's such a shame, and all, but I'm sure she'll be the same way once she starts dating or something. Now! She's one hot chick and I'm sure she'll have no problem 'getting a life', if you know what I mean."

"Just get back to doing what you do best, Connors," the caller said and disconnected the call.

"He must mean, fishing," Connors said and chuckled at his own sick humor when Officer Miller entered the office.

"You going fishing?"

"No, you know we have missing girls to look for."

"I know, Chief. Several of us covered the old Johnson farm, including what's left of the barns, sheds and farm house and as expected, we didn't find anything."

"We have to keep looking and by the way, I'm heading out to check the Overton Cave," Connors relied and left the office to continue his own search.

Chapter 14

The black Suburban approached the underground parking lot entrance to the Federal Building in Boston several hours after the arrest of Alex Lyons. Word of the capture of this most wanted fugitive spread like wildfire among the local and national news organizations. As typical in high profile arrests, media outlets swarmed, like bees, around the building in hopes of getting photographs of Alex Lyons, through the heavily tinted windows of the SUV and/or an immediate interview with an FBI spokesperson, to broadcast on the nightly news.

The Suburban approached the downtown garage at a high rate of speed and entered the enclosure, but not before several cameramen captured the event on film and others took still pictures on their professional cameras, all capable of taking close-up shots from a great distance away with the benefit of high powered lenses.

A larger crowd of curiosity seekers and media surrounded the Federal Complex because it was announced a short statement was about to be made on the arrest of Alex Lyons.

"Who the hell is Alex Lyons? Has anyone ever heard of him or been able to find what he's being charged with or any past criminal history?" a reporter for Fox News asked the other members of the press who patiently waited for the news conference to begin outside the Federal Building.

"No, I can't find anything on this guy. I have no idea what Federal charges he's allegedly committed. I do understand he was initially stopped by a...Chief Connors of the Longberry, New Hampshire PD for the possession of illegal weapons and drugs and there is some rumor that items from the alleged murders of...Constance O'Leary and Morgan Childress of Longberry, were also found in the trunk of his red Mustang," the reporter added after checking his notes.

"We'll have to wait and see what the spokesperson says, I guess," a reporter for the Boston Herald reasoned.

"Someone's coming out, now!" an observer commented and the crowd gathered around the microphones that had been placed near the front entrance of the government building.

"My name is Agent E.D. Foley...spelled E. D. F.O.L.E.Y, the smartly dressed, middle aged, slender blonde, federal employee began, in a careful and direct manner.

"I have a short statement to make and will not be taking any questions at this time. The charges against Mr. Lyons have not been completely filed at this early stage of our case."

"The man we have under arrest is thirty year old Alex Lyons whose residence appears to have been in Yarmouth, Massachusetts until today," the striking agent commented, displaying a smirk because of her own joke.

"Mr. Lyons has been Mirandized and has been appointed a public defender. He is without financial means to pay for his own defense in the serious crimes for which he has been and will be charged."

"Exactly what charges are they?" an over eager reporter from the New England Telegram asked.

Agent E.D. Foley looked over her glasses at the young gentleman who asked the question and continued without acknowledging the interruption.

"Mr. Lyons has been under surveillance for more than five years and will face charges including but not limited to the interstate trafficking of illegal assault weapons, and interstate distribution and transportation of drugs, including and not limited to Marijuana, Ecstasy, Heroin, and Meth, but his most recent activities include the alleged murder of a federal judge and two DEA agents. So, in light of those alleged facts, he is and will remain in federal custody."

"What about the rumor he was found in possession of items of clothing belonging to two murdered New Hampshire girls in his red Mustang?" the same over-eager reporter blurted out.

Once again, Agent Foley looked over her eyeglasses and ignored the question.

"I'll now conclude this briefing until there is more information, forthcoming. I'm asking the citizens of New Hampshire and Massachusetts, as well, to keep in mind the fact that our trials are conducted in a court of law and not in the streets and each person is innocent until proven guilty in that court of law. Thank you."

"Oh, by the way, I would like to see you," Foley said pointing to the reporter who asked the questions concerning the clothing found in the red Mustang inside."

Once inside the front door, Agent Foley spun around and approached the reporter; her finger not one inch away from the startled man's face.

"Where in hell did you hear that from; about items of clothing found?" she demanded.

"Oh, we've been talking with Police Chief Connors, from the Longberry, PD for a few months now, about the missing girls in the area," the man replied nervously. "He's most co-operative and eager for word to spread in the news media about those poor missing girls. He even gave us pictures of...let me check my notes...of Constance O'Leary and Morgan Childress to publish a while ago."

"What else did the chief have to say?" Foley asked with growing interest.

"He did make a rather odd statement, now that I think about it, when he gave us those pictures; he said, and I quote, 'Those were the pretty ones'. What do you make of that Agent Foley?" the reporter continued.

"We live in stressful times and I know that community has been rocked to the core because of those missing girls," was her reply and showed the reporter out the door.

At the same time FBI Agent D.E. Foley was conducting the outdoor press conference, Alex Lyons was dealing with his own issues inside the FBI agency.

"Did you have to treat me like a common criminal?" Alex Lyons snarled at FBI Agent Emerson.

The owner of the red Mustang waited for the federal agent to allow him to exit the Chevy Suburban and to have the handcuffs that bound his wrists removed.

"Because I'm not FBI, I expected to be treated a little better, you know."

"Come on, Lyons; buck up! We had to make it look authentic, didn't we? And we're all from the same brotherhood, right?"

"Yeah, but we left the sleepy little town near Lake Winnipesaukee hours ago."

"Stop whining, man. You had air conditioning, didn't you?" Emerson snickered.

"By the way, where's my Mustang?"

"Don't worry, it's being towed to the garage as we speak...and just like magic, here it is!" he added while the tow truck backed into the downtown facility to off-load the sports car.

"Okay, now that everyone in the world knows what my license plate is, you're going to get me new ones, right?" Lyons asked the federal agent. "No way in hell am I giving up my ride," he added.

"Of course, what plate would you like?"

"Maybe one from another state, to begin with."

"I'll look into it," Emerson said and walked toward the elevator. He had more important things to do than stand there and discuss license plates with this guy.

Chapter 15

Peering through the window, adjacent to the driveway, Levi noticed a modest Toyota Camry with Maryland license plates parked behind his own car; obviously the rental car Beckwith said he would obtain upon his arrival in Boston. Levi quickly holstered his weapon and opened the door.

"Mr. Beckwith?" Levi asked and stepped aside. This man was obviously Zenja's father; the man he had seen in the photos on the mantel.

"Interesting vanity plate," Beckwith growled and walked past the stranger."

"I got here as soon as I could," he replied and sat beside his daughter who was waking from a fitful sleep on the love seat.

"Thank you for coming, Dad," ZenJa cried and hugged her father.

"There's nothing I wouldn't do for you, ZenJa," he said glaring at the stranger who quietly stood off to the side of the doorway. "Nothing!" he repeated.

"My head is about the explode," she said.

"I have just the cure," Levi said and disappeared into the kitchen.

"Who in hell is that?"

"He's a student at Claybourne. He's in my one criminal justice classes."

"He looks a little old to be in college."

"Dad, don't start. There are grandfathers taking classes at Claybourne and I'm sure other colleges, as well. Age is immaterial."

"He sure has made himself right at home here," he added when Levi brought a tray of beverages, including mugs filled with piping hot coffee, cream and sugar, two aspirins and a tall glass of iced water for ZenJa.

"Most kitchens, I've noticed, are equipped with similar essentials," Levi said quietly and smiled sweetly at Tony Beckwith.

"Thank you, Levi," ZenJa said. "Water and aspirin are exactly what I need."

"I've suffered a hang over or two in my life, so I know the perfect remedy," he said goading ZenJa's father even more.

"Hangover...what are you talking about?"

"Dad, Levi is being the wise-ass as, he usually is. We had two shots of whiskey after the call you made, so I guess we have you to blame for that!" she said and chuckled in spite of herself.

"Okay...you got me," Beckwith admitted.

"So, enough of this shit! ZenJa began, coming to grips with the reason her father was in Boston. "Who's with Mom?"

"Our neighbor, Emily, is with her. I couldn't leave her alone, especially now."

"So, what's going on?" ZenJa asked. "You were so vague last night; so start over."

"If you folks want me to leave, I'd be happy to give you some privacy," Levi reasoned, though leaving was the last thing he wanted to do, in light of the fact he had more information than Mr. Beckwith most likely had concerning the latest developments in Longberry, New Hampshire. Not that he was going to divulge what he knew to anyone.

"Yes, please leave us alone," Tony Beckwith said.

"Dad, maybe Levi can help."

"You don't know anything about him, ZenJa."

"She knows I wasn't brought up with my family in a circus. She knows I believe in the death penalty, and I drive a black Camaro and she knows I love Molly's BLT's and onion rings."

"Speaking of the Camaro...what in hell does that vanity plate signify?" ZenJa asked. "I mean, come on, LAWLESS?"

"That may not mean what you think, ZenJa. Actually, I am rather an activist and want LESSLAW!"

"So you're a liberal?" Tony asked.

"Oh, far from it, Mr. Beckwith. I believe there are too many laws on the books now. Enforcing those we have are enough and if not..."

"If not?" ZenJa asked

"Matters have a way of taking care of themselves," Levi said and smiled with his boyish grin.

"I'm not sure what to make of you..." Tony began.

"No one does," Levi said, his grin widening even more.

"Oh, God! None of this is important!" ZenJa yelled.

"What did you find out yesterday, Dad?"

Tony looked at ZenJa and then toward Levi.

"He can stay, Dad! I need someone I can trust. There sure isn't anyone here in Boston, now is there?"

"What if he can't be trusted?"

"I can be trusted!" Levi replied forcefully; his childish demeanor disappeared like lightening. His once bright blue eyes now the color of dark cobalt and steel.

"Okay, I'll start with the events that unfolded yesterday," Beckwith said sitting on the love seat beside his daughter and Levi making himself at home in the black leather recliner, once again.

"Chief Connors, the state police and FBI were having a press conference, of course it was a waste of time; there was nothing new to report."

"Were you at the conference," his daughter asked.

"Yes, right up front."

"So, anyway, Chief Connors gave his little spiel and abruptly took off in his cop car, leaving the trooper and FBI guys to finish the media event. Not long afterward the police radios squawked and it was Connors asking for backup. He announced he was in pursuit of a red Mustang, the one seen in Longberry a while back. According to rumor, the man had weapons, drugs and...listen to this...a backpack that contained items belonging to the murdered O'Leary and Childress girls. The chief was watching the area where their bodies were found, in hopes the perp would show up...you know... return to the scene of the crime and low and behold, he did. So the chief called for back up and the guy was arrested. But the thing is, the Feds have him in custody. He's wanted on several felonies, one including a Capital murder charge, so he'll have to go on trial for the Longberry murders *after* the Feds are done with him."

"Oh my God! This is good news. They found the guy responsible for the murders and now I pray they can force him to tell us where Zippy and Olive are, not to mention the other two girls who are missing!" ZenJa expressed with excitement.

Expressionless, Levi continued to sit in the recliner without moving a muscle, his eyes hooded to conceal his thoughts.

"You said that the man they arrested was the man who owns or was at least driving the red Mustang Molly and Zippy said they had seen at the Café?" ZenJa shrieked?"

"Yes, why?" her father asked.

"Because I saw that same car, here in Boston when I first got back to the city!" she exclaimed, glaring at Levi.

"So?" her father asked.

"Because it so happens I saw that red Mustang screaming down Storrow Drive," she continued with eyes like fireballs, piercing into the face of the young man sitting in her recliner.

Levi realized what ZenJa was about to say and knew he was going to have to make up some sort of an excuse and shifted, uncomfortably, in his seat.

"Well, Levi, do you have anything to say or has a cat got your tongue?"

"What are you talking about?" Levi asked with the innocence of an altar boy.

"I saw you barrel-assing down Storrow Drive right behind that red Mustang the other day. You were racing with him, so I assume you know him and if you know him, you must be in cahoots with him, too?" she screamed.

Levi lived by the rule that says, deny...deny... deny and hope for the best.

"I have no idea what you're talking about. But I do remember this joker challenging me to a little race, so I took him up on it. It was no big deal."

"I also remember Molly and Zippy saying you *both*, the guy in the red Mustang and you, the guy in the black Camaro were at the Café at the same time and on the same day," ZenJa yelled. "Get the hell out of my house!"

"ZenJa, you have it all wrong," Levi murmured exiting the comfort of the recliner.

"You and that bastard are in this together, aren't you? Where's my sister, Levi?" she screamed.

"Dad move your car so Levi can leave," she demanded.

"ZenJa, please let me explain." Unbeknownst to Miss Beckwith, Levi Harris would have come clean concerning the whole situation, but this woman was not about to listen, he realized and drove from Isabella Street to his temporary apartment in Boston.

Before he exited his vehicle, his second cell phone rang.

"How's it going?" the caller asked.

"As expected, but I don't like the way this situation is progressing."

"Don't tell me you're developing a conscience?"

"It's too late for that," Levi replied and disconnected the call, packed Alex Lyons' and his own meager belongings and left the quaint city of Boston, but not for the last time. He'd be back. He had one more reason to come back...that reason was ZenJa Beckwith.

Chapter 16

"Where's Mr. Harris?" ZenJa asked Professor Smith after class the next day. She hadn't realized how fond she had become of him, until he suddenly wasn't sitting behind her in class.

"I understand from Dean Thompson, he has dropped out of Claybourne. I believe he said he had a family emergency. Other than that, nobody seems to know."

"Oh," ZenJa replied and started to walk away.

"You know, Miss Beckwith, it appeared you two really hit it off...if I may be so forward. I'm sorry he's no longer a student in my class. He certainly brought about a lot of interest and excitement for a class that can be rather boring, if I must say so myself."

"Thank you, Professor Smith. I agree," she said and walked toward the Dean's office.

"Please come in Miss Beckwith. What can I do for you?" the Dean of Students asked.

"I realize this may be a rather odd request, but I was wondering if you could check and see if Mr. Harris may have left any forwarding address. We had a discussion, the other night and I owe him an apology for being an idiot."

"ZenJa, that is highly unethical, but I'll at least see if there's an address," he said and scanned his computer for registration and other information that is required to be given by each student upon receiving an acceptance letter for Claybourne College.

"Well, this certainly is odd," Smith began.

"What?" ZenJa asked and tried, in vain, to see the computer screen for herself.

"There's no information for Mr. Levi Harris. It appears he either never registered or his information has been deleted from our system."

"You mean there's absolutely no information about Levi Harris in the computer?" ZenJa asked; the mystery about this man, deepening, by the day.

"No! His files have disappeared." Smith responded while scratching his head in confusion.

"Thank you, Dean. I'm getting the feeling this man is and has been involved in the disappearance of my sister, her friend, and murders and God only knows what else," she said and ran from the office.

Chapter 17

For many fruitless years, residents of Longberry searched for Zippy Beckwith, Olive Pickering, and two other missing girls, Ashley Winters and Rose-Ann Olsen. ZenJa Beckwith made the trek from Boston to Longberry during school vacations to join the search that now appeared to be senseless, but ZenJa made a promise to her sister and she wasn't about to stop her search now. On most occasions, she and her parents were the only ones looking, in hopes of finding any trace of their loved one...or any girl.

Thankfully, during that time, there were no other reports of missing girls in the state of New Hampshire and all the citizens of Longberry were assured there would be no more disappearances or murders because Alex Lyons was sentenced to life in prison for the murder of a federal judge and two DEA agents, three years after his arrest.

For her own curiosity, ZenJa searched through the Boston newspapers for the names of the federal agents who arrested Alex Lyons, the name of the prosecutor, and made appointments to meet all involved in his arrest and trial.

"Agent Emerson," ZenJa greeted the tall, handsome forty year old government employee who pulled out a chair for her to sit in, in his office. "Thank you for seeing me."

"It's my pleasure. What can I do for you?" he asked getting right to the point; the no nonsense man he was.

"I wanted to attend the trial of Alex Lyons, three years ago, but I was stonewalled. I was told because of the sensitive nature of the information to be brought out in that trial his case was to be handled behind closed doors. Personally, I find that to be bullshit."

"I appreciate your feelings, believe me, and I realize and understand your passion in regards to this case, in hopes of getting answers to your own questions involving your sister and others."

ZenJa looked like she had been slapped across the face, at this man's callous behavior towards her.

"How do you know about my sister and what my motive might have been regarding Mr. Lyons? Did he tell you something?"

"No, Miss Beckwith, Mr. Lyons has never mentioned his involvement in the disappearances or murders in New Hampshire and because I'm an agent of the FBI and was present in Longberry when Lyons was arrested, I'm more than aware of the situation there," he replied.

"He's never gone to trial for the murders of those two girl!" ZenJa exclaimed.

"I'm fully aware of that, but he won't be seeing the light of day, so it was felt it would be a waste of taxpayers money to try him on those charges at this time. It's also a good idea to have leverage over an inmate in case, due to extenuating circumstances and because of a technicality, if Lyons were to get out of prison, the other charges would be immediately drawn and he would go to trial for murder and again, be remanded to prison."

"There is no justice, is there?" ZenJa asked.

"No, I'm afraid this is the best system we have and it's far from perfect, I agree."

"May I at least see this Mr. Lyons in an attempt to find out where he may have left or buried my sister; I've accepted the fact that she is, indeed, dead."

"Inmates have a list of acceptable visitors and the inmate must request to see you or receive mail from you, so I would assume that won't happen. Mr. Lyons is in isolation and not a very social person."

"Well, thank you for your time, Agent Emerson," ZenJa said and rose from her seat.

"If I may, Miss Beckwith...congratulate you on your acceptance into the FBI academy and now our tight knit community."

"Well, thank you Agent Emerson. That truly was the greatest day of my life."

"What field office are you assigned to?"

"In D.C." she replied.

"I know you'll make our agency proud," the man said and showed ZenJa from his office.

One of ZenJa's classmates and a graduate with her class, at the Quantico facility, was a tall, dark haired, maybe thirty year old man, who ZenJa knew by the name of A.L. Smart. He who coincidently moved into an identical two bedroom condominium at Forest Haven Estates, next door to the lovely auburn-red haired woman, on the same day.

"Hello, ZenJa," A.L. greeted her, both struggling with items of furniture they were moving into their units.

"Hello, A.L.," she replied. "I hate moving, don't you?"

"Yes, indeed. Hopefully, we won't have to move anytime soon."

"If you need any help, let me know," A.L. offered.

"I had a moving company do the job this morning, and it's all done, now, but thank you so much for the offer."

"I'm glad these condo's have garages, aren't you?" A.L. asked. "I bet you're as protective of your nice new black Dodge Charger as I am of my red Mustang."

For moment, A.L. noticed a slight hesitation from his new neighbor, before she responded. Had she thought it a coincidence that a driver in another red Mustang had entered her life. He hoped not.

"Oh, yes. This is my baby and I don't even want to see a scratch on it," she finally responded, with a guarded expression on her face.

"Well, let me know if you want me to help you hang curtains or if I can be of any help," A.L. cheerfully said and entered his own condo.

"How's it going?" was the question asked when A.L. answered his cell phone.

"All's well here."

"Has the package been delivered?"

"Yup...all safe and sound."

"Will you have access... to install the G.P.S. unit?"

"No problem."

'Good."

"Hey! While I have you on the phone, are you gonna come and help me unpack this shit? I feel like a fucking gypsy."

"I can't tell you how much I want to. It'll all be over soon."

"Thank God!" A.L. replied.

"What's it to you? When this is over, there'll be another one. I'm the one with a stake in this deal," the caller retorted. "My life's been...," the stranger began, but abruptly ended the conversation.

"I may stop over, one of these days," the stranger continued.

"You'll be driving the F-150?"

"Yes; I'll let you know before I get down there, so you can leave the garage door open, so I can enter through the side entrance; out of sight."

"How do you know I have a garage?" A.L. asked.

"I know everything," the stranger replied and laughed.

"If you're coming down here to DC, who's going to be in New

Hampshire?"

"It's all covered," was the reply and the call was disconnected.

Chapter 18

"It's so good to see you Molly," ZenJa said and perched on a stool at the counter of the Café she had frequented over the years. "I can't believe you're still working."

"Hey, sweetie, what am I supposed to be doing? Retired, knitting blankets or some such thing," she added and hugged this beautiful woman who never forgot to stop and say hello when she was in town.

"So, what are you doing in town?"

"As always, I'm here to search for Zippy, but now that I've graduated from school, I've gotten a new condo, near my new job, so I came to pick up some items my mom and dad thought I might want."

"I see you have a new car," Molly mentioned.

"It's kinda spiffy, isn't it?"

"What is it?"

"It's a Dodge Charger."

"I can't help but notice it's black," Molly said, with a twinkle in her eye.

"Oh Molly! I haven't seen that guy in three years. He simply disappeared from the face of the earth, so it seems."

"So, what can I get ya?"

"I'll have one of your famous BLT's and onion rings and a Coke."

"Funny you say that, because remember that guy you were just talking about...the guy who drove that black Camaro, way back...?"

"Yes!" ZenJa replied, excitement evident in her voice. "What about him?"

"He was in here yesterday, and ordered the exact same thing you just ordered. What are the odds?"

"He was here?" she asked.

"What was he driving?"

"He had a spanking brand new black Camaro and he's been in here many times, over the years. You never met up with him while you've been here?" Molly asked.

"No, sadly, I haven't. Listen, Molly, if you see him again, please give him my card," she said and handed a business card that merely had her first name and phone number printed on it.

"That's a funny business card."

"Oh, just give it to him, Molly, he'll see the humor in it," she replied and smiled at the thought of the dark haired, blue eyed stranger who had come into her life as quickly and quietly as he'd left.

"Well, what have you been up to since you graduated from Claybourne College?"

"Oh, nothing much, Molly," ZenJa lied. "I'm a financial analyst at major bank in the city," she replied, purposely being vague, avoiding the truth at all costs.

"Do you love your work?"

Oh, absolutely!" ZenJa said in all honesty.

"Well, Miss Beckwith," Chief Connors greeted the young auburn-red haired beauty when he entered the café.

"You're a financial analyst, are you? That's wonderful. I know your folks must be so proud of you."

"Yes, they are Chief Connors. Is my order ready?" ZenJa asked. "If it is, I would like it to *go,* please. I have to get back to the city."

"Coming right up, ZenJa," Molly answered and bagged the order up and sent her friend on her way.

Chapter 19

Levi Harris was staked out on the hillside adjacent to Molly's café and with the benefit of binoculars, he watched ZenJa Beckwith and Chief Connors enter the establishment, a few moments apart. Only after both customers left Molly's did the tall, dark haired man open his cell phone and make a single call.

"Follow her," were the only two words he spoke before getting inside his black Camaro and driving toward Molly's for an evening meal.

"Good evening, Molly," Levi greeted the proprietor, moments after the chief and ZenJa left the establishment and sat in his usual booth with a clear view of the parking lot, out front.

"Oh my God!" You just missed her," Molly exclaimed.

"Missed who?" he asked snickering to himself.

"ZenJa; ZenJa was just here and she asked me to give you this," she said handing the business card with only her name and telephone number on it.

"Levi looked at the card and chuckled at the joke only shared by the twosome.

"ZenJa said you'd laugh when you got the card."

"She's right! What a wonderful sense of humor she has."

"She said she hasn't seen you in a long time and wanted to get in touch with you."

"I know. It seems when I'm in town, she isn't and when she is, I'm not," Levi carelessly replied still thinking of the business card he held in his hand.

"How do you know when she's in town, if you're not?" Molly suspiciously asked.

Oh, shit! Levi thought to himself. "I've been checking in on the progress with Chief Connors to see how the cases of the missing girls are coming along," he lied. "And he mentioned she and her family are still valiantly looking for them."

"Oh, well then, you know there hasn't been any progress."

"Yes, I'm afraid I do."

"Well, I gave you the business card she asked me to, so what would you like for dinner, tonight?"

"I'll have a steak, medium rare, and a garden salad with Ranch dressing and a large coffee. I've got a long drive ahead of me and I'll need the coffee to stay awake."

"I'll get your order right away," Molly said.

"I see you have a new Camaro," she yelled from the kitchen.

"Yeah, I'm kinda partial to them, I guess," he mentioned while keeping an eye on the parking lot, in hopes Chief Connors didn't return at this moment.

After gulping down his dinner, Levi paid his bill, gave Molly a handsome tip and accepted a large coffee to go.

"See you soon!" Levi yelled on his way out the door, knowing that wasn't going to happen any time in the near future. He would be coming back to Longberry and the surrounding area, but not driving his black Camaro, dining at Molly's or contacting ZenJa Beckwith.

Several days later, in the darkness of night, the black Camaro, with the District of Columbia license plate, *LAWLESS* and a new red Mustang, with the Virginia license plate, *WANTED* left the sleepy town of Longberry, New Hampshire, onboard a tractor trailer heading South, down Interstate 95; destination unknown. The two sports cars had been exchanged for less high profile, less conspicuous vehicles from the tractor trailer. One vehicle being a silver Ford F-150 and the other, that was tailing ZenJa Beckwith was a silver Chevy Impala, both vehicles displaying Washington DC license plates.

At the same time the sports cars left the border, of New Hampshire, Chief Connors entered Molly's Café, once again, on his way home, to grab a quick bite to eat.

"That friend of yours...the guy in the black Camaro was just here," Molly commented.

"What friend? What Camaro?" the chief asked, his interest peaked.

"The guy that said he calls you to find out how the search is going for the missing girls; the guy who was here the day Zippy Beckwith went missing, as a matter of fact," Molly recalled. He seems to know ZenJa Beckwith pretty well or I might say she seems rather interested in him. She asked me to give him her business card, just today, and I gave it to him about three hours ago. He was leaving town...or so he said."

"Where's the business card?"

"I just told you, I gave it to the guy. Aren't you listening?"

"Did you see what license plate it had on it?"

"Yeah, it was registered in DC and it said, *LAWLESS*."

"Sorry, Molly...I gotta go," the chief said and scurried back to his patrol car to make a call on his cell phone. "I need to run a tag, Miller."

"Okay, what's the plate, Chief?"

"The tag is DC and it's a vanity plate that says *LAWLESS*."

"I'll check it right out, Chief," Officer Miller replied.

Connors was leaving the parking lot and a nondescript silver, older model, Ford F-150, super cab, pickup followed the law enforcement officer, at a distance, but close enough to keep his car in sight and at the same time the man driving the pickup made a call from his cell phone. "I don't know why we just don't stop playing games, here, and do what needs to be done."

"Everything's going according to plan," was the response to the man in the F-150.

"Chief Connors?" Officer Miller called the man's cell phone.

"Yeah, what ya got, Miller?"

"There's no such Camaro with that tag, in DC or anywhere else."

"That's bull shit!"

"Chief, there is *NO* car registered with that tag, in DC or any state for that matter...Camaro or otherwise."

"What the fuck?"

Chapter 20

"I just had Miller check the stats on the black Camaro with DC plates...*LAWLESS* and he told me there is no such car, anywhere, registered in the United States with that tag," Chief Connors screamed into his cell phone. "Something's going on and I don't like it. That Beckwith girl has been snooping around, way too much for her own good. She needs to be taken care of, one way or another," Connors demanded.

"How do you purpose doing that?" the male on the other end of the phone asked.

"There's one way to get to her and maybe she'll finally give up and be thankful she's still alive and that's to eliminate her only reason to come back to this God-awful town."

"You're suggesting killing her parents?" the mysterious person asked.

"What's two more?" Connors replied with an eerie laugh.

"You're a sick mother fucker."

"And you're not? What if that doesn't keep Miss Beckwith away, after you've accomplished that?"

"Then she'll be next."

"How many victims do you think a small town in New Hampshire will tolerate before someone takes this seriously?"

"Hey, we got Alex Lyons in prison and everyone in town thinks he's the perp responsible for two murders and most likely the disappearances of the other girls. Miss Beckwith's parents deaths won't be classified as murders. Just get it done. This time, you're going to have to get your hands dirty," Chief Connors ordered.

While the occupant inside the silver Ford F-150 kept Chief Connors under surveillance on this damp, cold evening, an unknown person called the Beckwith residence.

"Mr. Beckwith, this is New Hampshire State Trooper Dominic Solari and I wanted to let you know your daughter, ZenJa, has been in an automobile accident and is currently in the emergency room at Lakes Regional Hospital."

"Oh my God! How is she?" Mr. Beckwith asked when his wife reached his side and he continued to speak into his cell phone.

"Her condition is not known, but the hospital staff would like you to come to the emergency entrance and I'll meet you there."

"Thank you, Trooper, Solari. We're on our way!"

"Hurry! Ann...we have to get to Lakes Regional. ZenJa's been in an automobile accident," he yelled while the couple scurried to get dressed and rush down the highway to the hospital, that was more than fifteen miles away.

The couple fought to keep their composure; but nonetheless speeding through the heavy fog, rain slicked, winding back roads. Out of the pitch black, as dense as velvet and dreariness like death, itself, an unidentified driver and vehicle, mysteriously parked in a secluded path, off the highway, suddenly turned on the headlights and lurched toward the Beckwith's car.

The Halogen headlights blinded the driver; and the mystery vehicle gunned it's engine and entered the roadway from the passenger's side of the small car.

Natural instincts took over and in an effort to avoid an accident, Tony Beckwith, swerved the car to the left, swerved crossed the center line and fish-tailed; slammed into a large elm tree before bursting into flames and careening over a fifty foot embankment with a horrendous and violent crash of twisted metal and breaking glass.

The mysterious vehicle vanished from the site; no one the wiser it had been there on the night Tony and Ann Beckwith perished, in a terrible automobile accident.

"Chief!" Officer Miller yelled into his cell phone at the scene of a horrible fire and car accident. "Wake up, Chief," he yelled while the sleepy law enforcement officer struggled to open his eyes and get his bearings.

"What's up?"

"There's a car fire on Blackberry Road. A car's gone over the bank and it's burning. The fire department's on its way; the car is over the ledge, but I'm going to go down there and try and see if I can get anyone out of the wreck!" Miller yelled before he dropped the phone and made a valiant effort to help anyone who may have survived the horrible accident.

Chief Connors slowly put his phone down and started to get dressed. He knew there was no sense in rushing. He knew Blackberry Road like the back of his hand and realized no one would survive going over that ledge.

"I'm impressed," he said to himself and put his coat and hat on. "That was fast," he said and smiled to himself.

Chief Connors entered his patrol car that was parked in his driveway and slowly entered the highway. Chief Connors wasn't the only vehicle on that stretch of road, that night; a silver Ford F-150 was following him, but this driver had the benefit of night-vision goggles, which enabled him to drive without benefit of headlights. The deep dense fog completely obscured the pickup while it tailed the police chief.

The police chief's vehicle and the silver F-150, close behind, approached a narrow, curved stretch of highway and the glare of emergency lights and rescue vehicles was apparent for more than half a mile away. The driver of the Ford pickup locked his night vision goggles away and turned on his headlights when both vehicles approached the accident scene.

The driver of the pickup parked his vehicle many feet away and cautiously made his way, undetected, toward the ambulances and the EMS attendants who were loading two bodies into the units.

Officer Miller was receiving oxygen and medical treatment for burns to his arms, hands, and face when the mysterious driver looked to make sure Chief Connors was otherwise occupied and approached the young police officer.

"You okay?" the man asked.

"Who are you?" Miller asked.

"Oh, I was just passing by and saw the lights and all. I thought I could be of some help," he replied dodging the question.

"Yeah, I'll be okay, just some minor burns. I did the best I could." Miller replied, tears rolling down his cheeks.

It was apparent, to the stranger, this man made a valiant effort to rescue the unfortunate people in the wrecked car. His burns were more serious than he admitted and his clothes were burned and ragged from scaling the ledge and his hands were severally scraped and bruised.

"Do you know who the victims are?" the stranger asked.

"Are you the news?" Miller asked.

"Oh, trust me, I'm not involved with any news organization,"

"Well, I probably shouldn't say this, until the family is notified, but the two victims are Tony and Ann Beckwith."

"Oh my fucking God!" the stranger said and grasped the side of the ambulance for balance.

"Does this look like an accident?" the stranger asked, after the ambulance left the scene.

"Too early to tell," Miller said as Chief Connors approached the two men; the stranger quickly walking toward his truck before the chief could see his face.

"Thanks for stopping, but I think we have this all under control now. The chief is here," Miller yelled after the stranger who left the scene, more quickly, than he'd arrived.

"Who the hell was that?" Connors asked glaring, through the fog, at the truck that was leaving the way it came.

"I don't know some guy who saw the wreck and offered to help, but I told him we have it all under control."

"Did he ask any questions?"

"Nope," Miller lied. Miller wanted to find out what that stranger knew or how he knew the Beckwith family. He wondered if maybe he was the perp they were looking for and he wanted to get the credit, if he was. Miller had every intention of finding out who the driver of that Ford F-150 had been. He wanted to become Police Chief of Longberry, one day and what better way to accomplish that, than to solve the mysteries that surrounded this small town.

The driver of the F-150 slowly approached the entrance to the emergency room of Lakes Regional Hospital after notifying his *people* that there was a situation. His *people* authorized him to proceed as he felt best, with the extenuating circumstances that had just taken place.

"You got Connors tail?" the stranger called on his cell phone to the man driving the silver Chevy Impala.

"I'm on it," came the reply. "Okay!'

"Make sure you let me know if he comes near the hospital. I have business and don't need him here."

"Got it!"

"Can you tell me where I can find Officer Miller?" the stranger asked when he approached the front desk of the hospital facility.

"He's still being treated for his injuries, but you can sit here in the waiting room and I'll let him know you are looking for him. Can I tell him your name?"

"You can tell him the name is... Ford."

"Okay," the nurse said and left to continue her duties.

"Mr. Ford?" Officer Miller said when he walked toward the stranger he had met at the Beckwith accident scene.

"No, that's my vehicle. What my name doesn't matter right now. I need your help. What can you tell me about the accident?'

"Oh, I don't know. I don't know who you are."

"What do you want in life, man?" the stranger asked.

"My goal, for now, anyway, is to one day be police chief of Longberry and maybe one day become a Secret Service agent."

"Trust me, I can help you, if you help me."

"Are you serious?"

"Deadly serious," the stranger replied, his eyes the color of steel.

"I have no choice but to trust you and I assure you, Miller if you fuck me over, you'll be lucky to be alive at this time next week."

"Okay! You have my word."

"Anything you and I talk about now or in the future will remain between the two of us; got it?"

"Come outside where we can talk."

"How are your burns, by the way?"

"They hurt like hell, but I would have done anything to save Tony and Ann. I love them like my own folks. They have been through so much...their daughter missing and all..."

"I'm glad to hear that, because I...we... need your help," the stranger added as the twosome left the confines of the hospital and sat in the Ford F-150.

"Hang on a second, Miller. Jesus Christ! I need to be in two places at once, damn it." the stranger said and opened his cell phone.

"A.L. wake up!"

"Oh! Okay, I'm awake, even thought it's, what, three AM?"

"Yeah, it's fucking three AM, but I've got bad news."

"Oh, okay, I thought you were messing with me at first. What's up?"

"ZenJa's parents were killed in a car accident tonight in Longberry. I need to be there to tell her, but I'm in the fucking out-back of New Hampshire, as we speak. I'm chartering a plane and will be there as soon as I can."

"Oh my God! She's going to freak out! She loved her parents more than anything in the world. If that news doesn't send her over the edge, seeing you will do it," A.L. said with a grain of truth.

"I know. Make sure no one reaches her before I get there. I have a connection on this end who'll keep a lid on things from here," the stranger said while looking intently at Officer Miller.

"I'll be in touch the minute the jet lands."

"You want me to pick you up?"

"And what, bring ZenJa with you, asshole?"

"You stay where you are and keep an eye on her. Sorry, A.L., I didn't mean to snap at you. Just keep your eye on ZenJa," he repeated and disconnected the call.

"Okay...what do you want me to do?" Miller asked.

"Well, it seems I have to break my cover, but I promise you, Miller, if you fuck me over, I will kill you! Do you have that straight?"

"Absolutely."

"I want you to know, first of all, that you've been under surveillance for a long while now, and with that said, I'm not willy-nilly trusting you. You were cleared a long time ago."

"Cleared of what?"

"The disappearances of the young girls from this area and the murders of the O'Leary and Childress girls."

"Oh shit!" Miller replied. Well, I thank you for that. God! I had no idea."

"That's the idea of undercover surveillance, Miller."

"Right now, while I'm out of town, I'm instructing you to keep your usual routine, but keep your eyes and ears open. I want you to be extremely active in the Beckwith accident investigation. In all likelihood, it wasn't an accident."

"You're kidding me?"

"I don't kid about death."

"I'm going to contact the state police, Trooper Daniel Alton, and ask him for his help and the state police accident reconstruction team. You will offer him any assistance he requires, without being obvious. He will be aware of your co-operation."

"Anything else?"

"No, just keep your eyes and ears open, for now. I'll alert you to the fact that there's one or more set of eyes and ears lurking around watching and waiting."

"Watching and waiting for what? For good or evil?"

"Both! So don't trust anyone and no one will trust you. I mean no one! You'll be better off that way."

"I'll offer you another bit of advice; I find I've received interesting information at Molly's. Keeping ones mouth shut and ears opens does amazing things."

"Call me at this number if you have anything important I should know about," the man said while Miller looked at the business card that simply had a phone number on it. "I'll be in touch," the man said and motioned for the officer to leave the vehicle.

"Okay, sir. I got ya...what did you say your name is?" Miller asked as he stepped from the truck.

"I didn't," the stranger replied and sped toward the nearest airport.

Chapter 21

Officer Miller spotted Chief Connors patrol car parked at Molly's Café and drove in to get his usual breakfast, only hours after the accident that claimed the lives of two of Longberry's most respected citizens.

"I don't know why the State is investigating the Beckwith accident," Connors was informing the customers who flocked to Molly's for whatever bits of news they could hear.

"Good morning, Chief," Miller said and sat beside him at their usual booth.

"Oh my God! Brian...you were hurt last night?" Molly exclaimed and rushed over to see for herself, how much damage he had suffered.

"Molly, it's nothing. I only wish I could have saved Ann and Tony. They were my only concern. I'll heal...they...they...won't," he muttered.

"This is an unbelievable shame," Molly stated, in obvious shock over the developments that, again, rocked the small community. How will ZenJa cope with this?" she wailed.

"Yes, we're all devastated by the accident." Connors tried, in vain, to sound sympathetic.

"How did it happen?" Lanny Williams asked.

"We don't know. It appears they were driving too fast around that nasty bend on Blackberry Road and in the fog and rain, lost control, hit an Elm tree, and went over the ledges and the car burst into flames," Connors replied.

"You were the first on the scene, weren't you, Miller?" Carol Williams asked.

"Yes, I happened to be driving down that same road, coming from the opposite direction, and saw the flames through the fog and rain."

"You were driving from the opposite direction?" Connors asked, obvious tension in his voice, that Miller noted and remembered he had been warned not to trust anyone by the stranger in the F-150.

"Yes, I was," he had to admit.

"Did you happen to see any other vehicles on the highway, in that area, at that time?" Connors continued to question the officer.

"Shit! As a matter of fact, I did," Miller answered honestly.

"Well, Miller, we need to go to the station and have you make out a report about the events last night, for one thing. We should have done it last night, while it was fresh in your mind, but hopefully, you haven't forgotten any important details," Connors said and ushered the patrolman out of the café.

Miller climbed into his vehicle and Connors walked up to him and asked," What kind of vehicle did you see?"

"It was a dark S.U.V.," he lied. "I have no idea what make, model or year it was. It was too foggy and rainy to see and I wasn't paying much attention to it. I was just cruising around the area.

"Okay, Miller. Type out your report and we'll document it with what the State Troopers find out. "I'll have to notify Miss Beckwith, I guess, also," the chief murmured. "I hope we have a number or address where she can be reached."

"I hope so," Miller agreed and continued to fill out his report concerning the Beckwith accident.

When Chief Connors left the office, Miller opened his cell phone and dialed the number he'd been given by the tall, dark stranger who drove the F-150.

"Miller here. Connors is going to try and notify Miss Beckwith about her parents. He's looking for a number or address for her," he said and closed the phone.

"Well done!" Connors spoke into his cell phone, and drove back toward the Beckwith accident scene. "You have my admiration...getting the job done so throughly and quickly. I'm impressed, but I'm really worried, idiot, that you forced the car off the road where there are some, shall we say, items that need to remain *missing*. What happens if someone snoops around down there, in a farther radius than the initial accident scene, and tragically stumbles across those *missing* things of interest?"

"Now that I think about it, you should have planned the *accident* a little more carefully, though the end result was what we wanted. We just have to get this *accident* scene cleared and the cause determined as it appeared...due to fog, wet roads, and speed.

"I know, I thought about that, after the fact, but we can't turn back the clock now and I was also thinking, Chief, this will bring Miss Beckwith back to Longberry and God only knows how long she'll stay or she might consider moving back here for good. I'm sure her folks left their house to her."

"She better just come back for the funeral and burials, if she knows what's good for her. We don't need her snooping around again," the chief replied.

"She is one determined lady," the caller confirmed. "Hopefully, she's not too determined for her own good."

Chapter 22

Levi Harris, the driver of the black Camaro and at times, the silver Ford F-150 and his pilot landed at Regan International Airport several grueling hours after the accident that claimed the lives of Ann and Tony Beckwith. On the trip, Levi was consumed about what he was going to say to ZenJa, about the death of her parents, who he was, where he'd been all these years, and God only knew what else would come up in the obviously tense situation that was about to unfold.

Taking a taxi to an underground parking lot, where his Camaro was being stored, Levi left the garage, with his beloved black Camaro and a migraine headache.

"I'm almost at ZenJa's," the phoned A.L. "She's home, right?"

"Yes, she is. I know you want me to stay clear, so you two can talk, so I will, but if you need anything just call."

"Thanks, I will."

Several moments later, Levi drove into the extra large driveway and parked behind A.L.'s garage door, but changed his mind. He knew how ZenJa was prone to flee when dealt uncomfortable situations, so he backed up and parked his car behind ZenJa's side of the driveway, behind her black Dodge Charger.

"Nice car," he thought, exited his vehicle and noticed a curtain, move aside from a ground floor window in her condo. "It's show time," he muttered when the front door of ZenJa's apartment opened and Levi slowly walked up the sidewalk; not the meeting he had planned for the last several years.

"Oh my God! Levi," ZenJa cried and ran toward the solemn man who walked toward her, before she came to an abrupt halt. Levi could see the wheels turning in her head and knew what questions were buzzing through her brain...questions like, how do you know where I live, where have you been for the last three or four years, and why are you coming to see me now?

"What is it?" she asked, knowing the answer before she asked.

"ZenJa, we need to go inside," Levi said, a tear leaking from his eye. The tear could have been from his migraine headache or sadness; either way it was genuine.

Levi's gaze swiftly noted the comfortable, richly decorated living room and recognized several of the paintings ZenJa had brought with her from her former rental property in Boston. Levi resisted reaching out to touch the woman he had fallen in love with years ago; now was not the time.

ZenJa, please sit down. I have some bad news to tell you."

ZenJa stumbled to a beige leather couch and awkwardly sat down; Levi sitting beside her, reaching for her hand.

"It's my parents, isn't it?"

"Yes, ZenJa. They were both killed last night in an automobile crash on Blackberry Road."

Surprisingly, ZenJa appeared to have turned into a stone statue, she did not react as Levi would have expected.

"I'm so sorry, ZenJa," Levi said and reached out to hold her in his arms, if she wanted him to, but she stood up and walked toward the kitchen.

"Can I get you anything to drink, Levi?"

The handsome dark haired man, with the ocean-blue eyes followed her and replied," Actually, ZenJa, I have a migraine, so if you have something for that, I'd be forever grateful and a strong cup of coffee, if you would.

"No problem," she replied, like a robot; opening the medicine cabinet in the downstairs bathroom, vomiting in the toilet, washing her hands, face and brushing her teeth, before retrieving a bottle of Excederine Migraine, while Levi poured himself a cup of java in the kitchen.

"Can I get *you* anything, ZenJa?" Levi asked following her to the sofa, once again.

"Levi...I'm overwhelmed, in shock, and my head's spinning," ZenJa whispered, curling her feet beneath herself, in self-preservation mode.

"The only important thing, now, is what happened? With my parents."

"ZenJa, the state troopers are investigating the accident. It appears to have been an accident, at least," Levi began, his headache easing somewhat.

"I can tell you right now, Levi, it was no accident. To be totally honest with you, I was wondering when someone was going to show up at my door to tell me my parents were dead of a car accident, a fire, or just out and out murdered."

"Why do you say that?"

"I've had threatening letters for years. I've been told to stay away from Longberry and of course, you don't know me very well, but no threats are...were...going to keep me from my family."

The fact that ZenJa told Levi, he didn't know her very well, felt like a punch in the stomach, but he knew she was right. But in truth, ZenJa simply was unaware how well Levi did know this young woman.

"You never told anyone about the letters?"

"No...I was handling it as best as I could. There was no one to trust," she said and looked directly into this man's eyes and began to cry.

Levi let out an exhausting breath; a sigh and feelings of remorse he could never explain.

"I haven't seen you in nearly four years, Levi. Why in hell are you here telling me my parents are dead? Do you just coincidently show up when people are murdered? What, are you the bastard who killed my parents?" she screamed at the man who remained silent.

Levi held his forehead and wiped his face, in an effort to extract a moment to think.

"ZenJa, it will take me forever to tell you the whole story, but right now I need you to trust me and we need to focus on your parents and their funerals. Everyone in Longberry is devastated, especially Molly and the folks at the café. They desperately are grief stricken and want to pay their respects. I also realize you have not had time to comprehend the accident or your parents deaths."

"No! There, you're wrong. Not everyone in that town is grief stricken or mourning the loss of my parents. One or more people wanted them dead, like my sister."

With nothing left to be said and Levi's head about to explode, all he could say was, "I want you to know, I'm here for you."

"Like last time?"

"ZenJa, not that it matters, but you threw me out of your house."

"You could have tried to come back."

"ZenJa, you'll never know how I wanted to, but events, out of my control, left me no choice."

"ZenJa, Molly did give me your business card, the other day," he whispered. "I loved it. I haven't laughed so hard in a long time, and it appears I won't be laughing again, anytime soon."

"Why didn't you call me, Levi?" she begged while tears consumed her eyes.

"I was going to very, very soon," was his simple reply and stood up from the couch and walked toward the front window of her condo, and noticed A.L. outside puttering around in his flower garden, in the blackness of the night; keeping surveillance of his neighbor's yard.

"I'll be right back," he said and quietly shut the front door behind him.

"How's she taking it?" A.L. asked.

"As well as can be expected. She said she'd been getting threatening letters for a few years now, but never reported them because she had no one to trust."

"That really sucks. Our jobs certainly fucking suck, don't they?" A.L. replied.

"Yeah...all we do is sneak around, lie, cheat and steal and hell, I don't trust myself half the time, how could I expect anyone else to trust me?" Levi asked.

"You were doing what you thought best, you had your orders Levi and you had your own problems."

"My wife was *not* a problem, A.L."

"I didn't mean it that way. I should've said, obligations."

"That woman was my whole life and I died the day she died."

"I know, Levi."

"Well, I have to get back inside and see what I can do for ZenJa. I just wanted to let you know you can take a break. You don't need to be glued to ZenJa, now. I'm going to have to tell her the whole story, so you might was well go out and have some fun, for a change."

"I must be getting old, Levi. I enjoy hanging around the house," he replied and went back inside his own condo.

ZenJa was watching the two men talking outside her home and stood to the side as Levi, slowly, walked back inside.

"You know A.L.?"

"Yes, ZenJa I do, but his name isn't A.L. Smart, as you were told at Quantico."

"Oh my fucking God, what in hell is going on?" she screamed.

"ZenJa, really, this is so very complicated and I can't sit here and simply spill it all out. It's too much to comprehend at one time, and again, I think my fucking head is going to explode," he said and grasped the arm of a chair and sat down.

"It's nearly three in the morning. Could I please have some more medicine and just catch a cat nap on your couch and we can discuss this tomorrow? Better yet, if you want, after a few hours sleep, we can both head north to Longberry in my car. It'll give us a chance to talk and I speak better when I don't have to look someone in the face; I have so much to tell you."

"You speak better to someone, when you can avoid their facial expressions?" she correctly analyzed, "When they listen to your lies?"

"That pretty much sums it up, ZenJa," he said.

"You don't have to sleep on the couch, Levi. I have a spare bedroom upstairs and you're welcome to sleep there. There's medication in the cabinet that may help your head. The spare bedroom has its own bathroom with plenty of towels, but I remember you have a way of finding your way around," she said and Levi thought he detected a slight smile on her face.

She left him standing there to lock the front door and take the coffee cup and drinking glass to the sink after he retrieved a small duffle bag from his car.

"Good night, ZenJa and thank you," Levi said and closed the door to his room and laid down on the comfortable queen size bed. Tears rolled down his cheeks while he thought about his wife and all the pain he had suffered in his heart and soul, all because of his job.

Levi woke up the next morning with a start and reached for his Glock, that had been under his arm in it's holster when he went to sleep. He found himself covered with a warm quilt and his weapon on the night stand, and smiled.

"I could have killed you in your sleep," ZenJa said, after opening the door to his room and brought her houseguest a breakfast tray of steaming hot coffee, orange juice, scrambled eggs, bacon and English muffins.

"You know, ZenJa, last night I might not have even tried to stop you," he replied honestly, but I'm so grateful you didn't. I would have missed this delicious breakfast," he said and smiled.

"Who said it was for you?" This is mine; yours is in the kitchen...in the trash," ZenJa said and a sad smile crossed her lips, but not her swollen eyes.

Levi realized, ZenJa had been crying, probably all night; he wasn't surprised.

"I understand," Levi said. I know I wasn't a very good host, last time. We never got to finish our dinner and I want to make it up to you, ZenJa."

"It wasn't your fault, but I felt the fact that the arrest of a murderer was more important than any dinner."

"I know."

"Well, here's your breakfast, Levi. It's nearly noon, so if you want to get going north before it gets dark, I suggest you eat up, clean up and get a move on," she ordered.

"Oh my God! I can't believe I slept so long."

"You were exhausted, I wanted you to get some rest, but you need to get going."

"You're coming, too, right?" he asked.

"My suitcase is near the door," she said and left the man to his own devises.

Levi used his cell phone and called A.L to update him on the plans he and ZenJa had arranged that morning and told him to keep an eye on ZenJa's condo while they were gone, up north.

"Please give her my deepest sympathy," A.L. said.

"I will and when she finds out who you are, you asshole, you're going to need the sympathy," Levi said sarcastically.

Chapter 23

"I imagine Miss Beckwith is on her way to Longberry?" Chief Connors asked.

"I imagine, but I'm not sure if anyone has been able to contact her about her parents deaths," Officer Miller replied as the two public servants completed their paperwork covering their investigation of the Blackberry Road deadly car accident.

"Are the Troopers still investigating down there?"

"Yes, from what I heard. I'm heading down there, myself, later to see if I can help out," Miller commented.

"Why not just let them do their job. They've pushed us aside; assuming we're not capable of investigating a simple car accident, I guess," the chief snorted.

"You have to admit, Chief, it appears to outsiders that the Beckwith family certainly has had their share of tragedy in the last few years. Maybe they're making sure there's no foul play involved in this *accident*."

"What? Have you heard anything to make you suspect the state police think this accident is suspicious?"

"No, of course not?" Miller replied, his interest spurred by the chief's sudden remark. He knew he, himself, had been cleared of any suspicion in connection to the missing and murdered girls, from what the mystery man told him, so that must mean *someone* was investigating others in town; most likely Chief Connors.

"Well, Chief, I'm heading down to Blackberry Road, so if you need me, call me on my cell phone, the rookie officer said and left the police station.

"What are you doing here?" Trooper Daniel Alton asked when Officer Miller drove to the scene of the fatal accident, the next morning.

"I know this area pretty, well, Trooper. I grew up here and know every inch of the terrain and road, having driven this in the snow, sleet, rain and fog. I thought I might be of some assistance. These folks, were like my family and I want to see if I can help," the officer said with the utmost sincerity.

"Okay, that sounds good. You hang out with the reconstruction team doing the grunt work on the roadway. They may miss something that you can catch, knowing the terrain so well."

"Thank you for letting me help out," Miller replied and started to walk up the highway from the direction the vehicle appeared to have driven before hitting the tree and careening over the ledges, but stopped when the wrecked automobile was raised from over the embankment with the assistance of two tow trucks and an oversized crane.

Miller walked over to the car and inspected the outer shell, what was left of it, as best he could.

"What are you looking for? Anything in particular?" Trooper Alton asked in his usual inquisitive nature.

"Paint," Miller responded.

"You think this vehicle was sideswiped or forced off the highway? You know something we don't?"

"No, absolutely not! Just wanted to make sure, but because this vehicle is completely burned, I guess there's no way of telling if it had been."

Trooper Alton watched Miller while he slowly walked up the highway, where he'd initially been walking to assist the reconstruction team.

"Odd!" Alton murmured and went about his duties, keeping an eye on the Longberry law enforcement officer.

Miller walked the last sixteenth mile up the winding, steeply graded roadway where the Beckwith's last drove their vehicle and remembered an old logging road, that was situated to his left. It had been used in the early 50's he remembered his grandfather telling him. He stopped and looked at what had once been that road, but was almost completely overgrown and an *outsider* wouldn't have detected it. Miller stopped short when he noticed broken branches and tire tracks deeply embedded in the ground, in that overgrown wooded area.

Under the watchful eye of Trooper Alton, Officer Miller opened his cell phone and called the mystery man who had driven the F-150. "I'm at the accident scene and remembered an old logging road, just to the right of where the Beckwith's went off the highway. It's nearly overgrown now, but remembered it being here. There are fresh tire tracks in the mud and broken branches as if a vehicle was parked here very recently; the tracks are fresh and undisturbed," Miller stressed, again.

"Excellent!" was the response on the other end of the phone. "Is Alton there?"

"Yes, he's...watching me, as a matter of fact," Miller replied.

"Okay...go and tell him what you just told me and show him what you're talking about. Do not...I repeat...do not let anyone fuck with that evidence, though I do want the Crime Scene Investigators to make castings of the tire treads, and I want them to see if there may be any evidence of a vehicle...a broken lens, paint or something the vehicle may have left behind, while backing...I'm assuming they backed into the roadway. They know what they're doing."

"Good work, Miller," the mystery man replied. "By the way, is there a silver Chevy Impala, hanging around?"

"Yes, as a matter of fact. I've seen that vehicle around the station."

"Good," was the reply.

"Is he okay?"

"Yes, he's one of *us*," the caller said and disconnected the call.

"Oh my God!" Miller murmured. "He said I'm one of *us*!"

Trooper Alton stood beside Miller, when he closed his cell phone and Miller simply pointed to the broken tree branches and muddy tire tracks buried in the overgrowth of a once prosperous logging era.

Alton nodded his head and called the CSI team to collect whatever evidence could be attained in that desolate area of New Hampshire.

"If I may," Miller asked. "I'd like to scale that ledge and see what I can find, if anything of value. Like I said, I know these woods like the back of my hand."

"Okay, but be careful," Alton said and left Miller to his own devices.

Chapter 24

ZenJa and Levi left Forest Haven Estates, on the outskirts of Washington, DC, in the brand new black Camaro by 2:00 p.m., minutes after he talked with Miller on his cell phone.

The young couple realized they weren't going to drive very far that day. Logically, they knew there was no hurry to get to Longberry. There was no family for ZenJa to visit, there, anymore. No more pleasant memories to be had...only sadness and heartbreak.

"ZenJa, I know I have so much to explain to you, but right now, the only thing that's important to me, is you and your well being and sanity."

"Thank you, Levi, but to be honest with you, I don't care about you, what you've been doing or anything. I simply want to die," ZenJa replied automatically and honestly.

"I know, ZenJa...I know."

"How in hell do you know how I feel?" Have you ever lost a loved one or your whole family?" she screamed insanely.

"I can never know how you feel," Levi lied. "I'm sorry to assume that I do."

"Okay, so please shut up and drive and by the way, how's your migraine?"

"It's better today, but that doesn't matter," he replied meekly.

"Do you want to stop for dinner or to use the bathroom?" Levi asked after three hours of driving.

"Yes, I guess that would be a good idea," ZenJa replied; the first words she had spoken in hours. She'd been listening to her MP3 player with headphones to discourage any conversation with the driver.

"I think the CD, "21" by Adele is great; have you heard it?" Levi asked.

"You could hear it?" ZenJa asked. "Did I have the volume up that loud?"

"It wasn't really that loud, but I could hear it," he admitted. She does have a wonderful voice."

"Yes, she does. So, what kind of music do you listen to?"

"I love almost anything, except Rap. Lady Gaga, Five Finger Death Punch, Motorhead, Sucker Punch, Taylor Swift, Toby Keith, Metallica, The

Rolling Stones, Areosmith, Black Label Society, Evanescence, Kings of Leon, and Linkin Park are some of my favorites.

"Good choices," ZenJa commented and waited for Levi to park the car at a McDonald's restaurant.

"Do you want to grab a bite to eat before we head out or do you just want to freshen up? I know this isn't as fancy as the last restaurant we visited, but this isn't like last time."

"I could use a large coffee and maybe a grilled chicken salad, with Ranch Dressing," ZenJa replied and went to the ladies room.

The couple both freshened up and Levi ordered their meal and sat down opposite ZenJa in a secluded booth.

"What no Happy Meal?" ZenJa tried in vain to sound cheerful to the man who was the only person she had to depend on and who was going out of his way to assist her in her time of dire need.

"I didn't know if you wanted a boy's or girl's toy, so I ordered a Big Mac, instead."

"I have no need of a boy toy, thank you," she said and the couple smiled at the joke.

The couple sat silently, and consumed their meals, each with their own thoughts, but overwhelmed with recollections of the events that had brought them together more than four years before.

"ZenJa, I noticed a nice park, across the street. Would you like to take a walk with me, so I can start to tell you a little about myself? I know I have a lot of explaining to do."

"Do you really think it's safe to be milling around an unknown park at this ungodly hour, in this neck of the country?"

"What? You mean Delaware?"

"Exactly!"

"I'm packing, remember?" Levi reminded her.

"And so am I," she replied pulling her Glock from her purse.

"Well, I doubt anyone's going to fuck with us, now are they?" Levi replied and ushered his friend across the street to sit down on a bench near a large fountain.

"I really don't want to go any farther north, tonight," ZenJa said. I'm in no rush to get to Longberry," she admitted.

"I understand. There's no rush..." he sympathized.

"ZenJa, what do you want to know about me? I do want to caution you, though, that it takes years to fully know someone you fall in love with, so I don't expect to answer all your questions tonight. There isn't enough time in the world for that."

"Fall in love with?" ZenJa whispered like it was a foreign language.

"So...what should you like to know?"

"Who are you?"

"My name is Levi Harris; I was born and raised in a small town on Lake Winnipesaukee, not that far from Longberry, actually, as you well know; I have a *small* house on the lake."

"Is that where you stayed while you were passing through going back and forth to school, before you ran away?"

"That's a fair question and yes, I was staying on the lake, but did have an apartment in Cambridge. Before we go any further, with the running away part, let me back up."

"Be my guest," ZenJa encouraged sarcastically.

Levi drew a deep breath before he continued. "I'm not sure how far back to start, but I'll begin within the time frame I met you. All I can say is, that I work for the government, I guess you've already assumed that."

"To be honest with, you Levi, I never thought that. I thought you were the perp behind the disappearance and murders of the girls from the Longberry area."

"I can see why you would think that."

"That's why I threw you out of my house that night."

"Why did you give Molly your business card to give to me, then, after all this time?"

"I don't really know. I think I wanted to find out, once and for all if you were."

"What were you going to do, put your life on the line to find out?"

"If I had to, yes."

"That's my girl."

"Now that I know you took the card, why didn't you call me?"

"Because, ZenJa, I couldn't help you and fall in love with you at the same time."

"What the hell are you talking about?"

"Hhhhhh," Levi sighed and held his head in his hands again.

"When the Winters and Olsen girls went missing so many years ago, I was fresh out of the Academy and was assigned their cases. I was located on

Lake Winni and would blend in with the locals." Levi never admitted who he really worked for; ZenJa incorrectly assumed it was the FBI.

ZenJa, continued to look forward, her heart breaking knowing where part this story was headed.

"Of course you know there was never any success with finding those girls, though I never stopped looking, watching, and listening. All for naught. Then, your sister and her friend went missing, and I again was assigned to the cases. We both know about Constance and Morgan and how those bodies were discovered..."

"So, is that all? You were just assigned those *cases*, as you say?"

"No, ZenJa. Since Zippy and Olive went missing, I've been your shadow and if I've not been there, for you, others have been."

"Why have you been stalking me?"

"Because we knew about the threatening letters you received. They were intercepted before you received them and as you can guess, there was no evidence to be obtained from them....no fingerprints, DNA, nothing."

"Why did you let me receive them...to scare the living crap out of me?"

"No, ZenJa, to keep you on your toes."

"So much for that...my parents were killed."

"They're investigating the accident, as just that, but I have some inside information that appears to be leaning toward homicide."

"ZenJa, it has taken us over five years to clear some suspects and others we can't."

"Who has been cleared?"

"Well, Molly, of course, Lanny and Carol Williams, Jim Bacon, and Officer Miller."

"You haven't mentioned Chief Connors," she replied quizzically.

"No, I haven't."

"Do you think...?"

"I'm extremely suspicious, but I have no evidence."

"ZenJa, let's call it a night. I think you've got enough to digest, for one day and I'm exhausted, but I admit, I'm so relieved to have you here, beside me. It's easier keeping an eye on you this way," he added and stood up and waited for her to also rise.

"I agree; I'm exhausted, too, but doubt I'll sleep, but I do need a warm bath and comfortable bed."

"I've made reservations at The Otis Inn, just off the highway. It's a very nice, family bed and breakfast."

"Okay, that sounds nice. I'm not going ask you how many times you've stayed there and with whom."

"Phew! That's a good thing," Levi replied; happy this woman continued to show some spunk.

"You're insufferable," ZenJa said with the slightest of grins in spite of her overwhelming sadness.

Chapter 25

"What you been doing today?" Connors asked his fellow law enforcement officer.

"I was just helping down at the accident scene. You know, marking the area with cones, directing traffic and waiting for the highway department to come and replace the guard rails that were knocked down."

"Any gossip?"

"No, it appears the Accident Reconstruction Team is nearly done with their investigation and the car has been removed to the state garage for an automobile autopsy. Just standard stuff," Miller replied, not offering any information other than the obvious.

"Well, Miller, you ought to call it a night. I've got some things to finish up here and then I'm heading out, unless something else comes up," Connors replied.

"Okay, Chief, see you tomorrow," Miller said and left the police station, but was aware of a silver Impala parked off to the rear of the parking lot, inconspicuous to someone not looking for it.

"Good...keep an eye on that bastard," Miller murmured toward the car that was hidden in the shadows and then drove to his own home.

"Silver Impala is on the target," Miller said into his cell phone...a call that was connected to another phone in the state of Delaware, at the Otis Inn.

"Good!" Was the reply before the call was disconnected.

"Well, if it isn't Officer Miller's brother, Jackson," Connors replied when the assistant school principal entered the police station, shortly after Brian Miller arrived at his own home.

"Just checking in to see how things are progressing. What a terrible shame...what happened to the Beckwith family, huh?" Jackson asked, not sure if the police station was *wired* or not.

"Yes, it truly is," Connors replied. "What can I do for you?"

"Nothing, really. I just wanted to know if there were any plans for the Beckwith's funeral, yet. I know the children at school are upset with the latest developments and events involving the Beckwith family and this brings back memories of their missing friends, Zippy and Olive. Maybe it would be fitting to have a candlelight memorial for the kids?"

The two gentleman exited the police station and before the duo left in their separate vehicles," Connors whispered, "Oh my God, Jackson, I think I'm going to cry. You're good...you're really good."

With the secrecy of a Stealth Bomber, the silver Impala and driver crept behind the police chief's vehicle; keeping him under surveillance, like he had for many days, now.

Police Chief Connors slowly drove down Blackberry Road, stopped at the accident scene and appeared satisfied with the clean up; any signs of an accident nearly vanished from the area, with the exception of the nasty wound to the mighty Elm tree and a few flowers that people from the community had placed that day, in memory of their friends.

The driver of the silver Impala, watching with high powered binoculars swore under his breath, "Get out mother fucker...I dare you."

Much to the driver's surprise, Connors did stop the vehicle and make his exit, but he wasn't looking at the immediate accident scene...he walked back up the hill, some tenth of a mile away and looked over the edge. Illuminating a flashlight for a moment, scanning the area below, the chief then walked back down to the police vehicle and drove away.

"That's interesting," the Impala driver murmured and marked the exact spot where Connors had stood, with a small pile of rocks, near the guard rail, in the pitch blackness of the night.

Chapter 26

"I've booked two adjoining rooms, ZenJa with two private baths," Levi commented after he brought ZenJa's suitcase and his own duffle bag up the stairs of the comfortable inn.

"I hope there's a lock," she retorted with Levi realizing she was exhausted and wanted to lash out at anyone and he was her only target. He understood. He'd been there, himself.

"I'll be right next door, ZenJa," he said softly and closed the door between the two bedrooms.

Levi heard the water running in the adjacent bathroom, and likewise, showered and flopped into his queen sized bed and promptly fell into a fitful slumber.

Hours later, Levi heard the door, between the two bedrooms open and smelled the alluring, provocative perfume ZenJa obviously wore at all times; this not being the first time she had mesmerized him with her delicious scent.

"Levi?" ZenJa whispered.

"ZenJa! What is it?"

"I'm afraid. Will you just hold me?" she begged.

"ZenJa..." he hesitated and then gently pulled the covers off to the side, to allow this woman, who wore a shimmering short purple negligee and smelled like heaven into his bed, arms, and his heart.

"I promise I'll be a gentleman," he whispered into her beautiful red hair as she snuggled into his arms and laid against his body.

"I know you will, Levi," she murmured in return and immediately fell asleep.

Before the sun rose, Levi slipped out of the queen sized bed, showered and dressed for the day. He did this out of respect for ZenJa, to give her privacy and not to emphasize the fact that she may be embarrassed, having come into his room. He went downstairs to the breakfast nook and helped himself to two cups of steaming coffee, cream, sugar, two blueberry muffins, butter and dishes of strawberries mixed with blueberries and returned to their rooms.

"I hope you like my selections for our breakfast," Levi simply said after placing the heaping tray on the small dinning table near the television set.

"Thank you. I have to admit, I'm starved," ZenJa said without an ounce of shame, for which he was appreciative.

"So, tell me, ZenJa, what have you been up to the last few years?" Levi asked looking over his cup of coffee.

"I'm sure you know exactly what I've been doing," she replied indignantly.

"Humor me," he retorted and smiled. "Or would you like a bullet to go with your Glock...I mean butter with your muffin?" he responded, his blue eyes twinkling.

"Well, after I threw you out of my house," she began with Levi nodding in agreement. "I went back to school the next day and you had disappeared off the face of the earth. I finished school at Claybourne, graduated third in the class and went to Quantico and like you, became an agent. My specialty is hostage negotiations, of course you know all this, don't you Levi?"

"Yes, ZenJa I do and I can't tell you how proud I am of you. I'm not simply proud of you...I admire you more than you'll ever know.

"I made a promise to my sister I'd find the bastard who made her go missing, if it takes me the rest of my life and now that I've got connections with the Bureau, I can accomplish this easier than by going it alone, on my own."

"So what's your story?" ZenJa asked sipping the last of her coffee.

In an effort to avoid discussing his own personal demons he stood and began to place the breakfast dishes back on the tray and walked to get his duffle bag.

"We have to get moving," he replied and packed the last of his belongings. Is your suitcase packed?" he asked.

"I can get it. I'll be down in a minute."

Levi paid the lodging bill and waited in the Camaro for ZenJa to put her bag in the trunk and the couple sped in a northerly direction toward New Hampshire.

"We should arrive sometime late tonight," Levi said when ZenJa put a Black Label Society CD in the car's Bose music system.

"Good choice," Levi remarked; the last words spoken between the couple for several hours.

"Are you going to speak to me?" ZenJa asked.

"What do you want to know?"

"I told you most of my story, that you already know, so what about you revealing a little part of your life to me?"

Levi was silent for several more miles, shook his head and began to speak.

"ZenJa, I'm very private about my life, my past, and probably will be about my future. I don't trust anyone, especially when it comes to revealing my inner self. "You were lucky to have a family you trusted, could talk to, and know they'd support you in whatever you decided to do or achieve."

"Indeed, I was," ZenJa replied softly, watching the intensity and strain that was vividly apparent on Levi's face.

"Can you start with something simple, like your childhood?"

Levi smiled, listening to Fade To Black, by Metallica, that played on the CD system, now.

"I told you I grew up, with a very wealthy family, on Lake Winni, I still reside in that home on the lake, on Governor's Island, in my free time.

"I went to private schools; the whole ball of wax. I excelled in school and sports, went to several different colleges and began working for the government."

"Okay, that's about as brief of a history as you can muster, *mister*?" she said and smiled.

"I'm trying," Levi replied and chuckled.

"Do I have to ask you direct questions to get answers?"

"How about using some of your hostage negotiating skills?"

"Okay, wise-ass. Would you tell me about your family, sir. Some of pleasant times in your childhood?"

Levi smiled again.

"My father and I went to every Yankee-Red Sox game there was in either Boston or New York, as long as I can remember. They were the best of times...my Dad and me," Levi began while the couple sped up the black ribbon of highway.

"Your mother?" ZenJa encouraged.

"My mother was a famous author. She wrote under the pen name, Olivia..."

"Olivia Swan!" ZenJa answered.

"Yes, Olivia Swan."

"I have several of her books."

"I noticed," Levi replied quietly.

"Oh my God! I remember there being a terrible tragedy involved with her," ZenJa said before she realized what she said out loud.

"Yes, ZenJa, I also remember that!" Levi growled at his passenger.

"Oh my God! I'm so sorry, Levi," ZenJa whispered.

"Levi, stop the car...pull over here at this rest stop!" she yelled.

"What the fuck?" he yelled in return.

"Please stop the damn car!"

Levi slid into the rest area, sideways, barely making the entrance without hitting a cement wall.

Levi jumped out the seat and ran around to open his co-pilot's door.

"What the fuck's the matter with you?" he continued to yell at ZenJa who shook uncontrollably in her seat.

Other drivers, stretching their legs at this busy interstate stop looked on the scene with interest and concern that someone was in danger. Several men began walking toward the black Camaro; Levi oblivious to the strangers.

"ZenJa, what's the matter," Levi asked a little more quietly than before and helped the woman from the car.

ZenJa immediately fell into his arms and both young people cried tears of sorrow they had not shed in years; the on-lookers stepped back a few yards, but kept an eye on the situation.

After a few moments the young couple composed themselves, somewhat, and got back into the vehicle.

"Levi, I don't want to go back to Longberry. I feel I'll die if I do."

Don't worry, ZenJa, no one...I mean no one will hurt you."

"I don't mean I'm afraid of being hurt or killed by some sicko, I'm already dead," she wailed and once again broke down in tears.

"What do you want to do, ZenJa?"

"I don't know. I can't go back to my parents house. I don't ever want to go there again."

There must be some items you want from the house...something to remind you of your memories."

"Do you have anything to remind you of your memories, Levi?"

"I've the most wonderful home in the world on the lake, but that's only a material thing, every other memories I cherish are in here," he added putting his hand on his heart.

"Exactly! I don't need anything material. I have the things I want, already; the pictures I treasure most."

"I want my parents bodies cremated," ZenJa said out of the blue. I'm not going to the house to select a suit for my father and a pretty dress for my mother to wear in their coffins."

"Okay, ZenJa, I think that sounds like a reasonable idea.

"My parents always wanted to be organ donors, but I guess that's all gone to shit; having been burned in a fucking car, isn't it?"

Levi simply nodded in agreement.

"Do you want me to call the funeral home in Laconia to have them make arrangements?"

"Is that where my parents are, now?" ZenJa asked in a whisper.

"Yes, I checked with a source I've on the ground there."

"Do you want to have a simple wake, with a few close friends or none at all? I think everyone in town wants to pay their respects. They all loved your folks and you, you know."

"I guess it would be rude and selfish of me not to let those who truly loved my parents not have a chance to say goodbye."

"I'll be right beside you the whole time, ZenJa. You can count on me."

"Thank you, Levi. I never would have made it through this without you."

"You're not through it, yet, ZenJa. A loss like this takes years, if not a life time to overcome."

Levi started the engine of the Camaro and slowly left the exit of the rest area and noticed the sun was beginning to set, again.

"Levi?" ZenJa asked.

"Yes?"

"What happened to your family?"

"I'm an agent and I only cry in the dark," he replied, avoiding the question and stepped on the throttle, wishing the past was something he could control as a gas peddle and sports car, or the bullet coming from his Glock.

ZenJa laid her head on her driver's shoulder and tears leaked from her eyes, again. The darkness of the night enveloping them, like a cloak of midnight, on the highway, ahead.

ZenJa woke from a fitful sleep, in the Camaro, when Levi shut off the engine and slid his seat back and closed his eyes, without moving a muscle.

"Where are we?" ZenJa asked.

"At my house on the lake," Levi said, his eyes still closed.

"Here," he said, handing ZenJa the key ring that had a remote that appeared to be for the car and house.

"Fiddle around with this and turn on the lights, if you can," he said, holding his hands over his eyes.

"You have another migraine?"

"No, I'm just getting old, I guess. It's never taken me two-three days to get from DC to New Hampshire."

ZenJa held the remote and aimed it in the darkness toward what appeared, in the moonlight, to be a house.

Without warning, the car alarm sounded, the trunk lid opened, the headlights flashed and the exterior and interior lights of the house turned on and off and dogs in the neighborhood began to bark.

Tears cascaded down Levi's cheeks after ZenJa threw the keys and remote back at Levi, who howled with laughter...much need laughter.

"Your insufferable," ZenJa cried and laugh as well. "Do you trick all your guests like that?"

"No, not everyone, just people I care about," Levi said as simply as if he were commenting on the weather.

Levi exited the vehicle and ran over to open ZenJa's door. When ZenJa stepped out, Levi turned on the exterior and interior antique coach lanterns of his majestic Post and Beam home, which had once been a humongous barn.

"You can see, the entire ground level is comprised of a two door garages on the back side," he said waving his hand, to proudly display the incredible structure that was accented with various dated gable roofs, complete with four copper weather vanes. "And on the lake side, the lower level has a slate floored game, music, and weight rooms, complete with indoor swimming pool...once we get that far, you'll see all that," he continued and ushered her inside the door, separating the garage doors, and directed her toward the stairway that led to the second floor.

"Oh my God, Levi! This is beautiful and as you mentioned before, it's on Governor's Island," she said while the couple sauntered toward the wrap-around porch that encompassed the entire home, from the second tier.

The couple peered out the glazed glass doors that led to the balcony, outdoors and Levi said, "Welcome home, ZenJa."

"This is paradise! One whole wall is a granite and black marble fire place and another, facing the lake and all four sides of the barn is nearly all glass and open living area with cathedral ceilings," she cried, her hands clutched with glee. "This is amazing and I love how the windows are pitched toward the center, accenting the arcs in the ceiling and roof and the old coach lanterns."

"Did you design it?"

"Oh, no, my father did. I was just a kid when it was built."

ZenJa spun around, like a fairy princess, swirling across the pine floors and strategically placed earth tone, patterned throw rugs, dodging and darting around the haphazardly situated sofa groups, majestic grand piano, that encompassed one corner of the open concept living area. "This is the most perfect place in the world!" ZenJa exclaimed, running her fingers up and down the keyboard.

"You had a piano at your house in Boston. I assume you play?"

"Yes, actually I'm rather an accomplished pianist," if I do say so myself," ZenJa replied. "Do you play?"

"No, that was my mother's piano," Levi said with no emotion in his voice.

"What a wonderful built-in bookcase. It blends in with the rustic flavor of the hand-hune beams, rail road ties and weathered wood and I can't help notice there's quite a collection of books and artwork, here."

"Of course all the books my mother wrote are here and pictures of our family."

ZenJa wandered over and glanced at the nearly fifty books written by Olivia Swan and stopped in front of several shelves that displayed who appeared to be his parents, Levi, himself as a youngster, and an even a younger brother. One other photo startled the young woman; it appeared to be a fairly recent wedding picture of Levi and a gorgeous blonde woman. ZenJa remained silent; she realized this was not the time to discuss his family at length.

"Come on, ZenJa, let me show you the rest of my little shack," Levi suggested, knowing ZenJa had seen his wedding photo.

"This kitchen is amazing, Levi. It's larger than some homes, I've been in. I mean, look...a six burner, two oven stove? A center island worthy of Martha Stewart or Rachael Ray. Copper pots and pans; this is amazing."

"The hanging copper pots and pans are only for display. I'm sure as hell not cleaning those after each use," Levi said with conviction. "I've a nice set of cookware I use, under here," Levi said opening the doors underneath the center island that was enhanced with a black, streaked with purple veins, marble top.

"Well, these aren't too shabby," ZenJa commented.

"You can see they're almost new. I'm never here long enough to use them."

"These cabinets and cupboards are awesome. They are handcrafted, I assume."

"Yes, I wanted something that wasn't solid wood, that's why I asked to have glass panes put in the doors and had them stained a rustic, antique finish of cranberry. The wrought iron hinges and latches were handcrafted, too. It kinda accents the marble counter...you think?"

"Indeed...these are gorgeous. I also love the idea of having the double sinks and raised faucet-sprayer and look...a brick pizza oven in the wall and my God, the frig is big enough to accommodate a restaurant.

"How can you even think about leaving this gorgeous home? I'd want to be here every single day and never leave," ZenJa said without thinking.

"Good, then that's settled. You better start packing your things."

"I'm going to pretend I didn't hear that," ZenJa said and quickly added, "I love the slate floor, here in the kitchen, too. I always wanted flooring like that."

"It's easy to clean," Levi teased. "I just bring in the garden hose and spray it down."

"Oh my God! You're impossible! Come on, show me the rest of your lake-side *shack*."

"Toward the rear of the house, also on the second floor, is my office...plenty of windows and sunlight, you'll notice in the day time. I love this great old oak desk. It was my father's and of course I have a nice comfy executive desk chair and of course a Bose stereo surround sound system, throughout. Other than the desk, my most prized possession is my father's, grandfather's clock."

"This is awesome...I mean the entire inside of the house is all rustic, oak flooring and beautiful throw rugs. It's very tastefully decorated," ZenJa continued to marvel.

"Well, there's a full bath over here, walk in closets, laundry room, styled from what would have been horse stables. You like the idea of having the wooden doors open from both the top and bottom? Do you like the concept?"

"The only thing missing is the hay on the floors and horse blankets draped over the railings," ZenJa replied and chuckled.

"Speaking of hay, I have breakfast out on the deck on most mornings. I love to watch the white caps on the lake and the sail boats, drifting by. It's very relaxing."

"You obviously don't have much time to relax, do you, Levi?"

"No, but I'm thinking of cutting back on my schedule. I'm financially secure, so I'm obviously not working for the money. And before you say anything, ZenJa, I'm not bragging. Money means very little to me."

"Now, let me show you the third floor," Levi said leading ZenJa toward the center of the open living area that had a rustic stairway and balcony.

Once on the landing, ZenJa looked over the edge and admired the living expanse from above. This is a masterpiece, Levi. It's the most beautiful home I've ever seen."

"I'm glad you like it. I'd hate it if you weren't comfortable in your new *digs*."

"So, anyway, ZenJa, this is the master suite, complete with walk out deck, and of course, overlooking the lake."

"From what I can see, even though it's dark outside, your house pretty much is surrounded by beach and a view of the lake.

"Indeed, it is. There's only a small private driveway leading up to the garages, but there's over three acres of lawn, surrounding the house, that's raised and held in place with an eight foot stone wall. Then there are stairs leading to the private beach and boat launch."

"So, to get back to my bedroom, as you can see there's a very comfortable king-sized bed, and plush dark gray carpeting," Levi said while sweeping his hand like the models on the television show '*The Price Is Right*', do.

"I've made quite a collection of abstract art I display here and more contemporary art downstairs. I call this my *freak* room. I only have two Picasso's though, but I'm working on collecting more. My father bought theses many years ago..." Levi replied and drifted off. "I've also started collecting art from an unknown artist, from New Hampshire. His work is quite remarkable and who knows, maybe one day they will be priceless."

"Who's the artist?"

"His name is Shawn F. Cherbonneau and if you noticed I have many of his folk-art prints in my office and as you will soon see, in the two other bedrooms, up here."

"He's an amazing artist," ZenJa replied. "They're what...; they aren't water colors or paints, are they?"

"No, they're colored pencil."

"Oh my God...look he's drawn each blade of grass, each leaf in the trees and every petal of every flower. These are incredible. I want you to give me his number so I can check out what others artwork he has in his collection."

"Will do, ma'am."

"Well, ZenJa, here's one of the two spare bedrooms, each with private bath. Pick out the one you want. I'll finish showing you around in the morning. I'm beat and I'm about to fall down, so if you'll excuse me, I have to get some sleep."

"Yes, of course. I'm exhausted, myself. I can't thank you enough for everything you've done for me," ZenJa said and took her suitcase Levi had placed at the top of the stairs to the room next to the master suite and closed the door.

"You're welcome," Levi whispered and closed his own door, took a shower and collapsed in his bed, but not before making a call on his cell phone.

"You holding down the fort?" Levi asked the man driving the silver Impala, in Longberry.

"Yup. I saw something very interesting a while ago and will update you tomorrow. I know it's late and you sound beat."

"Yeah, I am. I just got home on the lake, so we'll be around tomorrow."

"We?"

"ZenJa came back with me."

"Be careful, Levi. You can't go through *that* again."

"I know. See you tomorrow."

"Yo!"

After making one more cell phone call to A.L., letting him know he and ZenJa arrived safely, Levi literally passed out from exhaustion.

Chapter 27

Just before dawn, the sun slowly drifting above the mountainous terrain and burning off the heavy thick fog, Officer Miller parked his patrol car on Blackberry Road and slowly walked along the highway at the scene of the Beckwith accident. Surveying both sides of the road. He noted there appeared to have been evidence taken from the overgrowth, across the street from the initial impact point of the Beckwith vehicle, at the Elm tree. He was convinced the staties had taken impressions and castings of the tire tracks and whatever evidence they may have found among the broken and matted branches of the surrounding trees, by a vehicle, most likely an S.U.V. or truck, that he had informed Trooper Alton about.

Moments later, Miller walked across the road and noticed a small, but obvious pile of rocks that apparently had been carefully placed near the guard rail, a few hundred feet before the accident site.

"Hmm, wonder what those signify?" he murmured and looked over the edge at the heavily wooded area between the guard rail and mountainside that began to slope upward, from a deep crevice only a foot or so from the safety rail. "I know those weren't there the other day?" he said out loud.

"No, they weren't," a man said, scaring the living devil out of the officer in uniform.

"Jesus Christ! Where in hell did you come from?" Miller asked ready to drawn his weapon from his holster.

"I've been watching this area and some of you folks from town for a while now," the tall, dark haired man replied, lighting up a cigarette.

"I've got to give these damn cancer sticks up," he casually remarked, ignoring Officer Miller, walking closer to the edge of the guard rail and rock pile.

"Who in hell are you and where did you come from?" Miller asked, still holding his weapon in his right hand.

"I have no name and do you want to know where I was born or where I came from within the last three minutes or so?"

"I don't give a flying fuck where you were born, but you just didn't appear out of the blue."

"No, I didn't. Look through those trees over there. See the sun reflecting off that silver car over there?"

"Yes?" Miller replied.

"That's my car."

"Okay, so why are you snooping around here and checking out some of our residents?"

"I'm looking for a murderer, someone who has abducted girls from the area, and anything else illegal going on around here."

"They arrested that Alex Lyons guy for the murders. We only have missing girls, that I know of, anyway."

"*Only* missing girls?" the man asked.

"I don't mean to minimize that; I didn't mean it to sound like that,' Miller explained.

"Well, enough of this shit. What are *you*, doing here," the stranger asked.

"I can't say. I was told not to trust anyone and I only have one contact I make."

"Who might that contact be?"

"I can't say."

"Well, tell me this...what was he driving the last time you saw him?"

"How do you know it's a *him*?"

"Oh, fucking A! Call the guy and let me talk to him, if you have his cell phone number," the stranger demanded.

Miller nervously opened his cell phone and dialed the number of his contact.

"This is Miller. There's someone here who wants to talk to you. He's asking a lot of questions and I'm not telling him shit!"

"Okay, let me talk to the asshole."

"Here! He said let me talk to the asshole," Miller said and thrust the phone at the stranger.

"Yo?" Levi asked.

"What time you showing up?" the stranger asked, smiling at Officer Miller.

"In a few hours. I have a lovely lady, here making me breakfast and I'm not about to leave before I finish my coffee," Levi said and laughed. ZenJa kicked him under the table, where they were dining, facing the lake, in the early morning hours.

"Miller's okay. See what he's looking for. He's only doing what I told him to...not to trust *anyone*."

"Well, finish your damn coffee, fucker, and tell Miller to confide in me.

I'm tired of wasting my time watching and waiting..."

"You ever say that again, asshole, and I'll see you're written up or fired! There's nothing we do that's a waste of fucking time! There are missing and most likely dead girls out there and you'll waste your fucking time until they're found, you got it?" Levi hollered into the cell phone, loud enough for Officer Miller to hear.

"I'm sorry Levi. I didn't mean it like that. I'm just exhausted, I guess," the man said and handed the phone to Officer Miller.

Levi? I finally have a name, Miller thought to himself.

"The asshole you're talking to, Miller, is okay." Just don't trust anyone else, except Trooper Alton. I should be in Longberry in a few hours."

"Okay, Levi," Miller responded and smiled and thought, I finally have a name.

"Miller just called me Levi," the agent said over his eggs, bacon, and toast.

"I think the asshole you were talking to, Levi, mentioned your name," ZenJa commented and smiled over her glass of orange juice.

"Yeah, he did. He really is an asshole."

"By the way, Mr. Harris, how is it your frig is filled with fresh groceries, when you haven't been here in weeks or months?"

"I have someone who comes here and takes good care of me," he replied not thinking how that sounded to the young woman he was sharing breakfast with.

"Your *wife*?" ZenJa snarled.

Levi slammed his silverware onto the table, scraped his chair backward and picked up the dinnerware he was using and stormed into the house.

"Get your shit together, ZenJa. We're leaving in half an hour. Oh! And by the way leave the shit in the sink, my *wife*, will clean up this mess after we leave."

Silently, Levi locked up the house, set the security system, parked the Camaro in the garage and backed a new black Lincoln Navigator, with tinted windows and a New Hampshire vanity license plate that read *GOT'YA* from the other side of the parking *lodge,* and threw ZenJa's and his own luggage into the rear of the large S.U.V.

After the couple climbed into the vehicle, Levi cut ZenJa off, just before she was about to speak.

"Levi...I'm..."

"My *wife's* car," he replied, glaring at her with his steel blue eyes.

ZenJa realized she had met her match where stubbornness was concerned; she knew not to utter as much a single word while the couple drove toward Longberry.

Levi and ZenJa closed the gap on the miles between Lake Winnipesaukee and the small rural town where Molly's Café /convenience store/ gas station, the largest establishment, other than the feed store, was located.

Officer Miller and the unknown man who drove the silver Impala traversed across the accident scene on the highway. An hour later the two men took the initiative to scale down the steep roadside where the Beckwith car finally rested.

"That's one fucking steep embankment," the stranger said.

"Good place for an *accident,* ya think?" Miller commented.

"I agree and it makes sense, what you showed me about the overgrown area across the street where some vehicle has been obviously parked, recently. At least after the last rain we had...or during."

"It was raining and a heavy fog, that night," Miller reminded the stranger.

"Yeah, I remember."

"I noticed that pile of rocks, near the guard rail, up there," Miller said pointing several yards away, at the top of the bank.

"Yeah, I want to go over there and see what Police Chief Connors was looking at last night."

"What did you say?" Miller asked.

"I said, I was keeping your boss under surveillance last night and he just so happened to drive up here. Now, I may not be the brightest lightbulb in the package, but he wasn't looking at the area where the car went off the road and landed...he walked up that way," the stranger said pointing north, from the accident scene, "about fifty or a hundred yards away. After he left, I marked the spot with that seemingly innocent pile of debris, to find the exact spot today, but you removed them," the man said as he and Miller walked toward that destination along the bottom of that crevice.

"It was about here, I saw him stop," the stranger said. "I should have marked the inner side of the guard rail, so I'd know exactly where the hell the spot was."

"I already did that," Miller said. "See the black X over there?"

"I'm impressed," the man replied and both men walked horizontally to the X marked on the safety rail above.

"I should have brought a tree trimmer, to cut back some of this roughage," Miller said while both men struggled to make any headway through the thick brush, overgrown trees, swamp and traversing brooks and streams.

"Remind me to bring some bug repellant, next time," the stranger remarked.

"Watch out for ticks and...; holy fuck!" Miller yelled.

"What is it?"

"Oh my God! Oh my God!"

"What the hell is it?" the stranger barked and struggled to make his way toward the area, sloshing in the mud.

"It looks like a skeleton!"

"Get back...don't touch a fucking thing," the stranger yelled. "Turn around and retrace your steps backward, in the mud."

"Okay," the young officer said while what would appear to a child, like someone playing the game Twister, the man pivoted on one foot and, as best he could, stepped in his own footprints toward the dry embankment near the stranger.

The stranger was on his cell phone before Miller made it to the edge of the swamp.

"Get your ass here, pronto, Levi. We got ourselves a situation. I'm on Blackberry Road."

"I'm ten miles out," he yelled and floored the S.U.V around the twists and turns of the country back roads.

"Do you want to go to your folk's home or do you want to go to the Café?" Levi snarled, not giving ZenJa any other option.

"What's going on?" she asked indignantly.

"Nothing you need to know and frankly, I don't know myself, yet. So, where are you going to go?"

"God! Levi, please don't make me go to my parent's house. I can't go there, knowing there are probably a few dishes in the sink, the beds are unmade or whatever..."

"Maybe you should go there. There maybe something, as a clue, why your parents left their house that late at night. Have you thought of that?"

"No, I never thought of that. Okay, I'll go there, but please don't leave me there. I can't stay there overnight."

"Will there be anything for you to eat, or do you want to stop at the convenience store, first?"

"I'll be okay. I know my folks always have *stuff* in the freezer."

"I assume the power is still on ?" Levi asked reasonably.

"As far as I know. I'll check before you *take off*," ZenJa hissed.

Moments later, ZenJa removed her suitcase from the back of the S.U.V and slowly walked up the sidewalk that led to what used to be her parent's home and reached for her key in her purse. Without ZenJa being aware, Levi walked behind her and took the key from her hand and opened the door for her.

Without a word, Levi turned the lights on and off, searched the house from top to bottom, for ZenJa's safety, and was moved beyond his ability to demonstrate, the pain ZenJa was suffering. A pain he was more than aware of...his own painful demons.

"I'll call you when I'm finished with whatever my partner has in store for me today," Levi said and softly closed the door behind the woman who had tears streaming down her cheeks.

Moments later, Levi drove the black S.U.V to Blackberry Road and noted the only two vehicles in the area was Officer Miller's patrol car and the silver Impala.

"Why don't you have Connors under surveillance, Agent Wyman?" Levi barked at the stranger.

"Jesus H. Christ, I can't be in two fucking places at once," ATF Agent Brent Wyman growled in return.

"Sorry; each fucking day gets worse and worse, doesn't it?" Levi asked; his way of apologizing.

"Well, your day's about to get a hell of a lot worse that it started out."

"Chief Connors is in Concord today. He has some paperwork to file with the Department of Motor Vehicles. He's expected to be gone most or all of the day," Miller offered to appease the tension.

"We still have the GPS on his car," the stranger reminded him and I have him right here on my I Pad. He's still in Concord," the man said and showed the internet screen to Levi.

"Okay, keep an eye on it to make sure he doesn't come flying by here, anytime soon. What we got?" Levi asked.

"Miller said he thought he saw a skeleton down there," the stranger said and both men pointed down the embankment where they had recently struggled to reach the roadway, again.

"Oh fuck me!" Levi said and opened his cell phone again and after a few quick calls, he explained what was about to happen.

"Take your patrol car half a mile south of here and block the road. Take this asshole with you," Levi said pointing to his friend/co-conspirator. "I'll block the road from the North."

"What if people want to drive by…I mean this is a public, not well traveled, but a highway, just the same," Miller asked.

"Tell anyone who wants to drive through, there's been a landslide and road's blocked. They'll have to use alternative ways to get around this area."

"More Feds and the New Hampshire Troopers will be here shortly and will completely block off this area. The State Medical Examiner will be here, too, and of course CSI."

"Good job, Miller," Levi said and dismissed the duo.

After Levi blocked the highway with his S.U.V. he called A.L in DC.

"I think this shit is about to explode up here. Can't verify anything yet, but if you want to be involved in the action and become the ghost from past to the present, you might want to get your ass up here."

"You want me in Longberry or at the *shack*?"

"Let me know when you get here and I'll let you know. Get a rental from the airport."

"It'll be nice to get out of prison," the man chuckled. " I'm on my way," Alex Lyons replied on a serious note and left the condo the government rented for him.

Chapter 28

ZenJa forced herself to wander, aimlessly, through her parents home. Once she got the courage to enter their bedroom, she realized her parents must have been woken from their sleep and quickly dressed for some reason. Their pajamas were scattered all over the floor, her mother appeared to have dropped her purse, spilling some the contents on the floor, but not bothered to retrieve the items. She noted her father's cell phone on the floor and picked it up. The battery was dead, but she plugged in the charger and while it was charging, she noted the last phone number that was listed under, received calls.

The number wasn't familiar to her, but she took note of it, copied it into her own phone. Her parents had no computer in their home, but utilizing her own I Phone she contacted Google Search and requested a web site, Reverse Number Lookup and plugged in the number that was last received on her father's cell phone, the night her parents died in the accident. No surprise to her, the number was unlisted. She assumed, it was a cheap, throw away phone, people buy every day to use once or twice and then dispose of. None the less, she dialed the number from her phone and was relieved to note it did ring; whether anyone heard it ring or would ever answer it, was anyone's guess.

After stripping the sheets from her parent's bed and collecting the other dirty clothes left scattered around, she did a load of laundry and noticed her father's cell phone was now fully charged and without thinking, placed it back on her father's dresser.

The afternoon wore on and ZenJa decided to walk the same path Zippy would have taken, the last time she went to Molly's Café, with her friend Olive. She hoped to get a feel or become connected to her sister, like some psychics do. She remembered the dream she had, so long ago, about running water, wood, and mud.

ZenJa also wanted to visit with the proprietor and get a fresh cup of hot coffee and something substantial to eat. She desperately wanted to see a friendly face; she certainly hadn't seen one, today.

The FBI hostage negotiator slowly walked toward Molly's Café, glancing right and left, looking for something to draw her attention to running water, mud or an enclosure. ZenJa had walked this path a thousand times before and never felt anything *pull* her in any one direction. She was well aware that Zippy hadn't been abducted on her way to the Café and in all actuality no one knew when or how her sister had become missing. She was aware that her abduction had taken place between the time she left her house to walk a quarter of a mile down the road to catch the school bus. Her parents hadn't been informed of the missing girl until she never returned home from school that day and they called the school to find out where she was.

When Zippy hadn't gotten on the school bus or arrived at school, the logical thing to assume was that the girl stayed home from school and the school hadn't notified the parents or called to find out why she hadn't arrived. Those were simple days when innocence was the devil in disguise. ZenJa was happy to have been informed the schools now were required to notify parents if children don't arrive at school and parents were likewise required to call the school and notify the officials the children wouldn't attending school on a certain day. This cross-reference was needed; no child was safe in the society today...no child was safe anywhere, anymore.

As ZenJa approached Molly's Café, a stream of New Hampshire State Police units, a mobile State Police crime lab vehicle and a black Chevy Suburban, with tinted windows, screamed down the highway.

ZenJa walked into Molly's and being she was the only person inside the café, with the exception of the cook and Molly, herself, Molly ran over to the young woman and wrapped her arms around her, cried and hugged her until her tears had subsided.

"I'm sorry, ZenJa. I swore I wasn't going to do that when I got to see you," Molly apologized.

"Here, let me wipe your eyes," ZenJa said after grabbing several napkins from the holder near the salt and pepper shakers.

"Okay, that's better," ZenJa said trying to comfort the woman she had known all her life.

"What's going on, outside?" ZenJa asked. "A whole bunch of law enforcement vehicles just sped down the road."

"I don't know, I haven't heard anything. It's been quiet here today."

"Well, Sweetie, what can I get you? You look like you've lost weight. You look like you need a BLT, onion rings, and a Coke."

"Oh, no, Molly, thank you, but I couldn't eat all that. I'll just have a slice of your homemade apple pie and a slice of cheddar cheese on it and a cup of coffee."

"Okay, my dear," she said and went into the kitchen to get the order, herself, because the cook was out back having a smoke break.

While ZenJa waited for her order, she tried calling Levi's cell phone and it immediately went to voice mail.

"Shit!" she swore and threw her phone into her purse.

When Molly brought ZenJa's coffee and dessert to the counter, Lanny and Carol Williams entered the Café.

"Hello ZenJa," the couple said. "We're so very sorry about your parents and their accident. We are truly sorry. You're folks were the best! If there's anything we can do, please...please let us know."

"Thank you so much. I appreciate it."

"We've been driving by, kinda keeping an eye on the place, to make sure there's no vandalism going on while you're away, not that we expect any, but just to be on the safe side..."Carol drifted off.

"I can't thank you enough. Let me give you my cell number in case you ever want to get in touch with me," ZenJa said and handed Carol a blank business card that simply had her first name and number on it.

"How are you holding up?" Lanny asked.

"Oh, about as well as I can expect and doing my best to hang in there."

"What can I get you, folks?" Molly asked the new arrivals.

"Coffee and some of that apple pie for me," Lanny said.

"Ditto!" Carol said and sat down beside her husband and ZenJa, at the counter.

While Molly was serving her customers, Assistant Principal Jackson Miller, Officer Miller's brother, entered the café and acknowledged ZenJa and the Williams' with a nod and proceeded to sit at a booth near the front window, but behind ZenJa and the others who occupied stools at the counter.

"What can I get you, Jackson?" Molly asked.

"Just coffee," he responded, smiled, and gazed out the window.

"We just tried to drive over Blackberry Road, but both ends of the highway are blocked off," Lanny said to initiate a conversation with ZenJa and Molly. "The authorities are there and said there was a landslide on the road, somewhere and the road will be closed until they can shore up the sidewall of the mountain and clear away the mess."

"Well, it's probably because we've had so much rain lately," Molly added and handed the assistant principal of Riverview Middle School his coffee, cream and sugar.

"Thanks, Molly," the man said and began to fiddle with his spoon while drinking the hot beverage.

After a moment, Jackson removed his cell phone from his coat pocket and sent a text message. Several seconds later his phone vibrated, indicating a message had been received on his end. He quickly opened the phone, read the message, returned the phone inside his pocket and continued to drink his coffee and less than two minutes later, the man stood up.

"Can, I get you a refill?" Molly asked.

"No thanks, Molly. I'm all set. I want to be able to sleep tonight," he replied and smiled and left a five dollar bill on the table.

"What's up with him?" the cook asked, having come inside from his smoke break, entering the dining area and watching the educator drive away.

"Why, what do you mean?" Molly and ZenJa asked in unison.

"I was watching from the kitchen...I can't put my finger on it, but Jackson sure seemed interested in your conversation about the landslide on Blackberry Road. He texted someone on his phone and shortly after he sent the message, he got a reply. I don't know much about cell phones and that texting crap, but I got one of them things and I know how they work."

"Interesting!" ZenJa murmured and tried to call Levi, once again, only to reach his voice mail account.

"ZenJa, did you ever meet up with that guy in the black Camaro," Molly asked to change the subject.

"Yes, as a matter of fact I did. I was just trying to call him."

"That's great! He seems like a really nice gentleman," Molly commented. winking at ZenJa.

"He's something; what, I'm not sure, yet?" she growled.

"At least you got to catch up with him. He sure chuckled when I handed him the business card you asked me to give him."

"Oh, yes, he's a regular clown, he is," ZenJa sputtered.

Carol and Lanny looked at each other and smiled. "I used to feel the same way about Lanny before I fell head-over heels in love with him."

"Love is about three hundred and sixty degrees the opposite of what I feel for that insufferable creature."

"There's a fine line between love and hate, you know, ZenJa," Molly teased.

"Oh...please," ZenJa said and left her stool and walked over toward the window.

"It's going to be dark soon," she said softly. "I can't go back there," she whispered. "Where are you, Levi?"

Chapter 29

The New Hampshire State Major Crime Unit vehicle, known as MCU, was parked along beside a dozen or more law enforcement vehicles, from Officer Miller's patrol car, Levi's Lincoln Navigator, ATF Agent Brent Wyman's Impala, six state trooper's vehicles, and a small collection of FBI Chevy Suburbans. The entire length of Blackberry Road had been cordoned off and diagrams had been drawn up for an initial search, beginning at the immediate site where Officer Miller had inadvertently stumbled upon the partial skeletal remains of what appeared to be a tall child or small teenager.

A team of forensic pathologists and anthropologists were on scene and taking over the intimate details of the microscopic search that had begun, with a vengeance, only moments before.

Officer Miller, who knew the area like the back of his hand, was in charge of sectioning off at least an area equivalent to a mile radius into a grid to be searched inch by inch for what other remains and/or evidence would be found.

Levi was persistent and demanded to know, from the 'ologists' as he called them, what information they could give him, from their brief, but careful first assessment for any clues as to the identify of the victim that had been found.

"This is rather unusual," one 'ologist' began. "There are two tibias, here but they are both different lengths."

"You thinking there was more than one body dumped here?" Levi asked.

"It could very well be. Even though these remains have been here...I would estimate between five and ten years, it appears one of these tibias might have been broken at one time, prior to the death. I see what appears to be a bone that was healed."

Levi never heard ZenJa mention Zippy having had a broken leg at any time, but there was no reason to for her to have mention that, he realized.

A female 'ologist', said, in the deadly stillness of the crime scene, "I found something over here!"

"Everyone stay back and freeze! What you got?" Agent In Charge, Emerson, from the Boston Field Office, asked.

"It looks like the skeletal remains of a small hand and there's something inside it, I think."

"I've got my evidence bags and I'll keep the evidence in tack, if I can," Deirdre Roberts, the pathologist said into a tape recorder to document the search. "Shi..," Roberts began. "Whatever was inside the hand just fell out!" the woman declared, desperately trying to keep from swearing.

"Okay, I'm using my gloved tweezers and will pick it up and put it in a separate bag."

"Can you see what it looks like?" an unknown person asked.

"It's pretty rusted, but it looks like it might be a metal name tag. It's about the size of a name plate you might find on a...."

"On what?" Emerson yelled.

"On a law enforcement uniform or jacket. Like I said, it's pretty rusted, but I can see there was once a clasp and pin on the backside. The clasp is still there, but the pin is missing."

"Okay, I'm leaving a marker and retracing my footsteps back to the MCU vehicle with the evidence," Deidre Roberts spoke into the recorder, once again.

All available eyes were focused on the evidence the young female pathologist discovered.

"Levi, being taller than some of those close by, had the advantage and could see the rusted bit of metal as well as could be expected.

"Can you make out a name on it?" Levi asked; the question everyone else wanted to know the answer to, as well.

"It's in very poor condition, but in reference to the three letters I can make out, that appear to be what would be the right hand half of the name tag, I can see the letters ORS," she said with conviction.

"Oh my God!" Miller said, covering his mouth.

"Okay, people, let's get back to work. It's going to be dark soon and one more thing, anyone who is at this premises is more than aware we have a murder and/or dumping ground here and I know this goes without saying...if I find anyone here opens their mouth to anyone...and that includes the President of the United States, I'll see that you are fired and brought up on federal charges," Emerson hollered. "We'll spend another hour here and then we'll call it a night. I have fresh eyes coming in to keep this site secure until we come back tomorrow at six hundred hours."

"What's up with the name plate?" Levi asked Miller while they continued their search, in close proximity to each other.

"At the same time Ashley Winters went missing, back in 1999, I remember Connors' police issue winter jacket had a rip on the left chest area and his name plate was missing. I was sitting at Molly's, having coffee that morning, and Molly and I both asked him about the rip and he laughed and said he was checking the oil in the cruiser and got hung up on the radiator cap and ripped the jacket and name tag off. You can ask Molly. I know she'll remember...we all teased Connors about it for a long time. Even Jim Bacon, the local mechanic, told him he should leave the heavy stuff to him and let him check his oil from then on."

"Well, that certainly makes sense...I mean the letters that are visible are ORS, as in CONNORS," Levi murmured.

"That fucking son of a bitch!" Miller said and vomited. "I worked with that bastard for the last, what, fifteen years."

"Okay...I want you to report this to Emerson before you go and after you tell him what you just told me, go home. You've earned my respect and I can assure you that's almost an impossibility. That never happens. Good job, Miller. See you at six," Levi said and slapped the officer on the back.

Levi was relieved that it might appear the victim or victims here in this muddy, dumping ground was not Zippy Beckwith, but either way, it was or had been someone's child and there was no joy in that.

The attending law enforcement officers gathered around to discard their white coveralls/clean suits, hair and foot coverings and gloves into a large dumpster that had been brought to the scene by the highway department earlier that day. Once all the contents had been secured, the dumpster was securely locked for the night.

The fresh team of New Hampshire Troopers and FBI agents arrived to secure the area for the night and the weary search teams went their separate ways.

Officer Miller entered his patrol car and Levi Harris walked up to him and knocked on his window. "You did real good, today, Miller. If you need someone to talk to, about this, you have my number. Emerson said we can't talk about what we found today, but he didn't say we couldn't talk to each other. I know this is the first time, in your career you've been involved in something of this nature, and it's pretty nasty stuff...I know."

"This has been one hell of a day, Levi. I appreciate you kinda looking after me and am grateful you notice how hard I'm trying to solve these cases. No one should have to go through this. I'll call you if I need to," Miller said and slowly left Blackberry Road.

FBI Agent In Charge, Edward Emerson, walked up to Levi. "I understand your brother, Alex Lyons, a.k.a A.L. Smart, has been released from federal prison," Emerson said and laughed.

"Yeah, he's been enjoying his freedom, keeping an eye on ZenJa, for me and by the way, he's heading up here, as we speak. I'll have him stay at the lake house because he can't been seen in the area, yet. Miller saw him when he was *arrested* in the O'Leary and Childress cases and of course Connors knows him, *personally*."

"You think we'll have enough evidence for an arrest, soon?" Levi asked.

"We have to make sure all the pieces fit. I don't want that mother fucker walking on a technicality. He's under twenty four hour surveillance, so he's not going to commit any more murders or there won't be any more missing children," Emerson said.

Levi wasn't so sure and with good reason.

"You think Alex and I should continue to hang around?" Levi asked. "This really is your territory, now, FBI, not ATF."

"Yeah, hang in there. You don't have anything better to do, do you?" Emerson asked and smiled.

Chapter 30

Levi left the crime scene and while heading down Blackberry Road, he checked his messages on his cell phone. There was one from Alex and two from ZenJa. He called his brother first.

"Yo! What's up?" Levi asked.

"I'm at the lake house."

"You're going to have to stay there, too. You can't come to Longberry, now. There are people here, obviously, who'll recognize you, like Officer Miller and Chief Connors," he reminded his younger sibling without breaking his pledge to remain silent about today's developments on Blackberry Road.

"What time will you get here?"

"I don't know, I have to pick up ZenJa, first."

"What ya been doing all day?" Alex asked.

"Nothing much," he lied "How about you starting up the grill and making some steaks? That should keep you out of trouble, until we get there."

"Okay, sounds like a plan."

After disconnecting the call with his brother, Levi called ZenJa.

"Sorry, I couldn't get back to you before now, ZenJa. I've been tied up all day. Did you get some things taken care of at your folks house?" he asked cheerfully.

"Yes, I did Levi, but after being left to my own demise, for so long, I walked to Molly's and had lunch. Now that's it's nearly dark, Lanny and Carol Williams offered to take me to River View High School where their children and other interested students and parents are going to hear our illustrious Police Chief give a speech on the evils of Bullying. I figured I'd go, because it appears you are going to leave me stranded," ZenJa sobbed. "I told you I couldn't stay at my parents house tonight."

"I'm sorry, ZenJa. I had no idea I was going to get caught up in...a situation that took longer than I planned. I'm on my way to the school now."

"Okay...We're waiting to go inside the gymnasium, so why don't you come in, when you get here."

"Okay...I might just do that."

The doors to the River View High School gymnasium were unlocked moments later and ZenJa, Carol, and her husband were the first to walk inside and find seats while their boys scampered around, near the stage, burning their bottled up energy.

Chief Connors was setting up the microphone system and podium on the stage when his cell phone rang and he held the device to his ear that was near the microphone. Unbeknownst to Connors, the broadcasting system had been activated and several words of the whispered conversation were spoken. Words that the other party murmured exploded inside the athletic center, "...skeleton...Blackberry Road...we're fucked!"

"What the hell?" ZenJa yelled at the same time Connors jumped off the stage, pulled out his service revolver, and grabbed the closest hostage/collateral he could reach...Carol and Lanny's two sons and dragged the children into the men's locker room.

"I'll get him!" ZenJa hollered to Lanny, and pulled her menacing weapon from her shoulder holster. "Get Carol and yourself out of here and make sure no one comes inside the gym or school and call 911!"

ZenJa was aware of what was taking place...a hostage situation, that she had never had to handle on her own, but realized she was up to the challenge. She had one advantage most agents don't have, initially. They aren't usually acquaintances of the hostage taker or the interior of the building where the event was taking place.

ZenJa ran toward the locker room, with her Glock drawn. She heard Connors yelling at the children to, "shut the fuck up," while she clearly heard the youngsters crying.

"ZenJa, Levi just showed up,"Carol whispered.

"Okay, now *GET OUT* and make sure no one comes near the school, from the entrance. We don't want any more people here than we already have."

"What about my children?" she screamed, tears running down her cheeks and she trying to keep her wits about her, with her husband forcefully removing her from the school.

"Carol!" ZenJa bellowed with the voice of a seasoned Federal Agent, "I got this! Do as I say, *now!*"

Carol Williams, who was on the edge of hysteria looked Levi Harris square in the face. "Don't you let that bastard kill my children," she yelled.

"ZenJa and I both work for the government," Levi reluctantly whispered, out of earshot to any other witnesses. "I can't promise you anything, Carol, but I'll die before I let anything happen to your children and I know I speak for ZenJa, as well. The Feds, SWAT, and State Police are on their way," he said and ran inside the gymnasium with his weapon drawn.

Levi overheard what appeared to be children crying and a man yelling, the sounds bouncing off all four walls of the hollow expanse of the gym, and the AFT agent was momentarily confused where the people, behind the voices were, located. He silently crept along the outer edge of the north wall, fanning the direction of his weapon along with his ever vigilant eyes.

Less than a minute later, Levi was aware of the direction the sounds were coming from and immediately recognized ZenJa's authoritative voice speaking in a composed and calming manner.

Levi was also aware that ZenJa had no idea about the developments that had taken place on Blackberry Road today or that fact that Officer Connors had been under surveillance for many months, regarding the murders and disappearances that had plagued Longberry for many years. But the law enforcement agent remained hidden in the shadows of the school gym to allow ZenJa Beckwith to do what she had been trained for, as an FBI Hostage Negotiator and being an HN, her only goal was the safe release of hostages, everything else was moot.

"Connors, this is ZenJa Beckwith.

"What are you doing here?" he shouted.

ZenJa knew Connors was not aware she was an FBI agent, so she decided not to elevate his distress by stating that she was...at that moment.

"I came with Carol and Lanny and the kids to hear your conference of Anti-Bullying," she calmly explained. I know that must be a cause you're deeply passionate about; you volunteering your time and expertise for the benefit of the community," she consoled the agitated man.

"Now, why not come out and let the children go and play on the swings while we talk. I have no idea what's wrong, but I do know what has gotten me through my bad times; talking to someone I trust, is what I needed."

ZenJa waited for a response from the police chief, to no avail.

"Is there someone you want me to call, so you can talk to them, Chief and while we're waiting, please let the children go. Their mom and dad really want them to be safe. You know you don't want them hurt or involved in this."

While ZenJa waited for a response from Connors, she detected movement that appeared to be on the roof of the gym and knew the SWAT team must be setting up a command center above and she noted movement behind her and out of the corner of her eye saw shadows racing by the windows in the direction of the locker room.

ZenJa had stationed herself outside the heavy metal locker room door and cautiously and ever so slightly opened the door in hopes of getting a *visual* on Connors. She peeked inside, but couldn't see anything other than lockers and empty wooden benches, basket balls and baseball equipment laying in disarray.

"Connors, please talk to me. There's nothing we can't talk about and we need to bring this to a close before anyone gets hurt. This situation hasn't escalated to a serious situation. Please just send the children out first and then come out yourself."

Nothing...no response, only the whimper of two small, terrified children held captive, inside.

"If I come in and talk to you face to face, Chief, will you let the children leave? I'm no cop, Chief, you know I'm a simple financial analyst. I have no weapon," she lied, "so you have nothing to loose by letting the children go and talking to me."

"You don't have a fucking clue!" Connors screamed hysterically.

"What don't I know, Chief?" ZenJa asked showing as much respect as she possibly could muster to this man she had always despised.

Before Connors replied, Levi made his presence behind ZenJa, known to her and she signaled to him that she had it under control and not incite further stress on the situation. She hoped Connors thought it was he and ZenJa involved and not local, state and federal law enforcement personnel surrounding the school.

"Speak to me, Chief. What don't I know?" she repeated.

"It's too late," he murmured.

"It's not too late, Chief. Please send the children out and we can talk as long as you want. I'm here for you."

Unexpectedly, two small boys came running from the locker room and out the door where ZenJa was waiting.

Levi quickly and quietly escorted the children from the gym into the welcoming arms of their parents and into an ambulance that sped to a local hospital.

"Thank you, Chief. That goes a long way to your credit. I know you'd never hurt any child," ZenJa replied softly, watching the man come toward the door.

The FBI negotiator noted the man was shaking and appeared to be incoherent.

"I don't know how it happened," Connors began.

"Why don't you let me come inside, Chief and we can sit on the bench and talk. It's not very comfortable talking through this door, is it?" she asked. "Just throw your weapon outside the door and we'll talk. You know I don't carry a gun," she lied again and placed her Glock in the back of her blue jeans, in the waistband, covered by her sweatshirt.

Minutes passed and there was no response from Connors who remained inside the locker room.

"Chief? Can you hear me?"

"Is there anything you want? A soda, cigarette or a friend you want to talk to?"

"There's no smoking in a school!" Connors insanely responded; not making sense with a trivial detail like smoking in school and the seriousness of the situation he had gotten himself, in the last half hour.

Another few moments of silence and ZenJa knew time was on her side. There was no one in danger of being injured or killed...only she and/or Chief Connors and that didn't matter to her.

"Please let me come inside, Chief, so we can sit and talk," ZenJa calmly suggested.

"No! You stay outside the door."

"Okay, that's fine. We can talk from here," she agreed.

"You don't know what happened today, do you ZenJa?" Connors screamed. "You don't know anything, do you?" he hollered again.

"No, Chief, I don't. Why don't you tell me so we can work something out. If I don't know what's wrong, I can't help you."

"Where were you today, Chief?"

"Oh, I was in Concord, doing some business at the DMV."

"Okay, that's a good place to start. What happened at the DMV?"

"Nothing!"

"Okay, what happened after you got back from the DMV? Only a few minutes ago you were setting up the microphone and podium on stage and you received a call on your cell phone, right?"

ZenJa covered her mouth, recalling the words that now echoed through her mind...skeleton....Blackberry Road...we're fucked.

ZenJa wiped the perspiration from her brow and continued the negotiations.

"So what was the call about, Chief? Who called you?"

"Do you know what's funny about the media, ZenJa?" Connors rambled.

"No, what Chief?" she asked quietly removing the weapon from her waistband, now that she and Connors apparently were not going to converse face to face.

"Have you noticed that when there's a crime, let's say, involving children, especially girls, the news stations seem to focus only on the pretty ones; the pretty, slender, blonde, cheerleader types? How often have you heard or seen any constant reminders of a young black child missing on a nightly basis on those evening /lawyer talk shows? Not very damn often, right?"

"I couldn't agree with you more, Chief. I've said that a million times about Olive and Zippy," ZenJa said while tears streamed down her face. She knew Connors had something to confess and in her heart she knew what it was, but her job, her career was what mattered right now. She was not Zippy's sister...she was now FBI Agent ZenJa Beckwith. She had to Mirandize Connors before he did make any kind of confession, so the bastard couldn't walk on a technicality. ZenJa knew all was fair in love and war and when it came to playing ball between the cops and perps, there were no rules.

"Chief, it's only you and me here," she lied. "I do have to tell you that I've dabbled, somewhat in law enforcement, I did take some paralegal and some very interesting classes in justice." She neglected to mention the words, criminal justice, but simply voiced the word justice. "And it's my duty to read you your rights, just to protect you and me. Is that okay?"

"ZenJa, I don't care. Go ahead, read me my rights. I have nothing to hide," he said. "It's all over now."

ZenJa read Chief Bob Connors his rights to remain silent, anything he did say could be used against him in a court of law and the usual bit about lawyers and ability or inability to pay...

"Okay, Chief, now that's all done, can we talk; is there anything you want to talk about? If not now, with a lawyer present?"

"I don't need a lawyer," Connors replied.

"Talk to me, Chief. You'll feel better when you get whatever's bothering you off your chest. You're living with something that's eating you alive."

ZenJa glanced over at Levi, who stood to her left and gave her the thumbs up.

"What was that phone call about, the call you received a few minutes ago, Chief?"

There was no response for several minutes, but ZenJa saw Connors sitting on one of the benches, his head in his hands.

She began to open the door, ever so slightly in what Levi rightly assumed ZenJa was about to entire the locker room. Levi, touched her hand and shook his head, in the negative. ZenJa backed down and continued with her negotiations.

"Talk to me, Chief. I can help you."

"You'll be the last one to help me when you hear what I have to say."

"What's done is done, Chief. Nothing can change that, no matter what it is. All we can do, all of us, is ask for forgiveness. We've all done things we regret and pray someone will forgive us," ZenJa continued looking at Levi.

"The phone call was from someone telling me they found a skeleton on Blackberry Road today."

"Do you know who those remains may be?" ZenJa asked leaning against the cement wall.

Again, there was no response so ZenJa was going to us another tactic. "Are the remains of my sister, Zippy or Olive?" she asked with surprising compassion.

A deafening silence exploded in her head. "Were you and Alex Lyons responsible for the murders of Constance O'Leary and Morgan Childress? I know he was found guilty and has been in prison for years now. Is that what you want to tell me, that he didn't commit those crimes by himself?"

Levi noted ZenJa was struggling to contain her composure, but she carried on like a trooper and nodded his encouragement to her.

"Alex Lyons didn't kill those girls."

"Do you know who did?" she asked.

Bob Connors, once again remained silent.

ZenJa was aware that the chief was seated within her visual range, but the SWAT team would be unable to get a perceptible on him, where he presently sat, surrounded by cement blocks and no windows...ironically, ZenJa thought, like a prison cell.

"I gotta take a leak?" the chief said and started to walk toward the men's bathroom. ZenJa, having grown up in that small town, knew the rest rooms were located just around the corner, near the showers. ZenJa knew the entire lay-out of the school...even the underground passageway that led to the football field, a tenth of a mile away.

"He's going to the tunnel," ZenJa whispered under her breath...not loud enough for Levi to hear.

"Okay, chief, I'll wait right here," she lied.

Once Chief Connors took three steps toward the other end of the locker room, ZenJa quickly slid inside the heavy metal door, slammed it shut and locked it from the inside; Levi was pounding on the door, demanding ZenJa open the door and come out.

"ZenJa, get the fuck out of there!" "I'll shoot my way in, if you don't!" he exclaimed uselessly and he knew it.

ZenJa was in a hot pursuit of Bob Connors. The twosome sprinted toward the underground tunnel and seconds after ZenJa closed the door behind her, once inside the tunnel, a bomb blast decimated the interior and exterior of the gymnasium.

ZenJa knew instinctively that everyone on the roof, around the building and Levi had most certainly been killed.

"Okay, fucker! It's just you and me, now," ZenJa swore at the law enforcement officer while she continued to chase him down the tomblike structure that was as black as midnight and velvet. "You want this to go your way? Well, my fucking friend, you got it!"

The only sound that came from the chief's end of the tunnel was the shuffle of his feet and an occasional thump; his body hitting jagged rocks and stumbling.

"You just murdered about thirty SWAT team members, FBI and State Police Troopers you fucking son of a bitch and I'm going to blow your fucking head off when I get you and I'll give you an extra bullet for my sister, you slimy piece of dog shit!"

Connors simply laughed and reached the end of the tunnel, opened the exit door, but accidentally dropped his service weapon inside the door that had automatically locked behind him.

ZenJa reached the door seconds later and heard the clatter of the weapon falling on the stones and opened the locked door and with the benefit of the moonlight, spotted the weapon and retrieved it before entering the football field and closing the door behind her; again it was locked from the inside.

The overwhelming acrid scent of smoke, dust and the flames were only second on her list of priorities at this time. She suddenly realized Connors had, obviously planted the bomb in the building, hoping to attract people from the community to the school and had purposely parked his own sports car away from the building to make his escape after his intent to murder more innocent people.

ZenJa's first priority was to take care of Connors, whatever it took. She owed that to Zippy, the other girls and now it appeared other law enforcement officers and Levi as well. It was apparent no one survived that blast.

Chief Connors jumped into his Dodge Viper, struggled to find the keys, in his pocket and ZenJa opened the passenger's side of the door and jumped in...training her weapon at the subject.

"Drive!" ZenJa ordered.

"Where are we going?" the whimpering man cried.

"Oh, lets go to Blackberry Road."

"We can't go there. There are cops all over the place there."

"Pray, tell me why that might be, Chief?" ZenJa asked holding her weapon against the man's head.

"I heard someone found a skeleton down there," he said and started the engine and slowly left the ball field.

ZenJa was aware of fire trucks, ambulances, and commotion at the gymnasium, but was unable to see anything amid the smoke and flames that consumed the area.

While still directing her Glock at Connors' head, she tried, in vain, to reach Levi on his cell phone.

"Okay, pull over here," ZenJa said and pointed to a dirt road several miles out of town.

"Now, get out!" she ordered. "I'm going to blow your brains out and I don't want to dirty up the interior of this nice fancy sports car. It'll reduce the retail value of the car."

"ZenJa! Please don't kill me. We didn't mean to do it!" the man cried, but not exiting the vehicle.

"What do you mean...*we*?" she asked. "You mean Alex Lyons, the guy who's already in prison for the murders of the O'Leary and Childress girls?"

"He didn't kill those girls," he screamed.

"You mean to tell me, you've allowed an innocent man to go to prison for crimes you and who the hell else, committed? You're the most vial piece of shit I've ever known. And before we go any further, of course I'm not going to kill you, that would make me a piece of shit, just like you, now wouldn't it? But there is something I need to know and you'll tell me, otherwise I'll blow your brains out right here."

"You want to know where Zippy is, right?" he asked sweating

profusely and shaking nervously.

"Obviously! "Where is she?" ZenJa commanded.

"I don't know. I wasn't responsible for her disappearance."

"Who the hell was?" she growled.

"I can't tell you that."

"It's kinda late to be worried about covering up for someone else, who has already turned on you, isn't it Connors?" ZenJa explained not knowing or caring if it was true or not. She realized the man sitting with her in this car was close to having a mental collapse.

"It was Miller," he declared, not explaining which brother it was.

"You and Miller?" ZenJa asked.

"Did he take all the girls or were you involved as well?"

"He didn't...we both, were involved."

"Get the fuck out of the car."

"ZenJa...please," the man begged and opened the driver's side of the door and ZenJa pushed the broken man from the car.

The FBI agent exited the vehicle, walked toward the man who was sprawled on the ground, weeping like a three year old child.

"Did those girls cry like you are right now, you bastard?" she asked pulling back the hammer on her weapon.

"After I blow your brains out, I'm going after your co-hort, Miller," ZenJa declared and shot one round inches from her target...purposely missing the man.

At that moment, ZenJa heard a car slide sideways next to the Viper and come to a screeching halt.

"Drop the weapon ZenJa. You don't want to do that," Officer Miller said.

"It's you!" she screamed aiming her weapon at the officer. "This mother fucker just said you were the one responsible for the disappearance of my sister!"

"No, ZenJa, not me, my brother!" the officer shouted, standing as large as life, not drawing his weapon and not fearing that this agent was capable of shooting him where he stood. He knew better. If she was going to kill someone, she would have murdered Chief Connors before this.

"Please put the gun down, ZenJa. It's over."

"No, it's not over, Miller! My sister and the other girls, yes, even some of the pretty ones are still missing," she cried and holstered her weapon, but remaining to eye this officer with suspicion.

"I know, ZenJa and we will find them, I promise you."

Miller handcuffed Bob Connors, read him his rights and placed him under arrest and seated him inside his patrol car.

"The gymnasium!" ZenJa cried while she and Miller stood between the Viper and patrol car.

"There was extensive damage, ZenJa. We may have lost at least five SWAT team members and an unknown number of state police. I regret not being there to help, but I was busy arresting my brother."

"Levi!" ZenJa cried.

"Levi made it. They dug him out and med-flighted him to Dartmouth Hitchcock Medical Center in Lebanon.."

"How is he?" she whispered, holding on the side of the Viper for support.

"I don't know ZenJa. I think you better get up there. You know where it is?"

"Yes, of course," I'll leave right away, but I don't have my car here.

"Okay, drive the Viper back to the gym. If my guess is right, I would imagine Levi left the keys in the Navigator and I don't think he'd mind you driving it up there to see him."

"Be careful with my Viper," Connors warned.

"Oh, where you're going, asshole, you're not going to be needing it...ever!" ZenJa spewed at the man in handcuffs.

By the time ZenJa arrived, at what was left of the gymnasium, the fire had been extinguished, but an arsenal of fire trucks and man power remained at the sight. Members of the Federal Bureau of Investigation and Alcohol, Tobacco and Firearms, and Explosives Administrations, both divisions of the Justice Department, were investigating the bombing site, while another NH Major Crimes Unit arrived to assist.

Numerous television camera crews had arrived and even more news helicopters swarmed overhead, informing the public of the disastrous events as they unfolded.

"Miss Beckwith, Officer Miller said you were in need of transportation to Lebanon. If you don't feel up to driving yourself, I would be happy to escort you to the hospital," a New Hampshire State Trooper offered.

"I need to see if Levi left the keys in his vehicle and if he has, I'll be fine," ZenJa replied thanking the trooper for his offer.

"The keys are here," ZenJa shouted over the commotion. "I'll be all set, now," she said and climbed inside the large S.U.V and sped off toward the hospital, still shaking from the day's events that had unfolded, so far.

Several minutes into her travel, west toward Lebanon, a cell phone that was laying on the front seat rang. "Hello," ZenJa answered.

"Who's this?" the man asked.

"It's ZenJa...who's this?"

"Where's my brother?" the man asked.

"I can't say, right now, because I'm not convinced who you are," ZenJa replied, tired of playing guessing games, being lied to and deceived at every turn.

"How can I convince you who I am?" the man asked.

"Tell me where you are, for starters."

"I'm at my brother's fucking house, cooking steaks for you and my brother, wondering where the hell you both are!"

"What's your name?" ZenJa asked, thinking she recognized the voice of the caller.

"My fucking name is Alex Lyons."

"You're in prison!" ZenJa replied, having difficulty keeping the Navigator in the roadway, becoming more confused with each passing moment.

"Yeah, okay, I'm in prison, if that makes you happy! Now where the hell is my brother?"

"If you check the news you'll find out," ZenJa replied. "I don't have time to talk now, I'm on my way to see him at Dartmouth," she said and disconnected the call.

Chapter 31

The events that literally rocked and destroyed the River View High School gymnasium, before the arrest of Police Chief Bob Connors and Officer Brian Miller's brother, Jackson, devastated the patrons who crammed into Molly's Café. The locals gathered to catch up on the latest news; the areas surrounding the school and Blackberry Road were completely off limits to anyone other than specialized law enforcement personnel. It was standard practice for the towns-folk to gather at the café to compare notes, get the latest news, and gossip as well. Today was no exception, there wasn't an empty booth or stool at the counter, not to mention the line of patrons who patiently waited outside to get the next empty seat.

Lanny and Carol Williams were seated on their usual stools, having left their two boys in the care of their grandmother and grandfather in nearby Laconia, for the weekend. The parents knew the boys would enjoy escaping the glut of media and attention that was to descend on the town. And the boys were promised trips to The Whales Tail and other amusement parks in the area over the weekend in an effort to dull their minds of the experience that would live with them for many years to come.

"It was like something out of a movie" Lanny began to the hushed audience he had, the only sound heard was an occasional spoon or fork clanking against the china. "We entered the school as soon as the doors were open, to hear the anti-bullying seminar the chief was going to deliver. All of a sudden Connors received a cell phone call and we heard part of a conversation, because the microphone was accidentally turned on.

"What did you overhear?" Molly asked, sipping her coffee near the cash register.

"He said something about a skeleton, Blackberry Road, and we're F'ed. Then Connors ran into the locker room, after grabbing our boys and taking them in there with him. He kidnaped our sons!"

"ZenJa stepped in," Carol began, not revealing the fact that she and Levi worked for the government. "She told us to get out of the school and make sure no one else came inside or drove to the school for the seminar. She obviously didn't want any more innocent people to become involved in what, we had no idea, yet. She began talking to the chief and begged him to let the boys go, and that's all I know. I was outside. Finally, the boys came running outside and that's all any of us knew, until the bomb went off inside. As far as I knew ZenJa and her friend, Levi, and of course the chief were the only ones still inside, but after looking on the roof, we could see a SWAT team up there and so many other state troopers arriving at the school, along with ambulances and fire equipment. It was the most scary thing I've ever witnessed or been involved in."

"When the bomb went off," Lanny continued. "We knew this was a real emergency situation. I actually saw some of the SWAT team fall through the roof and some of the troopers were hit with bricks, glass and God only knows what else that came flying out because of the explosion."

"Oh my God!" Molly exclaimed. "This is horrible." she continued making the rounds filling up empty cups of coffee, while roaming the interior of the café.

"So there's no word about ZenJa?" one customer asked.

"No! Nothing yet, about anyone from the scene. No one is talking, they're all tight lipped, but I did hear a rumor Assistant Principal Miller has been arrested," Lanny confirmed.

"Well, his arrest must be because of that skeleton that was mentioned on Blackberry Road?" the cook asked. "I'm not surprised he was involved in something shady. I knew something was up the other day when he was in here and he found out they have closed off Blackberry Road because of an alleged rock slide and he flew out of here like a robin with his tail feathers on fire."

"He must have known it wasn't a rock slide, but that someone had found something suspicious down there where the Beckwith's died in that car accident." Jim Bacon concluded.

"This is horrible," Molly wailed with new customers making their way into the café.

"Can I help you?" Molly asked not recognizing the newcomers.

"We would like a booth, please," the man said while holding a camera in his hand.

"Are you Thomas Blake, with the television station WYCC?" Molly asked.

"Why, yes I am," the man replied, flattered that he was so well known in this small town.

"Well, I'm sorry, Mr. Blake, but there are no booths or empty seats now, I have a reservation list, as you can see, for any of the next seats that become available," Molly said, holding up a piece of paper that had nothing but gibberish on it. Molly was not about to have her local customers privacy invaded by the media and to have the reporters use her customers as sources for their stories. Molly knew what the media was like and how they twisted the truth in their stories to gain the most publicity.

"Oh, I'm sorry to hear that," Blake replied. "Is there anyone here who would like to speak with us, on camera, about the developments, that you know about, that have taken place over the last day or so?"

"Nope! We're all set," everyone replied in unison.

"You won't get anyone outside to tell you anything else, either," Lanny added. "Your best bet is to hang around the police station and wait for a news conference."

"Thank you, I will," Blake replied, disappointed that there was no one in this town taking the *bait*.

While the media waited for a new conference, Jackson Miller and Bob Connors had been placed under arrest and had been transferred to a jail in a nearby town, were they waited for their attorneys to arrive. Longberry had no secure facility to house the alleged criminals from either themselves or the towns-folk if they should decide to take matters into their own hands.

Their arraignments would take place in a matter of days, but much to the disappointment of Officer Brian Miller, the ATF, FBI, and state authorities, neither man was disclosing any tips about the whereabouts of the missing girls. They were as tight lipped about that as the towns-folk were about giving interviews to the media. This was a close community and they wanted their business to remain their business, but they wanted answers about their missing loved ones and would seek whatever justice the system allowed. That was the only way to resolve their heartbreak; to bring closure and heal from the wounds inflicted by two of their own.

Chapter 32

The federal authorities and Office Miller obtained warrants to search both Jackson Miller and Bob Connors homes and vehicles.

"I commend you, Officer Miller," FBI Agent Jonathan Drew said.

"About what?" Miller asked, resting his weary head in his hands, at his desk.

"Seeking answers to the crimes that have taken place in this town and surrounding areas and to have to arrest your own brother..."

"There was no question about it. I would arrest my own mother if she did something as heinous as this and frankly we don't even know exactly what Connors or my brother did, yet. I'm afraid what we do know is only the tip of the iceberg."

"All I wanted to say is, you're one hell of an upstanding guy," Miller.

"I take my job very seriously and like I told Levi, I want to be an FBI agent one day, myself."

"I know you'll be very well recommended," Drew said and smiled.

"Any news on the tire track impressions that were taken across from where the Beckwith's vehicle went over the ledge on Blackberry Road, yet, in comparison with Jackson's truck?" Officer Miller asked.

"Not yet, but now that we have a vehicle in question it shouldn't take long, now."

"This has been a nightmare for so many in this area, but especially for ZenJa Beckwith," Miller said shaking his head. "I can't imagine what she's been going through and I'll do whatever I can to convince my brother to tell what he knows. If he doesn't give it up willingly..." Miller continued but stopped short of explaining exactly what he'd do, if given a chance.

"He'll realize, I hope, that he's nothing to gain by keeping the folks around here in their living hell any longer. I'm rather confident they'll be facing the death penalty, so only the devil will be able to help them," Agent Drew said.

"Well, I suppose we better head out to Blackberry Road and see if they need our help in searching for any more remains. We only found two shin bones, a hand and that name tag," Miller said.

"After all the time the remains have been there, most likely animals have scattered, what bones were there, all over the place," Drew reasoned.

"Well, let's get going," Miller said and stood, locked the police station door and drove behind Agent Drew toward Blackberry Road.

"Any news about Levi and the others who were brought to Dartmouth?" Miller asked upon his arrival at the secured crime scene.

"Nothing yet. I've been waiting for ZenJa to give us an update, but nothing yet," FBI Agent Emerson replied.

"Anything new down there?" Emerson asked pointing down the steep ledge below.

"We've found some more items of clothing and items that would have belonged in a child's book bag. We also found a science book, what's left of it. CSI is looking to see if they can enhance a number that was on the inside cover. All school books are assigned to each student and their numbers are kept in a log at the school, not that this book we found, may have actually been in possession of the person who was left here," Emerson reasoned. "We have to start somewhere," he replied in a tired and strained tone.

Chapter 33

While ZenJa sped on Interstate 89 she called Dartmouth Hitchcock Medical Center in Lebanon, NH and asked what section of that humongous hospital to approach and park to check on the condition of her *brother*. Now was not the time, she realized, to be completely honest. Truthfulness wasn't what was important to her; finding out how badly injured Levi was and what she could do to help him recover, was the only important thing on the agenda now.

Once she parked at the North Entrance, ran inside and announced she was there to see her *brother*, she was met by her neighbor from Forest Haven Estates in Virginia.

"What are you doing here, A.L?" ZenJa asked shaking her head in confusion. "Are you following me?"

"Don't give yourself so much credit, ZenJa. No, I'm not following you. I'm here to check on the condition of my brother, as are you, I assume?"

"You're Levi's brother?"

"Yes, and from what I just overheard you tell the receptionist at the front desk, you're my sister."

"You're Levi's brother?" ZenJa asked again, overwhelmed by the mysteries that continued to unfold with each passing moment of her life.

"Yes, and my real name isn't A.L. Smart. It's Alex Lyons," he announced, while the couple walked toward the elevator that led to the fourth floor, intensive care unit.

"You're Alex Lyons?" she exclaimed to the annoyance of others who occupied the same elevator.

"Let's wait to continue this conversation when we get out of this box," Alex suggested.

"I'm really more interested in seeing Levi, if possible, but I suppose I need to explain who I am and why you think you know what *is*, but really *isn't*."

"You're in prison for the murders of Constance and Morgan. I tried to visit you in prison..."

"That was a scam, ZenJa. The whole incident was a sting operation targeting Chief Connors. I was the bait! I had been meeting up with Connors over a period of months. He was giving me weapons and drugs and we were hoping he might gain my trust and eventually confide in me about the murders and other disappearances of the girls from the Longberry area. We hit pay-dirt when he put the weapons, drugs and the backpack that belonged to one of the girls in my car! We never dreamed he would walk right into the trap, that he did, and so easily."

"I can't believe it! You were suspecting him for a long time?" ZenJa asked startled by the information she was given.

"Yes, we did, but we didn't know if or who his accomplice was until just yesterday, as a matter of fact, when all this shit happened," he continued walking with his *sister* toward the reception desk to introduce themselves and see what condition Levi was in and if it was possible to visit him.

"We are family members of Levi Harris and would like to know his condition; if and when we can see him," Alex announced.

"I will let you speak with his nurse, over the phone and she can give you the information you are requesting," the clerk replied. You may dial #6 on this phone and that will connect you to his nurse."

"Thank you," Alex replied and dialed the number.

"I'm Alex, Levi Harris' brother and I would like to know his condition and if we may come in and see him?"

"Mr. Harris is still in surgery and if you'll wait in the waiting area on this floor, we'll come out and get you when he comes into his room or the doctor will come out and talk with you when he's out of surgery."

"Thank you very much. We'll be right outside the door," Alex replied and ushered ZenJa to a secluded corner of the crowded waiting area and sat down.

Alex relayed what little information there was and asked her if she wanted a cup of coffee or sandwich.

"Yes, actually, I could use a large coffee and something to eat. I can't remember when I ate last. Thank you, Alex. I'll wait here, if you don't mind."

"No problem. I'll be back in a few."

ZenJa's head was swimming, she closed her eyes, and visions of the last few days played before her like an old fashioned movie.

ZenJa wasn't sure what the truth was, any more and all she did know, for a fact, was that A.L. Smart had been a decoy and his arrest had been *arranged* in an effort to find the real culprit or culprits who had become the most despicable human beings in New Hampshire history.

While ZenJa waited for news about Levi or Alex to return with some lunch, she thought about her parents and how she hadn't begun to acknowledge their deaths, not to mention plan a service. But the important thing right now was Levi. Everything else she would deal with one day at a time.

Twenty minutes later, Alex returned with a bag filled with sandwiches and two cups of coffee.

"Any word?"

"No, nothing yet and thanks for the food. I didn't realize how hungry I was until you mentioned it," ZenJa said and sipped her coffee and selected a BLT from the bag and Alex chose a ham and cheese on rye.

"Any word on how many, if any, deaths there were at the gymnasium explosion?" ZenJa asked.

"No, the only thing I've seen was on television before I headed out to come here. If it hadn't been for you, I wouldn't have known about Levi, until Emerson called me, while I was heading up here."

"Well, obviously if you hadn't called his cell, I wouldn't have known who you were, other than my neighbor in Virginia."

"Levi called me just as he was going to pick you up from Molly's and I told him I was at the lake house and he asked me to put on some steaks for us. That's the last I spoke with him."

"So tell me, why have you been following me or at least seemingly watching every move I make?" Obviously, Levi was my guardian for a few days at Claybourne College and then disappeared. What was that all about?"

"Well, Levi was *assigned* to keep you safe and then when you threw him out of your house, I was assigned to keep you under surveillance."

"Just exactly why were you tailing me?"

"It was for your own protection. There were rumors about someone attempting to keep you from returning to Longberry to continue to search for your sister and it now appears that those people, who we presume to be Connors and Jackson Miller, were the people responsible for your parents deaths. That's what the CSI and we Feds are investigating now. Actually, Officer Miller was a big help in tracking down the tire prints that were made by what we think was his brother's truck. He noticed a vehicle had been parked in the underbrush across the road from where your parents car went off Blackberry Road. That was obviously where the perpetrator parked, on that dark and rainy night, in an effort to spook your parents into believing they were about to be broadsided by another vehicle and as any person would do, they tried to avoid the vehicle and sadly, they fell for the ruse and went over the ledge."

"Oh my God! I've been left in the dark about this whole thing," ZenJa wailed.

"I only learned these latest facts, myself, on my way up here. I spoke with Emerson and he filled me in on what Levi and the others had been investigating, today.

"Nothing was said to you, until today, because we weren't exactly sure who the perps were and until that was confirmed at the gym and what little we've been able to get out of Connors and Miller, we couldn't divulge what we knew. Now you can add more to the evidence with whatever Connors said to you in the gym, that night and while you had him in his Viper."

"My God! This just keeps getting more weird with each passing minute," ZenJa exclaimed. "It seems Connors and Miller would go to any lengths to keep their dirty little secrets, huh?"

"Yes, it seems so."

A few minutes later, FBI Agent Emerson walked into the waiting room, followed by who appeared to be three other agents.

"I see you've met Alex Lyons," Emerson said and smiled.

"I was just telling A.L. that I had indeed tried to visit him in prison, but it appears he simply didn't want to have visitors, it seems he was otherwise engaged," ZenJa said and tried to find the humor in it.

"I did explain the reason why," Alex replied and shrugged his shoulders. "I don't think she has had time to comprehend all the events," he added in her defense.

"Any word about Levi?" Emerson asked.

"No, nothing yet," Alex responded.

"What about the *others*?" ZenJa asked realizing there were many visitors, waiting news on their loved ones, sitting only a few feet away.

"Sadly, we lost two SWAT members and one state trooper," he whispered. "Who was the trooper?" ZenJa asked holding her breath.

"Trooper Daniel Alton," Emerson replied quietly.

"Oh my God! This is terrible. He played such an active roll in the search for my sister and the others. Does he have a family?"

"Yes, he is...was married with two boys, ages ten and twelve."

"There are no words to describe this and all the tragedies that have happened because of those two bastards," ZenJa continued.

"Alleged bastards, ZenJa." Alex reminded her.

"Yes, alleged bastards," she murmured.

"You said two SWAT members were killed? Anyone I may know?" ZenJa asked.

"No, I don't think so; they were summoned out of Concord. There were five injured SWATS and four state troopers. They've been taken to two hospitals, according to the severity of their injuries. Three SWATS are here and one trooper, the others were transported to Lakes Regional. I've been making the rounds," Emerson added.

"How are the patients you've gotten any word about?" Alex asked.

"Everyone is or has been in surgery. It appears everyone will survive, by the grace of God. Several have broken bones and burns."

"Where in hell do you start prosecuting Connors and Miller?" ZenJa asked.

"It'll be a hell of a mess for a while until the charges are all brought to the forefront and then we have to wait for evidence in the disappearances and murders. Let's just say *if* Connors and Jackson Miller are convicted they'll never see the light of day again, not that it will bring any satisfaction to anyone for their losses," Emerson continued.

"No, it certainly won't," ZenJa agreed.

"We're going down to check on the trooper and we'll be back in a while," Emerson said and he and his fellow agents walked toward the elevators.

The couple were finishing their lunch when a surgeon entered the ICU waiting room. "Are you members of Levi Harris' family?"

"Yes, we are," both replied in unison.

"I'm Dr. Goss, Chief of Surgery," he continued nodding toward ZenJa and Alex. "Mr. Harris is in serious, but stable condition, at this time. He received multiple broken bones in his left arm and shrapnel that embedded itself into a majority of his left side. This shrapnel contains pieces of metal and cement, from the blast, it would appear. Some of the metal pieces barely missed a vital artery in his arm. He is very luck," the doctor continued.

"How long do you anticipate his being hospitalized," ZenJa asked.

"We're going to keep an eye on him for several days. We want to make sure there'll be no infection rearing its ugly head. Metal fragments embedded in the body are nothing to fool with. I'll keep you informed and you can always speak with whatever nurse is on duty in his room."

"Thank you, Dr. Goss," Alex said and shook the surgeon's hand. "May we go in and see him?"

"Only for a few minutes," he replied. "The nurse will show you to his room; just enter this door, turn right and take the first left. His room number is 405."

"Thank you again," ZenJa said and followed Alex through the doors.

ZenJa and Alex quietly tip-toed into Levi's room. The man's arm was in a cast and in traction and he had various intravenous lines running into his right arm and hand and what appeared to be oxygen being delivered through his nose. His eyes were black and blue and his nose was swollen, otherwise neither ZenJa or Alex could tell what other injuries there were; he being swaddled in cotton and bandages and ice packs.

ZenJa reached out and touched his right hand, but he remained perfectly still because of his medicated from the surgery.

A nurse entered the private room and checked various charts and machines to make sure everything was working properly and her patient was as comfortable as possible.

"Will he sleep for a while?" Alex asked, the look of concern evident on his face.

"I think he'll be asleep until morning. It's best he get his rest. He's been through quite a lot for one day," she added.

"Do you think he can hear us, if we speak to him?" ZenJa asked.

"I truly believe people who are heavily medicated do hear those who speak to them," she replied and left the room.

ZenJa stood back and allowed Alex to talk to his brother.

"Hey, champ," he said softly. "You're going to be up and at 'em in no time. You just get your rest now, that's the only important thing. I love you bro," he added and wiped a tear from his eye and moved away from the bed.

"Levi, this is ZenJa," she also whispered. "I love you," she said without thinking and stepped out of the room, a Kleenex wiping her eyes.

After a few more moments, Alex met ZenJa back in the waiting room. "Good God, it's almost noon," he said looking at his watch. "What if we rent motel rooms, down the road and take turns getting a nap. You're exhausted, ZenJa. You've been through hell and back and you need to keep your strength up for yourself and for Levi."

"I don't want to leave," she begged.

"It's only down the street. You saw it coming in right. It's a Motel Ten or something, if I recall. Get us a couple of rooms and I'll call you when Levi wakes up, but only after you have a few hours of sleep and a shower."

"Do I smell that bad?" she asked and laughed.

"Well, I wasn't going to mention it, but running through that tunnel that hadn't been used in years, kinda covered you in mud, dirt, spider webs and what-not."

"Okay, I can't argue with you about that," she admitted. "I'll run to the local K-Mart on the way and get some clothes and other items. You want me to pick you up some, too? We may be here for a few days."

"No, thanks. Actually, I still have my bag inside the Mustang. I hadn't had enough time to bring it in the lake house, yet when Levi asked me to throw some steaks on the grill."

"Okay, I'm leaving now, but if anything changes, please call me," she said and slowly left the hospital.

Shortly after ZenJa checked into the motel she quickly grabbed a shower, tossed her dirty clothes in a laundry bag, threw on a nightgown and collapsed on the queen bed and a flood of tears poured from her eyes. Tears for her sister, the other girls, her parents, Levi and the others who were killed or injured in the collapse of the gymnasium and a few tears for herself. Sleep didn't come easily. She tossed, turned and was consumed with fragments of nightmares, woven into a smoked filled collage of terror and sadness. Horrors of murdering Chief Connors and Jackson Miller, herself, in cold blood and not caring.

Several hours later, there was a knock at her door and it took ZenJa several seconds to realize where she was.

"Who is it?" she asked looking out the peep hole in the door.

"It's me, Alex."

"How are Levi and the others?"

"Here, let me put these things down," Alex said putting several paper bags that appeared to be filled with Chinese food and a selection of beverages on the kitchenette counter.

"Levi's doing better. He woke up a few minutes ago and was coherent enough to know I was there and I think he comprehended the fact that he'd be okay, eventually. I figured it was a good time for me to take off for a while and get us something to eat and to get some rest. His nurse said he'd most likely sleep for several more hours before he'd waken again.

"Did you get any rest?" Alex asked while digging into the various containers of take-out and noting ZenJa was wearing a short bathrobe that apparently covered a nighty.

"Let me get some clothes on," ZenJa said shortly after she realized she wasn't appropriately dressed for dinner or with a basic stranger in her motel room and headed toward the bathroom.

"Okay! I'll dish out the goodies and by the way, I asked them to put four fortune cookies in the bag, in case the first ones, we open, aren't that good," Alex said and chuckled.

"Your room is next door, by the way. I'm assuming it's just like this one," ZenJa said to make small talk. "Your key is on the dresser, mine is in my purse."

"Thanks! I'll put it in my pocket and reimburse you for the room."

"That's okay, it's on the taxpayers dole," she said and left the bathroom wearing a clean pair of blue jeans and a black cotton turtleneck, her freshly washed red hair tied in a pony tail.

Once the twosome started eating their dinner, the subject of the bombing at the gymnasium came up again.

"The trooper and three SWAT's who're in the hospital will be okay, eventually, like Levi. They all suffer from broken bones and burns. Emerson told me they are in serious, but stable condition and their families have gathered around, as have their fellow law enforcement family.

"How come it's only you, me and Agent Emerson here to encourage Levi? How come there aren't hundreds of FBI out there to make sure he's going to be okay?" ZenJa asked while eating a crab ragoon and concern etched in her face.

"Levi isn't like the rest of us. He's...how should I say it? He's deeply 'underground' and if he had to take a bullet before admitting he was Alcohol, Tobacco, Firearms, and Explosives Federal Bureau of Investigation, Central Intelligence or National Security Administrations, he would. No one really knows who he works for. I don't and sometimes I don't think he does either!" Alex said and laughed.

"Oh my God! He certainly is a complex person."

"What about his...your family?"

"Anything he wants to divulge about his family is his business."

"His family isn't yours?" she asked nibbling on a egg roll.

"Let's just change the subject, if you don't mind."

"I'm sorry, I really wasn't trying to intrude, I was only trying to make conversation."

"Well, I've stuffed my face enough for now, I'm going next door and get some sleep. If you want to go back to the hospital before I get up, that would be nice; just in case Levi wakes up again," Alex said and picked up the trash and left ZenJa's room to go to his own.

Several hours later, after ZenJa had another quick nap, she quietly left her motel room and drove the Lincoln Navigator to the North Entrance of the hospital, again and walked inside to visit Levi.

"Oh, I'm glad you're here," Doctor Goss said. "I just left Mr. Harris and he seems to be improving. He was awake while I was there and he seems to comprehend what has happened and even though he's heavily medicated, he seems extremely restless. That's fairly uncommon, for someone who's been injured as he as, to be this *irritable*, this early in their recovery.

"He may simply be anxious to see his loved ones and know they're okay," ZenJa reasoned. "There were several of us near the *accident* scene and he may calm down when he's able to see us and on the other hand, he usually is irritable, so he must be improving by leaps and bounds," ZenJa said and chuckled lightly.

"Oh, that makes perfect sense," Dr. Goss said, but eyed ZenJa with a sense of curiosity, in hopes she truly was just joking. He wondered about some people and their weird sense of humor.

"May I please go in and see him now?"

"Of course, Miss Beckwith, but again, as I told you earlier, please keep your visit short. Mr. Harris needs his rest."

ZenJa entered the semi-darkened room and switched on another small light near the bedside. "Hi Levi, it's ZenJa," she whispered not to startle the sleeping man.

Levi's eyes flickered and with considerable effort he forced them open.

"ZeeenJa?" Levi mouthed her name as tears started to flow from his eyes.

"Levi, I'm so glad you're going to be okay and so very soon," she murmured.

"You okaaay?"

"Yes, Levi I'm fine," she said and could see her friend breath a painful but welcome sign of relief.

"We got them," she added. Connors and Jackson Miller have been arrested."

Levi simply nodded his head in recognition.

"Now the only important thing is that you get better. I know how much you want to get home to your house on the lake."

Once again, he nodded his head and drifted off to sleep.

His nurse came in and checked the monitors, injected his medicine and checked Levi's vitals. "Is there anything I can get you, Miss?"

"No, thank you. I'm fine. If you would like me to leave, I'll understand. I don't want to tire my frie...my brother," ZenJa corrected.

"If you simply sit quietly, I'm sure you'll be fine."

ZenJa spent the remainder of the afternoon sitting by Levi's bedside and held his hand when she could. Even though he was heavily medicated and was virtually hog-tied he had moments of fitfulness and struggled to free himself from the confides he found himself in.

Just before dinner time and the change of shift, several nurses came into the room. "We're going to change the sheets and give Mr. Harris a sponge bath, if you would like to step outside and get something to eat. That should give us enough time to take care of matters."

"Thank you," she replied and went to the nurses station to find out what rooms the state trooper and SWAT team members were in, in hopes of visiting them in her free moments, when Emerson met her in the hall.

"The nurses are busy with Levi right now, but I was hoping to visit Trooper Armand Porter and the SWAT members, Vernon Woo, Greg Mitchell and Thomas Frey. Would you please come with me; I realize I don't know them and they may find it a bit awkward and me as well."

"No problem. I know they'll be happy to see you."

Chapter 34

"What charges are Connors and Jackson Miller facing?" ZenJa asked Agent Emerson after their visit with the law enforcement officers who remained at Dartmouth Hitchcock Hospital.

"Oh my God, ZenJa, it would be easier if I told you which laws and statutes they haven't violated. The federal charges mostly involve weapons and drug charges, from what Connors provided to Alex, in that sting operation. Interstate transportation in receiving and selling illegal weapons and drugs for example.

The state's attorney's office is still compiling the charges that we know about for both Connors and Miller. Until we find more evidence of the missing girls it'll be hard pressed to charge them for the disappearances of your sister, Olive, Ashley and Rose-Ann, though I don't think you're aware of what was discovered on Blackberry Road, yesterday, were you? Everything's been so damn crazy and all this shit is happening all at once," FBI Agent Edward Emerson.

"What *was* found on Blackberry Road? I remember hearing something about a skeleton. That's what they found there, yesterday?" ZenJa cried a mournful wail.

"Actually, Officer Brian Miller and Agent Wyman were up there scouting around the day before and discovered what appeared to be human remains and after the pathologists and anthropologists arrived on the scene to further investigate the area Doctor Roberts, of the M.E.'s office, discovered the bones of what appeared to be a child's hand and inside the hand appeared to be a name tag, or badge, if you will. They've been sent out for forensic testing."

"The name tag or badge...was it perseverved enough to determine what it once said or read, as the case may be, and did you actually see it?"

"Yes, ZenJa, I did see it. The letters we could make out were to the right, of the center, of a metal rectangle and the letters were **ORS**."

"Connors!" ZenJa exclaimed.

"I would tend to agree with you."

"So that's where Levi was all day, yesterday...on Blackberry Road?" ZenJa asked in a whisper.

"Yes, ZenJa, that's where we all were and that's why the road was blocked off. There was no landslide."

"Oh my God! That's why he insisted I go to my parents home or somewhere...anywhere but to remain with him for the day. I was so angry with him for dumping me off like a extra piece of luggage and now I know he was only protecting me," she added while tears streamed down her face into another Kleenex.

"I'm sorry," ZenJa said in an effort to compose herself.

"It's understandable. You've been under an extreme amount of duress in the last few years and I'm amazed at how well you've continued on with your life and gone on the become an agent. That's something I'm sure your sister and parents would be so proud."

"That's the least I can do for some other family, in hopes no one has to go through anything like this...ever and with that said, exactly how will the cases against Connors and Miller unfold?"

"This is going to be a very complicated case. Usually, the most serious offenses come to the forefront, and those are usually federal charges. It appears the only charges we have that would be considered federal are the weapons and drug charges against Connors, that we know of, so far.

"Obviously those charges are insignificant as apposed to kidnaping and murder charges and the explosion at the gym. Crimes that actually took human lives," ZenJa reasoned.

"We've traced serial numbers on the weapons Connors gave Alex, in the string operation, and some of those have been involved in murders as well and those weapons were taken across state lines, that would constitute federal charges, especially if they can be traced to murders."

"Are you going to find out if Connors had anything to do with the actual usage of the weapons that were used in the murders," ZenJa asked Agent Emerson.

"That'll obviously be more difficult to prove."

"So why not just get those two bastards on the charges they allegedly committed here in New Hampshire and be done with them!" ZenJa exclaimed. "Maybe one of those weapons was used to murder the Childress and/or O'Leary girls?" ZenJa asked hopefully.

"We're investigating all that, ZenJa."

"We're trying to discover who was the more relevant figure in these crimes. We're in hopes of having one SOB turn on the other."

"You mean to tell me the prosecution may let one asshole get off scott-free?" ZenJa asked raising her voice at the absurdity of that statement.

"Oh, no, ZenJa. There's not a chance in hell, *if* these two creeps are responsible for any of these crimes, either of them will walk. One may simply save his own skin and not face the death penalty. That's all…either way, again, *if* they are responsible, they will spend the rest of their miserable lives in prison and/or on death row."

"You keep mentioning *if*. I'm assuming you're simply using the term *if*, instead of alleged?"

"Exactly! It's so common place for experienced law enforcement officers to use alleged or if, we simply don't think about it or how it sounds to others," Emerson explained. "The more experience you have, ZenJa, it'll come naturally to you, also."

"I know both of those assholes have gotten lawyers, but can you tell me if either of them has done any talking? Have either of them confessed to anything?" ZenJa asked and noticed Alex approaching them from the elevator on the fourth floor.

"I don't know anything about that at the moment, ZenJa, but when I do, I'll let you know. These are serious and a vast number of alleged crimes we're talking about. It could take years to sort it all out, so don't be discouraged."

"Years?" ZenJa asked in shock.

"Yes, years, but be comforted to know they surely won't be getting bail and will be sitting in a not so nice jail cell from now until eternity, if my guess is right."

"Yes, and be assured cops don't fair very well in a jail cell. I should know. I truly felt like a murderous convict during my stay in a Boston jail cell,"Alex mentioned, overhearing their conversation and laughed.

"Be thankful those fellows didn't know you indeed were a cop!" Emerson replied and smiled.

"So you can guarantee me that you have a solid case against Connors?" ZenJa asked Alex.

"Oh, for sure! We were stringing him along for a while and of course he was under 24/7 surveillance not simply for the weapons and drug charges, but in case he decided to kidnap another child."

"So, enough of that for now. How's Levi," Alex asked.

"Nothing new. He's resting and we were just having a snack, waiting for the nurses to finish what they have to do to our boy," Emerson replied.

"Mr. Harris would like to see you now," the nurse said only seconds after Alex sat down next to ZenJa and Emerson.

"You two can go first, if you like. I saw him for a few minutes, earlier," ZenJa said.

"Okay, we'll see you in a few," Emerson said.

Chapter 35

While ZenJa waited for her opportunity to visit with Levi her thoughts were interrupted by the appearance of Officer Brian Miller, who took a seat beside her in the ICU waiting room.

"ZenJa, I'm sorry it's taken me so long to get up here to see Levi and the others and I especially wanted to see how you're doing."

For a moment ZenJa was confused, on guard, and unable to forget this man's brother was most likely responsible or partly responsible for the kidnaping of her sister and God only knew what other horrendous crimes.

"Oh! You startled me," ZenJa said shaking her head to clear her brain.

"I'm sorry, I didn't mean to. If you want to be alone, I'll understand."

"No, that's fine. I wanted to see you too, but we're both aware things aren't normal, anymore."

"I know, ZenJa. How are you holding up? Is there anything I can do for you?"

"I have only one thing to ask. If you have *any* influence over Jackson, I beg you, please *persuade* him to tell you what he did, what Connors did, and where the missing girls are."

"He's refused to see me or any member of our family, yet, but I assure you that will be my top priority."

"What other members of your family are there?"

"Only my mother."

"Do you think she'll be able to convince him to talk?"

"My mother and I, of course, are devastated by these developments and will do whatever we can to convince Jackson to do what's right. We plan to strongly remind him of the fact that God forgives those who truly ask for repentance."

"You and your family are religious?"

"My mother goes to church every Sunday and on most occasions Jackson accompanied her, as odd as that may sound. They usually sat right up front, if that isn't another irony. I, myself, go to church when I can, but I don't feel a person needs to attend church to believe in God. I live by the Golden Rule."

"Obviously, attending church doesn't mean squat when an *alleged* criminal sits right up front, knowing he's going to commit another crime whenever the opportunity presents itself," ZenJa concurred.

"As soon as I convince Jackson to see me, I'll let you know what he tells me."

"Thank you, Brian, I pray you're successful."

"Me, too."

"While we're at it, ZenJa, I wanted to let you know I admire you for how you handled Connors during the hostage situation with Carol and Lanny's sons and of course the aftermath when you had every right and reason to blow that mother fucker away, but you didn't. I can't say I would have been able to handle myself in the same way, under the same situation."

"Who told you about what I did during the negotiations inside the gym? You said you haven't seen or talked to Levi, yet?"

"Carol came to me and told me all about what she had seen and heard. She admitted she left the building, like you instructed, but came back inside, following Levi and overheard your conversation with Connors, until Lanny came and dragged her outside. Thankfully it was before the blast, otherwise she would've been injured, too."

"My God, I'm glad she's okay and the boys, especially."

"I owe you an apology, Brian. I admit I didn't handle myself well, with Connors away from the school. I truthfully can't say I wasn't about to blow his brains out."

"I have no idea what you're talking about, ZenJa," Officer Miller said, smiled and stood to stretch his legs.

"I had my weapon pointed right at his..."

"Like I said, I have no idea what you're talking about. There are some things, I believe, and one of those things is I can be trusted with confidences and would hope for the same in return. Did you ever go to school or work with someone, ZenJa, who you told something, in confidence, of course or the confidence was implied, and that person couldn't wait to run and tattle? Well, that's how I feel about shit like that. When someone tells me something or I see something that has no relevance or had no impact on the situation, I'm like a priest," Miller replied and laughed.

"You're really an upstanding guy, Miller. I admire you."

"I was telling Levi, a while back, that I wanted to be police chief one day, but that seems rather tame in comparison to what I think I want to do now."

"And that would be?"

"I want to either be FBI or CIA," Miller replied, proudly.

"You'll have my vote of confidence," ZenJa replied at the same time Agent Emerson and Alex Lyons entered the waiting room.

"Hello, Miller," Emerson said and shook his hand.

"I wanted to get up here sooner, but with everything that's happened in Longberry..." he murmured. "We have many long days and nights ahead of us," he continued.

"I've spoken with the town selectmen in Longberry and they've decided you should be acting police chief until a vote can be taken at a later date," Emerson said.

"You know, before all this happened I thought that's what I wanted, but now I'm not so sure if hanging around Longberry is such a good idea. I know I'm not responsible for what my brother did, but it'll always be a cloud hanging over my head, I think."

"You know, I sympathize with you, Brian. I have no desire to come back to Longberry, myself. I just want to take care of my parents affairs and never come back."

"You know, people in town really want to offer you their condolences and were asking if you planned to have a service or memorial for your folks," Brian mentioned.

"I'm really not planning on having any kind of service, but I'll promise them, if someone finds my sister, I will have a service for my parents and her as well. There will be no closure until she is found and now, especially with this *accident* my parents had, that appears to be a murder instead, this really connects the two cases into one, as far as I'm concerned. What I'll do, is stop by and personally speak with the people in town who have meant so much to me and my family. I'll find that less stressful. I know I can't run away from anything or anyplace, but for my own well being, the less time I spend in Longberry the better I'll feel."

"If there's anything I can do, ZenJa, let me know," Miller said.

"What do you plan on doing, if you're not going to take the chief's job?" Emerson asked.

"I was just telling ZenJa that I want to check out the FBI or CIA. I want to do more with my life than spend the rest of it in a small town."

"One way to get training and experience to lead is to join the military," Alex said.

"I think I'll do that. I've always wanted to be a Marine or a Navy SEAL. I don't know if I have what it takes to be either, but I'd sure like to try."

"Well, Officer Miller, let's take a walk and we can talk about that while ZenJa goes inside to visit with her *brother*," Agent Emerson said while he and Alex Lyons directed Officer Miller to a more private area in the Chevy Suburban, with tinted windows, that was parked outside the hospital entrance. The vehicle with non-traceable license plates from the state of Massachusetts.

Chapter 36

"Mr. Harris has been given more pain medicine," Levi's nurse began. "He may sleep for a while, but feel free to sit by his side, if you like."

"I will, thank you," ZenJa said while walking up to the sleeping man, touched his face and then his hand.

"Levi, this is ZenJa. I'll just sit here and I want you to know I'm here if you need me," she whispered and noted what appeared to be a slight nodding of his head.

While sitting in a comfortable lounger that had been brought into Levi's room, ZenJa dozed off herself after a few minutes.

Without warning, Levi appeared to be having a nightmare and woke ZenJa from a deep sleep. She jumped from the chair and began to stroke his forehead while trying to comprehend what he was saying while he was thrashing around.

"Don't leave me, Isabella!" he cried in agonizing pain. "I'll be right home. Wait...! Don't lee..." he continued.

ZenJa grabbed a cool cloth and moistened the patient's forehead, checking for a fever, that he didn't appear to have.

Without warning, Levi grabbed ZenJa's hand with his right hand and yelled, "I'll blow you're fucking head off if you ever touch me again. I'll kill you, like you killed..." he began and stopped thrashing around and fell back to sleep but not before the alarms on his blood pressure and oxygen monitors sounded an alarm.

ZenJa was crouched back in the lounge chair, scared and horrified at what she had just witnessed.

"He...seemed to have a nightmare," ZenJa cried; the nurses and Dr. Goss rushing to attend their patient.

"That's not uncommon, Miss. Mr. Harris has been given some serious medication. Having nightmares or flashbacks are very commonplace," Dr. Goss assured the frightened woman.

"Do you think they're simply hallucinations or real events from the past?"

"From what I've read and heard testimony related from other patients and their families, in all likelihood they're fragments from ones past experiences," Dr. Goss explained. "Like I said, they're probably bits and pieces of events coming together as one. It's difficult to say."

"Is he okay, now?" ZenJa asked sincerely.

"His blood pressure and breathing are back to normal. He doesn't appear to have disrupted his cast or his traction unit. He seems to be fine, now," Dr. Goss confirmed.

"Thank you," ZenJa said and continued to sit in the lounge chair, wondering who Isabella was or is.

Was she the lovely blonde woman in the wedding picture with Levi? His bride? Did she desert him? Who was Levi going to blow their f'ing head off? And what happened to his mother? So many questions and no answers and she realized she knew nothing of the man who risked life and limb to help her.

A few moments later Alex Lyons came into Levi's room. "How's the patient doing?" he asked.

"He seemed to have a nightmare. The doctor said it's probably because of all the meds he's on."

"Most likely; that's not uncommon."

"Who's Isabella?" ZenJa asked out of the clear blue.

Alex looked like he'd been slapped across the face. ZenJa was unable to describe his expression. Was it anger, fury, pain, or worse?

"That is none of your damn business!" Alex replied. "I only stopped by to tell you I'm checking out of the motel and heading back to the office. I have things to do,"

"The doctor just told me Levi should be released into the care of private nurses in another day. I know he doesn't want to stay in the hospital, so I'll check in with him when he gets to the lake," Alex stated and left the room.

"He spoke with you?" ZenJa asked.

"Yes, ZenJa he spoke to me and told me he wants to get the hell out of here! Maybe he's only pretending to be sleeping when you come in his room," Alex retorted in unnecessary anger.

"Take his Navigator back to the lake and rent a car and go home."

"Oh...I had no idea," ZenJa whispered and left the room shortly after Alex. In her rush to exit the room, she neglected to see Levi raise his index finger in an effort to stop her from leaving.

Once outside Levi's hospital room she began to weep uncontrollably and whispered out loud, "I don't know where home is. I don't know where I belong, any more."

ZenJa slowly left the hospital, picked up her belongings at the motel and noticed Alex had already checked out. She called for a rental car to come and pick her up at Levi's house in an hour or so, while she drove the Navigator to its home. She parked the vehicle outside the garage and left the keys under the seat. Thankfully, she also noticed Alex wasn't here, as well. She wasn't up to having any further confrontations with him, now.

Once the rental car arrived, she drove back to her parents home in Longberrry, against her better judgement. She knew this would be the last time she went to that small town. She would meet with her parent's attorney to deal with whatever issues were involved with their financial business and she'd made arrangements to pick up her parent's urns, that contained their ashes from the crematorium and she wanted to say goodbye to Molly, one last time. ZenJa knew in her heart her sister would never be found...she just knew it.

Bright and early the next day ZenJa drove the rental car to the office of Jerry Johnson, her parents lawyer, where he read her their Will that obviously left all their worldly possessions to her. Much to her surprise, her parents had invested wisely all their lives and had acquired an impressive portfolio of financial assets that was equivalent to well over two million dollars.

"This amount does not include life insurance policies," ZenJa, that are rather modest, but total approximately another half a million dollars and the value will be doubled; it having been an accident, as their policy was written," the attorney stated.

"Is murder considered an accident?" ZenJa asked abruptly.

Somewhat taken aback by her statement, the attorney replied, "ZenJa, I'm sorry to hear that their tragic deaths evidentially weren't accidental, but in the eyes of the insurance company, it will be considered an accident. It was allegedly the fault of someone else, not intentional or death by natural causes. It will be considered a chance event."

"Again, ZenJa, I'm so sorry for the losses you have endured in the last few years. I have the utmost respect for you and your family felt like my own. They were good people."

"Thank you, Jerry. I know my parents felt the same way about you and your family and thank you for all you've done for me during this most traumatic time."

"Will you be keeping the house or haven't you decided about that yet?" Attorney Jerry Johnson asked.

"I know I shouldn't make any rash decisions now, but to be honest with you, Jerry, I have no intentions of ever coming back here again. There are only sad memories for me here so I think it best if I sell the house and property. I would like to buy a place somewhere else and start over, if that's possible."

"Any idea where you'd like to relocate?"

"I've always wanted to live on a lake and in the last few days I've been driving around the Lake Winnipesaukee area and have seen several homes that have caught my eye. These homes were not for sale, but I decided that I might like something architecturally similar.

"Would you want to build or buy?"

"I don't want to be bothered with the hassles of building when I won't be around that much; my job keeps me in DC most of the time. I'd like to buy something."

"I think I can help you on several of these fronts. Actually, your parents house and the three hundred acres of land that surround it have been of interest to a developer for several years and since your parents died, another person has expressed interest in the property, too. I tried to convince your parents to sell and move to some warmer place, like Florida, but they simply refused; the only reason being, they were adamant about not leaving until your sister was found."

"I had no idea."

"I know; they didn't want you concerned about this, so they asked me to keep quiet about the interest in that property.

"What does this person want with the property?"

"The newest person of interest, wants to develop it into a small, elite gated community with a golf course and condominiums; something similar to the retirement community of The Villages, in Florida. An all year-round resort attracting skiers, summer people, a snow mobile crowd and some of the rich and famous in Hollywood."

"Interesting!" ZenJa replied. "It would bring some life to this God forsaken place, wouldn't it and now that the *alleged* criminals in our presence have been arrested, that should bring some peace to the folks in town and who might want to invest in this development."

"Do you know what kind of an offer they have made?"

"As far as I know it's a single investor. He's offered ten million dollars which is equivalent to thirty three thousand dollars an acre. The land really is worth more than that, ZenJa, but the majority of it is wooded acreage and very hilly, rugged and rocky terrain, with numerous boulders and the trees and stumps that would have to be removed."

"Okay, so what was the other aspect of my situation did you say you could offer assistance?"

"I'm personally acquainted with a real estate agent who has access to some very impressive homes that are for sale, many of which are in foreclosure, with the devilish state of the economy, you are well aware of. You could purchase a home for a fraction of the price it's worth with only a small portion of the money you have the potential of having or actually do have without even selling your parents property. If you forgive me for saying so, you are a very wealthy young lady."

"Okay, I would like to meet with this real estate person and see what's on the chopping block, for starters," ZenJa replied. "I want something right on the lake with it's own private beach and plenty of privacy and maybe on Sander's Bay."

"Who knows, I may decide to write a book one day," ZenJa said and smiled for the first time in weeks.

"If you can arrange a meeting with yourself, the potential investor, and myself, I would consider the offer he has made. I have no use for that property. Like I said, I don't want to come back here for a long time."

"This investor wants to remain anonymous, ZenJa."

"Do you know who he is?"

"Yes, I do and I respect his privacy as much as you do, yours."

"Probably some rich asshole from Hollywood?" ZenJa asked trying to get some indication of who it might be.

"You're probably right, ZenJa. He probably is from Hollywood and I'm sure you'd most definitely find him an asshole," the attorney replied and smiled.

"My kind'a guy," ZenJa said and stood to leave.

"Where would like your money from your parent's estate, insurance policies, and if and when this property transaction takes place, sent?"

"You can wire it to my bank in Virginia. Here's a voided check with my bank's information," she said ripping out a check, cancelling it and handing to the attorney.

"You're going to want to have some sort of financial assistance, ZenJa," the attorney cautioned. "But from what Molly says you're a financial analyst so you know all about that."

"Yes, I do," ZenJa replied and smiled thinking she would have to actually take some courses on financial planning, now. It would be in her best interest if she did.

"I'm heading over, now, to see Molly."

"Tell her I said hello," Attorney Johnson said.

"I will and thank you again, Jerry for all you've done and you notice on the voided check I gave you, my address and phone number are listed."

"Got it, ZenJa," the elderly lawyer replied and watched this striking, auburn/red headed, young lady leave his office. "I wish I was about forty years younger," the man said before answering an incoming call.

"Hi Molly," ZenJa said and entered the crowded café at noon.

"Oh my God, it's so good to see you, I was hoping you weren't going to forget all about me," Molly cried.

"I will never forget about you, Molly."

"ZenJa!" The cook behind the counter said. "We want to thank you for everything you've done to protect our town and get those bastards arrested. We never would have done it without you," he continued, wiping his hands on his apron.

A deafening applause broke out along with a standing ovation from all the well wishers, Longberry's townsfolk, who were having lunch at the café.

"Thank you, all so much and I want to thank you for being so helpful during these sad years. You were the rocks that held my family together and helped us through the bad times. I will never be able to thank you enough,"

"You must know, ZenJa, that Oscar, here, was somewhat helpful in the demise of Jackson Miller," Molly said waving her hand toward her cook.

"What did you do, Oscar?" ZenJa asked while a couple moved over, to give the new arrival a stool at the counter.

"He noticed something fishy about Jackson's behavior and notified the state police. He had a feeling going to Chief Connors wasn't a good idea."

"I just had a feeling something wasn't right," Oscar said, blushing with the unwanted attention he was receiving.

"I can't thank you enough, Oscar. Thank you from the bottom of my heart."

"It was nothing," he said and walked back to the kitchen where he felt more comfortable.

"What can I get for you?" Molly asked.

"The usual BLT, diet coke and onion rings," ZenJa replied.

While ZenJa waited for her order to arrive she stood and made a statement on behalf of her parents.

"I've decided to leave the area, at least for a while. I'm not planning a memorial service or burial for my parents, now. Their remains have been cremated and they will come with me to DC. My wounds are too deep at this time and I simply want to distance myself from the town, but I will never distance myself from you, my friends, who made my life a joy. I will never forget you and I just heard that my parents never wanted to leave this town because...they loved you all so much," ZenJa explained, knowing in all honesty that was the truth.

ZenJa sat down and Lanny and Carol were the first of many customers who came over and gave her hugs while she wiped the tears from her face with a napkin.

"Thank you all, again. I love you all, as well."

"Lanny and I'll never be able to thank you, ZenJa!" Carol exclaimed. "You saved our boys!"

"I wish I could have done more," she replied thinking of the three law enforcement officers whose lives were taken the day of the bombing.

"Those men will never be forgotten," Lanny said with all in the café in agreement. "What people like that do, we can never imagine; saving lives of people they don't even know."

"Will you be going back to work at the *financial institution* you work for?" Carol asked looking at ZenJa with a knowing glance.

"Yes, I will, Carol and I promise to keep in touch," she said and nodded with their secret and confidence in tact.

After eating several delicious onion rings and taking a drink of her diet Coke, she decided now was the time to brooch the subject of selling her parents home and acreage. "While you're all gathered here I have something I'd like to discuss with you. I feel you're like family to me and my decision about what I'm about to consider effects you all, so I want to hear what your opinion is about a situation that has just arisen because of my parents passing."

"What is it?" Molly asked, taking a seat beside ZenJa, with a cup of coffee in her hand.

"There's a rumor that an investor wants to purchase my parents home and the three hundred some-odd acres surrounding it for a resort similar, from what I understand, to be built like The Villages, in Florida. It will be comprised of a golf course and condos and God only knows what else, in an effort to attract some rich and famous who love the four seasons that New Hampshire has to offer; skiing and other snow sports, fishing, hunting and of course the beautiful foliage we have. Now, I know that will alter life here in Longberry, big time and I wonder how you folks feel about it. Of course it will involve a new school, upgrades of sewer and water systems, power supplies and highways and I can't even imagine what else, but from what I know about financial aspects involved in situations like this, it can generate an immense amount of tax dollars and revenue to the area. Business could boom and employment could skyrocket and still have the feel of small town America."

"That sounds like a wonderful idea, but what about small places like this café, convenience store and gas station. The big guns will come in and wipe this all out," one man offered.

"Hold on, there," Molly retorted. "Who thinks I want to work my ass off here for the rest of my life? Maybe this will be the retirement I can look forward, too. If a new, bigger supermarket and a Mobil or Irving gas station wants to buy me out, maybe I'd want to sell. How many of you people are tired of traveling forty or fifty miles to get groceries each week not to mention household items and clothing in Concord? I know I am."

"Think of the employment opportunities," Carol added. "Our children are growing up and need to find part time work after school so they can save for a car or some items we can't afford for them, like their own computers, not to mention hundred dollar sneakers."

"Not just the kids," Lanny continued. "How many of us would like to work closer to home and what about our retirees who want some extra income they can earn working in stores that obviously will materialize from the purchase of the Beckwith Property."

"There would be employment opportunities in the resort of...well, what I'll call the Beckwith Resort, for lack of a better name, at the moment," Jim Bacon added. "There'll be a massive amount of work that'd be needed to clear out that mountainside, building the roads, and like you said, schools and other town systems. I could use the extra business at my garage or even expand and become that Irving...Mobil gas station...repair shop, auto repair, and who knows, a car dealership."

"Our schools would expand. We'd need to hire more teachers and of course now we have to expand our police department because Brian Miller has decided to leave the area and what did he tell us, this morning? Be all he can be." Oscar added.

"I think this has the potential to become a wonderful, fruitful expansion of our town, not to mention a prosperous advancement for our citizens," another person added.

"Brian Miller did mention he might be leaving," ZenJa confirmed.

"He still has to investigate and help the authorizes, both federal and state in the investigation concerning Connors and his brother and he said he'd be around long enough to do that," Molly said. "He mentioned something about he was *strong armed* into possibly going into the military or maybe becoming a financial analyst like you, ZenJa," Carol said and smiled.

ZenJa smiled and ate another bite of her BLT without daring to glance at Carol.

"With the possibility of all these new developments, around here, ZenJa, maybe we can use a *financial analyst* here in town," Carol mentioned. "If this plan develops, it seems to me we might even get our own bank," she added and smiled.

"So, from what I'm hearing, is there anyone here who might object to my selling the property? I'll be very aggressive, in the negotiations, that it'll be tastefully designed; no casinos or anything like that and hopefully it will raise the property values around, but with the added income from taxes, hopefully your property taxes won't be effected."

"I realize this will be a long process and all the proper legalities will have to be worked out with the town fathers and the state. I just wanted to get your feed back, for now," ZenJa continued.

"Thank you for taking our opinions into consideration, ZenJa," Molly said and left her seat to wait on two newly arrived customers, one of which was Officer Miller.

"Hi, folks. I just stopped by to get some coffee and peach pie, if you have any," Miller said.

"Coming right up."

"Wait, Molly. Remember when..." Miller began and looked around to make sure there were only trusted townsfolk in the café before he continued.

"Remember what?" Molly asked.

"Do you remember when Chief Connors came in here with his winter jacket that was ripped and missing his name plate?"

"Yes, I remember. He said he ripped it while checking the oil or something and the name tag got caught on the radiator cap."

"Exactly! You remember it exactly as I do!" Miller said and brightened considerably.

"So, what about it? I remember that, too!" Jim Bacon, the local auto mechanic replied. "I told him to let me do the heavy lifting," he continued while everyone in the café laughed.

"Do you remember when that was, Molly? Miller asked.

"Yes, I remember like it was yesterday. "It was in 1995."

"How do you remember that so well?" Miller asked sadly realizing the first girls that were reported missing were not until after 1999.

"Because that was the week I finally got divorced!" Molly said and laughed. "That was the best week of my life."

"You are sure it was in 1995?" Miller pressed.

"Yes, I have no doubt about it!"

"Shit!" Miller murmured, but loud enough for ZenJa to hear him.

"What?" ZenJa asked while everyone in the café held their breath.

"Ashley Winters and Rose-Ann Olsen were reported missing in 1999, weren't they?" Miller asked.

"Yes, that sounds about right," Jim Bacon replied.

"I have to go," Miller said without receiving his food order, but with ZenJa hot on his heels, both racing from the café.

"What is it?" ZenJa demanded.

"I have to call Alex and FBI Agent Emerson about something we found on Blackberry Road."

"You mean the name plate and with **ORS**, on it, along with the skeleton remains?"

"Yes, but ZenJa...Molly just confirmed what I had forgotten...she said that jacket was ripped in 1995 not 1999, when the first girls went missing. The name plate was found in the skeletal hands of the victim or victims we just found!"

"I have to get in touch with Alex and Emerson so they can get the ME to get moving on the autopsy of the remains and I have to get back to the office and find out who else was missing and maybe never reported or they were from another area. This shit just keeps getting worse, doesn't it?"

"Yes, it certainly does. I have to get out of here!" ZenJa cried and quickly left the parking lot.

Before ZenJa left town, she called Attorney Jerry Johnson and told him she was interested in selling the Beckwith Property and told him to keep in contact after relaying the stipulations she had. Not allowing the property turned into a Las Vegas type circus, to which he completely agreed and assured her he didn't think that was the intent of the potential buyer.

ZenJa returned to her parents house and obtained what little she wanted from the house. Pictures, one of three file cabinets, containing personal papers and a few mementoes from each family member including a quilt her mother made for Zippy and another one for herself that remained on each of their beds, to that day.

Inside the file cabinet she found a key to a safety deposit box at a bank in Laconia, New Hampshire where, she was certain, what little jewelry her parents had would be inside and any stocks, bonds or other important papers. She knew there was no rush to see what was inside. Surprisingly, now that she discovered she was about to be a wealthy woman, money had very little appeal to her. What was valuable to her were the good memories she had of her parents, her sister and the decent people of Longberry.

Chapter 37

"I hope you're comfortable, Mr. Harris," a pretty thirty year old, black haired, green eyed nurse asked her patient upon his arrival at his home on Lake Winnipesaukee.

"Thank you, Mrs. Patten," Levi replied. "I love it out here on the deck, watching the waves, the boats, and catching some sunshine," he continued while he relaxed on a oversized, padded, outdoor lounger.

"It's good to get rid of that traction device. I don't like being confined," he added while he sipped the lemonade Mrs. Patten brought out for him.

"Dr. Goss said you're recovering very well and within a few weeks, you'll be out of the cast and up and at 'em."

"You know, I may not heal as fast as the good doctor thinks. I like simply relaxing at home for a change."

"I can understand, perfectly. This is a beautiful spot and you certainly have a lovely home."

"If you don't mind my asking, what occupation do you have?"

"I've been called a pirate, a spy, a detective, an FBI, ATF, CIA and DEA agent, murderer and a double agent," he said and smiled.

"Oh! I see by the collection of books you have inside, you're a writer," the nurse said innocently.

"Exactly!" Levi offered and smiled. "And because my writing is so secretive I keep my office locked. I wouldn't want anyone stealing any of my mysterious plots...not that I'm in any way suggesting you'd steal any of my good ideas, but I do have a relative who comes by and has been known to snoop into my private affairs," he added, his crystal blue eyes turning the color of cold steel.

"Some relative," Nurse Patten replied.

"Oh, he's an innocent asshole. He just can't help himself. He thinks he knows what's best for me."

"I can hear the affection you have for him, even though you try to hide it, Mr. Harris."

"I'm not sure affection is the word I'd use, but we'll leave it at that."

"I notice you have a fondness or liking for books written by the famous author Olivia Swan. It appears you have them all. I've read every one of her books and I love the way she intertwines mystery, dark secrets, and murder and mayhem all in one."

"I know. It seems she actually lived the lives she wrote so knowingly about, doesn't it? They give me great ideas for my own books. I especially love the one she was working on, at the time of her death. I vaguely recall someone saying it was called, *'Swinging From The Rafters'* where a woman named Misty Moyer, a rock star, hangs herself in the family garage. Nice huh? Nice to have the family come and find her fucking dead body *'Swinging From The Rafters'*, as she blatantly titled it," Levi said, his eyes once again the color of cold steel.

The nurse was slightly taken aback by the comment her patient made in reference to the book's theme and how the victim was found. "That book was never finished or published, was it?"

"No, it wasn't and forgive me, you can see how involved I get in the books I read and write," Levi offered in explanation of his minor melt down. "That's why she was one of my favorite authors. She was an inspiration in my own writing."

"Have you published any books?"

"No, not yet, but I'm almost finished with my third composition. It's a series about a rouge DEA agent, Harley biker guy, who investigates corruption within the administration. He's quite the ladies man and may roam around now and then, but he only lives for the one woman of his life."

"That sounds fascinating," Mrs. Patten replied.

"I'll give you an autographed book when it's published."

"I'd love that."

"Now, to get back to the business at hand, is there anything I can get for you? It's almost time for your medication and the sun is all well and good for you, but I don't want to you get a sunburn. Do you think you'd like to walk back inside now?"

"Yes, I think I will. It does get pretty warm out here when there's no breeze."

"After I take my meds, I think I'll go downstairs and work out in my gym. I want to get some strength back in my legs and back."

"That sounds like a good idea, but Dr. Goss doesn't think you should work out your right arm, even though it's not your injured arm. By working out one side, you may inadvertently injure the left arm."

"Okay, that makes sense," Levi agreed. "If you want to take off for the day, after you make me some dinner, I'll be fine. I never was a chef or cook for that matter, so a big salad and small steak sounds good, if you'd like, you can join me or feel free to go home. I can manage for the night. I don't need a nurse here to watch me sleep," he said and laughed.

Levi was comfortable having Abby Patten coming during the day, as she had for the last weeks and didn't want his home invaded by any other strangers. He was and always would be a private person...not a writer or author, but a private human being.

"I'll love to stay, if you don't mind, for dinner. My husband is a firefighter and will be on duty until tomorrow."

"Between your hours and your husband's long schedule, that must make for difficulties, finding time to be together," Levi remarked innocently.

"Yes, it does, but we both love what we do and of course we love each other. We've been married for twelve years and we plan on making this our first and last marriage," Abby said and laughed.

"I hear ya," Levi commented thinking he had done that once and never planned on getting married, again.

"Okay, I'm going downstairs and work out. Give me a shout out when dinner's ready, if you will."

"Roger that," Abby responded and went to work in the kitchen.

While Levi was working on his leg lifts, he tried once again to call ZenJa, but having been the case over the last few weeks, his calls went right to her voice mail and his phone calls were never returned.

"I just hope you're okay. That's all I want to know," he said, leaving another message on her phone.

"You trying to call me? I didn't know you cared," Alex said when he strolled into the gym at the house on the lake.

"No, I was trying to call...oh never mind," he replied.

"How are ya doing? You look better than the last time I saw you."

"I'm doing fantastic, thanks. You staying for dinner?"

"Yes, I just saw your *nurse* and asked her to throw on another steak for me.

"You know," Levi began while continuing his work out. "Now I know why the government assigns you and portrays you has a fucking douche bag, the lowest, scummiest creature they can; you fit the part so well. You really are a fucking pig. Mrs. Patten is my nurse and a very happily married woman, if you must know, so stop insinuating there's anything between us. I happen to respect the sanctity of marriage and speaking of which, when are you going to get married so you'll stop hound-dogging around. Aren't you a little old, now, to be running around like a dog in heat, all the time?"

"Hey, I love being a single guy. I don't ever want to be tied down," Alex began.

"It must be hereditary," Levi murmured under his breath but loud enough for Alex to hear.

"I'm not even going to distinguish that with a reply," Alex said and picked up some weights and began pumping iron, too.

"What's the matter, Alex, you don't want to be reminded of what *your* mother was...,"

"You mean *our*, mother?" Alex corrected.

Before Levi could reply, Abby announced dinner was ready.

"Be right there," Levi and Alex replied in unison and both men glared at each other.

The sun was setting and a peaceful wake glistened across the lake, while the trio ate their steak dinners and watched the boats listing slowly across the water.

"Just enough breeze for the sail boats," Levi commented while eating some of his chef's salad.

"Do you sail? Abby asked eating some of her own vegetables.

"No, I don't have time to waste, slipping across the water. I love my motor boat and once I'm better I'd be happy to take you and your husband out for a day of fishing."

"Can I come, too?" Alex asked and smirked knowing he was irritating his older brother, like always, simply for fun.

"You certainly can," Levi said and smiled with his devilish grin. "If we're going fishing we're going to need an anchor," he replied and laughed out loud for the first time in many weeks.

Abby couldn't resist the urge to laugh and did so without hesitation.

"You two are just like my two boys. They're always fighting and teasing each other, but my boys are only ten and eleven," she said and looked over her glass of iced tea at the two pranksters who sat around the table.

"Oh, good, make sure you bring the boys, too. We'll need some bait," Alex said and laughed at his own joke.

"I told you my brother was an ass; now you can see that for yourself."

"I have a feeling if something dreadful were to happen, each of you would be the first one there to help the other out. Am I mistaken?" she asked with the wisdom of a mother.

"I suppose you're right," Levi replied and without emotion to indicate that to be the truth, he continued to eat his steak.

"This is a delicious dinner, Abby," Alex commented to change the subject. "It sure beats eating in diners all the time."

"What do you do for a living, if I might ask? You're brother told me he's an author, are you one as well?" Abby asked innocently.

Alex sat at the table, covering his mouth with his hand and Abby was well aware of mannerisms and what certain personal reactions indicate and she knew covering ones mouth with their hand usually signifies a person who doesn't want to answer a question or someone who's stalling for time. "I didn't mean to intrude," Abby said. "I was simply making conversation."

"No problem. I'm really just kinda of a drifter," he replied.

"A drifter with a beautiful new red Mustang?" Abby replied before she realized what she was implying.

"Well, come on Alex. Why don't you tell Mrs. Patten what you really do for a living?" Levi egged his brother on and smiled. Levi could see the wheels turning in Alex's head and knew how uncomfortable he was at that moment and Levi was savoring every second of it.

"I'm an investment broker for a firm in Virginia."

"So, that explains the license plate you have, from Virginia, but what does the LQQKN signify?"

Alex sat for a moment, trying to think of an intelligent answer to questions this woman was firing at him, like an interrogator of the FBI.

"My brother is always *looking* for someone...some people to invest with his firm," Levi replied helping his brother out of the web of deceit he was creating for himself and not very well, he noted.

"If I make a suggestion, Abby. Keep your money under your mattress where it's safe. Don't let my brother get his hands on it," Levi said and laughed.

"Okay, I'll take that advice to the bank, thank you and if you gentleman are finished with your dinners, I'll clean up and get along home."

"Thank you, again, Abby for a delicious dinner. If it hasn't been for you, I would have starved to death by now."

"My brother and I are going into my office, now because I've a new section of my book I've written and I want to see how he likes it," Levi said and ushered his brother to his office.

"Okay. I'll see myself out when I'm finished,"Abby replied and once again went to the kitchen.

"Jesus, Levi, you need to get laid or something. You're a fucking bastard these days," Alex said in his usual, but callous manner.

Levi didn't take the bait and ignored the comment. "So what's new with the Longberry investigations?"

"I was talking to Brian Miller the other day with Emerson and you could say, he strong-armed him into becoming one of us, and I don't mean an author or financial investor." Alex retorted, but smiled.

"Excellent! He's a good man. If I can think of anyone I'd want on my team, it'd be him."

"How's ZenJa."

"I don't know, Levi. I don't have to pretend to live at Forest Haven Estates anymore, so I went back home. Last I knew she was still living there."

"I don't know if I should mention this or not, but while you were on your drugs, you must have had a nightmare or hallucinations or something."

"Why do you say that and why not mention it?"

"The nightmare or whatever you had was while ZenJa was in your room visiting you and you must have mentioned Isabella's name. She asked me who Isabella was and I nearly freaked out! I simply told her it was none of her business and that was about the last time I saw her. I didn't know what else to say. You know I'm not fond of Miss Beckwith and you and I may act like idiots around each other, but I do have your best interests at heart and I don't want to see you get hurt. I freaked out because I didn't know what you said or how much made any sense to her, if anything."

"Well, I guess that explains it."

"Explains what?" Alex asked.

"Come on let's go back out on the deck. I just heard Abby leave. I don't want to be inside anymore than I have to in this beautiful weather."

Once the men were seated in comfortable lounge chairs Levi continued where he'd left off inside the house.

"I've been trying to call her, simply to see how she's doing. She's been through hell and back you remember, right?" Levi asked his brother sarcastically.

"Yes, I do, Levi, but I don't want you to take another injured animal under your wing..."

"My wife wasn't an injured animal!"

"I didn't mean it like that and you know it. I never seem to know what to say when I'm around you, anymore, Levi."

"Then, maybe you should stay away more often. It's not like we're really close in any way, shape or form. As you know there's only one connection we have and that connection no longer exists."

"I know, Levi. We both had the same whore as a mother," Alex yelled and slammed his beer on the table and walked off the deck, got inside his car and began his journey back to Virginia in the red Mustang with the license plate, LQQKN, on it.

Chapter 38

"I've come to visit my brother, Jackson Miller and if I may, visit another inmate, I'd appreciate it. I realize these appointments are usually made ahead of time, but I was hoping to kill two birds with one stone," Brian Miller said and laughed before he realized what that sounded like to the correctional officer.

"Sorry, I didn't mean that. I'm just a little overtired and punchy, I guess," he explained and shrugged his shoulders.

"Your name, please," the rugged correctional officer asked at the Center Street Jail, where Jackson Miller remained in custody.

"Officer Brian Miller."

"Who's the other inmate you wish to visit?"

"Robert, Bob, Connors."

"May I see your license?" the man asked.

While Brian dug out his identification he realized this man did this job every day and sympathized with him knowing how incredibly boring and discouraging it must be to be surrounded by criminals and their families on a daily basis. He wondered if he was up to the challenge of involving himself in the world of crime, mystery, undercover operations, secrets, lies, and more lies. Brian decided, yes, he could do it.

He smiled when the guard handed him back his license and ushered him inside a secure visiting area where there were dozens of other inmates and their visitors, that included children vying for a few moments with their fathers.

"Here's your number," the guard said and handed Brian a card with the number eight on it. "You will sit in the number eight station and you must use the phone to speak with the person you're here to visit. All calls are monitored," he added and walked away.

Brian had been in jails many times, but not to visit. He was familiar with the procedures and saw no reason to mention it. The guard was doing his job, such as it was. Brian imagined that ninety nine percent of the time things were peaceful in jails and prisons, but all it took was a fraction of a second for all hell to break loose and he respected what any people in law enforcement did for a living. It's a nasty job, but someone had to do it, he realized.

Within ten minutes Bob Connors was brought into the visitors area and was escorted to his stool, that was bolted to the floor, as were all the stools and counters that were separated by bulletproof glass and phones on each side of the window for visitors and inmates to talk.

Brian watched his former boss, Police Chief Bob Connors walk behind several other inmates who also had people come to visit them. All of the men held their heads down and their eyes avoided looking at anyone. They had matching numbered cards in their hands with the folks who were visiting and simply sat down on the appropriate stool. Once seated, Connors looked up and seemed somewhat surprised to see his former employee sitting across the glassed enclosure and picked up the telephone.

"Thank you for coming," Connors said. "I don't know what to say."

"Is there anyone, any family, you want me to contact so they can come and see you or at least write to you? After giving it some thought, I realized I don't know anything about your family, except the fact you have no immediate family in town."

"Last I knew my daughter lived in Maine, but I haven't had any contact with her since she was a baby. Her mother divorced me more than 30 years ago. I don't even know if either of them are living, to be honest with you."

"Would you like me to try and find out?" Miller asked.

"If you want. You can check my address book, it's...well, it was in the top drawer of my desk,"

"Okay, I know where it is. I'll see what I can do."

"Brian...I'm sorry I've disappointed you like I have. I can see it in your face," Connors continued.

"I just wanted you to know I'm here if you need something. I don't have a lot of money, so I can't put any in your canteen fund, but if there's something I can do at your house or find you someone to be a power of attorney over your affairs until this gets straightened out, I'll be happy to do that."

"Thank you, Brian. That's very nice of you and I appreciate it, but I've given my lawyer power of attorney, so he'll see that I have money in my fund so I can make calls or write letters. Who in hell I'll call or write to, I don't know. At least my lawyer can get my subscriptions to magazines and puzzle books."

"I also, have another lawyer to take care of my financial affairs, including my house and stuff like that. I've instructed him to sell everything and put my money in my account here at the jail, for now and then he'll transfer it to prison, when the time comes," Connors sadly mentioned.

"What are you saying?" Miller asked. "You sound like you've already had your trial and been convicted."

"I'm not going to prolong the inevitable, Brian. I'm a sick bastard and

I have to pay for my crimes. It's as simple as that."

"Does your lawyer know and agree with what you *think* you want to do, now? Give it some time, Bob. You may have a change of heart, down the road."

"What are you saying, Brian? Are you saying I should try to get away with what I did?"

"I can't even begin to tell you what I think, at this point, Bob, but all the advice I can give you is to ask for a fair trail. Every citizen deserves a fair trial. The outcome will be decided and then what is...is."

"You're one hell of a guy, Brian. I wish I were half the man you are. You're fair, nonjudgmental, and respectable."

"Thanks, Bob. I'll be honest with you, though. I'm heartbroken for you and my brother, is all I can say. I'm really devastated. All I can ask is why, but I don't expect you to answer me. I'm sure you don't know yourself."

"I don't know."

"Are you going to become police chief, now?"

"I was thinking about it, at one time, when you retired down the road, but now I don't think so. I really don't want to stay in that small town anymore. I guess there are too many memories."

"Kinda like a cloud of gloom over the town?" Connors asked sadly.

"I guess you could say that."

"I'm sorry I'm the cause of that. I've done many things I regret."

"What are you planning to do, then?"

"I've been recruited to join the FBI," Miller said proudly.

"No kidding!" Connors replied. "I'm impressed and I know you'll be a great asset to the agency. I'd offer to give you a recommendation, but I guess that might not be a good thing," Connors said and chuckled.

"I think I'll let that pass, but thank you for the vote of confidence," Miller said and smiled. He was relieved to see Connors appeared to be handling his incarceration well, unless the shock hadn't worn off yet or the man really was insane and didn't know what kind of hell he was in for. Sometimes, ignorance is bliss, Miller surmised.

"I have to get a few minutes to see Jackson," Miller said. "I do hope you let me come and visit again, Bob."

"Yes, I'd like that. You'll probably be the only person who does."

"I'm going to be honest with you, Bob. One reason I'll be coming by is I'd like you to tell me what you know, I want to know. If you would rather confide in your lawyer about what you know, that's fine. People need answers and closure," Miller said and stood to leave.

"Take care, Bob and I'll see you soon."

Brian left the seating area and checked in with the correctional officer, once again, who handed back the number eight card he held.

"I'd like to see my brother, Jackson Miller, now if I may?" he asked.

"He'll be down in about ten minutes. You can take this same card and sit where you were before," the officer explained.

Brian was shocked at his brother's appearance. He was disheveled and disoriented, scared and confused. He had easily lost twenty pounds in the few weeks he's been behind bars.

"Thank you for seeing me, Jackson," Brian began as tears fell.

His brother didn't look him in the eye and kept his head lowered, but Brian hoped he was listening.

"Jackson, no matter what's happened," he began. "You're my brother and I'll do anything I can to help you get through this.

Brian was unaware if his brother heard him or if he was capable of comprehending what he was saying, but he continued to speak. He wasn't interest in details or confessions, at this point, he wanted to gain his brother's trust in hopes a deal would be made to save his life, if it came down to that and the most important aspect of this situation was to find the missing girls, if he had any knowledge about that.

"I just wanted to stop by and let you know Mom and I both love you. Mom isn't well enough to come, now, but maybe in a while. I also wanted you to know I've put some money into your canteen fund, so you can make purchases, maybe some treats for yourself. I know you always loved Snickers and Sky Bars," Brian added and smiled, noting his brother raised his head, slightly and looked in his direction. "I guess you have to buy pretty much everything, including shampoo and stuff like that and of course snacks and paper and stamps. I know Mom wants to hear from you and I do, too,"

"We're going to make sure you have a good lawyer, too."

"No! Jackson replied. I have a lawyer and it's free. I don't want you or mom to spend any money on that."

"You folks have two minutes," the guard announced over the intercom.

"Well, we'll talk about that at another time, Jackson. I have to go now, but keep your chin up. I'm here for you," Brian said and quickly left the enclosed jail that seemed to be sucking the very life out of him.

Chapter 39

ZenJa returned to her condo at Forest Haven Estates in Virginia and was eager to return to work.

Her lawyer, Jerry Johnson was in constant contact with her about the status of her parents estate and had successfully transferred the monies from the life insurance policies and financial assets her parents had into her account in Virginia. Overnight she had inherited over three and a half million dollars, not that money was going to relieve the pain and hurt she had in her heart. She knew she wouldn't be going to Vegas or spending the money on trivial things like vacations or spa treatments. She really had no idea what she would spend some of the money on, other than a nice home on a lake.

Her wish was to find several worthy causes to donate money to; causes and organizations that didn't spend a majority of their money on overhead, leaving little for the truly needy. Several causes immediately came to mind as she looked at the status of her bank account on her computer the first evening she'd returned to Virginia. The Salvation Army, Wounded Warriors, Disabled Veterans and Homeless Veterans were her first choices and she wanted to initiate a scholarship fund in her sister's name to be given to a deserving student upon their graduation from River View High School, each year.

Other scholarships she wanted to fund were for the children of the three law enforcement officers who perished in the explosion that devastated the River View Gymnasium. That was the least she felt she could do.

With these pending good deeds on the table, she felt her life finally had a purpose after all these weeks. ZenJa wanted to become an anonymous philanthropist; there was joy in giving to those she deemed the most in need.

In an effort to experience the art of giving on an impulse, ZenJa drove her black Dodge Charger to a local twenty four hour Wal-Mart superstore. She wandered around, with her own shopping cart, selecting many needed items for her empty pantry and while she toured the store, she practiced her surveillance skills and with the stealth of a panther, she targeted a young working class couple. The man, who appeared to be the husband, was wearing pants and shirt with his name embroidered above the front pocket and on the back of the shirt was the name of a local garage. The yong lady, who appeared to be the wife, was wearing a Dunkin' Donuts uniform. ZenJa noted the couple selected several different items, looked at the price and chose to return the goods to the shelves. The young couple appeared to be so much in love, they were oblivious to the woman who followed them and added the items they returned to the shelves into her own shopping cart.

The man and woman made their way toward the toy section. Even though ZenJa was at the other end of the aisle, she kept a watchful eye and ear out to discover why they were in that section of the store.

"Betsy would love this pink tricycle for her birthday and Rick was asking for this little electric sports car." the man mentioned. "He'd look so cute riding around in it, wouldn't he?"

"You know we can't afford those things, now. Maybe when I get a raise," the woman whispered.

ZenJa made her way over to the couple and struck up an conversation with them. "I'm interested in buying a few toys for my niece and nephew, for their birthdays. I have no idea what kids like today, maybe you can help me?

"You have children, I assume, because you're here in the toy aisle?"

"Yes, we have a three year old daughter and four year old boy," the lady replied.

"That's so special," ZenJa replied. "They're about the same age as my relatives," she lied. "Other than bikes, that all kids like, what else do you think kids that age might like?

"My son loves these electric sports cars. See, I work at a garage and sometimes on wrecker calls, I take him with me. He loves machinery and anything with an engine," the man said proudly.

"We just bought a house and the kids have been asking for a play set...you know the kind that have swings, slides and teeter totters. We're hoping to get them one next spring with our income tax refund check," the young woman said.

ZenJa was wondering how she was going to find out if the parents had a home or simply rented an apartment and she was thankful that subject came up on its own.

"Not to change the subject, but you know," ZenJa continued. "I've been looking for a good mechanic and dependable, reliable service in this area. I just moved here from up north and I need my car for my business and am looking for a place where I can call and get my car serviced right away, if the need comes up."

"What kind of car do you have?" the man asked.

"I have a new black Dodge Charger. It's my baby."

"No problem. Our garage just purchased all the new fangled equipment that's needed today because of the sensors and computers that operate these cars. I liked it in the old days when you needed your eyes and ears. I could tell what was wrong with a car as it drove into the garage bay, on most occasions. Sound was everything."

"I know," ZenJa said shaking her head in agreement. My father worked on our old 1978 Olds F-85. That was bigger than a tank! There were distinctive sounds for a water pump going, a wheel bearing in need of replacement, and of course the sound of muffler with a hole in it, hasn't changed any," ZenJa said and laughed.

"You know a lot about cars." the woman said.

"Oh yeah, I spend many wonderful afternoons working on cars with my dad," she said. We changed radiators, brake pads, mufflers, you name it," she added and wiped a tear from her eye.

"I apologize my parents just passed away and I'm still not used to the fact."

"I'm so sorry. Please accept our condolences."

"That's very kind of you, but enough of that."

I'll write down the name of your garage," she said, looking at the man's shirt and jotting the information on one of her business cards.

"Well, this is one smart woman and I'm not going to be able to take advantage of her, am I?" the man said and laughed.

"You're as honest as the day is long, Keith," the man's wife said. "He'd replace an engine in someone's car if he could...for free."

"That's why we're always broke," the woman said and laughed.

"Let me introduce myself. My name is ZenJa Beckwith and you are...?"

"I'm Keith and this is my wife, Darlene. We own the garage that's advertised on the back of my shirt. We're just barely making ends meet, but we have a wonderful family and that's all that matters."

"God love you two," ZenJa said amazed at what a truly happy couple this was. A match like her parents had been...back in their day.

"Here's my business card," ZenJa said and handed them one of her cards that simply had her name and number on it.

"Funny business card," Keith replied noting it simply had two details on it.

"I haven't decided what business I'm going to be in yet," ZenJa said and laughed.

"Do you have a business card?"

"Yes, and my cards have my business address on it, too!" Keith said and smiled, but you already wrote down the information," he said, but handed her a card, anyway.

Out of the clear blue ZenJa recalled what Molly and the other townees mentioned about the developer who was interested in the Beckwith Property and how business, including grocery stores, gas stations and obviously more mechanics were going to be needed in Longberry. Jim Bacon couldn't handle all the potential business that might infiltrate the small town in the mountains of New Hampshire. Something to keep in the back of her mind, she realized.

"Sorry, I was just zoning out for a minute," ZenJa explained.

"That's okay," Darlene replied.

"It's really has been a pleasure to meet you, Keith and Darlene. I'll stop by and schedule an appointment soon. I know I need an oil change."

"You can check your owners manual. It isn't necessary to get oil changed at every three thousand miles, like in the old days. Some cars are good for seven thousand or more miles."

"See, that's why we have no business," Darlene said and laughed.

"I do a lot of highway milage and I've been known to put the peddle to the metal, on occasion, so I try to get it done as often as I can."

"Where do you go, if you don't mind me asking?"

"I go to New Hampshire a lot."

"That's a great place. I miss the mountains," Darlene said. "I could tell you were from up north."

"That obvious?" ZenJa asked.

"Yes, I'm from Vermont, myself, and recognize the little drawl, if one can call it that."

"Well, we better get going; Darcy has to get home and get ready for her own job. She's been babysitting, so we could get out," Darlene replied.

"It really has been a pleasure to meet you," ZenJa said shaking couples hands and watched them walk to check out their meager items.

For the next two hours, ZenJa did some serious shopping at the Wal-Mart store. She asked the man in charge of the bicycle area to bring the pretty pink trike, the sporty electric Hummer lookalike to the front of the store. Then she wandered over to the birthday decorations and selected balloons, party favors, hats, table cloths, napkins, and a pinata for a boy and a girl. She selected the *Hello Kitty* theme for the little girl and *Spider Man* for the young boy.

When ZenJa got to the check out register she realized how big the electric Hummer was and knew it wasn't going to fit inside her car. She would have a difficult enough time to fit the tricycle and other party items and her own groceries inside.

ZenJa paid for her purchases and had an associate help her bring the vehicles to her car.

"I know they're not going to fit," she assured the clerk before he could say anything. "I'll be fine," she said and took out the business card Keith had given her and called the number.

"Keith's Automotive and Towing," a man answered.

"Hi, this is ZenJa. I just met you and your wife at Wal-Mart a few hours ago?"

"Yes, Miss, what can I do for you?"

"I just finished shopping and low and behold my car won't start. Could you come over and give me a boost and tow, if need be, to your garage. I've no idea why it won't start," ZenJa lied.

"Okay, I'll be over in a few minutes," Keith replied and hung up.

"Awesome! I hope he brings a truck!" she said out loud.

Within ten minutes a flat bed truck pulled up beside ZenJa's Dodge Charger, which she had opened the hood, to make it convenient for the mechanic to find her car.

While ZenJa was waiting, she lugged the Hummer and tricycle toward the rear of her car, out of sight.

"So, what seems to be the problem?" Keith asked jumping out of the truck and walking toward the engine compartment.

"Oh, I made a mistake," ZenJa began. "It's not my car that won't start, it's this one," she said and directed Keith toward the miniature Hummer.

Keith looked at ZenJa, his eyes appearing to be wider than golf balls.

"What the...? You can't do this," he began, choking on his words.

"Why only my name is on my business card is because I'm a secret Santa, of sorts," she lied again. "I'm sorry I had to call you on this ruse, but after buying these things, I realized I didn't have any way to get them to my house or yours for that matter," she said and laughed.

"This is too much. I can't...I don't know what to say."

"I always say, what comes around goes around. One day you can do something for someone else, but by the sounds of it, you already have. Running a business is expensive and I know it's easy to feel sorry for people and help them out and from what I gather, it's easy for you to give more than you receive. Am I wrong?"

"My wife can answer that," he added sheepishly.

"Now, how would you like to handle this? When are your children's birthday?" ZenJa asked taking control of the situation.

"We're going to celebrate them this Saturday. Rick's birthday is Friday and Betsy's is Saturday and of course we both have to work during the week and the only day Darlene could get off this week will be Saturday.

"Is your business adjacent to your house?" ZenJa asked, already aware that it was from the information she got on her GPS system.

"Yes, it's right across the street."

"Okay, so I'll tell you what we'll do. We'll load these *vehicles* onto your flatbed and you can drive them to my house. We'll put them inside my garage until the birthday party and in case it rains, we're going to have the party at my house! How does that sound?"

"Oh my God. You must be an angel. I can't believe you're real!" Keith exclaimed. "Why are you doing this?"

"To be totally honest with you, I had a sister, once and I lost her. Let's just say this is my way of passing a little bit of her heart on to someone else."

"I'm...I can't believe this," Keith said, sincerely.

"So, now if you'll follow me, I'll show you were to deliver these vehicles that appeared to have broken down," ZenJa said and helped Keith load the Hummer and trike onto the flatbed.

"Now, before we leave, I want you to stand beside the wrecker, here," ZenJa said and pointed to the direction she wanted him to stand. I'm going to get this on my camera phone! Don't you think this will make a great calendar for your business, next year?"

"This is outrageous," Keith said and laughed until ZenJa thought he'd fall over.

"I could print...*NO JOB IS TOO BIG OR TOO SMALL FOR US TO HANDLE.*"

"Oh my God! That's great. How about tee shirts?"

"Are you in advertising?" Keith asked.

"No, I'm a spy, but I think I should go into advertising," ZenJa said with a twinkle in her eye, knowing Keith never would believe that she was a spy.

"You're one funny lady."

"You know, I haven't had a reason to laugh or smile in a long, long time," ZenJa said with sadness in her eyes. "This has been more rewarding for me that you can imagine."

"Darlene will never believe this when I call her."

"If she'd like, she can come over Friday night, or anytime, actually, and we can get the decorations up. We'll set up in the my garage to take the weather out of the equation."

"Okay, I know you have a business to run, so if you'll follow me, I'll show you were I live."

"Lead the way," Keith said.

"Not only were Keith and ZenJa leaving the parking lot of the Wal-Mart Superstore, but another vehicle followed them down the highway, also.

Chapter 40

"You're here really early," Levi said to his boss, ATF Director Matthew Montgomery, also known as Monty, and looked at his watch to notice it was only six in the morning.

"I have a lot of work to do concerning Connors and Miller cases."

"Connors was the only person, as far as we've detected, involved in the Weapons Across State Lines operation," Levi reminded his boss. "The kidnaping and murders have been tied to both Connors and Miller, but we have no jurisdiction where Miller's concerned on that front."

"We're still trying to connect both situations together. Of course, having no confessions from either asshole, hasn't helped."

"Could it be that Zippy and Olive saw something going down and had to be eliminated?" Levi asked. "Something that Alex might have overlooked, while he had Connors under surveillance?"

"It's very likely," Montgomery replied.

"In Molly's statement she said Connors had given Olive and Zippy a ride to the restaurant the day Olive went missing and the day after, Zippy disappeared."

"Could it be possible one of the girls saw something in the Chief's car and Connors realized what one of them had seen?"

"Like what?"

"Maybe a weapon sticking out from under the seat of the car and Connors realized, after he let them out, they had to have seen it? If that's the case, we would be connected as the weapon or weapons would have been the single thread that ties their disappearances together, and we would have jurisdiction as well as the FBI," Levi said realistically.

So, let me guess, you're ready to come back to work?" Montgomery, the director of the ATF asked Levi, eyeing him cautiously.

"Yes, I've been slaking off long enough, don't you think?" Levi asked.

"Well, now that you mention it," Monty replied and smiled.

"Nice office," Levi commented. "So it appears taking down Connors got you a little promotion out of New York and here in Virginia, now?"

"Actually, I'd put in a request for a transfer long before the taking down of that cockroach. My daughter is going to Georgetown University, so I wanted to be closer to her and my parents have a house down here, so for the next four years, or so, my wife and I'll be shacking up with them. They have a small cottage and they're gone most of the time. They spend winters in Florida and go to Europe all the time."

"Well, enough of that...how are you feeling? How's your arm now?"

"I'm almost as good as new. I still have the cast, but I figured I could do something simple like surveillance, if you have anything around here?"

"Why down here? Why don't you want to work closer to your home?"

"I've got a little bit of business down here and thought you might have something that would keep me busy for a few weeks. I'm going stir crazy."

"What business might that be?" Emerson asked and smiled.

"I have a few things to settle with my brother and I thought I might check on ZenJa, to see how she's doing."

"I kinda figured ZenJa might be one of the reasons you're down here."

"Keeping tabs on her for so long became a habit, I guess. I just want to make sure she's okay and thank her for what she did inside the gymnasium and talking to Connors like she did. She really did an amazing job of negotiating with him, though the end result was devastating. If it hadn't been for her and the fact she knew about the tunnel between the gym and football field, Connors would have been long gone and I assure you we never would have found him."

"So you actually heard the conversation she was having with Connors?"

"Oh, yes...I sure did. She was cool, calm, and collected. She handled herself like a pro."

Well, you seem to be so anxious to get back to work, you can start by writing a detailed report about what you witnessed once you got to the gym. That will be vital for the trial and it'll be a good report to add to ZenJa's file. Being a newcomer, as she is, it'll help when it comes time to give her a review and consideration for a raise."

"I know I shouldn't mention this, but it's rather difficult for me to type on a computer, so if I may dictate my report...?"

"Absolutely! Once you finish taping it, let me know and I'll have one of the secretaries type it for you and I'll forward it to Edward Emerson, with the Bureau."

"Thank you; it sure feels good to get back in the swing of things and if you think of something else for me to do, before I get this damn cast off, let me know. You have my number, of course."

"Will do."

Where're you staying, by the way?" Monty asked the agent.

"I just got into town and haven't got a hotel room yet."

"Well, you know your brother's gone back to his house and the government has rented the condo next to ZenJa's for the next 6 months, so why not go and hang out there? I bet she'd like to see a friendly face."

"I don't know if *friendly* would be the word she'd use in the same breath when speaking about me, but what the hell, all she can do is break my other arm," Levi said and laughed.

"ZenJa has the keys to the condo, so you can reintroduce yourself to her when you pick them up and the other good thing about staying at the condo is that you can keep an eye on her and the place is all furnished. What could be better than that?"

"Sounds like a plan. I'll head over after I do a little shopping." Levi said and headed toward the local Wal-Mart Superstore.

Once Levi entered the parking lot of the shopping complex, he immediately spotted ZenJa's Dodge Charger, with the distinctive license plate that read, ZIPPY, on it.

Levi stopped toward the rear of the parking lot when he noticed a flatbed wrecker approach her car. Using his binoculars, the agent spotted what appeared to be a child's bike and a child's size electric car near her vehicle and he also saw her car was full of household items and other children's toys.

"Well, well, is *Miss* Beckwith keeping a secret?" Levi murmured to himself. Does this little Miss have children I don't know about?"

Needless to say, Levi never entered the Wal-Mart store. He observed, with a chuckle, the effort ZenJa and a man made loading the toys onto the huge tow truck and the fact she was taking pictures of the event with her cell phone and the fact she was laughing and smiling. Levi enjoyed seeing her smile. He realized she should do it more often.

Once the toys were fastened down and both parties entered their separate vehicles, Levi followed them, at a respectable distance until he realized ZenJa was leading the tow truck to her own condo. Parking up the street, to keep the on going events under his watchful eye, he noted the tow truck back into the driveway and off load the toys and park them inside ZenJa's garage and shut the door.

ZenJa appeared to hand the driver several denominations of dollar bills. The driver tried, in vain, to refuse the money, but ZenJa insisted and the driver finally conceded, waved and drove away.

Levi made a note of the name of the towing company and decided he'd drive by, shortly, and check out the establishment. Keith's Automotive and

Towing, he added to the contacts of his cell phone, along with the phone number that was stenciled on the truck door panel.

After grabbing a cup of coffee and a breakfast sandwich at a local restaurant, Levi drove by Keith's Automotive and Towing Company, after locating the establishment on his GPS system.

Spending a few minutes in a vacant parking lot, Levi was deciding how to approach this mechanic and find out what the deal was, with the children's toys.

Fifteen minutes later, Levi entered the automotive shop to fuel up his vehicle and hopefully meet the man who had driven the tow truck to Wal-Mart that morning.

It appeared there were only two men working at the establishment. One young man was working on a Honda Civic, in one garage service bay and another young man came out to pump his gas.

"Hi, there," Levi said after he exited his Camaro.

"Hello," the man said. "You want me to fill it up?"

"Yes, thanks. This is unusual, isn't it? A full service gas station. I can't remember seeing any of those around in years," Levi mentioned in an effort to begin a dialogue with the attendant.

"I've just taken over this business and I'm trying to attract new and old customers; going a little above and beyond, if you know what I mean," the man replied.

"I like your spirit. There aren't enough people in the world who do more than's expected of them, if they even achieve that," Levi remarked while the man filled his tank.

"You want me to check the oil?" the man asked after agreeing with his customer.

"Sure! Actually, if you have time, I'd rather have an oil change. I've done some long distance, high speed driving lately and it's probably due for a change."

"No problem. I'll call the local NAPA store and get an oil filter for it. It'll be here in no time."

"I've got plenty of time," Levi replied.

"I see you must have broken your arm?" Keith noticed.

"Yeah, I tripped over my dog," he replied and laughed.

"How much longer you expected to have to wear the cast?" the man asked and checked the engine size and make and model of the Camaro to order the proper oil filer.

"Another two weeks or so, from what the doctor says. I'm getting pretty antsy and want the damn thing off."

"I hear ya," the man said.

"Why not come inside and have a seat and a cup of coffee while I wait for the oil filter. I'll call the parts store now and it should be here in five minutes."

"Okay, thanks, I'll do that."

"My name's Levi and you're Keith, the owner?"

"Yes; it's always been a dream of mine to own my own business. Capitalism and all that, part of the American dream."

"You certainly have the attitude for it," Levi said and poured himself a cup of black coffee and sat down while Keith went to wait on another gas customer.

As soon as the proprietor finished serving his customer he came back inside the office. I've seen two very interesting vanity license plates today. Yours, with LAWLESS on it and another sports car, a Charger, with ZIPPY on it," he mentioned for strike up a conversation.

"I've seen that car around," Levi admitted and smiled.

"The lady driving that vehicle is an awesome person. My wife and I met her this morning at a store and she..." he began. "Oh never mind. I won't bore you with that."

"Today's paper's on the table, if you like and I'll get your car inside," Keith said and walked out the door to get the oil filter from the delivery man and drove the Camaro into the second service bay and raised it with the hydraulic lift.

While Levi waited for his car to be serviced he wondered what ZenJa had been up to this morning that made this man and his wife become so fond of her. Levi knew he, himself, was more fond of her than he should be, but he wasn't a married man...not any more. Knowing the red-haired, green eyed beauty, he realized she must have done some nice deed. She obviously hadn't called the wrecker to bring her car in for service, unless he hadn't gotten there in time to see if it had failed to start and she merely needed a jump-start.

Levi was, indeed, having an interesting morning and he just arrived in Virginia.

"Your car's ready," the owner of Keith's Automotive and Towing said and handed the set of keys to Levi, after removing it from the lift and drove it to the front of the building.

"Thanks a lot. That was quick. My schedule's so erratic, it's difficult for me to make appointments ahead of time for servicing my vehicle," Levi said and removed his wallet from his blue jeans pocket.

"That's what the lady with the Zippy car said this morning, too. She said she needs to have a mechanic get her car in at a moment's notice."

Levi smiled and said, "I know what she means. It's always rush, rush, rush and no one has time or patience to wait for anything any more. Everyone wants everything like fast-food...now!"

"How much do I owe you?"

"Because your car's under warranty and as you said you drive it as it's meant to be, a high performance vehicle, I used a high grade synthetic oil and it's a tab bit pricey, but it's what your manual calls for."

"Don't apologize, Keith. If I couldn't afford to maintain my car, I wouldn't have bought it. I don't look for deals. What I *am* looking for is a reliable, honest mechanic."

"Okay, I got it! I'm so used to feeling guilty about charging people for the work I do. I know money's tight for people."

"You need to make a living for your family and they're the most important people in the world, Keith."

"You know, I've only had this station open for less than a week and everyone who's come in here has given me the same advice. I feel encouraged."

"Good! That's what business is all about...making a profit."

"You're bill is ninety-five dollars...the oil filter was..." Keith began, but Levi cut him off.

"You don't need to explain in detail, either. I've had my oil changed before so I know what it costs," he said and laughed while handing him a one hundred dollar bill. Keep the five for the coffee, it really was good."

"Man! That's one nice car Camaro ZL1, 6.2, V-8, super charged, 6 speed stick with 20 inch wheels. I think I saw in a magazine it's called Barely Street Legal? What's it got for Horsepower, about 580? This sucker must move," Keith commented without allowing Levi to answer his questions. The mechanic admired the car, inside and out, he stopped short when he looked under the seat and saw Levi's Glock 9mm underneath.

"How the hell did that get there," Levi said and smiled. "Must be one of my little rascals left it there when they were playing with it," Levi said and laughed at the absurdity of that statement and put the weapon in his shoulder holster.

Keith was taken aback and stepped to the rear of the sports car. He was intelligent enough to know Levi wasn't old enough to have children of age to be *playing* with any weapon, not to mention a Glock, but he feared he was about to get robbed.

"Oh, don't worry, Keith. I only shoot bad people," Levi said, got into his car and peeled out of the automotive center leaving a trail of rubber more than one hundred feet down the highway.

"Who the hell was that?" Keith's employee, Randy, asked.

"I have no idea, but for some reason, he doesn't seem like a bad guy, in spite of the gun he has."

"Sure has good taste in cars," Randy agreed.

"I can't argue with that," Keith replied and went to pump gas for another customer.

Levi had initially planned to do some grocery shopping at Wal-Mart, so he drove back to the plaza and loaded up a shopping cart with items he wanted, including a simple charcoal grill, briquets, and lighter fluid.

His list also consisted of several steaks, fresh corn on the cob, salad fixings, butter, olive oil, and several varieties of soda, beer and other necessities for entertaining that evening. Before he headed back to Forest Haven Estates, he stopped by a liquor store and bought several bottles of wine, gin, and rum in case his guest so desired to have a beverage or two.

Shortly after his excursion, Keith drove his Camaro into the adjacent parking space, next to ZenJa's Charger and was relieved she was home. He didn't want to have to break into his own condo on the first day he was in town.

Before exiting his vehicle, the wounded AFT agent tooted the car's horn and waited for ZenJa to peek out the window to see who it was. As he expected she did look and frowned when she saw him in her driveway.

"Hello, my dear," Levi said and eased himself out of the car and waited for ZenJa to walk down the steps of her condo.

"What in God's name are you doing here?" she asked in an attempt to appear pissed off.

"We're going to be neighbors for a while."

"Oh, no you don't! I just got rid of your brother, I don't need you around here."

"I'm only doing as your boss has requested," he replied.

"And exactly what might that be? Are you still going to be on me after those two...", ZenJa began but Levi cut her off.

"ZenJa," he whispered. "Keep you voice down. We have neighbors, you know," he continued seriously.

"Yeah, sorry about that."

"Well, come on in. I have the keys to your condo."

After the couple entered ZenJa's home, Levi sat in a comfortable arm chair and put his feet up on a hassock.

"Why don't you make yourself at home," his hostess snarled.

"Are you always this pleasant, just before lunch?" Levi asked and smiled.

"Only because you showed up on my doorstep, otherwise I'd be a bitch!"

"I thought it might because you were awake and at Wal-Mart so early this morning, you might be in need of a little nap."

"You fucking son of a bitch! What the hell are you doing following me? Will you please get the hell out of my house and my life?" she begged ever so loudly.

"You're not very neighborly, Miss Beckwith. You haven't even asked me how I am or how my arm is healing."

"You're incorrigible! It's all about you, isn't it?"

"Well, not exactly. I bought us a grill, some steaks and other goodies. I know the new-comer to the neighborhood usually gets at least a cake or pie from the people next door, but in our case, I still owe you a nice dinner.

"Oh, by the way," ZenJa said without commenting on the dinner invitation. "Thank you for having my car delivered from the restaurant to my house in Boston, that night. I never even thought about that when we left."

"I know. I don't like leaving ladies in distress or loose ends behind," he added regarding the short dinner they never finished.

"So, if I have to ask, how are you feeling and how is your arm?"

"Now that I'm in your company, I feel fantastic. My arm is getting better and I should have the cast off in two weeks or so and speaking of that, I could use a hand bringing in my...our...groceries before they spoil. You can see I'm a cripple."

"I'll help you bring them into *your* condo; like you said, I went shopping this morning, so my pantry's full," she retorted.

"Thanks, I appreciate your help," Levi said and looked intently into the green eyes of the woman who stood before him; the auburn-red haired beauty who intrigued him more than he wanted to admit while ushering her outdoors with his right arm.

"I'm assuming you only bought food for our cookout? I don't see anything in the bags such as milk, eggs, bread or any other staples and of course you have enough booze here for a good drunk."

"Actually, I was hoping to get you drunk enough so you would...," Levi began.

"So I would what?" ZenJa growled again.

"So you would get drunk enough to make me breakfast in the morning and to become a fucking half-way decent human being! Get the fucking chip off your shoulder, you bitch! You're a real piece of work, you are!" he said and motioned for her to leave his condo while slamming the door after her.

Tears streamed down ZenJa's face while she ran toward her home and shut the door. She couldn't have felt worse than if Levi had actually slapped her across the face. ZenJa threw herself down on her couch and cried herself to sleep.

It was dark outside when ZenJa woke up and struggled to her feet. She dragged herself to her bathroom and took a shower and put on clean blue jeans and a burnt orange turtleneck sweater when she smelled the scent of steaks on a barbecue grill. Her mouth watered and realized she hadn't eaten all day.

"Come on ZenJa, swallow your pride and apologize to the man, make amends and let's try to start over again," she said out loud. "You've been a royal bitch for so long you don't know how to be anything else," she admitted.

ZenJa looked out her back window on her neighbor's patio and noticed Levi had the picnic table filled with all the necessities for a cookout; what appeared to be for two people. The charcoal grill was ablaze and the steaks were obviously cooking with the cover closed and ZenJa's stomach began to growl from the delicious aroma that was coming from next door.

ZenJa fetched an her iPod and brought the entertainment outside to the party.

"I want to apologize, Levi. You're right, I've been a bitch, like I told myself, for so long, I don't know how to be anything else. I admit it and again, I'm sorry. You've never done anything but be nice to me, other than spying on me.

"I guess I'm in charge of the entertainment committee, you've obviously outdone yourself with the food," ZenJa added and switched on the iPod and songs from the group, Five Finger Death Punch, started to play.

"I was hoping you'd smell the steaks and come outside," Levi replied without acknowledging or accepting ZenJa's apology, but rather dismissing it entirely.

"I fell asleep; I guess I needed a nap, like you mentioned, and I was awake and at the store early this morning."

"I guess you wonder what I was doing there and you obviously saw me with the toys..."

"Yes, do tell. Do you have children I don't know about?" Levi asked and smiled with his devilish grin.

"No, it's a long story, but I met this couple in the store and overheard them talking about what a difficult time they were having providing a birthday party for their two children and I just wanted to help, that's all."

"That doesn't surprise me in the least. You're much more generous and delightful than you lead people to believe."

"So, when's the party and am I invited?"

"Good grief! I suppose you'll come over whether you're invited or not, won't you?"

"Well, of course. I could order a pony, if you want, but you'll have to clean up the poop in the back yard. I have a bad arm, you know," he teased.

"Why not just have an ass come...oh wait, you'll already be here!" ZenJa said and laughed out loud at her own joke!

"Oh...that's a good one, my dear," Levi said and grabbed a beer from the cooler that rested on the table and offered ZenJa one, as well. "I so enjoy sparring with you!"

"Thank you, beer will be fine," ZenJa replied and ignored her neighbor's comment.

"I'm saving the fancy wine and other alcoholic beverages for another occasion."

"What might that be?"

"Oh, I thought we could celebrate at the birthday party and get hammered and then I can really be an ass," he teased.

"You can do that without drinking, from what I can tell," ZenJa said and smiled, but in a friendly way.

"I'm sorry, again, Levi. I promised myself I'd be on my best behavior."

"At least you're trying," he said while taking the two small steaks off the grill and placing them in plates along with steamed corn on the cob, while ZenJa dished out two bowls of salad.

"This really is delightful. I appreciate the effort you've made," ZenJa said looking shyly at the man who sat across from her at the picnic table.

"I enjoy entertaining, but haven't had any reason to for a long time. Between work and work, that's about all my life revolves around, now."

The couple sat silently for the duration of their meal and Levi offered

ZenJa another beer and took one for himself before sitting down facing her, once more.

"Can I ask you a very personal question?"

"You can ask, but it doesn't mean I'll answer it."

"I know so little about you and you practically know everything about me. That hardly seems fair especially since what you know about me is considered, I think I deserve to know a little about you. To even up the odds a little."

"Do you want to ask the questions or do you want me to tell you what I know, you want to know?"

"Please go ahead," ZenJa said and put her fork down, folded her hands in front of her and waited to hear what and who the real Levi Harris was.

Levi sat, with his head turned down toward his plate for several minutes before he began to tell some of his story.

"There's no sense in starting from the beginning; that's so boring, but I guess a good place to start is how Alex Lyons and I are related?"

"Okay, start where you like, Levi. I'm listening," she whispered softly.

"Alex and I have the same mother; Olivia Swan. Alex is three years younger than I am and my mother was married to my father, but the whore was fucking around with Alex's father and Alex is the by-product of that fucking around."

"I'm so sorry, Levi," ZenJa said and reached out to touch her dinner date's hand.

"Now you know why there is, how should I say it, some *animosity* between us. I've never liked the man and never will. He's like a bed sore that simply won't go away."

"Did he grow up with you and your father, or who?"

"My father and I never knew about him, ZenJa until my mother...died."

"How did she hide her pregnancy?"

"Coincidently, she was writing another novel and she convinced my father she needed to reside in Europe, at some castle, somewhere, in order to get the *feel* for her latest creation, for the last six or seven months of her pregnancy."

"Who did he grow up with?"

"The pool man," he said and laughed.

"Come on, Levi," ZenJa said and chuckled.

"No, I'm serious, she was fucking the pool man and he brought Alex up and I guess that explains why he's the way he is...crude, rude, and an

197

asshole."

"Did your mother have anything to do with Alex?"

"Probably the only time she did was when she was screwing his father. I really don't know, ZenJa and I never asked; I never cared."

"To be fair to Alex, Levi, it wasn't his fault who his parents were. You have to admit that. No wonder he's who he is today. He's been hurt all his life, shunned like a freak, no doubt. God only knows how he was treated in school. Children born out of wedlock can be treated so cruelly by other children. There were probably mother-son events at school that he couldn't attend because he basically had no mother, not to mention the fact he had no female presence or example in his life, unless there were other women hanging around, in and out of his father's life."

"To be honest with you, I think he's an ass, too, but now I can understand a little bit more about him and what makes him tick. What kind of female relationships does he have, now?"

"He's the love 'em and leave 'em kind of guy. I don't think he's had more than a two year relationship with any woman."

"So he basically just fucks around?" ZenJa asked.

"Pretty much."

"What a lonely life that is, Levi."

"Is it any more lonely than yours, ZenJa?"

ZenJa removed her hand from Levi's and looked down at her own plate without answering.

"Or yours?" ZenJa retorted sharply.

Levi sighed and hesitated before he responded.

"I have loved only one woman in my entire life and she's gone, ZenJa. There'll never be another woman like her in my life, *ever*!"

"She hurt you, so you've given up on finding happiness for yourself, again?"

"My wife didn't hurt me, ZenJa. She died," he replied while salty tears burned his eyes and he stood up to get another beer and one for his guest. Levi put her beer on the table and walked over to the grill and tightly sealed the cover to extinguish the charcoals and avoid ZenJa's gaze.

"Oh my God, Levi, I'm so sorry! It was callous of me to assume what I did and say what I said about your wife at your house. God, please forgive me," she cried and walked up to Levi and embraced him in her arms, a mutual embrace that lasted longer than either intended.

"It's okay," Levi said and pried himself away from ZenJa and sat at the table again.

"No, it's not okay, Levi. To be honest, I guess I was jealous..."

Levi looked at his dinner date and searched her eyes for sincerity, if it was truly there, and he realized it was.

"Her name was Isabella, just like the street where you lived in Boston," Levi said and smiled. "I knew the minute I found out you lived on that street there was something...something there...a connection, if you will. It was like Isabella was with me, surrounding me with her love, all over again. I could feel her presence, like I used to. I can't really explain it."

"I can almost feel her love surrounding you, as well, Levi. I've had the same feeling with my sister many times, sometimes I have nightmares, but other times I feel her smiling down on me."

"I know exactly what you're saying, ZenJa," Levi said and reached out for her hand.

"I met Isabella in fifth grade and we were in love from the first day I saw her. We got married right after high school and we both went to college together and graduated. We both worked for the government; not the same agencies, but we were both in law enforcement."

"We were married for only ten years. We were so much in love. It was a love no one could ask to ever have again. It would be selfish, greedy, and impossible to ask for another love like that."

"How did Isabella die?" ZenJa asked softly.

"She had cancer. I think she knew she had cancer a lot longer than she let on. She tried to protect me, or she was in denial, I don't know, but I was so angry with her for not sharing this dreadful time in her life so I could help her. She dealt with this mostly on her own. She only told me about it when she was so sick and it was obvious something was wrong."

"When I was visiting you in the hospital, Levi, you were having a nightmare and you shouted for Isabella not to leave you, to hang on."

"I'm sorry you heard that, ZenJa."

"What did you mean, not to leave you and hang on? I asked Alex about it and he nearly bit my head off and basically told me to mind my own f'en business."

Levi simply shook his head, regarding the comment Alex made. This man knew his brother and realized that was something he'd say.

"I was on assignment in New York City and she called me to tell me she was slipping away. I had no idea her condition had deteriorated as quickly as it had, in such a short time. I was telling her to hang in there and wait for me to make it all better; to tell her I'd be right at her side," Levi said and shamelessly cried into his dinner napkin.

"I never made it in time. She died alone and I'll never forgive myself for that...ever. I deserve to rot in hell and suffer every day of my fucking life," he swore. "I let my wife down."

ZenJa wiped her own tears away and silently walked up to Levi and offered him her hand and the couple walked inside his home to sit on his couch. ZenJa silently sat beside this tough agent and held him in her arms like she had her baby sister so many times when she had scraped knees or a broken heart.

An hour or so later, Levi had fallen asleep and ZenJa gently made him comfortable on the couch and covered him with a quilt she had gotten from her house. The quilt that had once been Zippy's favorite.

After making sure Levi was sound asleep, ZenJa went outside and cleaned up the remains of their dinner and put everything away and washed the dishes and as he had done with her, at her house in Boston, she sat in a lounge chair and slept with one eye open in case Levi needed her.

Chapter 41

Early the next morning, ZenJa was in the process of leaving Levi's house to get ready to go to her office. She had to catch up on some reports she needed to file, regarding the events that took place in Longberry, New Hampshire in the last few days.

Before stepping off Levi's doorstep, Alex and his powerful Mustang drove in the driveway.

"Good morning, Sunshine," Alex offered and climbed out of his vehicle. I see Levi's all moved in and it appears you have, too?" Alex asked, the sarcasm evident in his tone of voice.

Not to be baited into an argument with the jerk, that early in the morning, ZenJa tried to remember what Levi said about his brother and why he obviously behaved as he did and responded accordingly. "Levi had a rather difficult night," ZenJa said. "Actually, he told me a lot about you and your childhood, Alex, so I'm not going to let you drag me into any kind of altercation. I understand you better than you think, now that I know some of your history; I'm sorry about that," she replied and entered her house, leaving the speechless man standing on the sidewalk.

Alex got back into his car and left the neighborhood without stopping in to see his brother.

Just after ZenJa took her shower and dressed for work, she heard a knock at her front door and answered it with a cup of steaming coffee in her hand.

"Good morning, Levi. Would you like a cup of coffee? You look like you could use one," she said and smiled at the disheveled appearance the man had.

"You know, this is convenient...living next door to you. I can crawl over here without having to get all gussied up for a cup of brew and yes, thanks I sure could use one."

"Like you mentioned yesterday, I forgot to buy some and a coffee maker, too. I also want to thank you for cleaning up the ness outside, last night and especially for listening to me whine about my life. I'm very sorry about that. I *never* let my guard down like that, and again, I'm sorry."

"You know, Levi," she continued and handed him a mug of coffee. "Maybe you might be able to take a step, now and then, to move forward with your life, if you were to let your guard down, once in a while, but only, as I would do, only to someone I trust with my life," ZenJa continued and looked over her cup at her guest.

"I know you're right. I've just never met anyone, male or female, I trust enough to speak truthfully with or to be honest with."

"Until now?" ZenJa asked.

"*Maybe*, until now," Levi replied.

"If I'm willing to lay my life down for a stranger in hostage negotiations, I think you can trust me, don't you?"

"I'm working on it. So, enough of that shit for now, where you going all dressed up, this early in the morning?"

"I have to get to my office and finish writing reports on the events that took place in the gym in Longberry the other day. I should have done this sooner, but everything's moving along like the winds of a tornado."

"I know and thanks for reminding me, I have to write a report, too. So, thanks again, ZenJa for the coffee and..."

"Go home and get respectable," ZenJa said cutting him off before she got all weepy, again.

An hour later, Levi walked into his office at the AFT office in Falls Church, Virginia and began taping his long overdue report on the events that led him to be at the River View School and what he witnessed regarding ZenJa's exemplary performance in the hostage negotiations. He needed to give a detailed account of what he witnessed and the fact that ZenJa captured Chief Connors before he could flee and his impending arrest after the explosion that rocked the school; injuring many law enforcement officers and killing three others.

Listening to the recording of the report, for the second time, Levi was satisfied that everything he said was accurate and no facts had been eliminated. He realized ZenJa would be pleased with his report, not that any of it was slanted in any way. Levi was an honest agent, not to be distracted by any feelings he had for anyone he worked with, male or female.

Levi left his office with the recording of his report and happened to meet his boss outside in the hall. "Here's my report, so if you could have one of the secretaries type it up for me, I'd appreciate it."

"Good work, Levi. Now that you've completed that task, I'll have an assignment for you on Monday, so go home and get some rest."

"Okay, will do. Any hint what this assignment might be or where it will take me?"

"As a matter of fact, there's a rumor of a weapons and explosive running outfit operating out of New Hampshire. We stumbled upon it while we were in Longberry. Actually, there was an anonymous tip called in from the Lakes Region. Some woman was fearful her husband and brother might be involved and she wanted to end the operation, before someone got hurt."

"So the alleged operation originates in New Hampshire and ends up where?"

"Don't know, yet."

"I assume the 'informant' knows what will happen to the alleged perps when they're caught?"

"We haven't really figured out what her angle is, yet. You're going to have to meet her when you get to New Hampshire.

"Shit!' I just got all settled in my new condo."

"You're the one who's chomping at the bit to get back to work," his boss reminded him and left to deliver the tape for an office clerk to type and forward the document to the appropriate offices and departments.

"Oh! Wait" Levi yelled to catch Montgomery's attention before he entered the elevator.

"What do you want?"

"I was wondering how the investigation's going, regarding Connors and Miller. Any DNA come back on the bones that we found in New Hampshire and any reports back on the serial numbers or ballistics with the weapons we've gotten from Connors in connection with any crimes?"

"Actually, I just received some reports, but I haven't had a chance to look at them. It's Friday, go home, Levi. I'll let you know if there's anything substantial in the reports."

Levi stopped off and had a sandwich and Coke at a local restaurant and headed back to his condo. Dusk was settling on the area and he quickly noticed ZenJa's garage door open, her car in the driveway, and another vehicle behind hers.

Levi got out of the Camaro and sauntered over to his neighbor's garage and entered without notice.

"Hello, everyone," he called out in a cheerful greeting.

"Hello Levi. I knew you'd show up eventually and your timing's perfect. I need someone to help blow up the balloons," ZenJa said and smiled.

"I'm going to be the donkey for the party, I can't blow up balloons," he replied and laughed.

As soon as Levi joined ZenJa, the two guests who had arrived in the strange car appeared from behind the condo and entered the garage, too.

"Oh my God! It's you!" Keith exclaimed. "You said you knew the lady with the ZIPPY license plate. I guess you do," he said and welcomed the new arrival to the pre-party event.

"Yes, we're neighbors," Levi acknowledged and introduced himself to Keith's wife.

"I'm Levi and I assume, you, my lovely lady, must be Keith's wife and the mother of the birthday children?"

"Yes, my name's Darlene. "It's nice to meet you. Keith was telling me he had a most interesting day, thanks to ZenJa and he mentioned you and your *radical* car."

"That's the love of my life, that car," Levi responded and smiled at ZenJa who rolled her eyes and went back to decorating the interior of the garage for the birthday party that would take place the next afternoon.

"Well, you folks look like you've been very busy. The table's all decorated, streamers, balloons, the fishing pond, Pin The Tail On The Donkey, jump rope, and what's this? A Hummer and tricycle, dolls and a doll stroller, trucks, a toy kitchen set, Legos, and goodness gracious, what else?"

"Well, my friend, there's a wooden swing set, outdoor cabin, slide, teeter-totter, ladder and other items going to be delivered to Keith and Darlene's house to be erected, by the good folks at Home Depot, tomorrow, while the children are here at the party," ZenJa replied and smiled.

"Thank God, the pros are going to put that swing set together, I can't do much with one arm, you know," he explained, looking for sympathy.

"I was telling Keith, this morning, I tripped over my dog and broke my arm," he mentioned and smiled, again at ZenJa.

ZenJa returned the smile and once again, shook her head in disbelief.

"I was just going to ask you how you knew Keith and I'm sure I'm going to get an explanation?" ZenJa said curtly.

"I had to get my oil changed, ZenJa. Remember, I told you that a day or so ago? So, I stopped by and what a co-incidence, Keith's Automotive and Towing was where I stopped. It's like we're all connected, ZenJa," Keith said and laughed.

"We're only neighbors," ZenJa informed their guests.

"So, it looks like we've got all the decorations up, so, if you don't mind, ZenJa, we should be getting home. Our babysitter has to get some sleep, so she can go to work tomorrow."

"I can't thank you enough, ZenJa, for what you've done for us and the children. They're going to be thrilled beyond belief and like I told you this morning, you're an angel and I don't know why you selected us to watch over, but we're glad you did and we expect to do something like this for someone else, someday," Darlene replied and hugged her new friend.

"Good to meet you, Levi, also," she said and walked toward their car in the driveway.

"See you tomorrow at 2:00 p.m.," Keith said and waved to their new friends. "Thanks again."

"This looks very nice," Levi said admiring the decorations.

"Did you have birthday parties like this when you were a kid?"

"Yes, my mother and father always celebrated Zippy's and my birthday with a big party, with all our friends, their friends, and a few relatives and anyone passing by. We had great times," ZenJa replied softly.

"I had birthday parties, too. I guess Alex never did, not that I ever asked him."

"Do you think he might like to come over for the party tomorrow?"

"I don't think he's into children's events."

"Well, it might humanize him," ZenJa retorted.

"Who knows; he's like infection that simply doesn't know enough to go away. He may just stop over and the Lord only knows."

"Well, what I really came over to tell you is that I'm heading up north on Monday, so you'll be all by your lonesome."

"You're going back to work, so soon?" ZenJa asked with disappointment evident in her voice.

"Unfortunately, the bad guys outnumber us and we have to keep up the good fight, if we ever want to win the war."

"Sadly, that's true," ZenJa replied.

"Oh, and by the way, my boss said he's gotten a preliminary report on the ballistics and serial numbers of the weapons Connors was selling Alex, so he said he'd let me know if there's any connection with crimes that may have been committed with them and their origin, across state lines, of course."

"Do you know how the O'Leary and Childress girls were killed, ZenJa?"

"They were kidnaped, raped and shot," she replied sadly.

"I'm hoping we can connect the ballistics with the weapons Connors and possibly Miller were in possession of, at one time. All the serial numbers of the weapons Alex was dealing with, with Connors have been recorded and of course the ATF is in possession of those weapons; after all Alex was the *consumer* of them."

"Thankfully they're off the streets and can't be used in the commission of other crimes," ZenJa replied.

"You know, it's difficult to say who the bad and good guys are, sometimes, when you have the government authorizing weapons transactions over borders in the name of *goodness*, when in fact we have results like the murder of DEA agents with those same weapons. It's a travesty!"

"I agree and not to mention the fact that most of those weapons were *lost* in the shuffle. We can get to the moon and if we really want, we can monitor someone going to the bathroom in their own home, but the government can't keep track of deadly weapons?" ZenJa asked in disgust.

"That's why they need people like you and me, ZenJa. Someone has to do the dirty work and try to bring civility back to the country. It's a thankless task, but I feel I do the best I can."

"I have some chicken and rice heating up, in the oven, if you'd like to come over for dinner?"

"I already ate, but I'll keep you company, if you'd like."

"Don't you have to go home, first, and feed your dog?" ZenJa asked, again shaking her head at the lies that so easily slipped from the man's lips. She wondered if everything he verbalized, were in fact, all lies. Was this his way of dealing with his past. She imagined it might not have been as care-free as he indicated, in his younger days. He obviously loved his father and his wife, if he had indeed been married and she wondered if his whole life was an untruth. She hoped he trusted her enough, one day, to fill in the rest of the blanks.

Once the duo was seated, ZenJa dished up two small plates with her special chicken and rice recipe and beers for each of them.

"Levi dug into the meal, as if he hadn't eaten all day. "This is delicious, ZenJa. You're a very good cook."

"I enjoy cooking when I have guests. I never bother for myself. I usually only put something in the micro-wave for myself."

"How did you know you'd be having a guest for dinner tonight or is there someone else coming over, later?" Levi asked, raising his eyebrows to tease his hostess.

"I expected you to show up at dinner time. Most men do, from what I hear," she replied and smiled.

"I can see why they'd flock to your dinner table. This really is delicious," Levi said while eating another bite of his dinner. "Not to say men may not flock to you for other reasons," he added. "You're a very beautiful woman."

"My work is my life, at the moment. I have many things to accomplish before I think about any kind of relationships. I have to find my sister."

"Weren't you just telling me, yesterday, how I should try and get on with my life, not in so many words, but in your own way, that's what you were indicating."

"It's always easier to give advice to others, than it is to take ones own, Levi," ZenJa explained while she grabbed another beer for herself and her guest.

"You aren't going try and get me drunk and take advantage of me, are you, my dear?" Levi asked and smiled.

"Not on your life."

"I don't mix business and pleasure and for another thing, we can't be a couple, like you are probably suggesting. We both work for the FBI," ZenJa said, in hopes she could finally discover who Levi really did work for.

"Who said I'm FBI? Come on ZenJa, do you think I'm as dumb as I look?"

"Well, at least you have to give me credit for trying and I noticed you didn't dismiss that fact that we could be a couple?"

"I think I answered that question the other night, ZenJa."

"It's going to be a long day for me, tomorrow, so I'd like to thank you for a wonderful dinner and say good night, unless you'd like some help with the clean up and dishes?"

"No, thank you, I can manage and I'm glad you liked my recipe. It was one of my mother's favorites. Any idea how long you'll be up north?" she rambled.

"No...my boss hasn't said," Levi replied after realizing ZenJa was, again, trying to find out who his boss was. He let that slide, but smiled.

"Will you be coming to the birthday party, tomorrow?"

"I think I'd like that. Keith and Darlene seem like nice people. Can I bring gifts for the kids?"

"That would be a nice gesture. Maybe something for indoor activities for those pesky days it rains," ZenJa suggested.

"Okay, I'll pick up some puzzles, books and maybe a race set for the boy and a doll house for the girl?"

"That'll be a very nice thing, Levi. I know you're tough on the outside, but not so tough on the inside."

"I've never been accused of that, ZenJa. I wouldn't be deceived, if I were you," he warned and closed the door on his way toward his condo.

****

The birthday celebrants arrived promptly at 2:00; ZenJa and Levi had the gifts all arranged outside the garage, when the sun peaked out after a morning rain shower.

"Welcome! We're so happy you could make it," ZenJa exclaimed while the children scampered out of the car, ran up the driveway, and squealed with delight at the presents and the decorations. Only seconds later, they discovered the food and huge birthday cake that were spread out on the table before their parents left the vehicle.

"Is all this for us?" Rick asked with the excitement of a small child, his sister echoing him, as well.

"Mom! This is for us?" Betsy asked.

"It sure is," Darlene and ZenJa responded together.

"Let me introduce you two, to our new friends. The lady that made all this possible," Darlene said to her children.

"This nice lady is ZenJa and this nice man is her neighbor, Levi. And these two darlings are Rick and Betsy," Darlene said as the children walked up to their host and hostess and shook their hands. And this lovely young lady is my younger sister, the children's babysitter and real estate agent and secretary for an agency; may I introduce you to my sister, Darcy Peterson. Darcy this is Levi and ZenJa. I have no idea what their last names are..." Darlene mentioned and smiled.

"It's nice to meet you, Darcy. My whole name is ZenJa Beckwith and my neighbor is Levi Harris."

"My pleasure," Darcy responded and shook her new acquaintance's hands.

"Look, everyone! This is so great! You did this for us?" Betsy exclaimed.

"What do you say, kids?" Keith asked.

"Thank you so much," the children both said in unison.

"This is very nice of you do to this for us," Rick said, his sister shaking her head in agreement.

"It's our pleasure," ZenJa exclaimed and encouraged the children to try out their new vehicles, before opening their other gifts and having lunch and cake.

"I can't believe this, dad! Check out this new Hummer," Rick cheered and slowly began to drive the vehicle across the front lawn.

"Be careful, Rick," Keith warned and helped push Betsy on her new tricycle.

Levi walked along beside the father and daughter and the ladies grabbed lawn chairs and glasses of iced tea, watching with interest.

"You don't have any of your *children's toys* under the seat of your car, do you, Levi? I mean, I'm just asking. My children aren't used to playing with Glocks," Keith mentioned and smiled.

"No, my kids are out at the firing range playing with their AK-47's today," Levi said and laughed.

"Yes, they're out there with your *dog*, right?" ZenJa asked.

"Exactly! You know Rover get's bored just hanging around the house," Levi replied at the same moment Alex sped up the road and parked his Mustang on the street; the driveway, being full of cars and toys.

"Hello, folks. I heard there's a birthday party and I was hoping I wasn't late to have some cake," Alex said and sauntered up the driveway, avoiding the Hummer that sped across his path and once again headed toward the front and back yards with Betsy bringing up the rear on her bike.

Levi knew he hadn't mentioned a birthday party to his brother and when he glanced at ZenJa, he realized she, obviously, had.

"I even brought a pinata," Alex added proudly. "Instead of putting my face on it, I decided *Sponge Bob Square Pants* is the cartoon character of the season? Oh! I see you already have two other pinatas?" he replied, sadly when he noticed *Hello Kitty* and *Spider Man* attached to two tree limbs.

"That is very sweet of you, Alex," ZenJa began.

"We can never have too many things to smack around at a child's party," Levi added.

"With that said, you're just in time for the opening of the other gifts, the food, and cake and of course the games," ZenJa replied and glared at Levi.

"Let me introduce you to our friends you don't know. This is Keith, who owns Keith's Automotive and Towing and this lovely lady is his wife, Darlene. Their children, Rick and Betsy, are the rascals driving the vehicles," ZenJa offered while Alex shook hands with Keith and Darlene. "And this other lovely young lady is Darlene's sister, Darcy."

"This man's name is Alex Lyons," ZenJa simply said, not making any reference to Levi being his brother.

"It's my pleasure to meet you all," Alex replied while keeping an inquisitive eye on Darlene's younger sister, who was obviously attending the party alone.

"Do you folks have last names?" Alex asked and smiled.

"We are Keith and Darlene Morrison and my sister in law, Darcy Peterson," Keith replied.

The party progressed well into the evening, with music, games, and Levi, keeping his word, played the part of the donkey, with the bull's-eye on the cast he had on his arm and everyone took turns wacking all three pinatas before Alex cut them down from the tree branch and sliced them open with a steak knife, so the children could divide up the contents.

Alex and Darcy appeared to be comfortable around each other and both, Levi and ZenJa were happy to discover he could be civilized when he wanted to and had been on his best behavior.

The adults tried, unsuccessfully, to fit into the Hummer and ride the tricycle, while the food was enjoyed by all who attended. Last, but not least the children blew out the candles on the birthday cake after a rousing chorus of Happy Birthday. The cake and ice cream, was devoured and shortly after, the children fell asleep on the sleeping bags ZenJa had placed in several webbed outdoor lounge chairs.

The adults gathered around the outdoor barbeque pit, drinking iced tea and finally had a chance to get to know one another a little bit more.

"Well, I've discovered you work for a financial analyst, ZenJa," Darlene said. "What's your occupation, Levi?"

"Up until recently, I delivered pizza, but now I'm thinking of branching out and maybe having my own development company. I'd like to be in investing," he added and noticed ZenJa rolling her eyes again at the bold-faced lie, she assumed he was telling, again.

"You delivered pizza in that car?" Darlene asked while Keith looked on and also shook his head. He knew what Levi delivered wasn't pizza, but he really didn't want to know what, in fact, he did deliver, if anything. A man didn't need a Glock, under the front seat of his car, to deliver pizza, or after some consideration, he realized how the world was deteriorating and carrying a weapon might not be such a bad idea.

" What about you?" Darcy asked Alex. "What's your profession?"

"I'm a single, Virgo, who likes walks on the beach, dancing the tango, NASCAR, Ford Mustangs, and all kinds of music," Alex replied in his usual jovial manner.

"Idiot!" Levi whispered, but smiled.

"You love NASCAR?" Darcy asked, ignoring the other bologna she knew was his way of being cute and not divulging what his true occupation was. If he didn't want to disclose it, so be it. She had no problem with that. She hardly knew him and it didn't matter to her what he did. She just met him.

"Yeah, I do...do you?" he asked the lovely young lady.

"Oh yes! I go to the races here at Martinsville and Charlotte, I even went to a race in Loudon, New Hampshire, and Daytona Beach once, with Darlene, a few years ago. We had a blast. I loved every minute of it!"

"Who's your favorite driver?" Alex asked while the other adults watched, with intrigue, at the man who sat before them...who almost seemed to be human; his brother was comforted to see.

"Oh, are there any other drivers, but Tony Stewart and those who drive for Stewart-Haas Racing?" Darcy asked and laughed.

"Oh, my dear! You're so mistaken, Tony may have won a few championships, but this is the year Joey Lagano, again, will take home the trophy, and of course everyone is crazy about Dale Jr."

"I'll agree with the fact that everyone's a member of Jr. Nation," Darcy replied, while the other adults thought they were listening to someone speaking in a foreign language.

"Well, folks, I don't want to overstay my welcome, so I'll be heading out. Maybe we can take in a race, down the road, Darcy or at least go for a ride in my car," Alex said and stood to make his exit.

"That sounds like fun," Darcy said shyly.

"It was so nice of you to stop by, Alex. I'm glad you did," ZenJa said and meant it.

"I'm kinda glad I did, too," he said and smiled at the adults; his eyes lingering on his new friend, Darcy Peterson.

"Keep in touch," Levi said and waved his brother goodbye.

"Oh my God! This has been the best birthday party the children have ever had," Darlene expressed, looking at her sleeping children. "I'll never be able to thank you all enough."

"Just keep your children close to you. That's all I ask," ZenJa suggested.

"We'll have to be leaving, soon, too, but let us help with the clean up," Keith said as he and his wife began to gather the food to bring into the house.

"Let me put the left overs in separate containers and you're more than welcome to take all this home. I'll never eat all this and it'll just spoil."

"Only if you're sure. You've done more than enough, already," Keith mentioned.

"Don't forget, the children will have another surprise when they wake up tomorrow morning," ZenJa reminded the couple. "The fellas at Home Depot, called a while ago, and said the gym's all set up and ready to go."

"Wait until the kids see that when they wake up tomorrow," Darlene said and clasped her hands in glee.

After the clean up was complete, the exhausted children, their Aunt Darcy, and parents left to go home and recover from what had been an exciting and wonderful day for all.

"Do you want a beer?" ZenJa asked while leading Levi into her condo."

"Sure, I guess one or two will do," he replied.

"That was a wonderful thing you did for that family, ZenJa," he began after the couple sat on the couch, in ZenJa's living room. " It's nice to find a great family who appreciates the value of hard work, struggles along the way, and aren't too proud to accept an occasional gift from a stranger."

"Thank you, Levi. I appreciate that. But under normal circumstances, I wouldn't be able to afford such extravagances."

"What changed all that?" Levi asked, innocently.

"I haven't mentioned this to anyone else and don't plan to, but my parents lawyer contacted me and I've inherited a *small* bit of capital, so I want to do some charitable acts and make several donations to worthy causes, in my memory of my sister and parents."

"That's very generous..." Levi began when his cell phone rang.

"Excuse me, ZenJa. Oh! It's my *boss*," he added and smiled.

"Yo! What's up," he asked.

"Oh, I gather you're not alone?" Montgomery asked, knowing that was the response his agents gave him when it might not be safe to make any verbal responses with the exception of yes or no.

"Correct," Levi replied realizing ZenJa was looking at him intently.

"We got the ballistics back on the two murdered girls in Longberry...the O'Leary and Childress girls and they're a match of two different weapons that Connors exchanged with Alex."

"That's great news! But we don't know who the actual shooter was?" Levi asked. "The prints on the weapons can't be any use, can they? Not after all this time."

"I thought you weren't able to speak freely?" Montgomery asked.

"It's okay, now," the agent replied feeling ZenJa's eyes boring into his skin and put his cell phone on speaker, so ZenJa could listen.

"What about DNA? Any word on that, from the...victims?"

"It appears, from DNA we've taken from Connors and Jackson Miller, the O'Leary girl was, if not murdered by Connors, he was at least the rapist and the Childress girl was violated by Miller."

"So it isn't one-hundred percent proof positive who the actual murderer or murderers are?"

"Not at this time."

"No confessions yet?" Levi asked

"No, but we have Brian working on his brother. Very slowly and delicately, to gain Jackson's trust and make him realize once he gets his connection to these crimes off his chest, the better it'll be for him."

"Brian's doing a good job?" Levi asked to confirm the status of the case.

"Yes, he's amazing. I'm recommending him for the FBI or..." Monty began and Levi quickly shut the speaker of his cell phone off; " to join us in AFT, once this mess is sorted out."

"Sounds like a good plan. He's obviously proven his integrity."

"That's all I know, now. I just wanted to check in with you before you leave for New Hampshire."

"Wait! What about the DNA results on the skeletal remains found on Blackberry Road; you remember the remains that included the name plate with ORS on it?"

"Thanks for reminding me. We got that information back and it appears those bodies had been there before any children had been missing from that area. It was determined they had been abducted from Maine before the Olsen and Winters girls were reported missing."

"So who are these two victims?" Levi asked and turned his cell phone back on to the speaker, setting.

"They were two runaways, whose paths obviously ran across Connors. They were a brother and sister, twelve year old twins, named Josh and Eve Smithfield. Their families have been notified and as expected, are at least relieved to know their children have been found and so has the alleged perpetrator."

"I can tell you exactly when their bodies were at least thrown over the embankment!" ZenJa exclaimed, loud enough for ATF Director Monty Montgomery to hear.

"Brian Miller, Molly, and I were talking about the exact date Connors' police jacket was ripped and his name tag was missing and how he said he ripped it checking his oil. Both Molly and Brian said it was in 1995...before any children were missing from Longberry. Molly remembered the exact date because that was the day her divorce became final!" ZenJa added.

"Okay, I heard that and I'll check with my sources and confirm that statement," the ATF Director said. "Good work," he added.

"So, with that said and how those pieces are coming together, what's the plan, once I get back to New Hampshire?" Levi asked.

"Just go to Lake Winnie. Instructions will be there," Montgomery stated. "Agent Wyman is still in the area, in his Impala, and he'll give you the low down."

"Oh, okay. I know where he's hold up."

"And by the way, your brother will also be working this case with you. I know how much time you boys enjoy spending time together," Montgomery replied and chuckled.

"Oh! Fuck that!" Levi yelled into the phone; his boss continued to laugh before disconnecting the call.

"Thanks for that helpful information, ZenJa. I know there's been so much going on, it's hard to keep all this straight."

"I'm glad they are making headway with the Childress and O'Leary cases and am glad those parents in Maine will find some closure, after all this time, but my sister, Olive, Ashley and Rose-Ann are still missing."

"I know ZenJa and I pray you have some answers soon," Levi offered.

"With the actual evidence we have, I'm in hopes the jury will accept any circumstantial evidence and that will be enough for a conviction?"

"I'd hope this jury, when convened, will be more knowledgeable about the law and justification for conviction with the use of circumstantial evidence than the jury in another high profile case that was held, not so long ago, down south," Levi replied shaking his head.

"I couldn't agree more."

"I'm sorry to have to tell you this news, ZenJa, after we've had such a wonderful day."

"It gives me hope that there is a future for us, especially children."

"Well, Levi, I don't mean to scoot you out the door, but I'm beat and really want to go to bed."

"Okay, neighbor. I'll see you tomorrow. Maybe we can go for a ride, when I sober up," Levi said and laughed.

"I don't think two beers is going to make a drunk out of you."

"Good night ZenJa," Levi said and patted her hand, once again and walked toward his condo.

"Say good night to *Rover*, for me," ZenJa yelled before Levi closed his door.

"I'm going to have to buy a dog, now, so it seems. At least this way, something in my life will appear to be real and true," he said out loud and climbed the stairs to shower before he slept for the night.

Chapter 42

On Monday morning the skies in New Hampshire dawned on what was to be a gloriously sunny day. The air was fresh and fragrant, from the smell of spring flowers, Levi Harris noticed while he drove to the Center Street Jail. He'd been notified that Officer Brian Miller was scheduled to have meetings with his brother and Bob Connors and he wanted to witness the telephone exchange between the parties, per orders of his boss, Matthew Montgomery.

"I'm here to visit my brother, Jackson Miller and afterward I'd like to see Chief...I mean Bob Connors," Officer Brian Miller informed the corrections officer in charge of interviewing people, arriving to see their friends or family members, in the city jail.

"Here's my license," he continued.

"Yes, your name's on the list. Please step through the metal scanner."

Knowing in advance that such procedures were always enacted, Brian only brought in his license and the clothes on his back. His other possessions were locked, securely in the trunk of his car.

"Here's your ticket, number six. You know the routine," the guard said and opened the heavy metal door to allow the guest to see his brother.

"I'll give you fifteen minutes with Miller and the other fifteen with Connors."

"Thank you, sir."

"Hey...just asking," the correctional officer began. "Are you making any headway?"

"I'm trying," Brian answered and entered the cold, gray walls that felt like the inside of a coffin and sat down on the stark, metal stool.

Several minutes later, Jackson Miller sat down, on a stool, that was separated from his brother by bulletproof glass, and nodded before picking up the phone; their only means of communicating.

"How are you doing, Jackson? You look at little bit better than you did the last time I saw you."

"I'm doing okay. Thanks for coming."

"Did you get the magazines and books Mom sent?"

"Yes, thanks. Funny, being a teacher and assistant principal for so many years, I never read *In War and Peace*. I guess I'll have plenty of time to finish it, won't I?"

"Yeah, I guess," Brian said sadly.

"Have you seen your lawyer?"

"Yes, he was here yesterday."

"What's he say, if you want to talk about it, if not, I understand. You remember these phone calls are taped."

"I'm going to do the right thing, Brian. That's all I'm going to say."

"I'm glad to hear that, Jackson. It takes a lot of courage to do what you know, in your heart, is the right thing. I admire you for that."

"I want to get this over with as quickly as possible."

"I can understand."

"So, on a brighter note...remember the tree you planted for Mom for Mother's Day, so many years ago; the lilac? It's more than tripled in size and the color is brilliant. It's the deepest dark purple I've ever seen. She picked some, the other day and brought them in the house and put them in a vase with some tulips. She loves them and enjoys them so much, Jackson. She thinks of you every time she sees them," Brian said in an effort to cheer his somber brother.

"I'm glad she likes them. I always liked Lilacs, myself."

"So, what have you been up to, Brian?"

"Well, you'll be so proud of me, I think. I've been recruited to...work for the government. I can't say where or doing what, but I'm thrilled."

"I'm proud of you, Brian. I always have been. I wish I had followed in your footsteps, but I guess wishing doesn't produce results, now does it?"

"You can still do a lot of good, in here, you know. You do realize there are men in here who can't read or write? I know that may come as a surprise to you, but it's true. I remember one guy telling me, a while ago, that the inmates would charge him, money, cigarettes, snacks, or whatever, to read the letters his family wrote to him. That guy was blackmailed because he couldn't read. You can do something about that for people like him, Jackson. You're an educator. You can teach these men all kinds of subjects, not just reading and writing, but math, science and even about the stars. It might give them cause to find a reason to live and go out into the world to become a better person."

Brian detected a slight brightness in his brother's eyes, for a moment. Maybe he had successfully given Jackson a reason to live.

"I'm going to come back, when the front office is open and see what I can do to initiate a program like that here, or if there is one that's in operation, now, I'll see if you can become affiliated with it. You have a lot to offer."

"If that does happen, Brian, it'll be a while until I'm allowed to do that sort of work. You have to become a trustee, to travel around the jail."

"In the mean time, you can make up some lesson plans, just like the old days. It'll help make the time go by and give you a reason to look toward a new day."

"I appreciate all you're doing for me, Brian."

The corrections officer tapped Brian on the shoulder and told him he had two more minutes until Connors was coming down.

"Okay, Jackson, I guess our time's about up. I'll get right on the schooling idea and come back real soon."

"Thanks, again, Brian. I love you," Jackson said and was led out one door, just before Connors appeared through another; neither man seeing the other.

"I love you, too Jackson," Brian said and wiped tears from his eyes.

Brian's demeanor changed dramatically when Bob Connors took the stool his brother just left. This man, once his boss, was no friend of his, but he needed to get as much information out of him as possible. He wasn't concerned about their conversations being taped. He didn't give a fuck if Connors rotted in hell or not.

"Thanks for coming, Brian," Connors said in his usual larger than life, conceited self.

"Glad to come by. How have you been doing?" Brian asked to be civil.

"Okay. I get outside to exercise several times a day. We're lucky here, we get to shower each day and make phone calls and watch television."

"You're in general population?" Brian asked in surprise. "No one knows you're here or recognizes you?"

"No, I think they've kept anyone who may know me, away from me."

"Well, I hope it stays that way," Brian said not really caring if everyone knew who this man was or not.

"Has your lawyer been to see you?"

"Yes, he's been here almost every day. I know what he's trying to do."

"What's he trying to do, Bob?"

"He's trying to make me admit to things."

Brian knew exactly what Bob was referring to. Connors' lawyer was trying to get him to confess to his part in the disappearances and murders and hopefully, tell where the missing girls were...buried.

"Don't you trust your lawyer, to know what's in your best interest? Isn't it time to...find some faith and ask God for direction, Bob? To end this hell for everyone, concerned."

"Now, you're talking like I'm guilty of something," the man said and smiled evilly.

"Well, I think it's pretty common knowledge about some weapons and explosives, in your past history."

"Oh, that! Yes, that's true. I've already told my lawyer all about that stuff. He says that's petty stuff."

"Yes, I suppose those are petty crimes, with the exception of the murder of two SWAT members and one state trooper in that event at the school."

"So, if you're not talking about that, what are you referring to, Bob. Are you suggesting I'm talking about something else?" Brian baited the man.

"Oh, I thought you were talking about the missing..."

"Go on," Brian encouraged.

"The missing money from the petty cash drawer," the former police chief replied and smiled, again.

Brian knew there was no getting through to this son of a btich. He was as evil as the day was long and the man enjoyed the attention he was getting and Brian's visits even more, he assumed. He found pleasure in taunting him, much like he taunted his victims before he murdered them, no doubt.

"You think you're holding all the cards, don't you Bob? You think you're safe; that your life will be spared until you confess and tell us what we want to know, don't you?"

"Well, frankly, I do," he said proudly.

Levi had heard enough. He slammed down the phone extension, that was hidden behind a two way mirror, situated behind Brian Miller, unknown to any visitors or prisoners.

"What was that?" Connors asked when he heard the click.

"I don't know," Miller replied truthfully. "Static, I guess. You're aware, of course, these phone calls are taped and monitored, right?' Miller asked.

"Yes, of course I do. That just sounded funny," he replied looking around suspiciously.

"Well, to get back to our conversation, Bob, if I were you, I'd keep an eye on my back. You seem a little, how should I say it, cocky about your situation. As my mother used to say, "walls have ears," Brian said and left the man sitting on the stool, looking inquisitive and puzzled.

Once outside Center Street Jail, Brian walked to his car and got in, at the same time, Levi strolled over to speak with him.

"Hello, Levi," Miller said, obviously still upset with his conversation with former police chief. "I almost didn't recognize you with your sunglasses on."

"Visiting your brother, Brian?" Levi asked with the innocence of a small child.

"Yes, and that ass hole Connors. I'm trying to get some information out of him, but so far, no luck. That son of a bitch...I swear I'll kill that fucker some day."

Without divulging the fact he'd heard both conversations Brian Miller had that morning, Levi continued to play dumb.

"What about your brother? Have you gotten any useful information from him, yet?"

"No, but from the way he's talking he's confiding or will be confiding in his lawyer. I think, very soon, we'll find out what he knows. I pray he'll do the right thing, Levi."

"Have you had breakfast, yet?" Levi asked.

"No, I haven't, but I sure am hungry."

"Let's go over to the diner across the way and we can get caught up, if you want."

"See you there," Miller said and watched Levi walk to his Camaro.

"Are you fellas ready to order," the waitress asked after the gentlemen had studied the menu for a few minutes.

"Yes, I'll have the number three, over easy, with OJ and black coffee," Levi replied while the waitress stared, obviously curious about the fact he continued to wear his sunglasses.

"Hangover," Levi offered the inquisitive woman.

"I'll have the number four with sausage and hash browns and coffee. Plenty of maple syrup, if you please," Brian said and smiled.

"So, you just get back in the area?" Brian asked.

"Yes, I'm meeting a friend of yours, Brent Wyman."

"Oh, the guy in the silver Impala."

"I haven't seen him around in a few days."

"Oh, trust me, he's here," Levi said and smiled.

"I've no doubt. You guys are like the wind. One knows your around, but no one can see you."

"That's the way it should be Brian. Lesson number one," Levi said at the same time their orders arrived.

"Just to let you know, our Impala's been laid up for a while. Wyman *might* be driving something else, by now."

"Who knows, I may be driving something else, by tomorrow," Levi suggested, his eyes the color of cold steel, once again.

"I do remember the advice you gave me."

"What advice is that, Miller?"

"Trust no one."

"Exactly. Hell, half the time I don't trust myself," he said and laughed.

"You're one funny guy," Brian said.

"My second piece of advice, Brian, is don't trust anyone who smiles a lot," he said, smiled and ate a piece of his toast.

"You know, Levi. You actually scare the shit out of me, if you want me to be honest."

Levi peered over his sunglasses and said, "Good! Now you're learning. I heard those words of wisdom from my mother. She smiled a lot, too," he continued, his eyes nearly the color of coal.

"So, to get back to business; you're not making any headway talking to Connors?"

"Nope, that son of a bitch sits there smiling...yes, smiling." Miller began and realized what Levi was talking about.

"He sits there with a fucking smirk on his face. He's taunting us. I've no doubt the same way he taunted his victims."

"Alleged victims," he was reminded while Levi drank his orange juice.

"How's your mother taking Jackson being in jail?"

"She's not doing well. I know she'll never visit him, not where he is now."

"Did Jackson spend much time at your mother's house? Do you think he may have hidden items or anything of that nature on the property?"

"He usually went over there on Sunday for dinners, but when his wife left him, he started going over more often. I guess he was looking for free meals. He always hated to cook."

"When did his wife leave and do you know why she left him?"

"Oh, I don't know. It was shortly after they were married. He wasn't married very long and my guess is, it was about twenty years ago. Why she left, I don't know, but I think she met someone else and simply took off."

"Do you know for a fact, she actually did leave?"

"What are you asking?"

"Do you think she actually left on her own accord or could she have been one of Jackson's first victims?"

"Oh my God! It never dawned on any of us! I think I'm going to be sick," Miller replied honestly.

"No, you're not. Future agents do not vomit," he barked, under his breath and finished his eggs and toast.

"Finish your pancakes. Don't let good food go to waste."

From listening to the conversation between Brian and his brother, Levi was almost certain there were bodies or evidence buried on Mrs. Miller's property and he thought Brian might also have come to the same conclusion.

"Do you think he might have buried...stuff at my mother's house?"

"If I were a betting man, I'd say most definitely."

"Oh my God! What am I going to do?"

"How old is your mother, Brian. Is she old enough to want to go into an assisted living facility? Just asking."

"No, but she's wanted to go and visit her sister in Florida for a long time. Maybe now would be a good time for her to go?" Brian suggested.

"I think now would be an awesome time to visit."

"I don't know what her finances are, but if she needs some help with expenses, I'd be more than happy to help her out," Levi replied.

"No, she's fine. She doesn't have a *lot* of money, but she has my father's pension, social security and her own, so money isn't an issue."

"Okay, let's keep all of this just between you and me, for now. Go and convince your mother to go on a well deserved vacation."

"Thanks, I will. You know, you still scare me, but I can see you're a real decent human being," Brian said.

"Don't let that get around," Levi said, finished his juice, left the money for the bill and a nice tip and the two men left the diner.

"Okay, well, I'll let you do whatever it was you were going do, today, Brian. I have some things I have to take care of. See you later," the agent said before leaving the diner and Brian Miller to go his own way.

Levi had a lot of business to take care, before evening fell upon the great state of New Hampshire. His contact, inside the Center Street Jail, was due to report for work at seven that night and Levi had to be in police custody at about the same time.

"How's it going?" ATF Agent Wyman asked Levi and welcomed him into the government's rented home in Wolfboro, New Hampshire.

"Not too bad. How you been?" Levi asked while the men took seats at the kitchen table; in the nicely furnished two bedroom, country home, that bordered along Lake Winnipesaukee.

"You ever get out in the sun?" Levi asked before his host offered him some pizza and Diet Coke. "You're as white as a ghost," he teased.

"Unfortunately, there isn't much time to stroll along the beach in the sunshine, or darkness, for that matter. I'm usually trapped in my vehicle."

"Hopefully, soon, we'll all be able to take a vacation. I know it's been a long time coming for us all."

"I couldn't agree more," Wyman said finishing his pizza.

"You get home, often?" Levi asked.

"I've been back a few times, in recent weeks, what with Connors and Jackson in jail, but I'd like to see my son before he graduates from college and my wife before she goes on Social Security," he replied sarcastically.

"Your son is what...five years old and your beautiful wife can't be more than twenty one?" Levi asked and smiled.

"If she were here, she'd kiss you. Actually, she's twenty eight, one year older than me."

"I'll take her up on that kiss when we get together again. Speaking of which, as you know, I'm going to be around for a while. Why not invite your family up for a little vacation? They can either stay here with you, or if you feel safer with them somewhere else, we can arrange that. I can take over some of your surveillance duties while I'm still recovering from my *broken arm* you failed to mention or ask about, " Levi said teased.

"Stop whining! You always were a baby," Wyman said and laughed. "Trust me, I'm so sick of hearing about your damn arm, I could puke."

"Who's been talking about my poor injured arm?"

"That's all Montgomery's been talking about for weeks. Levi this...Levi that...His poor arm! Good God, one would think he was your father, for God's sake," Wyman continued to tease his friend and fellow agent.

"He's just concerned about his best agent, that's all."

"I'm glad to see your sense of humor wasn't injured or diminished in the bombing," Wyman added while he brought the remains of the food and drinks to the kitchen counter.

"So, what's up with the detail you're on now?" Levi asked.

"There's a local trucking company with two logging trucks. From what the informant tells us, it's her husband and brother who drive and operate the company. They've broken into several warehouses after dismantling the cameras, of course, and stolen approximately a thousand weapons, some being

AK-47's."

"They've also broken into large construction sites and stolen a vast amount of explosives, detonators and the whole nine yards."

"Why use the logging trucks?" Levi asked.

"To use as a cover. They actually do logging for a living, but when they make their drops, they use hollowed out logs, placed in the front of the trucks, masked among the real logs, in case they're stopped at a weigh station or for some other incident."

"So, I'm assuming they use the same fake logs all the time. In other words, they make their delivery and then take the hollowed out logs back to use again? It would be time consuming to keep making new ones for their drops?" Levi reasoned.

"We'll soon learn where this business is, I assume?" Levi continued.

"Yes, we're supposed to hear from the informant within several days."

"What makes sense is to view the property where the trucks usually are and where the bogus logs might be stored. If the logs are on the property when we visit, obviously they aren't making any drops, but the minute the logs leave on the trucks, it would be reasonable to assume they are packed with weapons and explosives aboard the truck for delivery," Levi continued.

"So you propose to do what?" Wyman asked.

"Put GPS systems on several of the logs and when they're activated, follow them."

"Follow them until they reach their destination?" Wyman asked.

"Probably, so we can see where the final destination is and who the recipient is."

"But what doesn't make sense to me, is, they can't drive log trucks on interstates and those trucks can't be driven major long distances, like across country," Wyman added.

"Exactly, so they must be making drops somewhere close to home."

"Hopefully, we'll find out soon," Wyman said.

"Not to change the subject, but we're still on for tonight?" Levi asked before he left the secure dwelling.

"It's a date," Wyman replied.

Levi spent the remainder of the afternoon at his lake front home. He wanted to relax before the events were to unfold at Center Street Jail, that evening, and he wanted to call ZenJa and see how she was doing. He, also, felt obligated to check in with his brother to make sure he was in New Hampshire.

With a glass of iced tea in hand, Levi made himself comfortable on the deck and watched the sail and speed boats cruise along the water before making his call.

"Hi, ZenJa. How are ya doing?"

"I'm fine, how are you? Are you in New Hampshire, yet?"

"I'm fine, also and yes, I arrived early this morning."

"I heard you leave in the afternoon, so I assumed you would have made it by now. I kinda thought you would've stopped by to say goodbye, but I know you're busy," ZenJa whined.

"I was going to, but I had to much to do, to get ready," he lied.

"I was thinking you were afraid to come over and say hello; maybe you were starting to peel away some of the layers of brick you've surrounded yourself with, in recent years; afraid you might be healing from some of your wounds?"

"Have you been taking some more of the psych classes, again, ZenJa?" Levi asked and laughed.

"There, that's better. This is the Levi I know and ...," she began and stopped short of finishing the sentence.

"The Levi you know and what, ZenJa?"

"The Levi I know and who's a jerk."

"Oh ZenJa, talking to you has made my entire day complete."

"I'm glad I could be here for you," she replied.

"Oh, by the way, I wanted to ask you, when I *do* get a dog, Rover, will you be able to puppy-sit for him while I'm on the road? Actually, I was thinking of getting a shelter dog, while I'm up here and bringing him home when I come back."

"No way, Jose'! I'm not watching any pet of yours while you wander all over the countryside."

"You sound like you miss me already!"

"Don't flatter yourself, mister."

"I love it when you talk dirty to me, ZenJa."

"You're incorrigible," she replied.

"See! There you go again, using those naughty words, when talking to me."

"Oh my goodness! Why did you call, just to bother me?" she asked.

"No, I wanted to ask you what kind of dog we should get, remember?"

"Levi, I really don't care what kind of dog, *you*, get. I have to go to work. Some of us have jobs, you know?"

"Oh, I have a job pending, at this very moment, so I will bid you farewell, my damsel in distress," he teased and disconnected the call.

What bothered Levi about this pending assignment was that having his arm still in a cast would make the details to be carried out most difficult, but he had the element of surprise on his side and a cast made a good hiding place for contraband.

A moment after that call, he placed a call to his brother to confirm, he was in New Hampshire.

Levi drove the newly acquired twenty year old *junker*, he purchased from a used car dealer that afternoon, across the alley that led to the Center Street Jail. Promptly at 7:00, that evening, dressed in his orange jumpsuit, that had been provided to him by his connection inside the jail, that morning, a second connection met him with a Sheriff's car, used to transport inmates on their way to the jail, court, or to receive medical treatment when it was necessary.

"You're going to open the door for me, aren't you *Sheriff*?" Levi asked sarcastically. "And don't forget to handcuff me," he added and laughed.

"Oh, I'll handcuff you, you asshole," the man replied.

"Don't make them too tight. I've a broken arm, if you remember."

"You really want to do this?" the man wearing a Sheriff's uniform asked.

"We all have things we have to do. They may not be according to the book, but just what book do we have to follow?" Levi asked.

"I didn't mean that you don't *want* to do this, I'm just wondering if now, with your arm as it is, the timing's right or not."

"The timing's perfect," Levi confirmed as the car and prisoner entered the underground garage. Levi Harris was about to become a resident at Center Street Jail for however long it took to complete the task at hand.

"I hope you ate good before you got here?" the *Sheriff* asked.

"I don't expect to be here very long," Levi replied and exited the car and was met by another *connection*.

"You guys look darling in your outfits," Levi whispered to the *Sheriff* and *Correctional Officer* after the trio entered the elevator, by-passing any and all official admittance procedures actual prisoners were forced to succumb to upon their arrival at the jail.

"Fuck you!" the *Sheriff* replied.

"See you back at the ranch," Levi replied and bid the *Sheriff* on his way. Oh! And don't forget to get the piece of crap, that just barely got me here, towed to the junk yard. It's no longer needed."

"Who's name was it purchased in, if I may ask?"

"Well, yours of course!" Levi said and laughed.

"You fucker!" the man replied and left the facility.

"We're on the second floor, as you can see. Coincidently, Connors was moved to this floor yesterday and he's going to be your cell mate," the *correctional officer* explained, needlessly, but as a ruse to conform to standard procedures.

"How long do you think you'll need?"

"Give me fifteen minutes and then we're out'a here," Levi replied.

"You're one confident bastard," the officer replied.

"Do you want to be here any longer than necessary?"

"Not on your life! And you're sure Connors has never seen you?" the *officer* asked, once again, so nothing would go wrong.

"No. He's never seen me and funny thing is, I'm going to be the last person he does see."

"Okay, here's the cell. Keep your head down. I'll leave the cell door unlocked and will be just down the hall," the *correctional officer* whispered.

"Well, Connors, you have a room mate, tonight." the officer announced out loud.

"I thought I was supposed to have a single cell?" Connors asked with apparent alarm.

"This ain't the Ritz Carlton and hell, this guy's harmless," the officer replied and removed Levi's handcuffs. "Hell, he even has a broken arm."

"What's he in for?" Connors asked.

"I forgot to return two library books last week," Levi replied and laughed.

Connors was visibly upset, his hands were shaking and his eyes were darting around the cell.

"Maybe I should ask you what you're in for?" Levi remarked.

"I... I've been wrongly accused of several misdemeanors," he lied. "I'll be out of here in no time," he replied and sat on his bunk, cowering in the corner.

"Well, before you go, let me introduce myself," Levi said after the *correctional officer* closed the cell door leaving the two men with the entire floor of the jail unoccupied, with the exception of themselves.

"Just to be social, I understand your name is former Police Chief Bob Connors?" Levi asked before the man violently began to shake.

"Who...who are you?" he pleaded.

"I'm the man who wants to know where you buried the missing girls from the Longberry area."

"Oh my God!" Connors began to scream. "Help me, somebody help me! He's going to kill me."

"Connors, calm down," Levi advised. There's no one here to help you. There's no one in this section of the jail. It's just you and me, so are you going to tell me what I want to know?"

"Who kidnaped the girls and who raped and murdered them?" Levi asked, always assuming the girls were dead.

"I'm not tell you anything!" he continued to scream, but shortly spoke again.

"It was Miller! He did it all. I was only into the weapons and explosives. Ask him, he'll tell you. He was a sick mother-fucker," Connors finally replied.

"We already asked him and he said it was you who did most of the dirty deeds. Who do you think we believe?"

Levi realized he wasn't getting anywhere this way. "Why did you have to dispose of Olive and Zippy?" They were innocent girls. What did they see that made you realize you had to kill them?" Levi suggested.

Connors was crying uncontrollably; a shadow of the obnoxious man he portrayed himself to be outside of the jail cell.

"Is this how the girls cried just before you killed them, Connors?" Levi asked, his eyes as black as coal.

"They...they saw a weapon I had hidden under the seat of my car and the ugly one, Olive, stole it when she got out of the car, the day I left them off at the restaurant."

"So? What was so special about that weapon?" Levi asked, intrigued by the events as they were unfolding.

"It was used in the murders of the Olsen and Winters girls, years ago."

"Why did you murder those girls?" Levi asked.

"It was...it was an accident," Connors stuttered.

"Accident my ass!"

"I didn't mean for it to go so far. I just wanted to kiss them and they broke loose and started to run..."

"So you raped and murdered them to shut them up?"

"I was young and they kept telling me how good looking I was."

"They were teasing you, right? They led you on?" Levi growled at this man who was putting the blame on two innocent girls for their own deaths.

"Yeah, that was it, exactly."

Levi thought he was about to vomit, but he recalled ATF agents don't barf."

"The Winters and Olsen girls were never found, so why risk murdering more girls?"

"I wasn't thinking...I mean, Miller convinced me the girls should be killed to shut them up," Connors continued to put the blame on another man.

"So, if Olive found the weapon and stole it, why kill Zippy?" Levi asked to confirm what he already knew.

"When I...I mean, when Miller confronted her about the gun, she told me...I mean, Miller, that she told Zippy about it and that Zippy actually was in possession of it, then.

"So you raped two innocent girls and shot them to death to make it appear to be an actual rape and murder, and nothing more? You're admitting that Olive and Pickles are dead?"

"I didn't...I didn't know what I was doing. I got so confused."

"What did Miller actually have to do with any crimes, if anything at all?"

"He buried the Olsen and Winters girls where they were found on Devil's Point."

"Why did he do that for you? What were you holding over his head?"

"He actually murdered his wife a long time ago and I helped him cover it up, so he was indebted to me. He owed me," Connors yelled in a violent rage.

"So Miller buried his wife on Devil's Point, also?"

"No. he buried her under some tree on his mother's property."

"Was the gun that Zippy, allegedly was in possession of, ever found?"

"No, I never recovered it."

"So you, no doubt, tortured those girls to find out where it was?"

"I'm not talking about it any more."

"WHERE ARE ZIPPY AND OLIVE BURIED?" Levi demanded.

"I'll never tell anyone. ZenJa, that bitch, is lucky to be alive, so she should be thankful for that, even if she never finds her fucking ugly sister."

"Times up," the *correctional officer* announced from the end of the corridor.

"Here, take this mother fucking gun, you fucker and blow your brains out or I'll come back and do it for you, you got it?" Levi glared, fire seemingly appearing from his eyes and threw the loaded weapon in the corner of the top bunk, to allow himself adequate time to leave the confines of the cell and walk toward the exit with the *correctional officer* in tow.

"Before Levi and his accomplice left the Center Street Jail, a shot rang out on the second floor of the jail. Alarms sounded and a chorus of footsteps pounded the hallways.

The two AFT agents left the facility and drove away in a sheriff's car that was later found, abounded, in Laconia, New Hampshire.

Chapter 43

"Thanks for the lift," Levi said as he and Agent Brent Wyman left the new red, Dodge Ram, duel cab, truck Alex was now in possession of for the assignment code named operation AK-47 in a 2x4.

"Everything go as planned?' Alex asked.

"I think so, but to make sure, let's check the nightly news. I don't want to miss all the excitement that was brewing when we left," Levi said and laughed, smirking at Agent Wyman.

Levi turned on the television and offered his guests beer and pizza he'd purchased on the way from the jail.

"You guys certainly looked much more slender in your uniforms," Levi ribbed his company.

"And you, asshole, looked lovely in your orange jumpsuit," Alex retorted.

"I must agree, orange does flatter my complexion," he replied. I think it also brings out the blue in my eyes, too."

Both agents simply shook their heads because the local news was about to be reported.

"We have breaking news from Center Street Jail, in Henderson, New Hampshire," a pleasant looking female newscaster reported.

"It appears there was a suicide attempt at the jail this evening. One lone inmate was shot in the head and has been taken to the Lakes Regional Hospital in grave condition. He's not expected to survive his injuries," the newscaster continued. "The identity of the inmate has not been released and we'll keep you updated when more news is available. The director of the jail has confirmed that this was an isolated incident and the public is not in any danger," the woman continued before speaking about another local story.

"That fucker better not make it," Levi barked.

"Did you get what you wanted out of him?" Alex asked.

"I got a lot of information; whether it's true or not, we'll soon find out. It sounds logical, if a crazy man can be logical," Levi continued questioning his own sanity.

"I got everything I could out of him, otherwise I wouldn't have let him have the weapon."

"What *did* you get out of him? Where Olive and Zippy are buried?"

"No, I'm afraid not."

"So, they're deceased?' Alex asked softly.

"I knew all along, they were. I felt it in my gut and I know ZenJa knows they are, too. She has to know," he continued with a deep sadness in his voice.

"We have an addition to the breaking story we reported, only moments ago, concerning the alleged suicide attempt at the Center Street Jail," the newscaster said. " It's been confirmed, the inmate who was shot has succumbed to his injuries and has passed away."

"Oh thank God! I didn't want to have to dress up in a nurses outfit and help him finish the job," Levi said and drank another beer and consumed another slice of pizza.

There were only two people on earth, who were presently alive, who knew what a dangerous man Levi Harris could be. His brother, AFT Agent Lyons and AFT Agent Wyman. They lived by the *Code of Silence* and had for years.

"Well, you guys better head out. I need to call ZenJa and I need some peace and quiet," Levi explained.

"What? I'm not hanging out here?" Alex asked.

"Hell, no! The government pays for your lodging, somewhere, so take advantage of it."

"You can hang out with me, if you want *for a few days*, until you find our own place," Wyman offered.

"Okay, that sounds fine. Frankly, I must be getting old like you, Levi. I like hanging out alone."

"Maybe you're growing up or maybe you're a little bit interested in Darcy Peterson?"

"She seems like a really nice person," Alex agreed. "I might like to get to know her a little better," he added as he and Wyman left Levi to his own devices for the night.

For an hour, Levi debated whether to call ZenJa about the developments that had transpired that night in New Hampshire or wait and let her get some sleep. He definitely didn't want her hearing about Connors' demise on the television or from someone else, so he thought it in her best interest to waken her and call.

"Hello?" ZenJa asked, having been woken from a deep sleep.

"Hello, ZenJa. I'm sorry to call so late at night, but I didn't want you to hear this news from anyone but me."

"What news?" ZenJa asked surprisingly fully awake and propped up on her bed.

"Shit! Where to start," he began and realized he hadn't fully thought about what and how he was going to tell her the news.

"What in hell is it?" ZenJa demanded.

"According to the nightly news, here in New Hampshire, Connors committed suicide tonight."

"Oh my God! That's terrible! Now I'll never..."

"ZenJa...it's not as bad as it seems."

"What in hell do you mean, it's not as bad as it seems?" she screamed into the phone.

"God damn, why in hell are you down there in Virginia. I can't talk to you over the fucking phone. I'm sick of this!" he yelled.

"What are your plans for the next few days? You have any assignments planned or paperwork you can do on a laptop from here?" Levi asked.

"Unfortunately, Levi, hostage negotiations usually aren't scheduled ahead of time."

"Well, let me go to my bank and hold myself hostage. Would you come and talk me out?" Levi said and began to laugh uncontrollably.

"Levi, are you drunk?"

"Hell, no ZenJa, I only get drunk when you're around!" he replied and continued to laugh; tears falling down his cheeks.

"What in hell is wrong with you Levi?"

"I really have good news for you, ZenJa and I can't wait to share it with you."

"You're referring to Connors, I assume?"

"Oh yeah. I wish you could have..."

"Could have what?" she asked fully awake now.

"I can't talk over the phone, ZenJa. I know my phone's secure, but I have no idea about yours."

"I have no idea, myself and I never felt I had reason the have one, frankly."

"Well, when you get up here, I'll make sure you get one like mine, so we can talk dirty to each other and no one will ever know."

"You're an ass, but other than what we already know about you, can you tell me one thing? Do you know where Zippy and Olive are?" ZenJa whispered, not wanting to hear the answer she knew she was about to receive.

"No, I'm sorry, ZenJa I don't, but I do have a pretty good idea, though," he spoke, ever so softly. "I also believe I have a motive. I know that's not the news you want, but I think I have some very good clues and I do believe we'll have answers, soon and I pray it'll give you closure," he murmured. "We're in this together, ZenJa, from now until the end," he added.

"I'm on my way, Levi. I have some vacation time coming to me and I do have some things I have to discuss with my parents lawyer."

"Don't drive, ZenJa. It'll take to long. Grab a flight and I'll meet you at whatever airport you can get a direct flight from. Probably Manchester/Boston Regional will be best. Let me know what time you'll be in and I'll be there. I need to take a drive, anyway, to clear my head," he added.

"God, ZenJa! I'm so excited! I wish you'd been there to see..." he said and disconnected the call.

Chapter 44

"You're here to visit your brother, Jackson Miller?" the Center Street Correctional Officer asked Brian, who walked to the front desk.

"Yes, thank you."

"I guess you probably heard there was a ruckus here last evening?' the guard whispered when he examined Brian's identification.

"Yes, I heard it on the news," Miller confirmed. "How did...?

"Sometimes, the less questions, the better," the guard warned.

"Is my brother's safety a concern?"

"No, I think he's fine. It appears he was better liked than Connors," the man whispered and showed Miller to the seating room.

A moment later, Jackson Miller walked into the secure side of the visiting area and took the opposite stool, across from his brother and nervously took the phone from the hook and began to speak. "I heard about Connors and his *suicide*."

"I just heard about it, myself, Jackson. What a shame," Brian replied sarcastically. "In some ways I'm glad the mother fucker's dead, but so many questions remain unanswered and only you can respond to them, Jackson."

"I've spoken to my lawyer and I've told him I'm afraid I'm going to *commit suicide*, too," Miller replied, nervousness evident in his voice.

"Jackson, are you insinuating Connors death was other than suicide?"

"Come on, Brian. It doesn't take a rocket scientist to figure it out."

"Jackson, if it was something other than suicide, you have to remember, you don't have enemies like Connors did. Everyone hated him and again, *if* it was something else, obviously someone found out he was here and had it in for him, but if it makes you feel safer, I'll personally speak to the director and voice my concerns."

"Thanks, Jackson, that makes me feel better."

"So, how have you been? You have enough money in your account for snacks and stuff and are the magazines and puzzle books arriving in the mail on schedule?"

"Yes, and again, thank you and Mom for that. It means a lot to me."

"Have you heard if you have any court dates scheduled?"

"No, nothing yet. I know it's going to be at least a year before a trial will start and of course you know I was denied bail."

"So how are you doing, Brian? Have you found a girlfriend, yet?"

"No, not yet, but you know how small Longberry is. I think I'll wait and find someone who's going to be living near where I am, when I finish my training at Quantico."

"That makes sense. When will you be leaving?" Jackson asked knowing that when his brother left, there would be no one to come and visit him, when he spent the remainder of his life behind bars.

"I haven't heard anything definite, yet, but don't worry and you know I'll come and visit as often as I can, when that happens."

"Brian, I wish I had everything to do all over again. I fucked up my life so badly."

"It's never too late to look to God for forgiveness and I think he'd be the first person or spirit, if you will, to tell you the first step is to confess your wrongdoings and move on from there."

"Do you know if Connors ever said anything or confessed to anything?" Miller asked.

"I don't know and as far as I do know, I would say no. I haven't heard otherwise, but even if he has or hasn't, that makes no difference regarding you. You're only responsible for you, not what he did."

"What if they think I did everything?" he asked nervously.

"The justice system isn't looking for revenge and just because Connors is dead, doesn't mean the courts are going to try to pin everything on you. Justice is only served when the truth is discovered. That's all anyone wants, Jackson, the truth, and that's all the families want."

"I guess you're right."

"Is there anything you want to talk to me about or tell me?" Brian prodded.

"No, not now. I have to get things in order."

"What do you mean, things in order?"

"Oh, I just mean things written down and then I'll give it to my lawyer."

"Okay, if you're sure that's what you mean. You aren't thinking of doing something stupid, are you, Jackson?"

"No, I couldn't do that to Mom and you," he said sadly; tears streaming down his face.

"I've checked into the possibility of you doing some teaching, while you're here, and it looks very promising," Brian said brightly.

"That would be nice," Jackson responded automatically.

"You have a lot to offer the others, who have no education, Jackson. You have a wonderful gift of teaching that needs to be given to those who are less fortunate," Brian encouraged.

"Time's up!" the guard called.

"Thanks, again, for coming Brian. I'll see you soon," Jackson responded, stood up, and waved goodbye.

Brian was unable to leave the confines of the jail soon enough. He felt like there was a noose around his neck and sped off down the highway. He was finding it more and more difficult to keep his brother's spirits up when his own were destroyed.

Not long after Officer Brian Miller entered the Longberry Police Station, Levi Harris walked in and sat down in a chair, across the desk, facing him.

"Good morning, Levi. Hell, you look like you haven't had much sleep. Can I get you a cup of coffee?"

"That would be great. I sure could use one and no, I didn't get much sleep. I had things on my mind and you know how that is."

"Yeah, I do. I'm glad you're in town. I was going to get in touch with you, to let you know I've discussed my mother going to Florida to see her sister and she's agreed. She feels everyone is looking at her and talking about Jackson, which they probably are, and any intelligent person knows she isn't guilty of any crimes, any more than I am, but she's getting more paranoid with each passing day."

"When's she leaving?"

"I think she's got a flight leaving from Boston on Friday. That will give her time to close up the house and pack."

"She has no idea why you really want her to take a vacation, does she?"

"Oh, no, of course not. That's just between you and me."

"Good! Glad to hear that."

"Have you had much of a chance to look around her house? I don't mean by starting to dig up the yard, but what about the house, itself?"

"I have complete access to it, why?"

"In order not to waste any more time, until your mother leaves, is there any way you can look in some nooks and crannies for a weapon? I'm not sure what kind or caliber. I'm thinking handgun, but God only knows it could be a rifle; something that could fit under a car seat."

"It's a big old farm house. There could be hundreds of hiding place, but I'll start looking around. Dare I ask where this bit of information may have come from?"

"Nope!" Levi said and smiled. "All I can assure you is that it didn't come from Jackson or Connors. I've never spoken with either one of them," he lied.

"There you go with that smile, again," Miller said and laughed, nervously.

"Just make sure, if you do find it, or any weapon for that matter, in the house, that you're wearing gloves when you remove it from its resting place and preserve it as you would any other evidence."

"Okay, I will."

"Here's your coffee, Levi," he continued and refilled his own cup and sat behind his desk, again.

"So, I guess you heard the news about Connors?"

"Yes, what a shocker, huh?" Levi asked and smiled.

"I'd like to know how in hell he got a gun while he was in jail."

"Maybe he had it stashed all along?"

"You think so?" Miller asked with the innocence of a child.

"I don't know how else he could've gotten one. I could understand if someone slit his throat or bashed his head in, but I have no idea where he would have gotten a gun," Levi commented in an effort to keep from smiling.

"Now, I suppose all his secrets will go to the grave with him. I just stopped by the jail to see Jackson, he of course heard the news, and he's afraid they'll try to pin all the dirty deeds that have been committed in the area on him. He assumes the townsfolk will seek revenge and it appears he's allegedly the only perp remaining alive."

"I don't think you give the good folks of Longberry much credit, Brian. All anyone wants is the truth and to find those who remain missing."

"Not to change the subject, but how's your arm healing?"

"It's almost all better. Another week or so and I'll have the cast off, thank God."

"That's great news."

"I drove by the school and I see they're erecting a new gym and repairing the damage that was done to some of the classrooms," Levi mentioned.

"Hopefully, it'll be ready in time for next year's session. I've heard rumors they're going to name it after the three law enforcement officers who died."

"That's awesome," Levi replied. "Sadly, that's an option, but at least those folks will be remembered.

"So, what brings you up to this neck of the woods?" Miller asked.

"Oh, I've some business to take care of at my house and around the area and I wanted to spend more time at the lake. I love it there."

"I've been trying to decide what field office I'd like to work out of, if I...you know," Brian began.

"Yeah, *if* you make it and *if* they give you a choice, I know all about that."

Shortly after midnight, Officer Brian Miller received a call from the authorities at Center Street Jail, informing him, his brother, Jackson was deceased. The cause of death was determined to be suicide by means of hanging.

Fifteen minutes after receiving that call, Officer Miller was contacted by Jackson's public defender, in an effort to also inform him of his brother's death.

"Thank you for calling me, Attorney Adams. I was contacted by the jail, regarding my brother's death."

"I'm very sorry to hear about this," Adams assured Miller. "I thought we were building trust and I was certain I assured him that he wouldn't be blamed for crimes he hadn't committed. I think that's what he was most concerned about."

"I know. I saw him today and we talked about the same concerns and I thought I had eased his mind, but I guess I failed him," Miller said as tears streamed down his cheeks.

"No, you didn't fail him, Officer Miller. I admire you for what you've tried to do for him. He talked about you all the time."

"I know this may sound rather callous, in light of this development, but did my brother happen to give you any message or written statement?"

"Yes, he did and he asked me not to open it until after his death. I suppose I should have violated that trust and opened it as soon as I received it, today, but if a client can't trust his lawyer..."

"I completely understand and I don't hold you responsible, in the least.

But now that it appears both offenders in the cases we have been looking at for so long, are deceased, what are you required to do with the statement?"

"After I read it, which I haven't yet, I'm required to hand this evidence to the authorities, which I assume would be you or the state or even federal authorities. You've all had a hand in this investigation."

"If I may, I would like to see the statement before you pass it along, if I might? I have a feeling it may contain something pertaining to the fact that some evidence from prior crimes may be buried on my mother's property and/or house in which my mother still resides. If possible, I'd like to eliminate the intrusion of her property until Friday, when she's expected to go on vacation in Florida. To be honest, with you, I spoke to Jackson, the other day and I got the feeling evidence might be in existence and the way he was speaking, today, I was pretty convinced of that fact, so I've arranged for my mother to take a vacation. She obviously has no idea what I suspect and I'd like to leave it that way, if I might. If you could simply wait a few days to read the statement, I would appreciate it, but if, in good conscience, you can't, I understand. Actually, the statement may not even tell us anything of value, I have no idea."

"I am going to open it now, Miller and we'll see where we go from here."

"Okay, I'll wait and if you could at least read the contents to me, I'd appreciate it."

The rattle of an envelope being opened, was evident over the phone, while Brian waited for Attorney Adams to read what was inside.

"This piece of lined paper simply says, *'Thank you for all you and Mom have done for me, Brian. I'm sorry* and *I love you.'*

"That's it?" Brian exclaimed. "How could he do this and not tell us what he knows we all need to know. What the families have to know?" he asked, before he was overcome with sadness, grief, and anger simultaneously. "Jackson...why?"

"I'm sorry, Brian," the lawyer said. "If there's anything else I can do, please let me know."

"Thank you for reading me the note and trying to help my brother," Miller expressed and hung up the phone.

There was one other note...a map, inside the envelope, that Attorney Adams failed to disclose to Jackson's brother. The man he'd called, prior to notifying Brian Miller of his brother's death, would be in possession of the information later in the day, after this man returned from picking up a passenger at Manchester/Boston Regional Airport.

Chapter 45

ZenJa's flight arrived on schedule and the couple was headed North to Lake Winnipesaukee, in the powerful black Camaro, shortly after midnight.

"It's good to see you," Levi began after the couple grabbed a cup of coffee at a drive thru restaurant.

"I'm glad I was able to get the time off and I agree that talking about important issues, that you're going to tell me about, should be said face to face,"

"So, if you don't mind, please tell me what's going on and how you're involved?"

"All I know," Levi began to weave his story to protect the innocent; so to speak. "All I know," he began again, "is that I heard from a contact that I have inside the jail, that the bastard, Bob Connors, committed suicide."

"You had me fly all the fucking way up here to tell me that?" ZenJa screamed.

"No, I didn't have you fly all the fucking way up here just to tell you that!" he yelled, pressing the gas peddle of the Camaro to the floor, sending the sports car rocketing up Interstate 93.

"Actually, there's more news, I have to tell you about, since we spoke last."

"What in hell is that?"

"Jackson Miller was found hanging in his cell just a short time ago. His lawyer called me and told me."

"Oh my God! This simply gets worse and worse."

"As odd as this may sound, I don't think it's all bad news. I think the taxpayers will be thankful they don't have to pay for those two bastards to remain in prison for the rest of their lives and the cost of appeals and all."

"You're worried about a few dollars? Tell me what I want to hear!" ZenJa demanded.

"Let me ask you; what does trust mean to you, ZenJa? In other words, are there some things you might hear that you're willing to take to your grave?"

ZenJa thought for only a fraction of a second before she replied. "Yes, there are things I'm willing to take to my grave and I'll also assure you I can tell you something you can take to your grave, if you want to or not, I don't really care," ZenJa yelled at the driver. "If it hadn't been for Officer Miller, Bob Connors never would have made it to fucking jail! Okay? I was going to blow his fucking head off while he stood right beside his Viper!"

"Wow! I've more respect for you now, ZenJa, than I ever have," wasn't the reply she expected to hear.

"So, what did Miller do to prevent you from doing what... hell, what I would've done, too?"

"He simply walked right up to me, in front of my weapon, and told me not to shoot. He was cool, calm, and collected and I listened to him."

"I knew I had him pegged right. He's one awesome guy and he'll make an excellent agent."

"Okay, enough of the stalling, Levi. Tell me what I want to hear."

"I can't tell you all the fine details, because it involved other people, but what I can tell you is I paid a visit to Connors. Remember, he never saw me before, so he didn't know me from Jesus, himself."

"While I was visiting him, he did a lot of talking and I got some very valuable information out of him. I'm assuming it's not all true, but I think I already surmised where there's some evidence stashed and/or buried. Brian Miller and I will be checking some stuff out shortly."

"So you're the link who supplied Connors with his suicide weapon?" ZenJa asked.

"If you're insinuating I murdered him, you're *dead* wrong. I simply convinced him he should kill himself when I realized I wasn't going to get anything else out of him."

"Where are *we* going to look for the evidence and maybe where my sister is buried?"

"What's this *we* shit?"

"Are you going to deny me access to help in finding my sister?"

"No, but there are a few complications, but only for a few days."

"What difference are a few days going to make?"

"To be perfectly honest with you, Brian and I think some of the evidence may be stashed or buried on his mother's property and in order not to upset her any more than she already is, he's convinced her to visit her sister in Florida. Her flight leaves on Friday. You don't think a few more days will make that much difference, do you ZenJa. Think about what that poor woman's been through."

"Why does Brian think that?" ZenJa asked.

"From some things his brother mentioned and the way he was talking, before he committed suicide and I assure you, no one aided in his death."

"While we're waiting for Friday, you and I are going to go back to your parents house and look around. I think there may be a weapon stashed there, somewhere. Before Connors met his maker he told me why he felt he had to murder Olive and Zippy," Levi whispered as the miles from Boston faded into the distance.

"What did he say?'

"I think you remember the day before Olive went missing, Connors gave both Olive and Zippy and ride in the squad car to Molly's?"

"Yes, I remember."

"Well, on the way it appears Olive found a weapon...not sure if it was a rifle or pistol, but I'm guessing it was a pistol because Connors said it was shoved under the seat and Olive wouldn't have been able to conceal a rifle in her backpack when they went into Molly's for ice cream.

From what I gather, from Connors, Olive found it and removed it from the car."

"A weapon was worth murdering two young girls?"

"He said that was the weapon he used in the murders of the Winters and Olsen girls. He said, as all perps do, try to make it sound like it was the victims fault. That bastard said how they kept teasing him, telling him how good looking he was and that fucker said he tried to kiss them and they freaked out and started to run away."

"He murdered those girls because of that?" ZenJa cried in anguish.

"It appears so."

"So he discovered the weapon missing from his car and assumed Olive or Zippy took it?"

"Yes, that's what he said."

"For the sake of argument, let's assume that's true. He then told me he confronted Olive about it and, according to him, Olive told him she gave it to Zippy."

"So he murdered Olive first and then Zippy?"

"I think so, ZenJa. I'm so sorry to have to tell you all this."

"I can't thank you enough, Levi for the risk you took and hopefully, finding out what happened to those girls."

"So you think the weapon may be stashed somewhere in my parents house?"

"I'm not a betting man, but I bet it is."

"If we can only find it, it may bring closure to those families," ZenJa murmured.

"That's where we're going after we get some rest. We'll start looking at your house and let Mrs. Miller leave town, before we alert everyone about what we know?" Levi asked in hopes of making a deal with ZenJa.

"Okay, Levi, I guess that's the least I can do for what you've accomplished in just a few days, while I wasted years looking for the same answers."

"You didn't have the connections I do, ZenJa. No one could have done this alone."

"You're right and I'll never be able to thank you enough."

"I also have some other news for you, too."

"What is it?"

"Jackson Miller's lawyer was the first person informed about his death and it appears Jackson had given the attorney a note to be given to Brian and his mother, upon his death. Attorney Adams called me after he hung up with the authorities, while I was on my way down here to pick you up."

"Why would he call you?"

"Because I asked him if he would, if something *should* happen to his client."

"Anyway, Adams told me there was a goodbye note to the family and a second page that included a map."

"A map?" ZenJa asked.

"Yes, obviously, I haven't seen it, but from what Adams told me, it appears it might lead us to some evidence that may once and for all solve the mysteries that have hounded the town of Longberry for so long."

"Oh! And by the way, Brian Miller doesn't know about the map, yet, though I'll tell him when I see him. After all he's already helping with the search, in the farm house, without his mother knowing about it. I simply didn't want him to start digging up the back or front yard before we notify the authorities. We can't keep this secret too long, or we'll be charged with tampering with evidence, but of course there's no one left to file charges. The alleged criminals are dead."

Neither occupants of the car spoke until they arrived at the lake.

"We're here," Levi announced to waken ZenJa, who had fallen asleep.

"You know, Levi, I can't tell you if I feel relief, anger, sadness or joy at the developments that have transpired in such a short time."

"I think it'd be safe to say you feel all of those things. It's perfectly normal to have mixed emotions at a time like this," he replied and opened the car door for his passenger and brought her suitcase to the front door.

"This is the most beautiful home, Levi," ZenJa commented when she and her host entered the lighted entryway.

"I agree and before we call it a night, do you want a bite to eat or anything?"

"No, I'm really exhausted, thank you. I'd really like to try and get some sleep. My head's spinning."

"Okay, your room's all ready. Same room as before, if it's suitable," Levi said and locked up the house and followed ZenJa to the guest room, with her suitcase.

"Goodnight, ZenJa," Levi said after putting the suitcase on the bed.

"Goodnight, Levi and again, I'll never forget what you've done to help me," she added and softly closed the door behind him.

Levi hoped all the alleged evidence they were seeking did indeed exist and the folks would have the answers everyone hoped to receive.

Chapter 46

"Levi, you awake yet?" Alex asked while his brother answered the cell phone by his bedside at 9:00, the next morning.

"Yeah, just barely. I had a long drive to the airport and back. We got here about two this morning."

"You heard about Jackson, I assume?'

"Yes, his attorney called me and with the information I got from Connors and info. Brian received, plus a map the attorney is in possession of, we may finally have some answers about the murders and missing girls. I hope so, so we can bring some closure to ZenJa and the other folks in town."

"You mentioned a map?"

"Yes, evidently Jackson left a goodbye note for the family and a map that I'm assuming discloses where evidence has been buried. Brian doesn't know about the map yet. I wanted to look at it first, to make sure we weren't being misled or we weren't going to be getting anyone else's hope up."

"Well, I'm still hanging out here at Brent's place so do you want me to fill him in on these developments?"

"Yeah, that'll save me from repeating the story again."

"Have you found any suitable places to live, yet?"

"I'm going to look at a beach front cottage, a few miles from Brent's, this afternoon."

"That'll be cool. Maybe you can invite Darcy up here and go to the NASCAR race in Loudon?"

"Yeah, maybe I will. It's nice to have someone I can rag on about the drivers!" Alex said and smiled to himself.

"Good for you, Alex. You deserve some happiness."

"I know and so do you."

"I know that as well. I'm trying to work on it, but at my own pace."

"Okay, well I just wanted to check in with you."

"When do you think we're going to get started on Operation AK-47 in a 2X4? Have you met with the wife, a.k.a informant?" Levy continued.

"I'm meeting her tomorrow."

"Where are you meeting her? I don't want you going off on your own. It could be a set-up, you know."

"Brent and I are going to meet her at Molly's café. I've made it known to Molly, we need a private booth in the back and not to be disturbed after we get our lunch."

"So you've told Molly you're not the creep she thought you were?"

"Yeah, I told her I was your ass-hole brother and after that, she fell in love with me," Alex added and laughed.

"At least you didn't lie to her,' Levi said and laughed as well.

"Okay, well keep me informed. ZenJa and I are going over to her parents house and look around for a weapon that may be hidden there."

"What weapon?"

"According to Connors he killed Olive and Zippy because one of the girls found a weapon under his car seat. The weapon that was used to murder the Olsen and Winters girls. He discovered it was missing after he gave the girls a ride to Molly's that fateful day. And according to him, he killed them because he was afraid Zippy was in possession of it and she would obviously give to ZenJa and he was certain the ballistics would come back and his life of crime would be discovered. He said he murdered Winters and Olsen because they were flirting with him and then when he tried to make a move on them, they ran. I figure that part is a lie and he simply raped and murdered them. Even so, whatever happened, he was a fucking perverted murdering bastard."

"You certainly found out a lot yesterday. That must bring ZenJa some peace."

"I think she's in a state of shock and hasn't had time to digest all the evidence and events, yet. I just hope it brings everyone some closure."

"So, you're driving the red Dodge Ram and what's Brent using for a vehicle on this assignment?"

"He's using an old blue, Ford pickup. Damn thing must be twenty years old. He's using that to blend in with the *lumber jacks* we're going to snag and he won't stand out so much, browsing around the wilderness. He'll be a good ole red neck," Alex replied and laughed.

"Okay, you guys set up a schedule, once you meet with *Mrs. Lumberjack*, at Molly's, and we'll figure out a way to put some GPS units on the fake logs and keep them under surveillance. Between the three of us, it should work out okay. Hopefully, this shit won't take to long. We have dead girls to find!"

Levi showered and dressed in his blue jeans and a black tee-shirt before going downstairs to his kitchen to make coffee and some toast.

Once he got to the stairway, the aroma of freshly brewed coffee and blueberry muffins gently caressed the air that reminded Levi of his childhood, when his father used to bake tasty treats for him.

"Good morning, ZenJa. Breakfast smells wonderful. I hope you slept well."

"Good morning, Levi and actually, I did sleep soundly, after I finally got to sleep. My head was spinning, as you can imagine."

"I've no doubt. Even though this is only a lake, and an extremely large one, at that, I find the smell of the salt water rather soothing and can sleep pretty well, when I'm here."

"I agree...it is a lovely place to live and actually," ZenJa continued as she poured Levi and herself cups of coffee and presented the freshly baked muffins with pats of butter, on the side.

" I have plans to buy a little cottage on the lake. I've asked my parents lawyer, well, I guess he's my lawyer now, to get me in touch with a real estate agent and schedule me to view some places that are right on the lake and possibly in foreclosure, to get a good deal."

"That's great...then we can be neighbors and you can come over and make breakfast for me on a regular basis. These muffins are the best I've ever tasted," Levi said and smiled.

"Oh, no! I enjoy cooking and all, but I cook when I want," she said and returned the smile.

"Just as long as, when you do cook or bake, you make enough for two; for me and you, that is."

"I'll try to make sure your portions don't have poison in them," ZenJa said and grinned from ear to ear.

"I'll remember that and now to get down to business, do you want to go to your parents house today and start looking around?"

"Yes, I really would. I want to get this business over and done with, finally, if we can, but first I'll stop by the lawyer's office and see what arrangements he's made with the relator so I can view some property. I didn't mention this to you before," ZenJa said while she poured second cups of coffee for them. "But the lawyer also mentioned there's an interested developer who wants to explore the possibility of purchasing my parents property."

"Really! That's great, if that's what you want."

"I've even discussed this some of the folks in town, to see how they feel about expanding their sleepy little village into a booming and hopefully financially profitable area. From what I've heard, everyone is pretty excited about the prospects of more employment, the development of expensive and tasteful condominiums and of course more people paying property taxes to bring revenue into the area. A nice golf course, new school and God only knows what else. That sounds exciting, doesn't it?" ZenJa said in a breathless whisper.

"It does indeed! I'm sure your folks would be so proud to know their property enriched their town, if the deal is made," Levi said and smiled.

Chapter 47

"If you're going to your attorney's office, you can use the Navigator," Levi said. He recalled the hateful and sarcastic comment he made to ZenJa as that being his wife's vehicle in a moment of anger when she insinuated he was still married. ZenJa had not forgotten that exchange; a pained expression overshadowed her face.

"I'll use my Camaro, of course. Do you want me to go to your parents house and after you're finished with the lawyer you can meet me there?"

"Okay, that sounds like a good plan."

"Here are the keys. ZenJa."

"I can't imagine where you'd start to look for a weapon, but my guess would be in Zippy's bedroom."

"I'll start there," Levi responded.

"There's a house key over the door frame at the rear entrance."

"Okay, I'll find it."

"I'll take off after I shower and change my clothes."

"Just shut the door; it'll be locked when you leave. I'll back the Lincoln out of the garage and that'll be locked also.

"Okay," ZenJa said and walked toward the upstairs that lead to her bathroom.

"Thanks for breakfast," Levi called and shut the door behind him.

An hour later, Levi entered the Beckwith home and noted ZenJa had obviously tidied up the residence when she was last here. Levi knew the parents left their home in the middle of the night, on the evening of their *accident* and it would have been sensible for them to leave their bed unmade and other items laying around. He browsed around the interior of the home and noticed all the linens, including towels and clothes the parents would have worn were washed, dried and put away. On the dresser, he found the cell phone ZenJa had left there, her father's phone and plugged it in to charge it up. He was curious if that phone may hold any secrets, not that it really mattered now. All the players in the dirty deeds were dead; or so he assumed.

Wearing gloves, Levi entered the room that was obviously a teenager's room and began carefully examining likely hiding places for what would be considered contraband, in the house. He began searching the dresser drawers, underneath, and behind the dresser before he moved the mattresses and looked under the bed before thoroughly checking her closet and searching for any hidden panels inside, or under the carpet.

His next destination was the girl's desk in which he searched the entire structure, to no avail.

Out of the corner of his eye, Levi noticed what appeared to be tiny amounts of plaster on the carpet. Plaster that would have fallen from the sheet rock on the wall, if there had been a picture recently hung. He removed the picture of a horse, Zippy most likely had put on the wall and quickly noticed a section that had been cut out and removed had simply been replaced with small pieces of duct tape. After carefully removing the tape and cut-out section of dry wall he placed the pieces into an evidence bag. In the hollowed out section of wall, Levi positioned his flashlight inside the crevice between the insulation and studs. While he was busy inspecting the inner wall of the bedroom for the weapon, he heard ZenJa enter the driveway and house.

"I'm in Zippy's room," Levi hollered.

"I'll be right there. I've got a call on my cell phone," she replied and sat at the kitchen table.

Five minutes later, Levy exclaimed, "Shit! Here it is," he added, having used a wire coat hanger to retrieved the pistol and carefully enclose it in an evidence bag.

"You found it," ZenJa said, once she entered the room, from the hallway where she's been watching for less than a minute.

"I didn't hear you come upstairs," Levi replied, having been startled by the woman who stood less than two feet behind him.

"How did you know where to look for it?" she asked

"I noticed some pieces of dry wall on the carpet, that came from a hole that was cut, behind that picture. Zippy must have cut the hole and put the gun inside."

"I vacuumed the entire house, the other day, Levi and there was *no* dry wall remnants, no matter how small on the carpet, in this room or any other," ZenJa replied with determination.

"Are you telling me, this carpet, in this exact spot, was completely clean?" Levi retorted in disbelief.

"I'll bet my life on it."

"Someone's been in this house, since Connors and Miller were arrested and died and planted it here. There's no other explanation, is there?" ZenJa asked in shock.

"Someone could be in the house as we speak," Levi whispered, removed his weapon and led ZenJa out of the bedroom and between the two of them, searched every inch of the house before sitting at the kitchen table for a break.

"That fucking weapon was the reason my sister and her friend were murdered and it appears not all the perps have been caught?" ZenJa, tearfully whispered.

"It appears so," Levi said sympathetically. "All those crimes were needless, as well as senseless. Makes me have so little faith in the human race; we're all turning into fucking animals!'

'Not all of us, I hope," ZenJa replied. "What are we going to do to find who else is involved in the disappearances and murders?"

"We have to keep digging and hopefully someone will talk, confess or be captured," Levi replied with a deep sigh. "There's someone involved in these cases who has fallen under the radar."

"We also have to keep this property secure, until we can get pictures of Zippy's room, prints off the duct tape, and get someone here to get some prints on the doors and whatever else is relevant. It seems we're not out of the woods as far as collecting evidence. There's still at least one perp on the loose. I'm calling Emerson and I'll have him send a team up here. We'll have to wait for them to show up, though if you want, I'll stay and you can head out, ZenJa."

"I'll hang around and where do you have to leave this evidence off? Who has jurisdiction at this point?"

"I'll also mention this to Emerson and see what he wants me to do with it when I talk to him," he said and dialed the FBI office in Boston.

"Sounds like a good idea," ZenJa replied not taking her eyes off the weapon. "This still seems like a nightmare and it'll all be over when I wake up."

"Emerson's team's on their way and he said he'll be right behind them and by the way I found this cell phone and charged it up while I was snooping around. I thought it might have some useful information in it."

"I charged it up, myself, when I was here and dialed the last number that was received on the phone. It rang to another phone, but there was no answer," ZenJa explained.

Levi picked up the phone and made a notation of the number and then called the number once again. As it had with ZenJa, it rang, but there was no answer.

"I'll get this number checked and find out who it belongs to," Levi said and dialed a number and handed ZenJa her father's phone to put in her pocket.

"Yo...I need to know who's in or was in possession of this telephone number," Levi said and he read off the number to the person on the other end of the call. "Get back to me as soon as you can," he said.

"Did you find the weapon?" Alex asked.

"Yes," he replied. "And I've got more bad news. It appears there were more people involved in the crimes that have been committed around here. The weapon appears to have been planted here at ZenJa's folks house in the last few days; *after* Miller and Connors died."

"Oh fuckin' A," Alex responded. "Who would benefit from both Miller and Connors being dead?"

"Obviously the remaining perp or perps."

"I would have several guesses to make, but again, they're simply speculation. I'm guessing someone who was anxious to help us gain access to Connors," Levi said as ZenJa looked wide eyed at the man who sat across the kitchen table from her. "I'm also thinking Miller's suicide probably wasn't a suicide after all," Levi continued.

"Well, I wanted to let you know, Emerson's on the way with his CSI team to check out this house. It's obviously a crime scene, more or less and I sure hope we can get some prints."

"When will you be at the lake house?"

"As soon as they show up."

Two hours later the CSI team arrived with Emerson close behind. Levi and ZenJa quickly brought the group up to date on their discovering of the weapon and it's location so the investigators could perform their tasks.

"I guess we can head out now and think about what we'll have on the barbecue grill tonight, if you want. I think we've accomplished quite a bit for one day and this house and evidence is in good hands, now."

ZenJa remained seated at the table and made an informal announcement. "Well, this day did have a little bit of good news. I have an appointment with a real estate agent tomorrow to look at a few homes on the lake."

"Are you sure you want to make that kind of an investment, now, ZenJa? Maybe you should wait until things settle down. This might be the last area you really want to take up residence in, for the long haul. The lake is so close to this house and memories or maybe one day, you'll meet someone who'll sweep you off your feet and provide a nice home for you."

"I'm not holding my breath on the later and being the independent woman that I am, I don't expect someone to support me for the rest of my life and I really would like to see this property develop into a thriving adventure for Longberry; if the property is sold."

"So you've decided to sell it to...I mean sell it?" Levi asked, standing up and motioned for ZenJa to follow suit and leave the house.

"I think so," ZenJa answered; a quizzical expression on her face.

"See you back at the lake," Levi said to ZenJa after bidding the FBI agents goodbye.

On the way back to the lake house, Alex called and informed his brother the phone number he asked him to trace, had once been a cell phone in possession of Bob Connors.

"I also have another bit of information about the tire impressions left on Blackberry Road. Those prints *did not* match those of any vehicle either Connors or Miller possessed."

"What the hell? I guess we simply haven't looked hard enough to find the vehicle, then, right?" Levi asked.

"It appears not," Alex replied solemnly.

"Do you think we're missing something or someone?" Levi pondered aloud.

"Obviously, nothing would surprise me in this case."

"So, at least we're fairly certain that Connors, that bastard, was the man who lured ZenJa's folks out of a dead sleep, in the middle of a dark, rainy and foggy night to their deaths. That fucking bastard will rot in hell, forever," Levi replied to his brother before calling ZenJa on her cell phone to tell her what he'd discovered.

"ZenJa, it appears the phone number I had checked out did, indeed, belong to Bob Connors and somehow, he lured your folks from their house, that night, and someone appears to have forced them off the highway. The ruse most perps use is to call a relative or loved one and tell them there was an accident and those at home are summoned to the hospital. My guess is that's what happened, but in light of the theory there were more than two people involved in the crimes, someone may have been using that phone with or without Connors knowledge."

"And also, from what I understand, the CSI team has been unable to find matching tires on any vehicle in possession of Miller or Connors that pair up with the evidence obtained from the tire tracks left in the mud, across the street, on Blackberry Road. The odd thing about those tire impressions is that one tire is not a matching set with the other three. There is one odd tire on the vehicle; the left rear. Hopefully, that will help us locate the truck more easily,'" Levi continued.

"There's no hell bad enough for someone like those evil sons'a bitches and what do we do, now, to find what vehicle that had been parked across the street?"

"We have to keep looking and pray for a miracle," Levi responded before disconnecting the call.

Chapter 48

FBI Agent Edward Emerson arrived at Levi's lake house shortly before dinner and once the evidence was secured in his vehicle, Levi, ZenJa and their guests sat on the deck, watching the boats cruise across the lake while they waited for Alex to finish making the barbecue feast.

"How many steaks are you planning to cook, Levi?" Alex asked.

"All of them, if you don't mind. We're having other guests, beside the four of us."

"Okay, the more the merrier," Alex replied and continued with the task at hand.

A moment later, the other guests arrived, with an assortment of salads and desserts to complete the menu.

"Hello, everyone!" Levi hollered when a family and one other guest arrived at the same time. "Let me get the introductions out of the way. I'm Levi Harris," he announced while shaking Abby's husband and two boys hands. "It's my pleasure to meet you."

"We're happy to meet you, also," Mr. Patten replied.

"And this lovely lady is, *was*, my private nurse while I was recuperating from my injuries. May I introduce you to Abby Patten," Levi continued and glanced at ZenJa, who appeared to be *more* than jealous, Levi noted and smiled at this obvious demonstration of displeasure by his house guest.

"Again, this is *Mrs.* Abby Patten," he continued after an awkward silence. "Also we have her brave husband, Firefighter Owen Patten and their two rambunctious boys, Rick and Dominic and our other new arrival is Brent Wyman, who's employed in the lumberjack business," Levi said and smiled, again.

"Abby, Owen, boys, and Brent let me introduce you to my friend, Edward Emerson; and my brother, for those of you who don't know him, Alex Lyons, and this lovely young lady is my...houseguest, ZenJa Beckwith."

All the formalities were performed and the party seriously got under way.

"Because, Levi's a writer, are you also authors?" Abby asked innocently, recalling the lie Levi told her upon one of their first meetings. "I know Alex is a financial guru, and the fact that Brent's a lumberjack, I'm wondering if you're collaborating on a book, together. And I'm also waiting for my autographed copy of the first book you get published and I truly wish Olivia Swan had finished,' *'Swinging From The Rafters'*, before she died," Abby continued.

Levi was obviously taken aback by the questions, along with the others who knew him and more or less what they did for a living.

Alex glared at Levi, before turning the steaks and turning his back on his brother, because of the title of the book hit so close to home.

The other guests innocently chuckled, and the group quickly gained their composure before ZenJa took it upon herself to reply.

"I can assure you, you're right on, especially where Levi is concerned. He is one of the most talented writers I know of. His special genre is fiction, of course," she continued and smirked in his direction.

""And, again, you're correct, Abby," Levi confirmed. "We're all here to produce the best novel since War And Peace.

Alex was standing close by and realized now was a great time to announce the steaks were done and it was time to eat. "If you'll all gather around, dinner is served."

"Can I see you in the kitchen, Alex?" Levi asked. "You can help me bring out more beverages," he demanded.

"I apologize for the title of the alleged book I was writing when Abby was giving me the third degree a while ago. When she first came here she questioned why I had all Olivia Swan's books on the bookshelf and I had to make something up. I'm sorry. I had no idea she would remember such an idiotic statement."

"No, problem, but this is the reason we have to stick to our *own*. Inviting *outsiders* into our lives is dangerous and causes us to constantly be on guard and lying. I'm sick of the lies," Levi.

"I know, Alex, but isn't it refreshing to hear about other people and their careers and take some of the drudgery, crime, and corruption out of our own? I know it makes me appreciate what others do for a living."

"Yeah, I guess."

"Anyway, what happens if and when you bring Darcy up here to go to the races and what if you become involved with her. Are you going to keep your occupation a secret forever?"

"Yes!" he responded without hesitation.

"Here are the drinks, on this cart, if you can wheel it outside. We better get back to make sure ZenJa isn't giving Abby the third degree about my body," Levi mentioned; the brothers laughed uncontrollably.

"What's so funny?" the younger Patten boy asked.

"Levi was just telling me about a time he was fishing and a big cat fish jumped into his boat and scared him half to death."

"Really?" both youngsters asked in unison; their eyes as wide as saucers.

"Yeah, well it was dark and I didn't know what it was. I thought it was a shark," Levi continued with the fictitious fish tale.

"There are sharks out in the lake?" Dominic asked in innocent wonder.

"Oh, no! I was fishing off the coast of Florida, back in the day."

"What else were you fishing for?" ZenJa asked and smiled politely.

"Actually, I found a pirate ship and an old sea captain with a wooden leg."

"Did he have a parrot on his shoulder?" Rick asked.

"He sure did, just like in the story Treasure Island."

"I love that book," Dominic replied.

"The importance of reading, boys, is that you can go to any part of the world, do anything, be what you want to be and not even leave your house. I sometimes pretend I'm a spy and go here and there finding bad guys."

"You're a really cool guy," Rick said.

"Tell you what. Next time you and your parents come over, we'll go out in my boat and see if we can find some treasure or pirates. How does that sound?"

"That's awesome," both boys yelled with excitement and enthusiasm.

The meal continued late into the evening and all those in attendance enjoyed themselves, especially now that the conversations were directed toward the Patten family and stories about firefighting, nursing, and the boys athletic endeavors. It was the mission of those who were in law enforcement to sway the conversation away from themselves and the event was a rousing success.

"Well, Levi, I hate to be the first to leave this very nice, peaceful, and pleasant gathering, but I've got things to take care of and along drive ahead, of me" Agent Emerson said after a few hours.

"Thanks for coming, Emerson and I hope you let me know what you think of the *story line*," Levi replied in code.

"It'll take a few days, no doubt, but I'll get right on it," he replied and made his exit.

The remaining group was ready to leave for their own residences, a short while later, with left overs wrapped in foil and Levi promised to take the Patten family out on his speed boat in the near future.

"Oh! By the way," Alex said as Levi walked him to his vehicle. "I rented a little cabin about a mile from where Brent has rented his house and if you have time, you can help me move my things in over the weekend."

"What things, pray tell, do you have? What in hell do you have to move in, with the exception of your shaving kit and a small suitcase with your underwear?"

"You guessed it! That's about all I have; I was just yankin' your chain, but you can stop by any time. The address is 649 Blackbird Lane."

"I will and by the way, aren't you tired of living like a gypsy?"

"Yeah, as a matter of fact I am," Alex, thoughtfully replied.

"Well, you and me both," Levi admitted and closed the door to Alex's red pickup truck and watched him drive away.

Levi made his way back into the house and he and ZenJa were left with the cleaning duties and a feeling of satisfaction of a job well done.

"So, I noticed you were a little jealous of Abby," Levi mentioned while he watched ZenJa load dishes into the dishwasher.

"You're insane," ZenJa snarled. "Why would I be jealous?"

"Maybe because Abby might have seen a side of me you haven't?" Levi said and laughed while he poured beers for ZenJa and himself.

"Oh! There's no part of you I haven't seen that I want to see, Mr. Harris," she growled and took the glass of beer from his hand and walked toward the deck.

"You leaving me with the rest of the cleanup?"

"Yes, you can finishing putting a few items of food in the refrigerator and turning on the dishwasher, can't you? I'll make sure the coals are extinguished," she added.

"I think someone was jealous. I really think someone was jealous," Levi sang; his way of teasing his house guest once more.

After the kitchen was clean, Levi wandered onto the deck, with his drink and settled beside his guest in a patio chair.

"You, know, I have to admit, I admire the courage and resilience you've managed to possess, with the disappearance of your sister and death of your parents, in such a short period of time," Levi said with sincerity. "You're spirit and drive are commendable."

"You've suffered from your own demons, Levi, so you know how painful and cruel life can be."

"It makes us stronger, I guess."

"I noticed Alex glared at you, when you mentioned the title of the fictitious book you had or are writing. What was the title? *'Swinging From The Rafters'*; what's up with that?"

"Oh, nothing. I guess he was thinking of Jackson Miller, hanging himself."

"You obviously mentioned the title of the book to Abby *before* Miller's demise," ZenJa prodded.

"I guess it simply struck a cord with him. How the fuck do I know what and why he does what he does?" Levi barked.

"I think I just struck a cord with you, too," ZenJa continued; regretting it the minute she said it.

"When's your flight back to Virginia? Don't you have to go to work?" Levi snarled defensively.

"I'm waiting for my lawyer to contact the potential buyer of the Beckwith Property, so we can discuss the possible terms of the sale."

"Well, call him tomorrow and hopefully you'll have an answer to your offer so you can go home. I've got a busy schedule up here and can't be distracted. I come up here for peace and quiet, not to be hounded with idiotic gibberish."

"I'm sorry, Levi, I didn't mean to intrude; I know what a private person you are. Again, I'm sorry."

"As soon as I speak with my lawyer, tomorrow, I'll go back to Virginia. I, also, have work to do. If you can drop me off at a rental car facility, close by, I'll drive myself to the airport," she added and left to go upstairs to the guest bedroom.

"That works for me," Levi said and continued to sit on the deck, wondering what situation *Operation AK-47 in a 2X4* would develop into and what to do about the mystery vehicle that had been parked in the mud, the vehicle with one odd treaded tire, and who had broken into the Beckwith home and hidden the weapon.

"So much for peace and quiet," Levi murmured and went inside to retire for the night.

Chapter 49

ZenJa was back at work in Virginia, after finalizing the details of the sale of her parents property, and Levi's cast had been removed and the ATF agent was currently the anonymous and current owner of The Beckwith Property.

Upon her arrival at Forest Haven Estates, after her first day back at work in the local office of the FBI, she checked her mail outside her door before entering her condominium. Inside the secured box was a single letter addressed to her. ZenJa noted there was no return address, but the post mark was White River, Vermont; the major postal delivery outlet in that state.

Once inside her home, something told her this letter was not any kind of miscellaneous advertising notice, but harassing notes, like others she had received, in the past. She quickly grabbed some latex gloves from a kitchen drawer and carefully slit the side of the envelope with a letter opener. The contents had been pieced together from words clipped and pasted on a simple piece of notebook paper from previously printed magazines and newspapers.

ZenJa read the message and immediately used her cell phone to call Levi.

"What's up, ZenJa?" Levi asked and waited for news on the encounter between his brother, ATF Agents Alex Lyons and Brent Wyman who were meeting with an informant regarding the *Operation AK-47 in a 2X4* Investigation.

"I just received a mysterious note, containing words cut from magazines and newspapers, in the mail today. The post mark is, oddly, sent from the White River mailing center, in Vermont. There is no return address and because I was suspicious of this, I carefully opened the letter, wearing gloves, of course."

"What does the note say?"

"It's in the form of a nursery rhyme and it says:"

Oh where, oh where has your sister been gone.
She's been to Heaven; with help of a con.
Roses are red, violets are blue;
She thought it was funny and so do you!

"That's all it says?" Levi asked.

"Yes, that's it."

"So it appears there's still someone who's been hiding under the radar, like we thought. A perv we missed and what's to prevent him from striking again?" ZenJa asked in terror.

"Why has this perv taken five years or more to send this? Has he been in prison or simply moved to another state and continued this murdering scheme?" Levi wondered out loud.

"Now that our other two criminals, Connors and Miller are dead, we have no way of getting any additional information from them," ZenJa commented.

"I guess we were in such a rush to solve these cases, we messed up, somewhat. I certainly have no regrets that Connors is dead, but I wish Miller hadn't committed suicide. He would have talked eventually."

"I'm going to call my boss, here at FBI headquarters, and have them pick this note up. Hopefully, we'll get some prints off it."

"Okay, that sounds good. Let's hope for some clues, but I have an idea, this person isn't stupid."

"This really freaks me out, Levi. Why would someone do this? Haven't they caused enough pain and suffering without this?" she cried in desperation.

"I know, but unfortunately, these freaks love attention and this guy, or gal, has either been out of commission, relocated, or disappeared for a while."

"Not to change the subject, ZenJa, but I heard from Brian Miller and he said he's been accepted into your family of FBI agents, of course that's if he passes all the tests and courses offered at Quantico. He's going to break in the new Police Chief, in Longberry, before he heads out."

"Who's the new chief going to be? Anyone I know?" ZenJa asked.

"He said the guy's name is Ivan Sweeney. He just got out of the military, but he's originally from Longberry and went to high school there. Does the name ring a bell or do you know if he's related to Wilber and Lily?"

"I vaguely remember the Sweeney family and do remember they have a son, but there are probably aunts, uncles, cousins and God only knows who and how they're all related. I do believe this Ivan might be about five or six years older than Olive and Zippy would be now."

"Well, I hope he's an asset to the community. The folks in that town deserve someone on duty they can trust."

"I understand the FBI just began their search of the Miller property for evidence concerning the missing girls and their bodies. So far, they've come up empty handed," Levi added.

"Anything on the prints on the weapon we found at my parents house?"

"Unfortunately, there were no prints on it. It had been wiped clean."

"This fucking stinks to high heaven. I'm sick of coming up with no clues!" ZenJa yelled into the phone.

"I know, ZenJa, but keep the faith. Somewhere, somehow, this person will screw up and we'll get answers."

"You have more faith than I do, Levi," ZenJa replied, her spirits dashed, once again.

"I have something else to tell you, Levi, before you hang up."

"What's that, ZenJa?"

"I've decided, now that I'm fairly well off, financially, after selling the property and what my parents left me, I'm going leave the FBI, buy a nice home, like yours, on the Lake and do what I always wanted to do. The only reason I joined the FBI was because I was so pissed off and wanted to take out my anger on any friggin criminal I could. I realize how close I came to blowing Connors away and that really scared me. I never knew I possessed that amount of anger and could come that close to murdering someone who wasn't armed and was giving themselves up for arrest."

"I commend you on making that decision. It couldn't have been easy for you. I also think you're too sweet; too nice of a person to be bogged down in the shit that has to happen to creeps like we're forced to deal with. I admire your courage and decision."

"You mentioned doing something you always wanted to do. What might that be?" Levi asked.

"I always wanted to be a writer and I guess I have enough material to write about, don't you think?"

"You going to be a mystery writer?"

"I think I will."

"Well, when you write about me, make sure you remind the readers that I'm tall, dark and handsome," Levi replied and laughed.

"What makes you think I'll write about you?"

"What better character could you develop for your novel?"

"You got that right, Mister. You *are* some kind of character, all right!"

"I actually want to continue snooping around Longberry, looking for clues under the pretense of writing a book. Good cover, right?"

"Yes, indeed, but be careful, ZenJa. Remember there's still someone out there who was involved, somehow, in the disappearances and murders."

"I will and now that we'll be neighbors, we can collaborate on our clues and my writing."

"Do I get a cut of the profits, from the book sales? You have to remember, I'm simply a poor federal agent, not a rich heiress like you," Levi replied and chuckled to himself.

"So, are you working on another case right now?" ZenJa asked.

"Yeah, Alex, Wyman, and I have just started on another explosives, gun running scheme around the area. We'll be pretty busy with this for a while. I'm hoping it won't take too long to bring this it to an end."

"Well, make sure you guys are careful."

"We will."

"Once I tie up the loose ends I have down here, in Virginia, I'll be back in New Hampshire. I may not desire to be in Longberry very much, but I truly believe, after giving it a lot of thought, New Hampshire is my home."

"It'll be nice to have you as a neighbor," Levi said regretting saying that out loud.

"Really?" ZenJa asked in shock.

"Thankfully, Lake Winnie is a big lake," he added, laughed and disconnected the phone before he said anything else to reveal what he felt about ZenJa Beckwith.

Chapter 50

"Congratulations, Police Chief Ivan Sweeney," Brian Miller said, shaking the hand of the long time resident of Longberry, after his swearing in ceremony.

"Thank you so much," Sweeney said, smiling from ear to ear. "It's my honor to serve my home town as a civil servant. My goal is to make this a safe, friendly, and welcoming place to live," he added for benefit of the few newspaper and television reporters who were in attendance.

ZenJa Beckwith was one of the many residents of New Hampshire who were curious to see who would be taking over the reigns of the small town police department.

"I hope you haven't forgotten the mission, in Longberry, to continue the search for the missing children in this God forsaken town," ZenJa said without any formalities.

"Yes, Miss Beckwith. Finding your sister and her friend is foremost in my thoughts and I'll do everything in my power to bring them home," Sweeney said with all the sincerity ZenJa had hoped for.

"I appreciate it," she continued and walked over to speak with Brian Miller.

"Congratulations on your success and your appointment in the FBI, Miller."

"Thank you ZenJa. I hope I do us both proud."

"Oh, I guess you don't know, but I realized I wasn't cut out for the Bureau. I submitted my resignation a few weeks ago."

"I'm sorry to hear that. I would have welcomed the opportunity to work with you."

"What are your plans, if I may ask?"

"I thought I might do a little private investigating on my own. Just call me a free-lancer," she said and laughed.

"Well, I see the mayor is motioning for Ivan and me to come to the podium, so I'll take off, but I want you to be safe, ZenJa and be careful," was all Brian said and left the young woman standing in the middle of the press room.

"Good evening, ZenJa," Levi Harris said, and led his friend away from the commotion, by the elbow.

"I see you made it in time for the refreshments," ZenJa said and laughed.

"Yeah, well I was hoping you'd run for the chief's old office, myself. You would have been a wonderful asset to this town."

"For one thing, I'm not a resident of Longberry and I have no desire to be in this town on a daily basis."

"So, you're all moved back to New Hampshire?"

"You know I am, Levi. Who are you trying to kid. You know every move I make."

"Well, I admit I try to keep my friends close and my enemies closer," he added and smiled.

"So, just were do I fit into that spectrum? Am I friend or foe?"

"You tell me, ZenJa, while we have dinner. We never did finish our first date, if you recall."

"Where are you suggesting we go?"

"How does a romantic dinner on my boat sound?"

"Not tonight, I hope."

"How about tomorrow evening? I have to prepare; to make sure I have the right menu planned."

"Oh, I guess that'll fit into my busy schedule," ZenJa said and chuckled because she knew Levi was aware she had no schedule or social life, for that matter.

"When I bring you home, after dinner, you can show me around your new house on the lake. I admit, I've driven by and am quite satisfied you made a great choice."

"I'm so glad you approve, Mr. Harris," ZenJa said and watched Levi walk toward the refreshment table and ZenJa thinking to herself how *hot* Mr. Levi Harris was.

Levi did not stop by to refill his plate with the delectable treats that called out to him, but continued to walk out the back door of the reception hall. He knew now was a perfect time to casually wander among the many pick up trucks and other vehicles parked to honor the new police chief. God only knew what one might find in the crowded parking lot, inconspicuous to all.

After walking along and winding his way through the haphazardly parked vehicles his eye was trained on an older model, heavily rusted Chevy Blazer. What immediately attracted his attention was the curious set of tires the vehicle displayed; three matching tires and one mismatched tire on the rear, driver's side.

"What ya' lookin' at?" Ivan Sweeney asked, having walked up behind Levi Harris.

"I'm just admiring this Blazer. Hell, it must be thirty years old."

"Yeah, this was the first vehicle I got, while I was in high school, for Heaven sake, and it was older than dirt back then," he said and chuckled. "It rusted quite a bit while I've been away, but I plan on sprucing it up in my spare time."

"Where've ya' been?" Levi asked nonchalantly.

"After high school, I enlisted in the Marines, became an M.P. and now I want to continue on in law enforcement, as you have already guessed."

"Must feel good to be back in your old home town, huh?" Levi asked.

"Yes, it's good to see the old gang, friends and unfortunately foes, as well," he continued and grinned.

Levi was most anxious to direct the conversation toward Olive and Zippy, but he intended to keep this conversation as light as possible, but he wanted to find an excuse to get an impression of the odd tire without raising suspicion..

"You ever take this bitch mudding?" Levi asked.

"Not since I've been back," Ivan replied.

"Well, I've got an old *beater* of my own and have been dying to take it up on the Beckwith property and let'er rip. You want to join me sometime this weekend?"

"That property is off limits, from what I understand," Sweeney replied guardedly.

"I happen to know the guy who just bought the homestead and he's given me permission to use it, until something is decided on what to do with it."

"Who bought it?"

"I'm not allowed to disclose that yet...not until the owner has a meeting with the townsfolk and he gives them a heads up on what he wants to do with the land. I think it's mighty nice of him to consider the people in Longberry and what this transfer of property may mean for the town, don't you?"

"You don't think this guy wants to turn those acres into some sort of swanky resort or start tearing up the land, do you?" Police Chief Sweeney asked nervously.

"That would be my guess," Levi said and smiled thinking he had just discovered who another party to the missing and dead girls might be. He looked and sounded exceptionally nervous about the prospect of anyone disturbing the land on the mountainside.

"Well, it's been nice chatting with you...Levi is it?" Sweeney asked.

"Yup...Levi Harris is the name."

"If you don't mind me asking, are you a long time resident of Longberry?"

"Or what you're really asking is what my business or reason for being in this delightful town is?" Levi questioned and smiled.

"Well, yes; being police chief, now, I like to know the locals and the drifters. Never hurts to know who's in the community."

"Absolutely! I couldn't agree more. Actually, I have a little shack on Lake Winni, went to college south of here and have a lot of friends in this town...from passing through and all. Trust me, I'm no drifter," he added and once again smiled his devilish, evil grin; the expression so few people knew its true meaning; that dark smile that turned his bright blue eyes into the color of steel.

AFT agents Alex Lyons and Brent Williams approached *Mrs. Lumberjack* at Molly's Café promptly on Friday morning, as planned. The trio were seated in the rear of the diner and their breakfast orders being prepared. The two agents, who donned their sunglasses and baseball caps, sat across from the female relative/informant of the two men allegedly involved in a explosives and weapons running operation from a near-by town.

"I'm not interested in your name," Alex began without an formalities. "And our names are of no concern of yours as well."

"Let's not sugar-coat any of this," the large boned, gray haired, fifty something year old woman barked while pulling her straw hat down over her face.

"Sorry," Alex continued while Molly brought the trio their breakfast orders, set their meals on the table, refilled their coffee mugs, and disappeared into the kitchen.

"It's easier for everyone, in situations such these, if people on both sides of the fence remain anonymous," Brent offered.

"Yeah, well I'm the one risking life and limb by coming here," the woman wearing bib overalls, a flannel shirt, and rubber boots remarked.

"And we appreciate this," Brent replied in an effort to sooth the woman's ruffled feathers.

"I've tried to get my husband and his brother to get out of this racket, but he refuses. He said the money is worth the risk, but I don't believe it is. I would rather have him in prison, rather than on a slab in some morgue."

"Do you think there's anyway we can get them to co-operate with the federal authorities and lead us to the *top dog*? I'm assuming they're only minor players in the scheme and there are others who have a lot more to gain and lose than your husband and a brother-in-law."

"Are you suggesting they may be able to get immunity for their cooperation?" the woman inquired with interest.

"We're not in a position to promise that or suggest that may be an option, but depending how significant this operation is and the depth and direction it leads, that could be a possibility," Alex replied in hopes this might have some influence over this woman's decision to continue to do the right thing.

The trio sat in silence while they dug into their breakfast selections and Molly noted the lull in the conversation and brought another coffee pot to the table, left more cream, and returned to her other customers in the café.

"I've never been to this café," the woman said while buttering more toast and chewing a piece of bacon she held with her other hand. "Good food," she mumbled while continuing to stuff her face and wiping the grease from her fingers with her shirt sleeve.

"We've never been here, either," Alex replied, with Brent nodding in agreement.

"Way out of your way?" the woman asked with interest.

"Yeah, we don't get down to these parts of the woods often," Alex replied with a *Down-East* accent.

"From Maine, I gather?" the woman asked eyeing the two men in an effort to find out as much about them as she could.

"We don't care where you're from and you shouldn't concern yourself about where we're from," Alex warned.

"What you should be concerned about is whether you want to convince your husband and his brother to cooperate with the authorities or if you want us to take this whole situation out of your hands. If that's what you decide, I'll assure you they'll not know you had anything to do with their demise," Brent stated.

"Give me a day or two to think about it," the woman said and got up from the table.

"Call me at this number when you've made up your mind," Alex said while handing her a slip of paper with a cell phone number on it. "We'll give you two days."

"Thanks for the breakfast," *Mrs. Lumberjack* said and left the café, climbed into a battered yellow Chevy pickup, complete with gun rack in the back window, and Hound dog waiting in the passenger's seat.

"Got the plate number?" Brent asked.

"Got it" Alex replied after he wrote the number on a clean napkin.

"She's a *real* lady," Brent noted and chuckled.

"Was everything satisfactory?" Molly asked.

"You bet ya," Alex replied and smiled at the owner while making a sizable contribution to the tin can on the counter that was being used to collect donations for the fallen officers families in the gymnasium catastrophe

"See you soon, Molly," Brent said and waved goodbye.

"You got a tail on that yellow pickup?" Alex asked Levi on his cell phone; he and Brent headed off in the opposite direction in an effort to leave *Mrs. Lumberjack* with the impression she was not being followed.

"Yup! Levi replied.

"You were able to hear the conversation, I gather?"

"Yeah! It was a good idea for you two to be wired. I also ran the license plate while you were feeding your faces. The truck is registered to...get this...*Shiver Me Timbers Logging Company*."

"You're kidding me, right?" Alex laughed.

"Nope! Give 'em an A+ for originality, at least."

"The owner's name appears to be Wilbur Sweeney".

"Any relation to the police chief of Longberry?"

"The police chief appears to be a cousin of some sort," Levi confirmed.

"Interesting, isn't it?" Alex asked. "I wonder if Ivan knows his relatives are underhanded, conniving scum-bags?"

"Nothing would surprise me and with that possible fact in mind, I suggest we keep the local law enforcement detail out of this," Levi said and continued to follow *Mrs. Lumberjack*, a.k.a. Mrs. Wilbur Sweeney, toward her residence.

"Roger that," Alex said and Wyman in full agreement.

The battered yellow pickup truck left the main highway and approached a nearly invisible dirt road, covered with an overabundance of tree growth, while Levi continued down the highway, but keeping an eye on the vehicle from his rearview mirror. The woman left the truck and unlocked a heavy metal gate before opening it and Levi was to assume she drove the vehicle inside and once again locked the gate behind her, because he had driven out of sight, around a curve in the road.

Several minutes later, Levi turned his vehicle around and approached the driveway from the east, slowed down and took pictures of the entrance and confirmed the fact the large gate was closed and locked.

Levi called Alex and then Brent on their cell phones and mentioned the latest facts he had discovered and told them to meet back at the lake house to organize a plan to initiate their next move forward.

"What if we order a helicopter to scan the Sweeney property from the air, initially?" Brent recommended. "This way we have a chance of eliminating as many possible surprises that we can."

"Good idea," Levi acknowledged. "Not that we can detect booby-traps from the air, but something tells me these people have big ferocious dogs, besides the hound dog in the truck, and these days, the property is no doubt covered with monitoring systems, if they're into really heavy duty shit."

The plan for helicopter surveillance was to be initiated for that evening, under cover of darkness, with the use of night vision goggles. The three ATF&E agents and a senior flight engineer from Plattsburg Air Force Base would accompany and command the aerial mission over the Sweeney property and then again during the daylight hours, the next morning.

"Hello Levi. I was wondering what you were going to be doing this evening?" ZenJa asked.

"Why do you ask?"

"I wondered if you want to tour my new, but empty abode and I wanted to try out my new outdoor grill and thought we could have some salmon steaks, red roasted potatoes and salad."

"That sounds very nice, ZenJa, but unfortunately I have an other engagement."

"Oh, sorry to hear that. Is it work related or pleasure?" ZenJa asked and wanted to cut her tongue off, afterward, for asking that question.

"ZenJa, ZenJa, ZenJa...if I told you it was work, would you believe me and if I told you it was pleasure, would you be jealous?"

"Oh! Get over yourself, Mr. Harris. I could care less either way,"

ZenJa lied.

"We're still on for tomorrow night, aren't we?" Levi asked, hearing the disappointment in ZenJa's voice.

"If you can find the time," she retorted.

"How about I *drift* over in my boat, to your boat launch about 6:30? I can see your dock from my house, you know, with my binoculars, so I'll know when your ready," Levi said and laughed.

"Why am I not surprised you're still spying on me?"

"Makes me wonder why you purchased a home so close to mine, one that I can clearly see from across the bay, if it bothers you so much," Levi commented and snickered.

"Oh my God! You're insufferable, like I've said so many times before."

"And you love me for it, don't you, ZenJa?"

"You make my blood boil!" she exclaimed.

"I think that's called passion, ZenJa," Levi chuckled. Okay, I don't have time to continue this bantering session, so does the menu I mentioned sound delicious?"

"Indeed it does and I'll bring the wine and something *special* for dessert."

"If I may be so bold as to ask what the dessert might be? I'm hoping you're not going to say it's some kind of body part, is it?"

"Oh my God! You're a delightful, evil, and sexy woman, now aren't you, my dear? I never would have thought you were capable of talking dirty like that! I like that, actually," he said after hesitating from his stunned silence.

ZenJa was horrified she had spoken her thoughts out loud and covered her mouth with her hand.

"I only meant..." she began.

"Oh, ZenJa, ZenJa, ZenJa, don't blush...I can tell you're blushing over the phone, now aren't you? I like that, too and just to ease your mind, I am thinking of using a body part or two of mine for dessert, but I was only thinking of using my fingers to feed you some fresh strawberries dipped in Swiss chocolate, but now that I think about it, I may change the menu and bring something else," Levi laughed and nearly choked on his own spit and hung up the phone

"Son of a bitch!" she yelled and quickly closed her cell phone hoping the redness would soon leave her cheeks.

Chapter 51

Promptly at midnight a Blackhawk helicopter, a flight engineer from Plattsburg Air Force Base, and the three ATF agents, donning night vision goggles, hoovered over the Wilbur Sweeney property in an effort to capture the lay of the land. That included the main residence and various out buildings, along with vehicles, including log trucks, skidders and any other items of interest and to view potential hazzards that law enforcement personnel would encounter, if a raid were to take place. Levi and his counterparts were in hopes *Mrs. Lumberjack* would persuade her husband and his brother, who everyone called Junior, to surrender their operation and cooperate with the authorities to enable the *feds* to arrest and prosecute the *king pins* in this weapons and drug dealing enterprise.

"It appears Mrs. Sweeney's none to happy to see us flying overhead," Brent commented while the members of the airborne entourage witnessed the lady of the house run outdoors with her faithful dog at her side and shotgun in hand.

"She doesn't really think she's going to shoot this *bird* down with that weapon, does she?" Alex murmured and laughed.

"Maybe she thinks we're going to steal that lovely yellow pick up truck," Levi added and smiled.

"Have you got all the pictures of the property you want?" Brent asked while Levi continued to document, on video, the property and it's contents.

"Almost, but let's take another swing by those logging trucks and piles of logs, nearby. I want to come back, another time, within a day or two, and see if the pile has been moved around, trucks loaded, or if there appears to be any movement of the inventory, in an effort to see if Mr. Sweeney and company are about to make a delivery.

"Good idea," Brent commented, when the Blackhawk circled around and the camera continued to document the selected items of interest to the group.

"What's that helicopter doing, nosing around our property?" Wilber barked to his wife who had just come inside their farm house.

"I don't know; you don't think *they* got wind of our little operation here in town, do you?"

"Who would have mentioned it, Lily? Certainly not Ivan. He just made Chief of Police, I doubt he's going to turn in his own family and incriminate himself do you?" Mr. Sweeney growled sharply.

"No, but maybe he's decided to throw us to the wolves and save his own skin and look like Mr. Innocent."

"He isn't in any position to throw anyone to the wolves, Lily and you know God damn well. We're not murderers..." Wilbur began.

"All I know is that helicopter sounded like a military contraption...it was no simple sight-seeing vehicle taking tourists around in the dark of night,"Lily replied.

"I know what kind of helo it was; I ain't no dummy. We may not have had those fancy flying machines in Nam and I rather doubt that Blackhawk was bringing our boy's body back from Afghanistan tonight, do you?"

"Look, Wilbur, I don't like you and Junior getting so deep in this illegal shit. I want you both to get out while you still can."

"Who says we can get out now? You know as well as I do, we're in this about as deep as we can get."

"What if I found a way for you to help capture the real ring leaders and possibly get off from any charges?"

"You've been to the feds, haven't you, you friggin' idiot?" Wilbur screamed, but didn't raise a hand to harm his wife.

"I was asking around, but don't worry, they don't know who I am and besides, I never gave them my name and I didn't get theirs either."

"You simply think that helicopter was just flying overhead for the fun of it and just so happened to fly over our place, tonight?"

"I'm sorry, Wilbur. I don't want anything to happen to you or Junior. You're the only family I have left, after losing..." Lily began but stopped mid sentence.

"Either way we're going to go to prison or die. The feds will put us in prison or Ivan will kill us. What's two or three more?" Wilbur asked and sat down in front of the fireplace to warm himself against the chill that had overtaken the farm house.

"I'd rather see us in prison than dead and if we go to prison, Ivan will end up on death row, if I know anything about the law," Lily reasoned.

"Let me think about it," Wilbur said and stared into the fireplace and thought about the son he had lost, not long ago, in a war so far from home.

****

Levi returned to his lakefront home shortly before dawn, after leaving

Alex and Brent at their residences and collapsed, from exhaustion on his bed, and mentally listed several of the unanswered questions that still remained in connection with the murders and disappearances of the young girls from Longberry and the surrounding area.

"Fucking evidence takes so long to process," he swore out loud and noted any fingerprints or evidence gathered from the break-in at ZenJa's parents had not come back with any useful information. He also, hadn't had time to investigate and compare the tire tread impressions with the mismatched tire on Ivan Sweeney's Blazer, either.

He was also fairly confident there was no evidence found near or around the Miller residence where it was thought some or all of the missing girls might be buried. If there had been, he would have been notified of that by the FBI who where investigating the property, with cadaver dogs, without any involvement or assistance from the local law enforcement community, other than Brian Martin. "Nothing but dead ends!" he snarled and fell into a deep, but restless sleep with visions of his beautiful wife pleaded for him to come home and be with her as she passed from this world to the next.

Chapter 52

Promptly at 6:30, Levi positioned his boat beside the lakeside dock that bordered on ZenJa's property and clamored out with his arms full of cloth bags, containing various wines and desert for his dinner date that evening.

He noticed ZenJa standing on the deck of her newly built log cabin, that faced the water, waving in greetings while she tended the charcoal grill; her silky, pink summer dress and long hair blowing in the breeze.

"Nice place," Levi said and secured the contributions he brought for the picnic, on the round, oversized, picnic table before reaching out and giving ZenJa a slight peck on the cheek. Both ZenJa and Levi were aware this was the first meaningful physical contact either had between themselves since they had first met.

"You look lovely, tonight and I also might add the salmon steak smell delicious, also," he said while taking a seat at the table.

"Thank you, Levi and you look very nice in your jeans and I bet the wine is delicious, too," ZenJa said rather sharply realizing Levi was incapable of giving a meaningful compliment or words of passion to express emotion of any kind. God forbid he appear to give a crap about anyone, she thought.

ZenJa's date smirked, aware of the intended barb she had flung his way...just as he intended.

"Is there anything I can help you with?" Levi asked, but remained seated.

"I'll get the cork *screw* and you can... open the wine, if you wish."

"Oh, for a minute I thought you were going to tell me to go and screw myself," he replied with a twinkle in his eye.

"I was brought up to be a lady, Levi. I might think that, but I'll try not to say it," she said and went into her home to get the items she needed to finish setting the table.

Not a moment had passed when Levi quietly entered ZenJa's new home and snuck up behind her, grabbed her by the waist and turned her to face him, while burying his lips against hers, bruising the soft flesh she willingly offered him; the couple overcome with deep and ravenous amounts of passion that had been building for months. Levi roughly gathered her flimsy dress from her shoulders and lowered it below her waist while he continued to assault her lips with his own; his hands hungrily fondling her firm breasts and nipples and pressing his body against hers.

"Levi, I want you," she whispered between her swollen lips. "Make love to me," she added.

"I've wanted you for so long, ZenJa," he said and backed her against the butcher's block that was centered in the oversized kitchen.

"No! I don't want to make love to you ZenJa, I want to fuck you!" he continued.

"Fuck me, Levi...I want you to fuck me, too!" ZenJa pleaded, leading Levi to the carpeted floor in front of the blazing fireplace where the couple lay, naked, exploring each other's flesh with lips, tongues, arms and legs; raptured in what would be their world of raw, uninhibited sex, passion, and furor.

"Oh my God!" a voice was heard at the entrance to the kitchen from the deck outside, while Levi and ZenJa grabbed what few clothes were within their reach, to cover their bodies, at the same time Alex Lyons stepped inside, grinning like a Cheshire cat.

"What the fuck are you doing here?" Levi swore reaching out to punch his brother in the face.

"Oh...you almost got me!" Alex said, after jumping out of reach and laughing like a hyena.

"You fucking son of a bitch...and I do mean bitch," Levi yelled while pushing his brother out the door, onto the deck. "You ever hear of knocking, you bastard?"

"Sorry! I was just driving by and I noticed smoke on the deck and stopped to make sure the house wasn't on fire. I had no idea this was ZenJa's new house," he added laughing until tears streamed down his cheeks.

While the naked man and his brother were ferociously arguing between the sliding door and the deck, ZenJa ran to the bathroom to dress herself and hide from this most humiliating experience; the worst of her life.

"When is it not normal for smoke to be coming from a deck, in the summer time, on a fucking lake?" Levi growled and dressed himself.

"Well, if you'd look, asshole, you'd see the fire had pretty much consumed whatever you were cooking and the smoke was thick and black and had burned away the top of the grill. How much longer would that cheap grill have held up, before setting the whole damn deck on fire?" Alex asked, but continued to chuckle.

"Oh shit!" Levi said and realized what a devastating fire this might have been.

"I guess you guys were *smoking* hot in there and couldn't smell the smoke out here," Alex offered, wiping tears from his eyes.

"I guess I owe you a debt of gratitude and thanks for putting out the fire before you came inside," Levi meekly commented.

"I think I got here and *came* inside before you did!" Alex mercilessly teased his brother. "And on that note, I think I'll leave before you kick my ass," he added and ran down the steps and drove away in his car.

"Get the fuck out of here!" Levi yelled and shook his fist at his brother as the dust from the driveway blocked his view.

"ZenJa, are you okay?" Levi asked through what he assumed was the bathroom door.

"Just go away Levi. Go away," she begged; tears streaming down her face.

"I'm sorry, ZenJa," he said and quietly checked the fire to make sure it was completely out, brought the items from the picnic table inside and slowly walked to his boat and sped toward his own house.

On the way inside his house Levi's cell phone rang and he noticed it was FBI Agent Edward Emerson calling. "What's up?" Levi asked; upon entering his home, after docking his speed boat.

"I just wanted to let you know, as you expected, there were no fingerprints of any interest to be found at the Beckwith proptery...inside or outside the home and there were no obvious signs of a break-in."

"Like you said, that's no surprise, but I've stumbled on an interesting bit of information and I've yet to have time to investigate this development."

"What is it?"

"It appears newly selected Police Chief Ivan Sweeney owns an old beat up Chevy Blazer and there are three matching tires and one oddly treaded tire on the driver's side rear."

"Well, now, that is interesting. How are you going to deal with that?"

"Ivan and I are going to become good friends and we're going *off-roadin'* in the mud this weekend and you can have someone standing by to get impressions of the rear tire to compare with the impressions we already have from the accident scene."

"Brilliant!" Emerson said. "Let me know exactly where and when and I'll have someone close by."

"The place has already been decided on. It's going to be on the Beckwith property...when I'm not sure, but maybe Saturday because it's supposed to rain Friday night, so it should be good and muddy."

"Keep in touch," Emerson said and disconnected the call.

Levi tried to call ZenJa, but not surprising, she did not answer her phone. "I'll give her some time to regain her dignity," Levi said out loud but left her this message. "Hi ZenJa...once again I'm so sorry about tonight and I know you're probably mortified with my brother showing up. He always appears when he's not wanted, but what I said...I meant," he confessed."

"I'm going *off roadin'* this weekend, Saturday, probably. Would you like to go? This isn't just pleasure, but mixed with business and I think you'll be very interested...not in me, but in something that may develop. Good night, ZenJa. Again, I'm sorry."

ZenJa heard the answering machine and replayed Levi's message several times in an effort to figure this complicated man out and what he was trying to say.

She realized she was indeed mortified with being caught red-handed, so to speak; her passion uninhibited and exposed for a stranger to see, but she'd faced life and death before, so after giving it some thought she realized this wasn't any big deal. Obviously, all three of them were adults and hopefully naked bodies weren't that uncommon to be seen. If she interpreted Levi's message correctly, he meant what he said about wanting to have sex with her. He didn't say he wanted to make love to her, after correcting her, but explained he wanted simply to have sex and she was and would be satisfied with that. Maybe he was ready to shed some of that armor he wore to protect his heart.

ZenJa was in no mood to speak with Levi, so she left him a text message and agreed to go *off roading* if he wanted on Saturday. Given Saturday was three days away, she assumed this embarrassing episode would be forgotten by then, but how she wanted his lips on hers again...oh yes, she did.

Chapter 53

"You got all the surveillance equipment you need?" Levi asked Alex and Brent as the trio made their toward the wooded lot that encompassed the Wilbur Sweeney residence.

"I wish I'd had some of this equipment the other night!" Alex whispered before Levi punched him in the face, sending him sprawling into the dirt.

"What the hell's up with you two?" Wyman asked in a hushed tone.

"Did you know my brother's a peeping tom?" Levi asked.

"Hell, no!" Alex snickered.

"He has no sex life of his own, so he has to snoop on mine."

"Oh, wow, I had no idea Alex was a perv."

"Hell, yes! He is and always has been."

Alex stood up, dusted himself off and continued to snicker at his brother's expense.

"What? Nothing to say, bro?" Levi asked.

"No, I guess not; but I do have to mention that I may not have sex life now, but it appears you don't either," he replied and chuckled at his own joke.

"Anyone I know?" Wyman asked risking the wrath of the man who faced him.

"Yeah...it's Zen..." Alex began when Levi grabbed him by the throat.

"Shut the fuck up, asshole or I'll fucking blow your head off!"

"Okay, gentlemen," Wyman said wisely. "We have a job to do and let's forget this silliness.

"It's called respect and I don't give a flying fuck about my respect, but no one disrespects a lady, Alex; don't forget that!"

"Sorry, Levi. I know I've razzed you enough about it and won't mention it again."

"Damn right you won't and you will apologize to the lady."

"I will Levi; I will the next time I *see* her," Alex added biting his lip in an effort not to smile.

Knock it off, you two, Mr. and Mrs. Lumberjack just left, with the dog, thank goodness, so let's hurry up and get this GPS attached to the log truck," AFT Agent Wyman suggested to change the subject from whatever compromising position Alex discovered his brother in, the previous day.

The agents neared the truck and noticed it had been fully loaded since they flew over the property in the helo.

"Well, it looks like the Lumberjacks will be heading out soon," Levi commented to no one in particular. "Looks like we arrived just in time."

Alex Lyon's cell phone rang shortly after the monitoring device had been secured on the logging truck.

"What?" he asked.

"Is this the man I spoke to the other day at Molly's?"

"Yes, it is and do you have any information for me?"

"Yes, I do. I discussed the *situation* with my husband had he's agreed to find a way to resolve the *fix* we've gotten ourselves into."

"That's very wise, but what about your brother-in-law? Is he interested in ending this situation?"

"I...we haven't mentioned it to Junior, that's what we call him. There's someone else involved and I don't trust Junior to keep his yapper shut. I know he would like to end this, peacefully, but I'm not sure if he won't want to help this other person attempt to escape justice and I...we...my husband and I have no interest in saving his sorry ass."

"Who is this other person?"

"I can't say."

"Okay, when will the truck be making a delivery?"

"I guess there's no sense in pretending you don't know what vehicle or items are used in this *situation,* is there?" Mrs. Sweeney asked.

""I guess it was rather difficult to hide the fact we flew over your property the other night, is it, Mrs. Sweeney?" Alex asked and smiled at the two agents who quietly stood by and also smiled, having the good fortune to learn of the positive turn of events that were unfolding.

"Where are you now?" Alex asked.

"We're in town on errands and I thought it best to call from a pay phone and you know how few of those there are around here."

"I believe Molly's Café is the only place in the area that has one, am I correct?"

"Yes, my husband and I are having a nice dinner here at the café."

"What if I come and join you for dessert?" Alex asked.

"I guess that'll be okay. There aren't too many customers here, right now."

"I'll bring my partner, if it's okay?"

"Yes, I guess so, if he has to, come, too."

"See you in fifteen minutes," Alex said and disconnected the call.

"Could this operation, *2X4* have come to a better conclusion?" Alex asked while the men clamored back into the old Ford pickup Brent Wyman was using for this operation.

"It's not over, yet," Levi cautioned.

"You think something's not right here?" Wyman questioned.

"Seems to simple to me. I'm not new at this business and there's always something unexpected that happens or could potentially happen. This seems to easy."

"She only knows about you two guys, right? You and Alex?" Levi asked to confirm his assessment.

"Yes...we never mentioned you or anyone else." Alex stated.

"Let me off behind Molly's, inconspicuously, of course, before you drive in the parking lot," Levi began. I'll come in after you two get yourselves seated. I'll be simply another customer, sitting by myself enjoying some of Molly's apply pie."

"What if Molly mentions us not sitting together; she very well knows, by now, our connection," Alex asked.

"I'll give her my *look*. She's one smart cookie and she'll know to keep her lip zipped."

"Okay, sounds like a plan and it'll be good to have back-up," Wyman agreed.

"Let's do this," Alex said while the trio drove to the local café.

The trio of ATF agents arrived at their destination and the group noticed the café wasn't as peaceful and quiet as one could hope.

"Looks like everyone in fucking Longberry is here," Levi swore, noting ZenJa's black Dodge Charger and Ivan Sweeney's patrol car were also parked in the lot, along with the Lumberjack's yellow pick-up truck.

"Shit! This is fucked up," Levi continued and bailed out of the truck, behind the café.

Once inside the restaurant, Alex and Brent ignored ZenJa, who was seated at the counter, chatting with the proprietor, eating a hot fudge sundae and also by-passed Chief Sweeney and the Lumberjack couple, too.

"What you want for dinner?" Alex asked his partner, while seating themselves directly across from the woodsman and his wife in booths at the rear of the establishment.

"Can we get some coffee, first?" Brent Wyman asked, eyeing the duo to their left and Molly who approached from the counter.

"Coming right up, gentlemen," she responded with no recognition in her manner or conversation.

Seconds later, Levi sauntered in the café and slid on a fountain stool next to ZenJa. It would have been rather irregular, Levi knew, if he had ignored ZenJa, knowing Ivan Sweeney was aware they were acquainted.

"This fucking sucks," Levi murmured under his breath and reached for a menu.

"If it's so fucking bad to sit next to me, you bastard, why not sit somewhere else?" ZenJa barked, also under her breath.

"No, ZenJa...this isn't what you think," he replied in hushed tones. "That isn't what I meant. This has nothing to do with you," he whispered at the same time Ivan Sweeney seated himself next to Levi, on his other side.

"What can I get you, two?" Molly asked Ivan and Levi.

"Well, Molly, you can get me a hot turkey sandwich with fries and a diet Coke," Levi said. "Ivan and I are not here on a date, so what he orders is on his own tab," Levi said and smiled, his evil grin, at the law enforcement officer who sat next to him.

"Are you always this quick witted?' Chief Sweeney asked and smiled.

"Oh, he's quick and slick," ZenJa added and ate another spoonful of ice cream.

For the first time in his life, Levi was unable to think of a comeback to that snide remark, but simply continued to smile and sip his water.

"Where's your car?" ZenJa asked noting he must have arrived with his brother and Wyman. She surmised their visit to the café was not a coincidence and wondered what the situation was.

"It broke down the road a ways and I walked here," Levi replied but kept his eyes forward. "I called a tow truck and hope they've come to get it by now," he quickly responded knowing if Sweeney volunteered to tend to the vehicle there was no vehicle to find.

"Here's your dinner, Mr." Molly said and placed the steaming hot meal and cold drink on the counter.

"Thank you," Levi and winked at the hostess.

"We still going off-roading Saturday, Levi?" Ivan asked.

"I wouldn't miss it for the world. You all set to get all muddied up?"

"Can't wait to see what vehicle you bring to the festivities. You just make sure it's all legal, inspected and licensed, now."

"It won't be either licensed or inspected," Levi said and laughed.

"What you bringing?"

"A new Polaris 4X4 I bought the other day, so I guess it's my vehicle against your old pickup, huh?" Levi smirked.

"We'll see who comes out on top!" Ivan said and sipped his coffee.

"Who do you think will come out on *top*, ZenJa?" Levi asked.

Before she could reply, Levi asked, " Hell, ZenJa, why don't you come with me on Saturday? It will be good for you to get some fun in the sun."

"I may just take you up on that, Levi," she said and left the counter to go to the ladies room.

"You have a liking for Ms. Beckwith, Levi?"

"She's only a friend and speaking of friends, do you have any in this town, now that you 're back?"

"I haven't had much time for socializing since my return. There's so much to get caught up on and stuff like that."

"You haven't forgotten the townsfolk are still looking for missing girls, right?" Levi callously reminded the man.

"That's my number one priority."

"Miss? We're ready to order now," Alex yelled from the corner of the café.

"Be right there, gentlemen," she replied only seconds after Mrs. Sweeney raised her voice and a chair was overturned in the corner of the café where Alex, Brent and the Sweeneys were seated.

"Put the fucking gun away, Wilbur, you ass," Mrs. Lumberjack ordered the man who stood, facing her.

Alex and Brent drew their guns, discreetly, from across the aisle at the same moment Chief Sweeney ran around the corner, from his seat at the counter.

"Drop it, Wilbur," Ivan yelled and fired without giving the man a chance to lower the weapon, which caused the man to shoot his helpless wife.

Alex and Brent quickly concealed their weapons, to guard their identities as officers of the law, but ran over to assist the wounded couple.

"What the fuck did you shoot him for, you fucker? Wilbur tripped as he was handing the gun to me for safekeeping!" Mrs. Sweeney screamed, before she expired.

"I've called 911," Molly yelled and she fled to the kitchen while ZenJa ran from the bathroom toward the crime scene.

"What the fuck's going on?" Levi yelled and grabbed, the still smoking weapon, from the police chief's hand.

"He was going to shoot her!"

"You know that for a fact, do you?" Levi questioned.

"You never gave him a chance to put the gun away and it appears the weapon only had one bullet in it," Levi remarked after examining the pistol using a napkin to refrain from leaving fingerprints on the handle.

"I obviously didn't know it wasn't fully loaded."

"The ambulance is on the way," Molly cried.

"Tell them not to rush, Molly. They're both dead," Levi said while Alex and Brent kept to the background under the pretense of having been at the diner as simple guests and having no other motive to be there.

"I'll have to investigate this," Ivan said softly.

"No, I think this will come under the jurisdiction of the State Police, if I know anything about police protocol," Levi reminded the chief.

"I'll call them," Ivan offered.

"That would be a good idea," Levi warned and asked Molly to lock from both front and back doors of the café to contain the crime scene.

The state police arrived and all those in the café would be required to give their statements, before they would be allowed to leave, well after midnight.

The café would be closed until further notice, at Molly's request and until all the evidence was obtained.

Alex and Brent gave their statements, outside in a state police vehicle, in an effort to keep their statements from being overheard by Chief Sweeney.

"So, what's your view of what happened, Mr. Lyons?" the trooper asked.

"Off the record, I don't want to divulge too much information right now. My partner and I are Feds and we're here to meet with Mr. and Mrs. Sweeney about a *situation*."

"So, now *for* the record, Mr. and Mrs. Sweeney were sitting at an adjacent booth at Molly's Café and we overheard them discussing their *logging business* and the fact they were interested in getting out of that *business*."

"Did this so called *business* appear to have illegal implications?" the trooper asked.

"I don't want to comment on that. I can't pretend to know and I don't assume anything," Alex replied with Brent nodding in agreement.

"I will tell you exactly what I saw the moments leading to the shooting."

"Okay," what happened?"

"The Sweeney's were talking and I overheard her tell her husband he didn't and wouldn't need his gun and she told him to, "Put that gun away,

Wilbur, you ass!"

"Those were her exact words?"

"Yes, that's just what she said and laughed, I might add," Brent added.

"I would say he was handing her the weapon, unfortunately, the barrel was facing Mrs. Sweeney and he started to hand it to her, he tripped over his shoe lace and lost his balance, knocking over a chair." Alex continued.

"Okay, come to the state police barracks in Commerce Station. I want to get separate statements from you two," the trooper said.

"Okay, as soon as I get my own car, we'll be there," Alex said and were allowed to leave the confines of the police vehicle.

Ivan Sweeney was the first to vacate the establishment and sent home on administrative leave; the State Police would be in charge of the town's security and needs until the investigation was over.

The bodies were removed to the coroners office before the AFT trio and ZenJa left the scene, well into the late morning hours. Once they walked outside, they were finally free to talk honestly.

"You need a ride home?" ZenJa asked. "I remember you saying your car broke down."

"Yes, I could use a ride, but my vehicle isn't broken down. The three of us came here together on a case, that has just fucking gone to shit!" Levi growled from anger and lack of sleep.

"So that's what you meant when you said, "This fucking sucks? You really weren't referring to sitting next to me?"

"Yeah...we were there investigating something and having you there and low and behold having the police chief there really messed things up. I didn't want you around for safety reasons and I wonder what the odds of the Chief being there at the same time we were going to meet the couple who happens to be related to the Chief and who just shot them in cold blood...more or less," he continued, without taking a breath.

"Alex and Brent are on their way to the police barracks in Commerce Station and we have to follow, to make out statements, too."

On the drive to the barracks, Levi explained, to ZenJa, what he knew about *Operation 2X4*, so far and hinted that there was more to Ivan Sweeney than met the eye and also explained the reason for his interest in going four wheeling with the chief.

"You think he was involved in the murders of the Childress and O'Leary girls and our missing Zippy and Pickles?"

"I think he is the missing link we've been looking for all these years, yes, but he may not be the only person left."

"Hell, he would have been only fifteen years old or so, when these crimes were committed and they stopped for years, now."

"That's exactly why he's more of a suspect now, than ever. He graduated from high school here in Longberry and then went to college and then enlisted in the military, so he's been out of the area for years and the evidence found at the scene of your parents murders indicated there was an odd tire on a vehicle that most likely forced them off the road, the night they died."

"That tire is on his old beat up pickup?" ZenJa asked coming to the realization where this conversation was heading.

"You got it," Levi replied after the couple drove into the parking lot and parked beside Alex and Brent.

"This is going to be one long fucking day," Levi commented, while the group entered the front door, to give their statements to law enforcement.

Chapter 54

"Thanks for the lift, ZenJa. Do you want to come in? I want you to know, though, that I'm not going to be very sociable; I'm only to crash in my bed, but you're welcome to sleep in your old room, if you want," he suggested and left the comfort of the Dodge Charger and opened the door to his home. ZenJa, slowly followed behind, after an exhausting interview at the State Police barracks in regards to the shootings at Molly's Cafe.

"I'd like that," she whispered. "Let me go out to my car and grab some fresh clothes I have in my overnight bag. Moments later she followed Levi up the stairs and each entered their own bedroom, closing the doors behind themselves.

ZenJa peeled off the jeans, tee shirt and underwear she had worn since the previous day, turned on the shower and eagerly entered the stall, basking in the warmth of the hot water as it streamed over her body.

Moments later, ZenJa heard the bathroom door open and watched Levi enter the luxurious, black marble tiled room, strip off his clothes and open the frosted glass door and barely had time to close it before the ravenous couple embraced; Levi forcing ZenJa into the corner of the stall and feverishly swept his hands over her soapy body and pressing his lips, consuming her mouth with his own.

"Oh ZenJa! I've wanted you for so long," Levi muttered; his lips sweeping over her own before moving to her ear and neck; his hands cascading over her firm breasts and pinching her erect nipples. "I've wanted to fuck you ever since I first met you, ZenJa," he hungrily admitted, his hand finding its way between her thighs.

ZenJa pressed her own wet and wild body against his, her own arm wrapped around his neck and the couple moaned with sexual frustration, hunger, and anticipation.

As wild animals in the jungle, the couple greedily and savagely explored each others naked, soapy bodies. Tantalizing, aggressively, and passionately expressing their desire that had long festered into insanity of need and desire.

Moments after the couple rinsed the shower jell from their bodies, Levi shut off the water and the couple stepped out of the confines of the stall and grabbed oversized fluffy towels from the heated rack. Quickly wiping each other's naked bodies down, Levi ushered ZenJa into the master bedroom and the couple embraced, lips and hands exploring each other's most sensitive and private body parts before collapsing onto the king-size bed.

Sounds of rapture, groaning with pleasure, and fierce uninhibited pure and raw sex escalated to a fever pitch for the rest of the late afternoon and the entire night. Only the necessity of another cooling shower, moments to catch their breath, and a shared bottle of wine interrupted other experiences of lust and passion, not coming to a conclusion until the sun was rising over the lake.

ZenJa slipped out of the king-sized bed and quickly grabbed a shower in her own bathroom, across the hall, in an effort to allow her bed-partner to get some well deserved sleep.

Completely refreshed, although exhausted from this sexual encounter, ZenJa dressed in a cool and crisp yellow summer dress and matching sandals before entering the kitchen to brew some coffee and prepare breakfast.

Sitting on a outdoor lounge chair, on the lakeside deck, ZenJa sipped her coffee and heard the water from upstairs running and realized she and Levi would soon meet, face to face in the familiar existence they had, had before last night. Would there be regret, shame, another fierce argument...like many they had in the past? Would last night simply be a mistake in Levi's eyes or would he accept the reality that he needed someone in his lonely life; not to replace the woman he loved, but to begin a new adventure, with life continuing and being what one makes of it? ZenJa was frightened at the prospect of what this morning would bring.

While he showered Levi thought about the night he had spent with ZenJa, in lust, and realized what his brother said was correct. He needed another good woman in his life and he even admitted he'd been sexually frustrated since the day his wife died, so many years ago and what a bastard he had been, but being a son of a bitch, in his line of work, was essential. He had to learn to separate the two lives.

Before Levi made an appearance downstairs, the bell to the front door rang and ZenJa went to answer it. She peeked out the window and noticed a van parked in the driveway and a delivery man standing on the steps with a large bouquet of multicolored roses and Lily-of-the Valley in an oversized crystal vase.

"Hello?" ZenJa asked and opened the door and received the generous bouquet from the young Tele-Florist associate.

"For you Miss," the man replied, smiled and left the doorstep.

ZenJa closed the door and put the lovely vase on an end table and read the enclosed card:

My Dearest ZenJa,

I don't know where we go from here, but I want you to be a part of my life, through the good and bad. I know I don't deserve someone like you, but I ask you to accept me for what and who I am.

Levi

ZenJa tenderly unwrapped the delicate paper that enclosed the bouquet and place the card in her bra, close to her heart before turning around, with tears in her eyes, she faced the man who had written these words of declaration to her. They were not words of love, but she realized Levi was Levi and wasn't about to change him. She loved him and if he never loved her in return, she would accept that.

Without words, Levi embraced the woman who stood before him and tenderly kissed her on her swollen lips.

"The flowers are beautiful, Levi and the gesture is lovely," she whispered and continued to hold this tall, dark, mysterious man who had entered her life and soul.

"I rather assumed this morning would be a little awkward, so I hoped to minimize the tension to prove to you I'm not a completely callous cad.

"Thank you again, Levi. I also thought this morning might be a little...shall I repeat the word you used, awkward and thought about leaving before you got up?"

"If you had done that, my dear, I would have had to accept the flowers and weep all over them, as you are, and read the card that was meant for someone else," he replied, laughed and again held ZenJa close to his body.

ZenJa was grateful for Levi's ability to handle any situation with grace and break the nervous energy that had encompassed the lake house.

ZenJa cheerfully picked up the bouquet and walked with Levi to the kitchen; their spirits and hearts light and happy.

"I made you some breakfast and it's warming in the oven," ZenJa said placed the flowers on the picnic table, on the deck.

"I hope you made enough for two."

"I already ate," ZenJa said serving the freshly brewed coffee.

"I don't mean for you; I'm ravenous and could eat a breakfast for two or a horse, if you have one on the grill; all by myself," he said and again laughed.

"Speaking of grills..." ZenJa began.

"No worries, ZenJa. We'll pick up a *real* grill at Home Depot or Lowe's when we venture out for our muddin' adventure with Ivan."

"You still think Ivan will want to go muddin'?" ZenJa asked.

"That's a good question. I'll have to find out, later."

"I hate to come back to reality, but what's the scoop on the shoot-out at Molly's yesterday?"

Levi sipped his coffee and took a bite of his toast and again was sadly brought back to real life.

"Mrs. Sweeney said her husband and brother-in-law, were involved in some weapons running scheme and she contacted Alex and Brent and wanted a day or two to convince her family members to end their part in the operation in hopes of saving their lives and hoping to get immunity for their cooperation.

"They had met at Molly's and were again going to meet in hopes of getting an affirmative response from the couple. But, when you and Ivan were both at the Café, that put the shits to any conversation they might have had. I showed up as backup and Ivan is still oblivious to the fact that Alex, Brent and I are affiliated or connected and we wanted to keep it that way. "

"So that's why Alex and Brent keep a low profile once the shooting started?"

"Yes, and I truly believe the Sweeney's were going to cooperate and that's why Ivan stepped in, so they couldn't."

"What makes you think the three of them are in cahoots over this scheme?"

"Something Mrs. Lumberjack said."

"Mrs. Lumberjack?"

"That's what we fondly called Mrs. Sweeney."

"And now you think Ivan is or was involved in the missing girls and murders, also?" ZenJa asked with great interest.

"Yup! I think so."

"So that explains the muddin' adventure we're going on?"

"Yes, ma'am and I've already contacted the FBI and there'll be someone standing by to take tire impressions once our fun and games are over."

"Do you think Ivan's the only one left, who was involved?"

"Well, no; like I mentioned Wilbur Sweeney's brother appears to be involved in the weapons running scheme, at least. I can't swear that he might not be involved with the missing girls, though Mrs. Sweeney never mentioned that, but did suggest there is more to Ivan than meets the eye, ZenJa. It seems like the cockroaches just keep coming out of the woodwork, around here."

Before Levi finished another bite of breakfast his cell phone rang.

"What?" he barked into the receiver.

"You better get your ass over to the Sweeney place."

"Why?" he growled shoving the last bite of scrambled egg in his mouth.

"The log truck and logs are gone!" Alex yelled.

"You got the GPS on?" Levi asked.

"Yes, we just turned it on and we're on our way to locate it."

"Who the hell...?" Levy began.

"I don't know, but my guess is Mrs. Lumberjack's brother-in-law; his name is Junior, by the way, and God only knows who else," Alex continued.

"Yeah, Junior and maybe Ivan?"

"That would be my guess."

"Where are you, Brent, and the truck, now?"

"I'm in my Mustang and Brent is in the old pickup. The log truck is heading up Ragged Mountain Pass."

"They'll never get to the bottom of that pass with a fully loaded truck," Levi surmised. "Not without turning it over and/or losing the brakes.

"I just hope both Junior and Ivan *aren't* in that fucking truck and die together," Levi yelled at the same time ZenJa and he began to quickly clear the outdoor table of food and flowers, grab their personal items, weapons, and painfully jump into the Navigator and headed toward Ragged Mountain Pass.

"Is Brent anywhere near you?" Levi asked.

"He's right behind me," Alex confirmed.

"Pull over and have him ride with you. That fucking piece of shit, he's driving, will probably crap the bed on the way and I want you both together so we can keep in constant contact."

"Okay; I'm pulling over and so is Brent."

"Also, keep away from that mother fucking truck. Don't try to pass it, or approach it from the front and keep the hell back! Those logs, if and when they let loose, will kill anything it's path."

"Okay, and I'll have Brent notify the state police, on his cell phone, in hopes they can set up road blocks to keep other cars off that mountain," Alex added.

"Sounds good," Levi replied and the couple and Navigator sped through the small towns and hamlets in Vermont at over ninety miles an hour.

"Here, ZenJa! Put the phone on the dash and on 'speaker' and we'll keep in touch with Brent when he's finished calling the state police."

"Oh my God, Levi. This just keeps getting worse and worse, doesn't it?" she cried and held onto the safety bar over the passenger's side door.

"Yes, but our sex life is going to get a hell of a lot better...ya think?" Levi asked and smiled.

"If it gets any better, I won't be able to move," she groaned and shifted her battered and bruised body in the seat, tightening her seat belt.

"Me either," Levi said, avoiding a fire hydrant and swung the S.U.V. around another vehicle by driving on a sidewalk.

"Adventure turns me on...how about you?"

Yes, I admit nothing turns me on more than a handsome, muscular man who looks for trouble and always finds it."

"Look! It's a log truck and the load is top heavy and weaving back and forth!" ZenJa cried into the cell phone to inform Alex and Brent of the developments.

"What side of the mountain are you on, Levi?" Brent asked.

"We're approaching from Suicide Point," he yelled above the roar of the engine.

"We're coming from the other side," Brent acknowledged.

"Well, that truck's headed your way, but I don't think he's going to make it in one piece. You better turn around and get the hell out of there, Brent," Levi warned. "If that load let's go, God only knows how far down the mountain those logs may travel."

"Are there any cars in your area?" ZenJa wisely asked. "If there are, you better warn them and tell them to get the hell out of there and maybe set up a road block until the State Police get there," she added.

Levi nodded and once again maneuvered the S.U.V. over the treacherous and narrow mountain road that was bordered by flimsy guardrails and cavernous cliffs on the descending side of the highway, while their vehicle climbed the steep and curving slope.

"What do you plan to do?" ZenJa cried, hanging onto the safety bar and seat with both hands. "You can't pass the truck or overtake it, Levi!"

"I know, but I'm going to try and persuade the driver to pull over and let him know the *gig* is up!"

Smoke was bellowing from one side of the truck and Levi shouted into his cell phone, "Oh fuck! A tire fire! That whole bitch'll be going up in flames in no time."

"Call the fire department, Brent, and tell them it's more than likely we're going to have a full blown forest fire here soon!"

"Roger, that!" Brent acknowledged.

The logging truck rounded a forty-five degree curve and as the driver bailed from the front of the cab, the truck ran up the right side of the highway, slammed into a rock ledge and buckled before the load and truck careened to the left and exploded into a fireball and slammed against the useless guard rails and rolled the nearly half mile to the bottom of a ravine; with logs, metal, flames, and smoke erupted the mountainside into a wall of fire of death and destruction.

Levi slammed the vehicle's transmission into Park and watched with horror, the scene that was evolving so far down the mountain, toward the quiet village that lay beyond the ruins.

ZenJa and Levi quickly exited their vehicle and checked the driver, who lay lifeless in the middle of the highway, for signs of life.

"He's still alive," ZenJa stated and pulled her cell phone out of her pocket and called 911 for an ambulance.

"Who is it?" she asked Levi who was checking the victim for an ID.

"This appears to be Mrs. Lumberjacks's dear brother-in-law, Junior," he said scanning the driver's licence that was in Mr. Sweeney's wallet.

"What's going on?" Brent yelled into the cell phone that remained in the Navigator. "The whole fucking mountain's on fire!"

"Yeah...I can see that!" Levi barked sharply into the phone when he and ZenJa climbed back into the vehicle.

"Get the fuck off the mountain!" Levi ordered. We're heading out, too!"

"We called the fire department," he added.

"We can't leave this guy here," ZenJa cried looking at the lifeless figure laying in the road. "We can't wait for an ambulance," she reasoned.

"Come on, grab this fucker's legs and we'll throw his ass in the back," he suggested and jumped from the front seat to open the tailgate of the S.U.V.

The couple struggled for several minutes to load the patient into the high-rise vehicle, while flames were licking at their heels.

Quickly, Levi slammed the Navigator into reverse and nearly crashed into the rock ledge before he made a 180 degree turn in the narrow roadway.

Moments later, the black vehicle sped down the mountain and was met by an ambulance and fire trucks from several neighboring towns.

Levi flagged the vehicles down, helped off load the patient into the ambulance and quickly gave the fire department chief the low-down on what had happened and what to expect on their arrival where the forest fire originated.

Shortly after, Levi and his passenger, Alex and Brent met in the parking lot of Molly's Café. Overhead, they noticed two C-130 Hercules aircrafts, depositing flame retardant chemicals on the fire zone and another smaller plane circled behind it, in an effort to extinguish the fire before it enveloped the whole town.

"Good work! We got Mrs. Lumberjack's brother-in-law, Junior," Levi said and gave a high-five to his male comrades and shyly smiled at ZenJa and shook her hand. "I'm so proud of you all," he added and continued to gaze into the lovely auburn/red haired woman's eyes, who stood before him.

"You can kiss her, if you want," Alex suggested, fully aware of the flirtatious exchange that had passed between his brother and the lady.

"If I didn't know better, I think he already has place a kiss on her lovely face," Brent added noting the whisker-burn and swollen lips ZenJa displayed, having had no time to hide the evidence, with makeup, before their departure from the lake house.

ZenJa blushed and Levi silently took her hand and helped her back into his vehicle.

"Looks like they have the fire under control," Alex mentioned, viewing the mountainside from the valley. "The smoke has turned white, so that's a good sign."

"It does appear they have it under control, thankfully," ZenJa agreed. "But I wonder how did those airplanes show up so fast?"

"I have no idea, but thankfully they did," Levi added. "Maybe they were on a training mission. It appears the plane, bringing up the rear, was monitoring the other two planes."

"If they were training, they got some useful experience in a big ass hurry." Alex said and smiled.

"The fire department will mop up the rest of the mess and I guess someone's going to have to haul what's left of the truck to the impound yard," Levi murmured and thought of Keith Morrison and his automotive repair business in Virginia. He wondered what the possibility of having he and his family relocate to Longberry and become a prosperous member of the community Levi had intentions of establishing on the Beckwith property, if he ever found the time.

"Who's going over to the hospital and check on Junior's condition and see what we can get out of him?" Alex asked.

"How about you and Brent go over and ZenJa and I'll check out the

Sweeney's homestead. I'm sure Junior will be at the hospital and I want him to remain oblivious to the fact that you, Brent and I are in any way connected. Let's keep him in the dark as long as possible."

"Okay, keep in touch," Alex responded and the two groups drove off in separate directions.

Chapter 55

"What in hell were you doing with that damn truck?" Ivan Sweeney yelled at the man who had, only moments before, been admitted to the local hospital; at the same time two AFT agents stood outside the door listening to the unfolding conversation.

"We'd had enough of this shit," Junior cried in pain. "We were getting out of this crap and hell, you knew it, as well," he continued. "That's why you shot Wilbur in cold blood!"

"Listen here, you piece of cow dung, I did no such thing!"

"You can fool everyone else in town, Ivan, but we know you better than anyone," he said at the same time Ivan reached over and grabbed the patient by the neck.

"I'll kill you, you fucker! You know damn well we'll all be killed because of you."

"No, you won't be killed," Alex said and burst through the door and knocked the police chief to the floor.

"It's all because of you, Ivan," Junior cried and whimpered in the corner of his bed.

"It's all right," Brent Wyman said to the patient. "You're now under protection, from this piece of garbage, by the ATF," he said while holding out his badge to the complete surprise of the local law enforcement officer.

"Get up, Ivan! You're under arrest," Brent continued and handcuffed the officer, while Ivan struggled and knocked over Junior's bedside table and chair.

"What in God's name is going on his this man's room," the nursing supervisor cried; entering the room that had the appearances of a barroom brawl.

"It's okay, now" Brent continued. "This man is under arrest and your patient is now under protection from the federal government."

"Oh, my!" she continued and went to her patient's side to render whatever aid she could to calm the victim.

"I'm okay," Junior weakly replied and fell into a deep sleep.

"You want me to stay here with Junior, until we get more help?" Alex offered.

"Thanks, Alex. That'll work, for now. I know we've been awake for, what...ever?"

"I can't remember what my bed looks like," Brent chuckled and led Longberry's Police Chief from the hospital.

"You know you're dead fucking meat," Ivan screamed through the halls of the hospital. "There are things you don't know and people who have a vested interest in the events..." he began but suddenly closed his mouth.

"Keep on talking, Ivan; I'm all ears," Brent encouraged. "But before you do, I'm going to Marandize you," he said and continued to read the prisoner his rights.

"I'm not saying another fucking word," he added while Brent frisked Ivan and removed the patrol car keys from his pocket and seated the town official in his own police car and the duo headed off to the local police station.

"You'll be nice and cozy in your own cell," Brent said, locking the cell door behind him.

"I'll kill you, mother fucker!" he continued to rant, while Brent closed the door between the cell and the outer office.

"Threatening a government agent, are you?" Brent yelled and laughed and picked up the phone to make calls to his superiors regarding the latest events that had taken place in Longberry, New Hampshire; but only after giving Levi an update, on his cell phone.

"Wow! That was fast," Levi said after disconnecting the call from Brent.

The couple entered the Wilbur Sweeney property in the Navigator and Zenja asked, "What's up?"

"Ivan's under arrest; exactly what charges, we don't know yet, but threatening Junior and I guess, Brent as well, and from the conversation Alex and he heard, Ivan was obviously involved in the *2X4 Operation*."

"So, Junior's in protective custody?" ZenJa surmised.

"Yeah, Alex is with him, until the Calvary arrives."

"I guess Junior also said Ivan shot Wilbur in cold blood, to shut him up and Junior also said he and his relatives wanted to get out of this weapons dealing mess they had gotten into."

"That will benefit Junior, down the road, especially if he comes clean with everything he knows and I surmise he knows a lot more about Ivan than just this weapons deal," ZenJa concluded.

"You know, I'm beginning to think this whole town is one big crime scene," Levi suggested while the couple exited the vehicle and began their search of the outside property, while waiting for a warrant for the entire premises and the assistance of crime scene investigators to arrive from Boston.

"I know what you mean," ZenJa replied with a deep and thoughtful sigh. "The FBI is still exploring the Martin residence, the hillside on Blackberry Road, my family property and God only knows where else...well, yes, now at Molly's Café and the mountainside where the log truck went off the road. Is this ever going to end?"

"Oh, by the way, not to diminish the severity of these crimes scenes, ZenJa, I have to correct you on one thing."

"What's that?" she asked.

"The Beckwith property is no longer your family property."

"And just what do you know about my family property or the new owner?" she asked sarcastically.

"I happen to know a lot about the new owner," Levi said and smirked.

"You! You bought that property?" ZenJa demanded.

"Yes, ma'am. It's now in my possession."

"Are you truly going to develop it and make positive additions to Longberry?"

"Absolutely, my dear and I'm going to need your help in that venture."

"You're going to retire from...well, from whatever agency you work for?"

"I'm thinking about it; I think it's time I settled down and became a family man," he added and reached out and held ZenJa in his arms and planted a strong, but tender kiss on her eager lips.

After a few moments of passion captured in each others arms, the young couple realized several federally authorized vehicles, from a nearby FBI office, were quickly approaching from the main highway, speeding up the driveway of the Sweeney property, with Alex leading the pack in his bright red Mustang.

"Looks like we got here just in time before the *lovefest* got out of control," Alex said and smiled while brushing past the blushing couple, with the FBI agents close on his heels.

The search of the Sweeney property lasted well into the next day, with agents removing box after box of evidence from the house, including computers, cell phones and any potential evidence they deemed valuable and secured it before transporting it to FBI headquarters they had established in Concord.

More FBI and ATF agents descended upon the small town of Longberry to secure any available evidence from Ivan Sweeney's property, to question Junior Sweeney, and to continue investigations at Molly's Café, the Martin residence and with Levi Harris' permission, to search the former Beckwith property for any clues to the disappearances of Zippy Beckwith and Olive Pickering.

Chapter 56

"You two need to go home and get some sleep," Emerson told ZenJa and Levi after another shift of investigators were combing the various potential crime scenes in the quiet town of Longberry. "Ivan is at the county lockup and isn't talking, even though he has a court appointed lawyer, so there isn't much you two can do now and you're obviously exhausted."

"What about Ivan's pickup? Have they secured that to match the tire impressions?" Levi asked.

"Yes, it's at the impound facility in Concord and it shouldn't take long to get a yea or nay on the tread pattern compared to the evidence we found on Blackberry Road," Emerson elaborated.

"I just know, somehow he's involved and probably the missing link about the disappearance of my sister and Olive and most likely connected, in some way, with the deaths of the O'Leary and Childress girls."

"It would seem as if you're correct," Emerson suggested while ushering the couple to the Navigator to send them on their way.

"I have an idea," ZenJa said when she and Levi sped away from the Sweeney property.

"What's that?"

"I want to go to the Pickering residence and ask Olive's parents if they have some information, they might not even known they had, all along, concerning Ivan Sweeney."

"Good idea; I mean hell, no one ever suspected that creep, who was, what about fifteen at the time, of ever having been involved in any crimes; no doubt her parents didn't either."

"I know my parents or Zippy never mentioned Ivan to me, but you know how some kids keep secrets...," ZenJa said and trailed off.

After a twenty minute drive, Levi and ZenJa arrived at the Pickering residence and knocked at the door of a small, quiet and tastefully cared for white clapboard home, surround with lovely flower gardens.

"Hello, Mr. Pickering, I'm ZenJa Beckwith and this is my friend Levi Harris. I was wondering if we could have a moment of your time?"

"Hello, ZenJa, yes, please come in. My goodness, you're not the little girl I remember running about the candy store, when we owned it, so many years ago," Mr. Pickering said and welcomed the couple to the living room, when Mrs. Pickering entered the back door, from the garden.

"Yes, that was so many years ago, wasn't it?" she asked sadly.

"I'm sorry we never got to stop by to give you our condolences when your parents passed away, but we were in Europe and then when we got back you were out of state, working at your financial company, so Molly mentioned." Mrs. Pickering said.

"Thank you, but you...we all have suffered and it's difficult to verbally express sorrow...I know."

"Let me get us some coffee," Mrs. Pickering offered grabbing a Kleenex from a box on the end table where Levi and ZenJa had made themselves comfortable.

"So, this is your friend?" Mr. Pickering asked with interest and lit up his pipe.

"Yes, he is a friend and we are both continuing the search for evidence in the disappearances..."

"First of all, I wanted to let you know, unless you have already heard, Ivan Sweeney has been arrested for various alleged crimes, as has Junior Sweeney."

"I hadn't heard that, but I did hear about the deaths of Wilbur and his wife at Molly's Café. What a shame. I always liked Lily," Mrs. Pickering remarked.

"Lily was Mrs. Pickering's first name?" Levi asked rather surprised that the rough and ready, armed with a shotgun, country woman would have such a feminine name.

"Yes, I realize that's hard for people who didn't know her to believe that," she commented; everyone chuckling as their hostess set down a tray of coffee and cookies.

"Well, so what's the deal with Ivan?" Mr. Pickering asked rather angrily.

"Well, we can't divulge anything on the present state of affairs, in his regard, but what I wanted to ask you, is did Olive or Zippy ever mention Ivan, as a teenager?"

"Mention him like how?" the tired father asked.

"Did they ever mention his name or if he might have been flirting with them or harassing them? I know Zippy never mentioned him to me or my parents," ZenJa stated, without any doubt.

Mrs. Pickering sat with her coffee cup held in mid air; it was obvious to both Levi and ZenJa her mind was traveling back so many dark years ago, trying desperately to remember any of the many conversations a mother has with her daughter and her best friend.

"She never mentioned him to me," Mr. Pickering replied, but he was always in and out of the candy store, and I think half the time he was stealing treats for he and his friends."

"I also remember when Ivan's parents moved away, he didn't want to leave his friends or school, so he stayed here in Longberry."

"Who did he live with?" ZenJa asked.

"He stayed with...the Millers, as a matter of fact," he responded as if a light bulb had gone off in his head.

"Which Miller family?" Levi asked.

"Assistant Principal Jackson Miller...! "Oh my God, you think Ivan had something to do with Zippy and Olive's disappearances and the murders?" Mr. Pickering asked in anguish. "All this time, the answers were right in front of us?" he cried.

"We don't know anything for sure, Mr. Pickering, but we are investigating the possibility," ZenJa said.

"You said, we are investigating?" Olive's mother asked "You both are obviously not working on Wall Street, then," she cleverly asserted.

"No, we aren't," was all ZenJa offered.

"To get back to the question you asked me, ZenJa, I do recall Olive and Zippy talking while we were swimming at the lake and I overheard them talking about how *creepy* Ivan was and how he used to flirt with them, but they didn't like him because, for one thing he was a lot older than they were and you know how young girls are...they either like a boy or don't."

"Did you ever hear them mention him or anyone else who might have been *creeping* them out?" Levi asked.

"No, they were pretty quiet about their adventures, as most girls were back then. Times were different and we all felt so safe," Mrs. Pickering offered and wiped her eyes, again.

At that moment, Levi's cell phone rang and he excused himself and went to take the call in the driveway, while ZenJa stayed with the Pickerings.

"What's up?" he asked his boss, Montgomery.

"We got confirmation on the tire tread on Ivan Sweeney's truck and it's a match with the imprints found at the scene of the Beckwith accident; the impressions the FBI has on file."

"That was fast and thank God it appears we may be getting somewhere with those cases."

"Well, when there are clues, such as you presented to us and the FBI, it's easier to narrow the evidence down," was the reply on the phone.

"Anything found on the Miller or Sweeney properties" Levi asked.

"Nothing regarding buried bodies, that we know of yet, but we just started digging around Wilbur's property. I don't think there is any evidence of cadavers on Miller's property. The dogs have been searching and scanning all those acres and haven't had any hits."

"What about Junior? Is he talking?" Levi asked Montgomery.

"Yeah, he, Wilbur and Mrs. Lumberjack, as you called her, wanted to come forth and spill their guts, but were afraid of Ivan, but now that Ivan's been arrested, he's talking. Unfortunately, Wilbur and his wife won't be able to go on with their lives as, hopefully, Junior, will."

"You think with his co-operation, he will get a light sentence, if any at all?" Levi asked.

"Depending on how deep this case goes and where the evidence leads, he will probably walk."

"How deep do you think this goes?"

"It's too early to say, but from what I've heard it leads from the south to Canada."

"So they were part of a tag-team operation?" Levi asked.

"It looks that way," Montgomery confirmed. "It doesn't appear this case is too elaborate, just some local-yokels trying to make some cash by actually stealing the weapons and drugs from storage units along the way."

"How would they know the who, what's and where's of these units?

"This goes back a long way with the Chief, Jackson, and Ivan Sweeney. Chief Connors got the low down from cops, where evidence was being stored. in what various parts of the country."

"And they would go to these areas and steal the stuff?" Levi asked. "Were there other cops involved, too?"

"We just don't know, yet. It's only been a few hours, you know," Montgomery reminded his agent.

Levi walked back inside the Pickering residence and after a few more minutes, he assured the grieving family that he and ZenJa would never stop looking for their daughter.

The couple drove from the residence when Levi's cell phone rang.
"Yo!" he replied.
"You better get over to the Miller residence." Alex said.

"Why?" What did they find?" he asked and looked at ZenJa.

"The cadaver dog just found a hot spot."

"Was it under a lilac bush?" Levi asked.

"Yeah, how did you know?"

"There were several highlighted spots on the map Jackson's attorney gave me and one was under a lilac bush."

"You haven't even given that map to anyone yet, have you?" Alex asked.

"No, Miller's mother just left town, so now that I'm headed over that way, I'll find the map somewhere in the house; if you get my drift."

"Oh, good one. Wouldn't want anyone to accuse you of withholding evidence, now would we?" Alex retorted.

"We all know what happens to those who withhold evidence, now don't we?" Levi barked in return. "Or should I say, what *should* happen to those who do!"

"See you in a few minutes," Alex said and disconnected the call without responding to Alex's last question.

"ZenJa, will you put this map, someplace inside the house, where someone might hide something, like this. You're probably more astute to where that might be, than me and then pretend to find it?" Levi asked and handed ZenJa the map that Jackson had given his lawyer.

"Okay, if I can gain access inside the house, that is."

"I have confidence in you and know you can do anything you set your mind to."

"Well, here we are," Levi said and the duo left the confines of the Navigator and walked up the driveway, before stepping over the crime scene tape. ZenJa headed toward the house, with the map and Levi approached the lonesome lilac tree in the front yard.

"The backhoe should be here in a minute, Emerson told Levi."

"Have the dogs found any other hot spots?"

"No, nothing," the FBI agent replied.

"After they're done here, I would like those dogs to be assigned to the Sweeney residence."

"Why do you say that?" Emerson asked.

"I'm not sure, but I think it's worth the time and effort," Levi said.

"You know it's too bad that log truck and the contents were destroyed in that fire," the agent said.

"I know, but I'm hoping all those *phony,* hollowed out logs, weren't on that truck."

"Why, what do you think might have been in there, other than the weapons and explosives stolen from the evidence storage units?"

"I don't know, but when we were looking around the property, something just came to mind, that I never considered before," Levi said.

"What's that?"

"What if those logs were used to transport other things, not just weapons and explosives; but bodies!"

"Oh shit! You might be right, but what are the chances those same logs, there today, were used way back when?" Emerson reasoned, logically.

"I know, but maybe, just maybe."

"Even if the Cadaver dogs make a hit, we still will never know where the bodies are."

"No, unless they're still encased in them and laying around the property!"

"God! I never thought of that," Emerson admitted.

"I never did, either, until today," Levi admitted at the same time ZenJa alerted the detectives she had found a mysterious map in the Miller home, inside a recipe box, on the kitchen counter.

"Good work, ZenJa," Emerson said and everyone, but Levi stood around and examined the newly found evidence, when the backhoe arrived.

With the skill of a surgeon, the operator of the heavy piece of equipment began to carefully remove one layer of grass and top soil at a time that encompassed the lilac bush, while detectives stood by, peering into the crevices that were being unearthed.

After two hours the dogs were brought back to the tree and as before, made it clear there was evidence of there being a body buried there, or at least at one time in the past.

Moments later the Criminal Investigation Units were summoned to the site as human remains had, indeed, been found.

"Oh my God! Please let this be Zippy!" ZenJa cried in anguish as she knelt on the ground, in the driveway, while Levi rushed to her side.

"Come on, ZenJa, we have to leave!" Levi insisted.

"No! I am *not* leaving!"

FBI Agent Emerson walked over to ZenJa and Levi and asked one simple question after making a statement. "This is against every ethical standard the FBI stands by and nothing should be said until all the evidence has been examined, but do you know what Zippy or Olive were wearing the day they went missing?"

"You have found evidence of clothing or other items?" Levi asked and continued to hold ZenJa in an upright position.

"Yes," was the answer.

"I have every reason to believe the body we have found is not your sister or her friend," he said before ZenJa could respond.

"Why not?" ZenJa cried in anguish.

"The crime scene technician said from her initial examination, this body is wearing wedding and engagement rings and appears to have been buried wearing a house dress. I'm sorry, ZenJa," Emerson added and walked away.

"That would be Jackson Miller's wife, no doubt," Levi said softly.

"Come on, ZenJa we have to go," he added and led this woman from the crime scene.

"We'll take care of this," Alex assured ZenJa.

Chapter 57

While ZenJa wiped her tear stained face, Levi suggested something that just came to mind, having heard about rings.

"ZenJa, I want to go back to your parents house. I just thought of something and could kick myself in the ass, for not paying more attention to details while I was snooping around and discovered that gun in the wall."

"What is it?"

"Remember when I pulled that duct tape off that piece of wall board that had been recently cut out, after you cleaned the room?"

"Yes, why?

"I used my flash light to find the gun and was so excited about having found it, I neglected to look for anything else."

"Like what?"

"Just as Emerson mentioned rings, I remember having my flashlight reflect off something that looked like gold at the bottom of that wall space and floor."

"The Feds are finished with the house aren't they?" ZenJa asked with renewed hope in her voice.

"Yes, and now that I own the property, I have free reign over it, so let's go and really see what we can find," he added and patted her hand and sped toward the other end of town.

The couple walked into the house that, at one time, had been a loving and joyful place to reside, with dread and trepidation.

"Do you want to wait here?" Levi asked ZenJa when they entered the kitchen.

"Hell, no! I'm coming with you," she responded and Levi smiled, knowing this young lady had more spunk than anyone he had ever known.

ZenJa turned on the light and Levi took out his flashlight and began to tear away the wall, that had been left as it was when the gun was found.

"Here it is!"

"It's a gold high school ring."

"Let me guess from what school," ZenJa said and clapped her hands.

"Yup...Longberry High and guess what?"

"Might the initials inside the ring be I. S.?"

"You got it, sweetheart!" he said and watched ZenJa blush because he used a term of endearment in speaking to her.

"I've got the ring wrapped in plastic and we can stop by and give this to Emerson, at the Miller house. I'm sure everyone is still there."

Shortly after the ring was turned over to the FBI, the young couple left the crime scene, once again.

"Well, I say we've had enough for one day, how about we go out for dinner...a nice dinner I promised you so many times, before."

"Well, I planned dinner one night, too and the grill and deck caught fire," she replied and laughed.

"Yes, and that wasn't the only thing that caught on fire, was it?"

"No, we both got *caught*, all right, by your brother and yes, we were on fire!"

"Do you like being on *fire*?"

"I never thought about it like that before, but I guess I do," she said and laughed.

"I'll drop you off at your house, so you can freshen up and I'll stop by and pick you up about 7:00, tonight?"

"That'll be perfect and while you're on your way over to my house, please bring my lovely bouquet of flowers that some very handsome man had delivered, for me, at your house, this morning."

"Who in hell gave you flowers? Well, now, I am pissed!" Levi added and laughed.

"We know it wasn't you, now was it...I said the man was handsome."

"Ouch! That was a little below the belt, wasn't it?"

"You know I'm only kidding, right?" ZenJa said and looked at the wounded expression on Levi's face; one he made in an effort to appear injured.

ZenJa exited the car, smiled and waved before Levi headed to his own home.

Chapter 58

Just after Levi stepped out of his shower, his cell phone rang and he noted the person calling was FBI Agent Emerson.

"What's up?"

"I just wanted to let you know it appears there are no other bodies buried at the Miller residence."

"What about at the Sweeney place?"

"We haven't had the Cadaver dogs go there, yet, but I thought we could all go over there tomorrow. You still think they may some evidence on that property?"

"Yes, I think it has something to do with those hallowed out logs. That's what my intuition tells me, anyway and by the way, has anyone had a chance to grill Junior or Ivan?"

"They've both lawyered up, as expected, but I have a feeling Junior doesn't know anything about the missing girls or bodies. I don't think Mr. and Mrs. Lumberjack knew anything about that, either?" the agent replied.

"What makes you think so?"

"Frankly, I don't think Mrs. Sweeney or her husband would have wanted to end the weapons and drug transportation scheme, if it were to uncover or possible federal murder charges, for starters."

"It appears Ivan, Jackson and Bob were using them as pawns in the grander blueprint of things?" Levi agreed.

"Most likely, if the bodies were discovered on their property, those folks would take the fall for the whole situation."

"What are the people of Longberry going to do about electing a police chief, seems there is no law enforcement in the town, now, except the state troopers," Emerson asked.

"I don't know. I guess the town council will have to meet and hold an election; the sooner the better."

"You know, I think ZenJa would make an awesome Police Chief for that town, now that she has decided to leave the bureau," Emerson suggested.

"We have discussed it and she really doesn't want to spend much time in that town, if you know what I mean."

"Yeah, but from what I hear this town is about to explode and expand into quite a playground for the rich and famous!" Emerson said, coyly

"Where the hell did you hear that from?"

"I've become quite good friends with Molly and she happened to mention it to me, in private, of course."

"I didn't know ZenJa had decided to sell the property," Levi lied and smiled.

"Well, when you go out to dinner, tonight, why don't you ask her!"

"What the fuck, do I have a drone flying overhead, eavesdropping on every conversation I have?" Levi barked.

"Something like that," Emerson said and disconnected the call.

Chapter 59

Shortly before his expected arrival time, Levi drove into ZenJa's driveway and knocked on her front door, which she opened within seconds.

"You look stunning!" Levi said and admired the little black dress, that all women have.

"You like it?" she asked as she twirled around and the flippy skirt caressed the air around her. "It's a little something I bought the other day. It's the first Chanel dress and matching purse I've ever had," she added.

"My wife had a dress just like that," Levi said without thinking.

"I'm sorry, do you want to go change?"

"Oh, no, it's beautiful and I have to move on, but I'm happy to know you have the same wonderful taste in fashion as she did."

"I think your wife and I had more in common than great taste in fashion," ZenJa replied and slowly melted into the arms of her dinner date.

After a few moments of tender kisses, Levi decided they better leave, if they wanted to get to the restaurant for their reservations, or to make the restaurant at all, that night.

"Your wrap, my lady?" Levi said and gently put the silky shawl around his date's shoulders and proceeded toward their destination.

"I have one stop to make, first," Levi said and parked his Camaro outside, in front of a luxurious brand name outlet mall a few miles from the restaurant.

"I'll be right back," he said, without giving ZenJa an option of accompanying him or not.

"Ten minutes later Levi climbed back into the car and handed ZenJa a lovely small bouquet of pink roses and placed another parcel on the rear seat.

"I never went to the high school prom, so I thought we could pretend we're going, how about it?"

"You really are a romantic, aren't you?"

"Shhh! Don't let anyone know that, okay. You'd destroy my bad-ass image," he added while the couple sped away to their next destination.

Traveling on the interstate, toward Boston, ZenJa asked, "Where are we headed?"

"We have a date that we never had a chance to finish, in Boston; you must remember and the night we left, I asked Robert, the Maitre d, you remember, to hold our table and I think the wine might be chilled enough by now, though the rolls may be a little stale!"

"Thank God we didn't have a chance to place our order, because that would still be sitting on our plates," ZenJa said and laughed.

"You're probably right!"

"Can I put in a CD?" ZenJa asked.

"Sure, what do you want to hear?"

"I brought one with me," she said and reached into her evening bag.

"Oh, well, we must be feeling romantic tonight; Barry White?" Levi said after hearing the first strain of *'Can't Get Enough Of Your Love, Babe'*.

"I have no idea what you're talking about," ZenJa said and sat back in her seat and enjoyed the foliage that was exploding in the North East.

"Good evening, Mr. Harris," Mark, the Valet greeted one of his best customers. "Welcome back to *Les Paris'*."

"Good evening, Mark. It's good to see you again and how have you been?"

"Very well, sir and it's good to see you and Miss ZenJa once again. You don't get to Boston much, anymore?"

"No, we've been busy, but you'll know whenever we're in the city, we'll always stop and dine here."

"I'll take good care of your car, sir," Mark said while Levi reached into the back seat to grab the purchase he had made in New Hampshire.

"Thank you, Mark," Levi responded and handed the young college student a one hundred dollar tip and led his date into the restaurant.

"Good evening, Mr. Harris and Miss ZenJa," the Maitre d greeted the diners and led them to a private dinning area, in a quite, cozy section of the restaurant. "I hope this meets your satisfaction?" he added.

"This is fine, thank you, Robert; this is perfect."

"As you requested, your wine is here, and is perfectly chilled."

"Left overs from last time, right?' Levi asked and snorted with laughter.

"Yes, sir!" Robert said and laughed. "May I get you anything that I may have forgotten?"

"Do you still have those rolls we left behind. I mean, you know I'm on a tight budget!"

"Mr. Harris, it appears someone made an error and threw those away, just last night, as a matter of fact," the man said and the trio laughed at the silliness.

"Speaking of which, did you ever get to meet the dishwasher, the last time we were here?" ZenJa asked her date, while the Sommelier poured their wine.

"No, and I think we should don't you?" Levi asked and held out his hand to assist his date from her seat.

"Thank you, Francis for pouring our wine. We'll be right back," Levi said and the server nodded and smiled.

Bold as brass, Levi and ZenJa entered the busy, but orderly kitchen and walked over to the dishwasher, who appeared to be someone's beloved grandmother; not less than seventy years old.

"Good evening, Mrs. Vaccarelli."

"Oh, my goodness, Mr. Harris! It's so good to see you again. We've all missed you here," she said and reached out and hugged the ATF agent.

"I've missed coming here, too; but most importantly, I would like you to meet my date, Miss ZenJa Beckwith," he said to the old woman who had tears in her eyes and hugged ZenJa.

"It's my pleasure, Mrs. Vaccarelli," ZenJa replied, but was truly confused by the affection Levi had with all these people at this restaurant.

"What a sweetheart you are; I'm so glad Levi...I mean Mr. Harris has found someone as beautiful as Isabella..." she said and trailed off.

"Well, again it was nice to see you, Mrs. Vaccarelli and now I want to stop by and say hello to the chef," he said and smiled at the old lady, but quickly whisked ZenJa away.

"Pierre, my good man, how are you?" Levi said and gave the middle aged man a hug.

"Mr. Harris, how wonderful to see you, and I heard you were dinning with us tonight and I have made the necessary selections for your dining pleasure.

"Thank you, and I want you to meet my date, Miss ZenJa Beckwith," Levi said while the chef gently raised ZenJa's hand to his lips and kissed her fingertips.

"Good evening, Mademoiselle."

"It's my pleasure, Pierre," ZenJa said and smiled.

"Well, I'll let you all get back to work, but again it was so nice to see you all," Levi said and ushered his date from the kitchen.

"Well, now, here we are. How's the wine?" Levi asked ZenJa after she took a sip.

"This is lovely and I'm so glad it didn't spoil while it sat here for weeks at a time," she said and laughed.

"Hmm, this is a great wine, indeed, but before we get down to eating our *Happy Meals*, I have a little gift for you," Levi said while reaching for the wrapped box he bought at the mall.

"These flowers are more than enough for our prom date," ZenJa said wickedly.

"No woman I knows, who wears a Chanel dress, goes without a diamond necklace to adorn their lovely neck," he continued and handed the lovely silver papered and bowed box for his date to open.

ZenJa squealed with delight and opened the box and saw the most stunning array of delicate diamonds encased in an exquisite pink gold necklace.

"These are...so beautiful," ZenJa exclaimed in a whisper.

"Let me put this on for you my dear. This way I'll have a chance to admire your cleavage," he whispered and kissed her neck.

"Oh my God! This is too much," she said and gently felt the necklace with her delicate fingers.

"Nothing is too much for you, sweetheart," Levi said and once again sat down.

"Oh, just in time. It appears our waiter, Josh, is here to bring the first courses."

"Good evening, Mr. Harris and my Lady," the young African American said and placed a basket of homemade, warm rolls, their soups and salads on the table.

"Thank you Josh," Levi said and ZenJa nodded.

"This soup is delightful," ZenJa said and studied her date with interest.

"One of the wonders of the Fall season, Pumpkin Soup and Apple pies and if I may be so bold, what are you looking at?" Levi asked and smiled.

"I wish I knew a tiny fraction of the *real* Levi Harris."

"Ah, ZenJa, it will take you the rest of your life to find out what there is to know about me and there may be some details you would rather not know about, as well." he said, but did not smile.

"Well, can you begin to tell me something I would like to know?"

"As you know, already about my childhood, what else could there be to know?" he asked while be buttered a hot roll.

"Why did you decide to work for the government, what branch I have no idea, of course, but I am curious what makes people dedicate their lives for a thankless job, such as ours; I mean you know the reason why I went the route I did...because of my sister."

Levi sat for a few moments and ZenJa patiently waited for him to sort out his thoughts. She had no idea if what he would say was to be the truth or not, but all stories had some truth to them, she realized.

"I don't know where to begin, ZenJa; I really don't," he began just as Francis, the Sommelier came to pour the couple more wine.

"Thank you, Francis," ZenJa said and the man left their table again.

"Can you begin by telling me how many people really know Levi Harris?"

This caused Levi to chuckle, smile, and looked deeply into ZenJa's eyes.

"ZenJa, I don't even know who I am, half of the time."

"You have a very professional way of avoiding questions, don't you?"

"I was admiring you in that dress and necklace, that's all."

"My wife and I used to come here all the time and she had a very similar dress and necklace," Levi said softly.

"You loved her very much, didn't you?" ZenJa asked and reached out for his hand.

"She was the sunshine and the moon, in my life," he added quietly.

"The expression on your face is the most peaceful I've seen it, since I met you."

"All I have to do is think about Isabella and I feel an overwhelming sense peace overcome me," Levi added, still holding ZenJa's hand while the soup and salad dishes were removed and selections of seafood, steak and asparagus tips, in cream sauce were placed before them.

"This is lovely and delicious," ZenJa said and chose another broiled shrimp to eat.

"Pierre is a world known master chef and has been here at this restaurant for as long as I can remember. He studied at the prestigious Two Bordelais, in Bordeaux, France before coming to the United States."

"The sauces our meals are swimming in are so rich and smooth and that makes me wonder why you rarely see an overweight Frenchman?"

"Because they savor their wine and that keeps them skinny!" Levi said and laughed.

"How does drinking wine keep them thin?"

"They get all horny and have a lot of sex, from what I hear," Levi whispered and poured them each other glass of wine.

"Does wine make you...horny, as you say?" ZenJa asked and lifted the glass to her lips, again.

"It takes more than wine, my dear."

"What does it take?" she dared to ask.

"A beautiful woman and you know there are very few of those around."

"What do you consider beautiful?" ZenJa asked.

"It might not be what you think," he began and savored another piece of steak and sip of wine.

"So, pray tell, tell me," she encouraged.

"Number one on the list is loyalty."

"As in faithful?" ZenJa asked when she realized he wasn't going to offer more information.

"That's part of it, but loyalty to death do us part...that sort of thing."

"As in confidences?"

"Absolutely!"

"What else makes someone beautiful, in your eyes?"

After several minutes, while the couple continued to dine and stare into each other's eyes. Levi finally responded to ZenJa's question.

"You!" he replied and held her hand while they stood and danced in each others arms to the violins that played, not far from their table.

"I never thought I would fall in love again, ZenJa...never in a million years," he added and gently kissed her lips and caressed her neck with his fingertips.

"I love you, Levi, I truly do," ZenJa whispered between parted lips and kisses.

After the couple returned to their table, they looked off into the corner and noticed the entire restaurant staff was peeking from across the establishment with big smiles on their faces before they retreated to their work stations.

"What was that all about?" ZenJa asked and blushed while Josh brought a tray of deserts and a steaming antique pot that held a french coffee, to be served once he clean off their table.

"You asked me how I know all these people," Levi began and smiled broadly.

"Yes, and now I assume you will enlighten me?"

"The lovely woman, who is the dishwasher is Isabella's grandmother and the owner of this fine establishment."

"No!" ZenJa replied not believing what she had just heard.

"Yes, this is where I met Isabella, so many years ago, well I mean we went to school together and fell in love, forever, in the first grade and I came in here for dinner one night and left, shortly after, with her as my bride. We were married right after high school."

"This is a family restaurant, ZenJa. Mrs. Adrianna Vaccarelli, as I just told you, is (was) Isabella's grandmother and Pierre d'Artagnan is (was) her father."

"d'Artagnan was the last name of the 4th Three Musketeer, was he not?" ZenJa asked.

"He certainly was and that warrior was born and raised in the French province of Gascony; like Pierre."

"What a beautiful story," ZenJa quietly whispered with excitement.

"So your wife's name, before she married you, was d'Artagnan?"

"Oh, no! Her full name was Isabella Vaccarelli-d'Artgnan."

"They must have loved her at the Department of Motor Vehicles."

"She was the only person I have ever known who had an extension on her license. She had a difficult time fitting the license in her purse, it was so big!" Levi said and the couple laughed out loud.

"So what was her married name? Dare I guess?"

"She was simply Isabella Harris," Levi responded and smiled.

"I would love to know more about her family. What an interesting history," ZenJa said as they couple finished their coffee and prepared to leave.

"Maybe you can write a book about them," Levi suggested.

"Do you mean it? You wouldn't mind or feel I was intruding?"

"No, actually, I think Isabella would love that. God only knows what crooks and criminals her family left behind in Italy and France," he added and helped ZenJa from the table. "Just don't pen a family history on my family," Levi added. You *will* not like what you find," he said seriously, but smiled.

"Are the other employees related as well?" ZenJa asked while Levi put her wrap around her shoulders and led her toward the door.

"Yes, our Sommelier, Francis, the waiter, Josh and our valet, Mark are all cousins and as you can see, there are very few tables and only reservations are accepted and I can't recall there ever being more than ten parties here at a time, but that is the beauty of the place and trust me, this is essentially a private facility."

"Only the rich and famous come here, I gather?" ZenJa asked.

"I guess you could say that," Levi replied and led his date from the restaurant.

"You didn't pay for our meal!" ZenJa scolded while they waited for their vehicle to arrive at the door.

"My dear, in case you didn't notice, we were the only patrons here, at this time?"

"Yes, I actually did."

"Well, don't worry, they know where to send the bill," Levi said and laughed.

"You booked the entire restaurant just for us?"

"Either that or no one felt like going out to eat tonight. I have no idea,' Levi said and smiled.

"Here you are, Mr. Harris," Mark ran around to open ZenJa's door, after leaving Levi's door open for him.

"Thank you, Mark," ZenJa said while Levi handed him another hundred dollar tip before he climbed into the vehicle himself.

"Thank you, Mr. Harris," Mark replied.

"How is college going?"

"Very well sir. I'll be graduating this spring."

"Where does the time go?" Levi asked and smiled.

"I honestly don't know. Have a good evening," he said as the Camaro sped off into the night.

Several hours later, as Levi stopped the car outside of ZenJa's new home, he got out and opened the door for her and walked her to her door.

"Would you like to come inside?" she asked, facing her date.

"Thank you very much for the invite and for a wonderful evening, ZenJa, but we have a busy day tomorrow, so I think I better go home and get some sleep," he said and he tenderly kissed her lips.

"Would you like some help tomorrow at the Sweeney property? Do you want me to meet you there?" she asked

"We all plan to be there by eight, in the morning, but that may not be a good place for you to go. We don't know what we are going to find...if anything, but it's up to you."

"I'll think about it and may show up. I'm just not sure now and by the way you were very quiet on the way home; is everything all right?"

"Letting go of the past isn't easy for me, ZenJa and I seem to take two steps forward and one back. I'm not sure where I want my life to go, at this point and I don't want to hurt you," he said honestly.

ZenJa was, indeed, deeply hurt by these words, but she gave the man credit for being truthful and in all honesty, she was in no hurry to embark on any relationship at this time, either.

ZenJa mustered up a smile, touched Levi's face and thanked him for a wonderful evening, kissed him again, before bidding him a good night. She slowly closed her door and watched Levi drive off, into the night.

ZenJa leaned against the heavy wooden door, that graced the entrance to her house and knew she was taking two steps forward and had to take one step backward, also. Her heart had been broken enough for one lifetime.

Chapter 60

By 8:00, the next morning, the Cadaver dogs and their handlers arrived at the Sweeney property, along with ATF Agent Harris and his brother Alex, FBI Agent in Charge, Edward Emerson, ATF Agent Brent Wyman all assembled at the gate leading to the Sweeney property to begin their search.

Emerson brought a map of the property and each person was assigned a quadrant to search, while the Cadaver dogs were to approach the home and focus on the pile of logs and barn area.

"Before we all split up, I suggest we meet back here at noon, if nothing is discovered, we grab a bite to eat and then come back and I also wanted to mention it has been confirmed, the body found on the Miller property, was indeed Jackson Miller's wife, as we expected," Emerson stated.

Before Levi walked toward his section of the property, he kept looking back at the driveway in hopes of seeing ZenJa enter, but in all honesty, he didn't think she would or even should. He realized he had hurt her, by saying what he had said, the night before, but he had to be honest with her and he also realized the woman had been through enough and searching and finding what may be her own sister and friend's bodies was more than one could expect.

While these agents were searching the wooded area around the Sweeney acreage, ZenJa drove to the Center Street Jail in hopes of meeting with, the now, incarcerated Ivan Sweeney.

"Well, isn't this a pleasant surprise," Ivan said as he spoke into the telephone to his first and only visitor since his arrest.

"I simply came by to let you know Levi and I found your high school ring, you lost, on my parents property, when you tried to conceal the gun that Connors discovered missing from his police car...way back when." ZenJa said without any formalities.

"I have no idea what you're talking about, ZenJa." he denied, but smirked.

"Where are my sister, her friend Olive and the other two missing girls, Ashley Winters and Rose -Ann Olsen, buried. You remember them from way back, don't you?"

"It's funny, isn't it, the only girls to be found here were Constance O'Leary and Morgan Childress, so I would have to assume the other girls simply ran off to experience a new life, rather than stay in the Godforsaken town of Longberry, forever. The other interesting fact is, the girls that were found or anyone bothered to look for or reported on the local and national news, were *only the pretty ones*...the pretty girls."

"Where are they buried, Ivan," ZenJa asked calmly, not giving this degenerate the satisfaction of responding to his mockery.

"ZenJa, I wish I could help you, I truly do, but I have no idea what you're talking about," he denied once again.

ZenJa stood up to leave the confines of the visitors area of the jail and before she departed she said, "I bet it sucks, not having any family to put money into your canteen fund, now doesn't it?"

An hour later, ZenJa entered the hospital room, where Junior Sweeney was still recovering from his injuries. She showed her ID to the officers who were guarding the man and they left to stand outside the door while these two people conversed.

"Hello, Junior how are you feeling?" ZenJa asked after sitting in a chair next to the man's bed.

"I'm feeling much better and plan to go home in another day or so."

"Where are you going to go, or where do you call home?"

"At my brother's place...that's where I've been living for several years, now."

"You do know the authorities are still canvassing the property, looking for evidence, don't you?"

"What evidence?" Junior replied sincerely. "What do you think is there?"

"We know about the weapons being transported in the hallowed out logs, Junior"

"Yeah, so...all the evidence, I'm sure, was lost in the fire when the truck burst into flames and careened down the mountainside."

"Are you telling me there is nothing else to be found on the property?"

"Like what? I already told the feds, Lily and Wilbur and I were going to come clean about all that."

"There is reason to believe some of the missing girls, from town, might be buried on that property."

"Say, what? Oh no! We have...I have no fucking idea about anything like that!" he yelled.

"That may be and there may not be any evidence to indicate that, but I just wanted to let you know, they're searching with Cadaver dogs, as we speak."

"I'm not worried in the least; I know there are *no* bodies buried there," he said confidently and ZenJa truly felt this man was not going to be of any value in the search for the girls.

"Okay, let's say *you* never buried any bodies there, but could someone else have done so?"

"I can't say someone else didn't...I have no idea," he replied and broke out in a sweat.

"Why are you so confident that Wilbur or Lily might not have buried any bodies there?"

"I can tell you why; my brother lost his son; he died serving our country in Afghanistan and that destroyed him, ZenJa. He would never take a life, that's something I will swear on the Bible."

"Did you ever hear Lily or Wilbur speak of Ivan or some crimes or whatever, he might have committed."

"I never heard them or spoke to them about it, but I know they were deathly afraid of him."

"He must have thought you knew more than you appear to, because he came here and threatened to kill you."

"He may have, I truly don't know what it would be."

"Well, thanks for your help, Junior. If you think of anything, please let someone know and I'll speak with Agent Emerson and let him know you are considering going to the Sweeney property to stay, once you're out of the hospital. They may have to make other plans for you, if they're not done searching."

"Thank you, ZenJa and I am and always have been sorry about your sister, your parents and everyone," Junior said as a tear cascaded down his cheek.

ZenJa left the jail and drove to Molly's for some lunch, at the same time the men, who had been searching the Sweeney property, drove in as well.

Levi exited his car and rushed over to ZenJa's Charger. "Good afternoon, ZenJa, I was hoping your might stop here for lunch," he said and he opened her car door.

"I've been to see Ivan and Junior," she said without looking at Levi in the face.

"Did either one tell you anything of interest?" he said while the couple followed the others into the diner.

"No, but I think you're wasting your time at the Sweeney place. I don't think there are any bodies buried there. Junior told me, Wilbur and Lily lost their son in Afghanistan and his death destroyed them and I don't feel they were capable of murder or any coverup to the degree Ivan might have been."

"Well, it appears you may be right. We haven't found anything, yet."

"Here let's sit over here, in this booth, away from the others," Levi offered.

Levi reached out and held ZenJa's hand and said, "About last night, I wanted to spend the night with you more than you'll ever know, but I don't want to hurt you and because I don't even know what I want, at this time, I can't ask you to..."

"To care about you?" ZenJa offered.

"Yeah, that about sums it up."

"I know and I happen to agree with you. Until I find my sister and the other girls, I don't think I deserve a life of my own, either."

As the couple sat quietly, Molly came over and handed them their menus and glasses of fresh water.

"Well, have the usual," Levi said as ZenJa nodded to confirm the order.

"Coming right up, you two," she said and smiled.

A moment later, Alex approached the table and had an announcement to make. "I called Darcy and she and the whole family, you know, Darlene, Keith, and the kids are coming up next week for the NASCAR race at Loudon!"

"That's great, we hope you have a great time," Levi said in hopes of dismissing his annoying brother.

"I've got tickets for all of us, so we hope you both will come, too!"

"Does that mean the tickets you got are all together...in other words, do we have to sit with you?" Levi asked and smirked.

"Well, of course it does! We're all family and you, newbies, to the racing world, have to enjoy it with us."

"Where are they all staying?" ZenJa asked in hopes Alex hadn't offered Levi's home for their stay.

"They're all booked at a hotel, near my cabin on the lake, so they're all set."

"I have to admit, I haven't seen you this excited in a long time," Levi replied as their meals were brought to the table.

"Well, you two, enjoy your meals," Alex said and headed back toward the group of investigators he arrived with.

"He's almost giddy!" ZenJa said and she and Levi dug into their BLT's and Onion Rings.

"Maybe he's growing up," Levi offered and avoided looking at ZenJa.

Once the group finished their lunches, ZenJa and the other investigators parted ways. Levi and the others were going back to the Sweeney residence and ZenJa left, without as much a goodbye.

"Everything okay?" Alex asked his brother as the rode together in the Camaro.

"Yeah, everything's fine. Neither one of us want to rush anything," and for once Alex knew enough to keep his mouth shut.

The investigation on the Sweeney property lasted for three more days and as expected, no evidence of human remains was found on the property and Levi had not seen ZenJa since she left Molly's.

Levi had tried calling her cell phone, driven by her lake front house, checked out the Beckwith property to know avail. ZenJa was obviously having some time to herself, he correctly reasoned.

Chapter 61

Two days before the NASCAR race, that was to be held at New Hampshire Motor Speedway, Kevin and his family arrived at their hotel and Alex was there to greet them.

"Welcome back to the Live Free Die State," Alex said after the group checked into their rooms and caught up on the latest developments with the children and the garage before they went to The Fisherman's Catch; a popular restaurant nearby.

"Where are Levi and ZenJa?" Darlene asked after their orders were placed.

"Levi is supposed to show up soon, but he...we haven't seen ZenJa in a few days. He thinks she just need some time to herself," he added.

"What does she need time to herself, for?" Darcy asked and snuggled up next to Alex. "It's obvious those two are crazy about each other."

"You know what they say, the effected parties are always the last to know," Alex said truthfully.

"Can we go outside and play on the swings, until our dinner gets here?" Betsy and Rick both asked.

"Well, okay, but only because we can see you from the window, but stay right there," Keith warned.

"Okay, see you later," the two children say and ran outside to play.

"So did everyone have a good trip?" Alex asked.

"Yes, we certainly did and it's so nice to get back here to New England and especially this time of year," Keith replied. "I love Fall; there's nothing like it and we can't thank you enough for having us come up, but I've a feeling, Darcy's the one you really wanted to see," he teased while Darcy blushed.

"Well, if we're going to be family, one day, we need to all get acquainted." Alex brazenly suggested.

"As far as I know, the only thing we have in common, is our love of NASCAR," Darcy teased.

"How else are we going to know if we have anything else in common, if we don't get together, now and then?"

"You love my red Mustang, don't you?"

"I have no idea if I like it or not. I've never been in it!" she said and smirked.

Their waitress brought their meals; Kevin went to round up the children and Alex asked the waitress for a pitcher of iced water.

"Iced water?" she asked with a puzzled expression on her face.

"Yes, Miss...I think I'm about to spontaneously burst into flames," Alex replied and reached out for Darcy's hand.

"What did I miss?" Keith asked when he and the children sat back down at the table.

"Oh, nothing...just don't sit too close to Alex."

"Why not?"

"He's all hot and bothered," Darlene offered while the adults laughed and the children rolled their eyes in disgust.

"Actually, we were only talking about my *hot* car and how Darcy is dying to have a ride it in."

"If that's what you want us all to believe, so be it," Keith said and reached for one of his fried shrimp and two french fries.

"I left a message with Levi and told him we'd be here about noon, and I was hoping he'd show up," Alex said and looked out the window, but failed to see the black Camaro drive in.

"The race is Sunday, I hope he and ZenJa come," Darlene said. "They're family now and we've missed them."

Ten minutes later, Levi and his Camaro came screaming into the parking lot of the restaurant and ran inside, with a large circular cardboard tube in his hands.

"Sorry, I'm late, but I wanted to get this from the architect before his office closed for the weekend."

"Do you want to order anything," the waitress asked and placed a glass on water in front of his place setting.

"No, that's okay, I'll have what he's having," he replied and pilfered two scallops from Alex's plate.

"Yes, Miss, may we have one more Captain's Platter. I'm sure between all of us we'll finish it," Alex said and moved his plate away from his brother's reach.

"By the way, hello everyone," Levi said and patted the children on the head.

"What's all the excitement?" Keith asked.

"I wanted you folks to see this," Levi said and opened one end of the tube and pulled over an empty table and spread out a large drawing of what he had planned for the Beckwith property.

"That's ZenJa's family acreage," Alex mentioned, with a quizzical expression on his face.

"It *was* the Beckwith homestead, but it's now owned by none other than yours truly."

"No way!" everyone replied at the same time.

"Yup, and this is the property, as it stands now and this," he began and removed the top drawing and revealed what was underneath, "is what the future has to hold for Longberry and the Granite State."

"What the hell?" Alex exclaimed. "This is a whole new community and expanded town!"

"Exactly and why it was important for me to get these preliminary plans today, was so you folks can see what I have in mind and I need your input on it."

"Why us?" Keith asked.

"Remember I told you I need and want a reliable place to have my car serviced and trusted friends? Well, I'm about to run something by you and your family."

"Excuse me, here is your order," the waitress said and stopped to look at the building plans. "Cool!" was her comment before she left their table.

"This is a massive undertaking," Alex warned.

"It doesn't need to be done in one week," Levi replied sternly.

"But anyway, what I wanted to discuss with you is the possibility of you and your family relocating here and being the owner of this garage,"

"Oh my God! Look at that!" Darlene cried.

"If this town is going to attract the rich and famous and those who want peace and quiet, they're going to need a place to have their cars serviced, aren't they?"

"I would give anything to move back here," Darlene said.

"This layout even includes this huge wrecker and another five stall garage," Keith said.

"Well, you know how badly those city folks drive and with the winter roads we have around here, you're going to be pulling more than one car from the side of the road," Levi said before he realized the last car to go over the bank was ZenJa's parents car and looked knowingly at Alex, who remained silent.

The group stood looking at the plans for another few minutes before Levi spotted ZenJa driving and parking next to his Camaro.

"Here she is. I left her half a dozen text messages and hoped she would come," Levi said and held the door open for her.

ZenJa walked inside and immediately went over and gave the Morrison family greetings and picked up the children and swung them around, completely ignoring, Levi.

"I'm glad you made it," Levi said and sat down and began to eat more scallops and french friends...his own, this time.

"What is this?" she asked and studied the drawings that graced the adjacent table.

"This is a new town," Levi said without looking at ZenJa.

"This is...this is...was my parents property, isn't it?"

"Yes, ZenJa it is."

"You plan to live here?" she asked, sharply.

"No, I love the lake and have no interest or desire to live here."

"Would you folks like to bring the children over, so they can make their own ice cream sundaes," the wise waitress suggested.

"Hell, yes, if that includes me," Alex said and ushered Darcy from the table, to follow the others and left Levi and ZenJa behind.

"This is beautiful," ZenJa said and wiped a tear from her eye. "It looks like a paradise."

"A four season paradise, ZenJa."

"Can you imagine how much revenue that will bring to this area?" she said.

"Exactly! This is what this town needs to prosper and let the painful memories rest in peace, once and for all," Levi said and reached out to turn her face towards his.

"We're all dying inside, ZenJa. Is this what our loved ones would want for us?"

"Every time I reach out, you back away, Levi. I'm not risking my heart to be broken again. The pain isn't worth it."

"I know," he said with tears in his own eyes. "I need to take my own advice," he admitted. "I can't do it alone, ZenJa. I need you to share this new chapter of my life with."

Levi rolled up the drawings, put them into the tube and waved to the others before accompanying ZenJa from the restaurant.

"Follow me," ZenJa suggested. "I have some place I want to show you." she said while she climbed into her car and sped away.

Less than five minutes later, ZenJa pulled off the highway on a dirt road and Levi followed. They drove for more than a mile and suddenly came to a stop and each exited their cars.

"This is the quarry," ZenJa said; the couple walking and to the massive stone structure; complete with a cascading waterfall.

"This is beautiful," Levi said.

"Everyone from town used to come here to swim. As soon as I got my driver's license, I would bring Zippy, Olive and the others here to spend the day."

"Over there is what we called the *pit* and we'd build roaring fires, cook whatever we could steal from our kitchens, at home, and of course toast marshmallows."

He and ZenJa sat on a large rock before Levi asked, "What were some of the best things you stole from home?"

"I swear my mother used to purchase things at the store for us, knowing we would bring them here. The shit she bought was nothing we would eat at our house," ZenJa said and laughed.

"So what was the shit?"

"Cans of little sausages and Spam, cheap hot dogs, huge cans of baked beans, even larger bags of potato chips, gallons of soda and of course bags of marshmallows."

"That was fun, wasn't it." Levi declared.

"It was so much, fun," she said and another tear trickled down her face and Levi reached out and held her in his arms.

"I was so lucky to have the family I had, but they're all gone now."

"Maybe it's time to let them rest in peace, like I said, and begin a new life."

"I don't know how to have any other life," she admitted.

"Well, I guess that's something we're both going to have to learn together isn't it? I have no idea how to have any other life than the one I've led for so long, either."

Levi reached over and hungrily kissed the woman he assumed he would one day marry. "I've missed you ZenJa; I've missed you so much."

"You weren't worried about me...being missing and all?"

"No, I wasn't worried about you. I know you can take care of yourself and needed time to yourself. Everyone needs time, apart, sometimes. It makes the reunions much better."

"This is so peaceful here, isn't it?"

"It is and I can see why you all used to hang out here. Nothing like fun and friends."

"Who was your best friend?" ZenJa asked.

"My father, actually. He was like a big kid and we did everything together. He and I built my first tree house, taught me to hunt and fish and of course we went to all the baseball and football games, when I was older.

"Did you have any kids your own age to hang out with?"

After a few moments, Levi finally spoke.

"I had two good friends, Zakk and Aaron, but they're dead, now."

"I'm so sorry. Do you want to talk about it?"

Several minutes went by without a response before ZenJa spoke. "You have to let them rest in peace, too."

"I know...I know. I've made my life sound like it was all fun and games, but it wasn't."

"You mentioned that about your mother and Alex."

"That's part of another story, but the reason my father spent so much time with me, I think, was to keep me out of trouble," he began and stood up to walk toward the water pool and ZenJa came to stand beside him.

"What kind of trouble?"

"I can hardly remember a day when I wasn't in trouble of some sort, to be perfectly honest with you. I think I was into mischief since the day I was born."

"Why?" ZenJa asked softly.

"To be honest with you, I have no fucking idea, why!"

"You were looking for something and trouble was what you found, instead of what you truly wanted?"

"I guess so...like I said, I have no idea. There's just been part of my heart that's been missing since I remember."

"Do you think it was a mother's love you were looking for?"

"No, it's more than that."

ZenJa was silent, her mind wandering, reflecting about something she remember reading, at one time, during her studies of hostage negotiations.

"What is it?" Levi asked.

"I'm sorry, I was trying to think of something."

"Well, enough of this shit," Levi said thinking ZenJa wasn't interested while he poured his heart out to her. "Let's go; it's getting late and I have things to do."

Before he climbed in his car he opened ZenJa's door and asked if she was going to the NASCAR race on Sunday.

"I plan to, are you going? I think it'll be fun and we can have a tail gate party with Alex and his guests and by the way, I've been instructed to wear ear plugs," she said and laughed.

"Okay, call Alex and ask him where we'll all meet, if you want. I have no idea what the track is like."

"I thought we could go together."

"You might not like the noise or I may not, either, so we'd be better off taking our own cars, I think." Levi said without looking at ZenJa.

"Okay, I'll see you Sunday, then," ZenJa said and drove away, leaving Levi standing my his car.

While Levi headed up into the White Mountains, ZenJa slowly drove back to her own home.

Chapter 62

Dusk was just setting upon the tiny hamlet of Lord's Hill when Levi pulled off the highway where other travelers and hikers parked their cars to admire the views that expanded around them and scale the rocks in the area.

Levi walked toward the guard rail that prevented cars from accidently driving over the steep cliffs of solid rock and simply sat on the rail; other people walking by, without notice.

The edge of night was filling the valley below while the sun's rays still caressed the sky above; the first stars of the night peeking through the heavens above.

"Beautiful place here, isn't it?" a strange old man asked; Levi astonished to see anyone had come near him without him realizing it.

"Yes, it is one of the most beautiful places in New Hampshire," Levi responded while the old man sat down beside him.

"You come here often?" the old man asked.

"No, I haven't been here in almost twenty years."

"I come by here, at least once a year," the white haired, bearded man replied. "I come here to find peace."

"Do you find it?" Levi asked.

"Find what? Peace?"

"Yes," the younger man said.

"Yes, I do, to be honest with you. There's no place better to come back to than where our memories are."

"What memories do you have, here?"

"My wife and I were married here more than sixty years ago and we honeymooned down at the bottom of the ravine. We spent our honeymoon scaling these cliffs...well, part of it," he man said and laughed.

"Were you married for a long time?"

"Yes, son, we were married until my wife died, five years ago."

"I'm sorry about your loss."

"You came here to find something you lost, as well?" the man asked.

"Yes, I lost something very precious here, twenty years ago."

"May I be so bold as to ask what it was?"

"I lost my two best friends, here."

"I am sorry to hear that. How were they lost?"

Levi sat silently for several minutes, staring at the vastness before him, hearing his friends laughter echoing across the mountain range.

"I haven't thought about Aaron and Zakk for a long time," Levi replied, avoiding the question the old man has asked.

"What made you think of them today?"

"I was speaking with a very special woman, who I'm falling in love with, and we were talking about our pasts; good times and bad."

"Are Zakk and Aaron included in the less than happy times?"

"Yes, well actually, we had some of the best times, but the ending wasn't so good."

"What happened?"

"I had just gotten my driver's license and the three of us came up here to do some rock climbing. It started out as a beautiful day and we repelled down to the bottom and then a horrific thunderstorm came out of nowhere and Aaron and Zakk wanted to wait until it was over, to give the slippery rocks time to dry, but I had a date, that night, so I convinced them we had to get back to the top and get home."

"So you all started to scale the cliffs," the elderly man asked when Levi hesitated to continue with the story.

"Yes, we were almost at the top and I slipped and lost my footing, but regained my hold, but Aaron, seeing me slip, lost his own focus, for a second and fell and on his way down, his leg came in contact with Zakk and they both plunged to the bottom."

"You feel responsible for that event?"

"Of course I do and always have! It was my idea to ascend, knowing the moss covered rocks were slippery and I insisted because I had a date and hoped to get *lucky,* if you know what I mean."

"Yes, I know what you mean and I'm so sorry that painful experience has taken such a toll on your life."

"It's that obvious?" Levi asked, wiping a tear from his cheek.

"Yes, it is, but what's more important, is what have you done since or plan to do to be able to forgive yourself and find some peace in your life?"

"I've dedicated my life to fighting crime, in some sense and have rid society of some disgusting human beings, for starters."

"That's all well and good, for the community and country, at large, but what have you done for yourself?"

"I met and married the most beautiful woman in the world, but she died of cancer and I wasn't even there to hold her in her last moments. I've failed at everything I've done."

"You do know you suffered from survivors guilt, don't you?"

"No question about it."

"Do you think your two friends would want you to live your life in your own self-made living hell? I mean if you believe in God and Heaven, you do realize they are in a better place than you are, don't you?"

"I never thought about it like that, I guess. I blame myself for their not graduating high school and college, get married and have a family...stuff like that."

"They missed out on those things, indeed, but being in Heaven is much better than anything here that earth has to offer," the wise man continued.

"I truly never thought of it like that," Levi said and looked toward the old man who had suddenly disappeared, as mysteriously as he had arrived.

Darkness had long since settled in the area and the Harvest moon and millions of brilliant stars caressed the velvet sky and Levi stood and slowly walked toward his car.

It was over an hour before he started the engine and drove toward his home on the lake.

He drove into the driveway of ZenJa's home in hopes she might have still be awake, but he noted all the lights were turned off, so he backed out and continued to his own home for the night.

Chapter 63

Levi stepped out of the shower, after a fitful night of tossing and turning, dressed and walked onto his deck with a steaming cup of coffee, when his cell phone rang.

"Good morning, ZenJa," he replied noting the number.

"Good morning, Alex. I just called to ask why you didn't come up to the house, last night?"

"How did you know I was there?"

"I have a motion sensor positioned at the end of the driveway. If those Avon ladies, show up, I want to make sure I put my German Shepard outside," she said and laughed.

"You don't have a German Shepard," Levi reminded her and smiled.

"Well, I could have one...someday!"

"I thought we decided against having any dogs," he teased.

"What if I put a cardboard cut-out on the front lawn, with big piles of poop, to make it look like he's real?"

"That's one reason why I don't want any dogs. When I mow my lawn, I want to make sure I don't have to worry about stepping in that shit...literally!" he said and howled with laughter.

"Okay, I'll give you that one, Levi."

"What are you doing today, ZenJa?"

"Nothing, much, why?"

"How about if I pick you up in half an hour, take you to breakfast and then take you to my special childhood place; seems you took me to yours, yesterday."

"I'll be ready," she replied with glee. "The foliage is so beautiful and I'm assuming your special place isn't some dark mysterious cave filled with bats, is it?"

"No, it isn't and the foliage is just beautiful, there; I saw it last night."

"You went to visit your childhood place?"

"Yes, and I haven't been there in twenty years and I must warn you, my special place does not have as many fond memories as yours does," he said and disconnected the call.

Forty-five minutes later the couple entered a small, crowded roadside diner, ordered their breakfasts and simply sat, silently, and looked into each other's eyes.

Having had training in psychological studies, ZenJa knew Alex was about to peel away another layer of his personal history and she realized she had to give him all the time he needed to say what was, obviously, weighing deeply on his mind.

"More coffee?" the waitress asked when she brought their meals to the table.

"Yes, please," Levi said, but remained looking into ZenJa's eyes.

"Would you like to share this blueberry muffin with me?" she asked.

"You like sharing and sampling from each other's plates?"

"Yes, indeed, the grass always looks greener on the other side, doesn't it," she replied and smiled.

"My wife and I always did that, too. She always said she hated steak, but when I ordered one, she always shared mine. Of course I didn't complain because I ate most of her scallops and shrimp," Levi said and laughed.

"Actually, I did that the other day, and stole some of Alex's food when we were talking about the plans for the Beckwith property."

"Those are beautiful plans and I know my parents would be astounded to see what potential they had sitting right under their feet."

"I'm going to need help...a lot of help with this project, ZenJa and I want you to share this experience with me and I'm not talking financial." I'm not simply asking you to share this with me, so I can share your money...well, some of it's my money, now," he added and laughed.

"What hand or role would you like me to play in all this; will you still be working for...whoever you work for?"

"I sincerely love my job, but I've been thinking maybe it's time to start a new chapter in my life and leave the past, in the past and now that you have left the Bureau, now might be a good time."

"To what extent I would like you involved in all this, I haven't figured all that out, yet. There are professionals that handle most everything, these days, from the ground work, landscaping, building, decorating, etc, but just to know I have someone keeping an eye on things while I'm not around would be quite a relief, for me. I don't want this to be a 24/7 *job*. I want this to be an adventure and fun."

"Well, we better eat this before it gets cold. We have a long drive ahead of us," Levi said while the couple silently ate their meals.

Half an hour later, the Camaro was speeding up the highway, when

ZenJa's cell phone rang and she put it on speaker.

"Hello, Alex, what's up?

"I was just checking with you about the race tomorrow. You and Levi are going to come, aren't you?"

"Yes, we plan to be there. What time and where do you want to meet?"

"If you meet us at Swamp Hill Road at 9:00 am sharp, we'll have a police escort right inside. You do realize what an effort this was to plan this. I mean there'll be cars lined up for more than fifty miles in either direction, at that time of day, don't you?"

"No, I really had no idea this was such a big deal!"

"You're in for one real treat, here...you and Levi both. I can't believe neither of you ever went to a race before and you do realize once you go, you are hooked for life, don't you?"

"Like that first use of crack cocaine?" she asked.

"Exactly...not that I would know about that."

"So, exactly, who's arm did you twist to accomplish this mission of having us chauffeured inside?"

"Well, it so happens Agents Brent Wyman and Emerson are also joining us and of course our guests Keith and his family and Darcy, so it's imperative for Agent Emerson to leave at a moment's notice; there can be no traffic congestion where he's concerned, so he made the arrangements."

"Is that the only reason you invited Emerson, so we can have a free pass, inside the gates and your brother is nodding his head, by the way," she added.

"Oh, Levi is there?"

"Yes, we're taking a nice leisurely drive to see the foliage."

"That's cool. So deliver the message and let him know we'll load up Emerson's Suburban with all the fixings for a huge tailgate party, so you can bring stuff, too if you want."

"What do you want us to bring?"

"We have all the major stuff, like grill, charcoal, lighter fluid and ice chests filled with ice and meat and cold salads. Keith, Darlene, and Darcy have been cooking all night, just to get ready."

"This truly is an amazing and festive ceremony, isn't it? ZenJa asked and simply couldn't believe the excitement in Alex's voice and the preparations that seemed to go into this sporting event.

"It's like New Year's Eve at every race," he exclaimed.

"I have no doubt; I have no doubt," she replied with less enthusiasm than the caller.

"Well, I got to run, the kids just ran into the lake, with their parents behind them, so I have to go," Alex said and disconnected the call.

"He always was a little...immature," Levi said shaking his head.

"Well, sometimes, it's fun to be silly, don't you think?"

"I guess...it's been a long time..." he added while he drove into the same look-out point he had entered the previous night.

"Oh my! What a fantastic view!" ZenJa cried and quickly exited the car, before Levi could open her door. "I remembered to bring my camera, too."

"I wonder how far away you can see from here...how many states?"

"You can see into Canada, from here," Levi said and gently reached for ZenJa's hand. The couple walked, silently, along the winding path that surrounded the upper part of the cliffs and ledges.

"Are you okay?"

"Yes, I'm just absorbing the beauty, fresh air, and the leaves."

"The leaves are what is beautiful," ZenJa said and laughed.

"No, their beauty doesn't hold a candle to you, ZenJa," he said and gently turned her face towards his at the same time he wrapped his arms around her and kissed her passionately.

Another couple walked by and ZenJa asked them if they would take some pictures of herself and Levi, with the magnificent view in the background. With no fewer than a dozen photos taken, in various poses, from the serious to the outrageously funny faces, the couple continued on their way while ZenJa and Levi took turns taking more pictures of themselves.

"See, you said I can't be silly. I think I pretty much made an ass out of myself, in some of those shots, don't you?"

"I especially love the picture of you and I playing *horsey*."

"I was not playing *horsey*. I'm an ass, remember?" Levi teased.

"Well, whatever you want to call it, I loved riding on your back," she said suggestively.

"My back is not where I'd like you to be riding, me." he said even more provocatively.

"Right here?"

"Why not? Don't tell me you're one of those women who only have sex in the bedroom?"

"I never discuss my sex life unless it's with the participant, at the time," ZenJa said sharply. "I don't kiss and tell."

"Well, if I happened to be a *participant*, as you call it, could we talk about it?" Levi asked, defensively.

The magical spell, passion, and flame that, at one time, appeared to be developing between this couple in the last few moments, disappeared like a fog, in the early morning light.

The couple continued to walk along, picking up an assortment of colored leaves before coming to a private picnic table that was nestled in among several oak, pine, and maple trees.

"We can sit here for a few minutes, if you want. The view is specular from here." Levi said while the couple sat down, side by side, facing the mountains

"You said you came here quite often, when you were young?" ZenJa began in an effort to ease the tension that had divided the couple, again

"My friends and I used to scale these ledges and camp out overnight all the time."

"Oh, so you *are* used to having sex under the stars, in front of a camp fire?" ZenJa asked.

"I came here with my friends, Aaron and Zakk and because they were males, we never had sex, so I can't say I ever did have sex *here,* under the stars."

"I'm just teasing you," ZenJa offered.

"I know."

"You never mentioned why you came here last night," ZenJa said and gently touched Levi's hand.

"I came up here to meet someone."

"Oh, I see, well, I'm glad you brought me here today," ZenJa replied, not getting suckered into asking who he came to meet and starting another argument.

"Do you ever see your childhood friends, Zakk and Aaron, now?"

"No, they're deceased."

"I'm sorry to hear that."

ZenJa was aware something was troubling her friend, again, and she was going to patiently wait for him to confide in her.

After several long moments of silence, Levi said, "The last time I was here, other than last night was the last time my friends and I climbed that ledge, over there," he said pointing to the North.

"That's very steep. I've never been rock climbing. I hate heights, and that certainly looks dangerous," ZenJa said frowning.

"I never understood the lure of rock or mountain climbing, especially places like Mount Everest," ZenJa added.

"Didn't you ever play King Of The Hill, as a child?" Levi asked and smiled.

"Yes, we did, but that was on top of a large snow pile, not higher than the outer atmosphere."

"Where's your zest for life...the thrill of a challenge?"

"I always played it safe, I guess," ZenJa replied knowing that was true.

"Is there a time you ever feel like taking chances?"

"Yes, and what about you? When was the last time you took a chance, other than at work?

"Touche', my dear; touche'! I'm about to take a very risky chance, right now, for your information," Levi began and for the next hour, he explained the events that took his friends lives and how he had suffered every day, since and about the old man who appeared and disappeared out of nowhere, the previous evening.

"I'm sorry this event took place, in your life and can't imagine how that has impacted that life, since, but I want to thank you for telling me about it and trusting me enough to confide in me. Trust me, I will never speak of it...ever, unless you want to talk more about your friends and the positive adventures you shared with them."

"It's nice to get it off my chest. My father and Alex are the only ones who know about it...well, I mean everyone in the state knew about it at the time, but the only people who matter to me, know or remember it now."

"Are you saying I matter to you?" ZenJa asked.

"Levi simply looked in her direction, but didn't respond. He realized she already knew the answer to that question.

"By the way, who was the old man?"

"My conscience, I guess."

"I'd say maybe it was a guardian angel, like Isabella, who had to convince you that you have suffered enough?"

"Well, we better start back, it's almost dinner time," Levi said, without responding to ZenJa's analysis.

"Wait!" ZenJa and embraced Levi and the couple gently laid down on the bed of falling leaves and made love until the moon and stars shone down from above.

Chapter 64

The couple, riding in the Camaro entered the town limits near their lake front homes before they spoke, after their meal at another restaurant, nestled in the White Mountains.

"Do you have anything, at your house for a tailgate party?" Levi asked.

"I have no idea what one brings to a tailgate party, to be honest with you."

"Well, you heard Alex say they have ice, meat, the grill and all that stuff and some salads they've been making for two days..."

"How about we bring something everyone always forgets. Like paper plates, napkins, plastic wear, cups, salt, pepper, catsup, mustard, trash bags, chips, dip, pickles, sodas and deserts?"

"You sound like someone may have forgotten stuff like that, in the past?" Levi asked and smiled.

"We always forgot the small, but vital things, like plates!"

"If we bring a watermelon, we better make sure to bring a large knife, too. I don't want to have to bring out my switchblade to wrestle that to the ground."

Levi and ZenJa walked into the largest supermarket, in the area and quickly filled a shopping cart with the essentials for the festivities, the next day.

"The good thing about all this shit, is none of it needs refrigeration, so we can leave it all here in the car!" Levi said and laughed while they stuffed the back seat to the rooftop.

After leaving the shopping plaza Levi asked ZenJa if she wanted to spend the night at his house.

"I really don't feel like being alone tonight, ZenJa. Revealing one of my deep dark secrets about my past, to you, was more stressful than I imagined. I would love to hold you in my arms and sleep well, for a change."

"You can leave me off at my house; I'll grab some clothes for tomorrow and drive over, if you want. Like you said, we may want to take separate cars."

"I'll wait while you pack and we're not taking separate cars, unless we have a fight in the next ten hours!" he said and laughed.

"Oh, I know, you want me to help unload all this *shit,* as you said, when we get to the track, right?" she teased.

"Damn, was I that transparent?"

"Yes, Mr. Harris, you were," she said while she ran up the steps to her house, threw some clothes in a duffle bag and ran back outside to spend the night in the arms of the man she had fallen in love with.

Chapter 65

"See, I told you we would be here in no time!" Alex said as all those in the procession drove inside the New Hampshire Motor Speedway track; that followed a state police car that had it's siren's blaring and lights flashing.

The line of vehicles, that slowly drove on the outskirts of the track, found adequate parking spaces near the camping area, included one Chevy Suburban, with black tinted windows, that Agent Emerson wheeled, a black Camaro that included Levi and ZenJa, the red Mustang, where Darcy and Alex made themselves comfortable the silver Chevy Impala that Agent Wyman drove, and Keith and his family in their rental car, bringing up the rear.

"Holy Mackerel!" ZenJa and Levi both said at the same time after they climbed out of their car.

"This place is massive!" Levi exclaimed when the entire group gathered around to stretch their legs. "I mean I've seen the races on television, now and then, but I had no idea what a track is like, seeing it up close and personal."

"I see you're catching NASCAR Fever, already," Alex said while he and Darcy showed off their NASCAR shirts and hats that included the #14 car of Tony Stewart and the #88 car of Dale Jr.

"We're going to stick out like sore thumbs with our everyday clothes," ZenJa wailed.

"Once this day is over, you'll have to select your own favorite driver and suit up, properly for next time," Darcy said and smiled.

Brent wore his Kyle Larson, the # 42 shirt and hat and Emerson wore the #48 of Jimmie Johnson. The Morrison family were all wearing the #4 of Kevin Harvick, with the exception of Betsy who wore the #10 of Danica Patrick, the only female NASCAR driver in this year's series.

Without haste, the friends had the Suburban and all the other vehicles emptied of picnic supplies, the grill heating up and several large folding tables and chairs opened and food stuffs on display and then everyone sat down to wait for the meat and corn on the cob to cook.

"Instead of buying napkins that would obviously blow away, I brought us each our own rolls of paper towels and everyone has their own trash bags they can hook to their chairs," ZenJa announced.

"Excellent idea," Alex replied. "I also see someone remembered the plates, cups and seasonings."

"And I see you brought yourself," Levi teased.

"I'll have you known I have callouses on my fingers from peeling potatoes for the salad," Alex said before he turned back to speak with Darcy again.

"Did you see how they turned Kurt's car into a rocket ship, after the first two laps of trials?"

"All it took was a half a wedge and then another pound of air, in the right tire," Darcy explained.

"Sure did mess up the front end, though when he spun out into the grass, didn't it? He mowed that like my front lawn and it took them fifteen minutes to clean the sod out of the front end."

"Well, Kurt told his crew chief the car was *plowing,* and had no grip, so it's no surprise."

"What in hell are you two talking about? Wedge, pound of air plowing, grip, mowing the law, and sod?" ZenJa asked as everyone, but Levi laughed at the couple who were at the track for the first time.

"That's NASCAR lingo," Brent explained. "You'll catch on."

"Who do you think will get the checkered flag today?" Emerson asked.

"I know what that is!" Levi yelled proudly.

"God help us," Alex said and went to turn the meat, on the grill.

The sports fans had settled down to indulge themselves in the tailgate festivities and the children had met some new friends and were playing with Nerf toys around the vehicles while the adults began talking business.

"So have you given any thought to relocating up here, Keith?" Levi asked.

"We talked about it since you mentioned it and as frightening as it is to uproot your family, there's nothing like New England in the summer and fall. We've truly missed it up here, though I know how horrendous winters can be."

"You'll be coming along, with the family, won't you, Darcy?" Alex asked.

"I have to, I'm the babysitter," she said and smiled at her date.

"This is an amazing community here," ZenJa said; watching the children play, groups of people walk by and saying hello to people they didn't even know.

"Everyone involved in NASCAR, whether you're on a racing team or simply a fan, we're all family," Alex said.

"You won't believe the charities these teams and sponsors support.

They donate and raise millions for all kinds of causes, including the military, children, and animals," Darcy explained.

"Excuse me, do you happen to have a extra roll of paper towels?" a Casey Kahne fan asked. "Ours ended up inside the cooler," the woman said and laughed while rolling her eyes at her small son.

"Sure, there are some right over there," Alex said, pointing to the back of the SUV. "Do you need anything else?"

"You wouldn't happen to have some extra salt, would you? Have you ever had corn on the cob, without it?" she said and laughed even harder.

"See, I told you we'd bring something useful," ZenJa said and smiled, stood up and handed her one of the travel size shakers they had purchased the night before.

"Yes, they brought the salt," Alex teased.

"You're new here, huh?" the lady continued as the children continued to play.

"How can you tell?" ZenJa asked.

"You're not wearing a driver's shirt or hat."

"That obvious, huh?" Levi asked.

"We've all been to our first race, at one time or another, but I can assure you, though, this will not be your last," she said and thanked them for the towels and salt.

"These people are amazing!" Levi said and grinned from ear to ear.

"What did I tell you?" Alex said and smiled.

"You never told us where our seats are?" Brent mentioned. "I hope it's not more than a mile to the closest bathroom?"

"That's what we forgot...a port-a-potty," ZenJa said.

"You folks will be pleased to know I've reserved our own private suite," Alex teased.

"I don't want to sit in a suite, I want to sit with the *real* fans," Levi said.

"That's a good thing, because I was only kidding about the suite, but we're right across from the finish line, but high enough so we can see all the action and everyone better make sure they make their own *pit stop* before we ascend into the abyss of the stands."

With less than an hour for the NASCAR race to begin, the ten race fans climbed into the stands and found their seats, the whole row of seats, like

Alex had planned.

"I didn't want people climbing all over us back and forth, during the whole race," Alex explained. "I swear, some of these people only come to eat," he said and laughed.

"That's quite a hike up here in these stands, so I don't plan on going back to earth, until after the race is over," Darlene said

The opening ceremonies began with these words announced over the loud speaker, "Ladies and Gentlemen, please rise for the presentation of Colors and today's prayers delivered by the Reverend Otis Bradshaw."

Shortly after this announcement, the Star Spangled Banner was sung, by a local country singer and not to disappoint anyone, two C-130's flew overhead, after which the roar from the crowd could be heard for miles around.

"This is quite the elaborate festival, isn't it?" ZenJa asked Levi when all in attendance put their ear plugs in and sat down.

The crowd quickly rose to their feet, once again, when the forty three race cars made their way around the track and circled two times for the drivers to warm up their tires and get a feel for the track's surface.

Less than three minutes later, the green flag flew and was waved; everyone in the crowd standing and cheering their favorite driver on. The race had finally begun.

"Who are you going to cheer for?" Levi yelled into ZenJa's ear, over the deafening roar of the engines; the cars circling the track at speeds of over two hundred miles an hour.

"The winner!" ZenJa replied.

"Am I a winner?"

"You certainly are," ZenJa said and kissed the man in her life.

Four hours later, with sun burned faces and their voices hoarse from yelling and screaming, along with the entire crowd, the winner of this Sprint NASCAR race was Joey Lagano, who sailed across the finish line with the other contenders close behind, and celebrated with the usual *'burn out'* and waving the checked flag for the fans.

The race car fans fought their way through the crowds and once again, fired up the grill and began to have their second tail gate party of the day.

"No sense in trying to leave the track at this time," Alex suggested. "It'll be five hours or more before the herd thins out," he said and held Darcy by the hand while they went to go visit the mechanize trailers to purchase more Tony Stewart and Dale Jr. decals, tee shirts and hats.

"While Brent, Keith and Darlene took charge of the grill and food preparation, Emerson sat and visited with Levi and ZenJa.

"Have you picked your favorite driver or team yet?"

"I think we'll have to watch until the end of the season and by next year, we'll have it all figured out, right, ZenJa?"

"I think so and from what I understand Homestead, the final race is the place to be," she stated.

"Told ya!" Emerson yelled to Keith and Darlene. "They're hooked!"

"If you had told me that yesterday, I never would have believed it," Levi said truthfully.

"I see all these people with campers..." ZenJa began.

"Yes, these folks come, some of them, for the whole week for the festivities, the pre race trials, concerts, test runs and get pit passes to wander through the garages and even meet some of the drivers," Keith replied.

"Let's do that next year!" ZenJa exclaimed.

"What about if we rent a motor home and go to Homestead in November?" Levi asked.

"That sounds like so much fun and by then we will have decided who our favorite drivers will be and then we won't come to next year's race looking like newbies, like we do today," ZenJa concurred.

It was well after midnight when the racing fans collapsed in their beds for a good night's sleep.

Chapter 66

Bright and early the next morning, Levi's cell phone rang.

"Yo!" was the typical response.

"Hi, Levi, this is Brian Miller. I just wanted to let you know this is going to be my last week serving the fine town of Longberry. I'm heading out to the FBI Academy and the State Police will continue to cover the town, but the town fathers have decided to hold an election for Police Chief and I just noticed ZenJa's name is on the ballot. Did you know that?"

"You're kidding, right?"

"No, I just got a copy of the ballot...hot off the press."

"Who else is on the ballot?"

"No one!"

"I seriously don't think she has the slightest interest in that job, Brian."

"I can't speak for ZenJa, but from what she said, in the recent past, she has no interest in spending any more time in Longberry, than necessary, much less serve that community."

"When is the election supposed to be held?"

"In two weeks."

'Thanks for the heads up and I'll be speaking with ZenJa in a few minutes, so I'll see what her reaction to this is. I don't think it will be what the towns people want, but maybe I'm wrong."

"Okay, talk to you later," Brian said and disconnected the call and Levi called ZenJa on his own cell phone.

"Good morning, NASCAR fan. How are you this morning?"

"Oh, my, it's later than I thought, I'm still in bed," she said and scrambled out from under the covers and noticed it was past eleven in the morning.

"How about if I drive over for...well, it's almost lunchtime, now," Levi suggested.

"We'll, have to hurry because we have to see Keith and his family before they head back home."

"Well, to hell with lunch, I'll pick you up in twenty minutes and we can head over to Alex's shack."

"Okay, they must have tons of left overs from the tailgate party, yesterday, we can chow down on," ZenJa added.

Less than an hour later, ZenJa and Levi sped into the driveway that led to Alex's residence and were welcomed outside at the picnic tables that were, once again, piled high with food and beverages.

"Shit! What are you two doing here?" Alex asked. "I was hoping to keep all this food for myself, so I don't have to go shopping for..."

"Ever again?" ZenJa remarked with a smirk.

"Well, yeah," Alex said and sat down with his plate piled high with picnic goodies.

"We really wanted to stop by to make sure we saw you before you guys left and we also wanted to know if you two have given any more thought about relocating here...it won't be for a year or two, most likely, but this way you can get some plans of your own made. I mean it's going to take a long time to make a luxury town out of the Beckwith property and we haven't even begun to move any dirt."

"We honestly have considered it and think we may very well take you up on the offer," Keith replied. "We want our kids to grown up, away from the city."

"That sounds wonderful and I'm going to have copies of the plans made and will send you some, so you can keep abreast of what's going on and give us feed back about where you might want your service station to be located." Levi said.

"Well, we hate to eat and run, but we better get going," Darlene said.

"Where are the kids?" Darcy asked and began to laugh.

"They're in the lake again!" Keith said. "The water temperature must be less than sixty degrees, for Heaven sake.!"

"I hope you don't plan on taking them ice fishing in the winter," Alex said.

"Why?' ZenJa asked.

"Because they'll probably jump through the hole in the ice, to go swimming in January, that's why!" Keith said and rushed the children inside to change into dry clothes before putting their suitcases into the rental car.

An hour later Keith, Darlene, Darcy and the children were traveling south, to Virginia and Alex, Levi and ZenJa sat around the campfire, enjoying the peace and quiet surrounding the lake.

"I love it here, after the summer people go home," Levi said. "It's our private lake, once again."

"Oh, I almost forgot. Did you know there's going to be an election for Police Chief in Longberry, in two weeks?" Levi asked. "Brian called me this morning and said he's heading out to Quantico, shortly, and the town fathers have set the date for the election."

"Did he say who's going to run or who's on the ballot?" Alex asked.

"There's only one name on the ballot, from what Brian said."

"Who's the dumb ass that would take that job?" ZenJa asked and looked at Levi, who simply looked at her, without saying a word.

"Oh, no! Hell no!" was her response. "I told you I have no interest in spending much time there and certainly not to have a career in that town!" she yelled.

"If we're to become *partners* in the expansion and development of your parents property, you're going to be spending more time there than you did when you were growing up," Levi reasoned.

"Maybe that isn't such a good idea, Levi. I got all caught up in the excitement of the project and forgot where this creation of yours is going to be located."

"Okay, I can understand your reluctance and maybe you're right," Levi said sadly. "It probably isn't such a good idea."

"Sometimes it might be better to leave things they way they are," Alex suggested.

"Well, then if I don't become a developer, I'll have to continue with my current job," he said and shrugged. "It doesn't really matter to me, one way or the other," he said truthfully. "It'll mean less headaches for me so maybe I'll just put the property up for sale and another developer can see what he can do with it," Levi mumbled to himself.

"I hope you understand how I feel about this," ZenJa stated. "I've mentioned it many times before."

"Of course you're right and I appreciate that, but maybe I was hoping to bring some fucking life back into that town and help everyone heal and make it a thriving, happy place to live!" Levi retorted and stood up. "What are you really afraid of, ZenJa?"

"What in hell do you mean?" she screamed while Alex sat silently, afraid to intervene, for fear of having his head chewed off.

"Just exactly are you insinuating?" she asked again.

"Do you know where your sister and her friend are buried? Are they on that fucking property?" he accused.

ZenJa reached up and slapped Levi across the face. He simply stood there, without raising his hand to defend himself.

Levi slowly walked to his car, got inside and drove away, leaving ZenJa at Alex's residence.

"That fucking bastard thinks I had something to do with my sister's disappearance?" she screamed hysterically while Alex simply sat and watched her.

"What, are you just going to sit there like a moron?" she yelled at Alex.

"What would you like me to do, ZenJa?" he asked calmly. "Go and shoot him?"

ZenJa looked at Alex as if he had slapped her across the face and she burst into tears and sat back down in her chair.

"I'll warn you, though, the last person who slapped Levi across the face is buried, six feet under," he said and walked into his house and closed the door. Without saying more, Alex had a fleeting thought of he and Levi's mother and the secret these two men kept, to themselves, to that day.

An hour later, ZenJa knocked on Alex's door and asked him if he would give her a ride home.

"I suppose," he mumbled, not caring he one way or another and preferably hoped she would walk.

Once the couple got inside the car and headed down the highway, ZenJa asked, "Why would he think I had anything to do with my own sister's death? Is he crazy?"

"Well, you seem to think we're morons and crazy, so maybe we are."

"Is that why he's been nice to me, becoming my friend or having you keeping an eye on me all this time, because you both think I'm guilty of some sick crime?"

"Get the fuck over yourself, ZenJa! I hate to break this to you but the world doesn't revolved around you, you know!"

Tears slipped down the woman's cheeks; they continued on their journey, in silence, until they arrived at her home.

The vehicle drove past the motion detector and the alarm went off inside ZenJa's house.

"Shit! What the fuck is she doing back here so soon?" a man asked out loud, collected his wits and walked toward the front door, as innocently as a choir boy.

"Thank you for the ride home, Alex," she said, climbed out of the

Mustang and slowly entered her house and before she closed the door, Alex heard a horrifying scream from inside.

Alex pulled his weapon from his waistband and met ZenJa at the same time she ran back outside of the house.

"What the hell is it?" he asked, aiming his weapon toward the door at the same time a handsome, clean cut man, also ran outside.

"Who the hell are you?" Alex asked, aiming his weapon at the man's head.

"Who are you?" he yelled in return.

"What are you doing in my house?" ZenJa screamed.

"Your house? This is my parents house," he replied indignantly.

"This house was foreclosed on and this woman is the rightful owner now!" Alex replied without hesitation.

"Foreclosed on?" the strong and muscular man, dress in blue jeans and a light blue tee shirt replied.

"Yes, foreclosed on!" ZenJa yelled, once again.

"Oh my God, I had no idea," the man said. "I had no idea."

"Why don't you call your parents and ask them about it," Alex sarcastically suggested.

"I would, but they've passed away and I haven't been in the United States for several years, now."

"Well, obviously they left lose ends and the mortgage and back taxes were not among their priorities," ZenJa spewed, glaring at the dumb founded man.

"You have a key to this house?" ZenJa asked.

But before the man responded, Alex asked, "You never changed the fucking locks?"

"No, I never got around to it," she admitted.

"Okay, let's all calm down now and please put that weapon away," the man said and sat on the front step.

"May we be brazen enough to ask to see some ID?" Alex demanded.

"Yeah, sure," the man replied at the same time Alex noticed a weapon in the man's waistband.

"You always go visiting your folks with a gun?" Alex asked, raising his weapon, once again.

"I always *carry*; it's part of my job."

"And just what job might that be?" ZenJa demanded.

"I'm a private contractor."

"And obviously not for a land developer, now, right?" Alex asked.

"No, I work...I'm outsourced for the government."

"Do you have that ID and a name?" ZenJa asked.

"Here's the ID and my name is...Brody Black."

"Why the hesitation? Had to remember what ID you were carrying?" Alex asked.

ZenJa noted a slight smirk, on the man's face, but he remained silent.

"You didn't notice this Charger outside and it most likely wasn't your parents car; they being deceased and all? And if I may be so bold where in hell is your transportation or did you fly in by helicopter?" Alex wanted to know.

"Actually, I did notice the car and I arrived by boat, as you can see. It's parked at the dock," he added pointing to the dock to their right. "That's why I came over. I drove by last night, saw the car and wondered why it was still here this morning. At first I thought it was just someone walking around the lake, but became concerned when the car was still here this morning and I came inside to check the house."

"You had no idea this house was foreclosed on and sold?" Alex asked again.

"No, I had no idea. Like I said, I've been out of the country for a few years now."

"You came by boat and just where did you launch that boat from?" ZenJa asked sharply.

"I live across the lake...well, when I'm in the US."

"Is Black the name that was on the Deed," ZenJa?"

"Yes, as a matter of fact it was."

"Well, I guess this has all been a misunderstanding, but I can assure you, Mr. Black, I will check this bullshit story out and if I may be so bold to ask you for the keys, that you have, for this house, that is no longer in your family?" Alex demanded, holding his hand out for the keys. "And I would like *all* the keys!"

"You know, I owe you folks an apology and if I may be so bold, may I take you both out for lunch. I don't spend much time here, so I have few, if no friends and it might be nice to have a few beers with some folks, from the area," Brody suggested. "Can we start over?"

"My name, as you already know is Brody Black and you are?" he asked and smiled at ZenJa.

"Well, the identification I'm in possession of, today, is ZenJa Beckwith and this man is Alex Lyons...today, anyway."

"You still don't believe this is my real name, I gather?" Brody asked and smiled again.

"No, why would we?" Alex said sharply.

"Oh, so you're not a married couple?" Brody asked, failing to respond to the previous question.

"No, we are not!" ZenJa said and glared at Alex. "No way in hell."

"Well, so what do you say, we all go and have lunch and if you can recommend a good place to eat, that would be even better. You folks, being from around here, must know of a good place?" he asked and handed ZenJa three keys. One to each door of the house and one to the garage.

"I have one question," ZenJa said.

"What might that be, Miss?"

"How long were you snooping in my house?"

"I just barely shut the door when you drove up. You do remember, I was standing just inside the door and hadn't make myself comfortable or made a sandwich, yet!" he said and laughed. "You know you really should get a big dog."

"I know, I've been told that often enough," she replied; recalling Levi making the same comment, not so long ago.

"So, what do you both say, we meet for lunch?"

"Meet us at The Opera House Café, in an hour," Alex said.

"Okay, that will be fine...see you then," Brody said and walked to his speed boat and left the area; drove to a local boat launch, where he loaded up his boat onto the trailer he had attached to his Cadillac Escalade and drove away.

"Jesus, ZenJa, I can't believe you never had those locks changed. What ails you?"

"I knew the owners had died, so I didn't really think they would be coming back to haunt me," she retorted.

"He's hot, huh?" Alex asked and laughed.

"Yes, as a matter of fact, I do find him quite attractive," ZenJa replied.

"Well, I better get going, so I can change clothes and pick up Levi before our luncheon date."

"You're bringing Levi?"

"Of course. I want him to see what he's up against, now."

"What do you mean, what he's up against?"

"A little male rivalry for your affections, I would say; might not be a bad thing for my brother," Alex said and walked to his car. "See you at The Opera House in an hour," he hollered to the woman who remained standing in the doorway.

Chapter 67

Brody, the government contractor, arrived at The Opera House Café moments before ZenJa drove up, with Alex and Levi right behind her, in the Camaro.

Levi was livid, when Alex explained what had transpired less than an hour ago and was most anxious to meet this, Brody Black character who Alex described as being very handsome and about forty years old, with a little gray hair at his temples and strikingly devilish green eyes and as fit as a fiddle.

"You sound like you have the hots for him, Alex," Levi said when they exited the car and walked behind ZenJa, into the Café.

"Darcy is much more to my liking, thank you," he retorted.

Once the trio entered the door, Brody stood up, and motioned for his guests to be seated at a large table, he had commandeered in a small corner, at the rear of the dining establishment.

"You already know ZenJa and myself, and this is my brother, Levi, ZenJa's boyfriend," he added for Brody's benefit.

"Boyfriend?" ZenJa asked defiantly. "I believe this is the man whose face I recently slapped," she added a little too smugly for Levi's liking.

"Levi reached up and touched his still smarting cheek and looked into ZenJa's eyes before saying, "That will only happen one time. Only one time."

"Well, shall we place our orders?" Brody suggested and continued to smirk. "Shall we start with beers while our orders are being prepared?" he added when the waitress came to their table.

"May we have two pitchers of beer, please," Brody asked without a reply from the trio about any beverages being ordered. "That is if you're of drinking age?" Brody added and looked at ZenJa, who blushed from the not so subtle compliment.

"Coming right up," the young girl replied.

"So what do you recommend?" Brody asked and stared at the menu, while continuing to steal glances at the lovely auburn haired lady who sat across from him.

"The Club Sandwiches are the best, I've ever had," ZenJa offered.

"That sounds good to me, Brody replied cheerfully and set his menu down."

The waitress returned with the pitchers of beer and glasses and Levi said, "We'll, have four Club Sandwiches, a large order of French Fries and

Onion Rings that we can share."

"You like to share?" Brody boldly asked, not knowing who he was dealing with, at their table, but continued to stare at Levi, without flinching.

"My father shared only one thing in his life and unbeknownst to him, it was our mother, but I assure you the only things I share are the rounds from my Glock."

"Ohhh!" Alex whispered and smiled.

"Oh, for God's sake, will you two stop it!" ZenJa hissed while she poured herself a glass of beer before passing the pitcher to Levi.

"The moment I saw you, coming into *your* house, ZenJa, I knew I had seen you somewhere before."

"Where have you seen me?"

"Someone handed me this campaign picture when I first got into the area. I commend you for running for Police Chief of Longberry. I've heard they've had their share of criminal activity in that area, over the years. What a shame."

"What do you know about that criminal activity, may I ask?" Levi demanded.

"Oh, just what my parents told me now and then. I know they were happy to learn the perps have been found," he added without thinking.

"How long did you say your parents were dead?" Alex asked, raising his eyebrows. "Come on you might as well tell us, we can find out easily enough, on our own."

Brody realized he had made a dreadful mistake and miscalculated the intelligence of these two men.

"The perps that you're referring to have only been identified in the last few months...when did your parents pass away, Brody?" Levi demanded when the waitress brought their orders. "I mean a house does not get foreclosed on in only a few months," he added for good measure.

"To be honest with you, my parents sent me yearly subscriptions to the local and state newspapers, so I actually read about the events that have unfolded, recently," he said, smiled and thanked himself for being quick witted.

"So now, if the brow beating and interrogation is over, I suggest you read me my Miranda Rights or we move on to less intense topics," Brody said and looked over his glass of beer, he held to his lips.

"So let me begin by asking what do you do for work, ZenJa?" he asked politely and smiled.

"I'm a...writer," she said.

"Wonderful! You look like the type of person who writes for the National Review or some political journal. Am I right?" he asked knowing that was not the truth.

"No, I'm a mystery writer, actually," she lied.

"So, you're going to run for Chief of Police and write about your adventures?"

"I have no intentions to run of that office...never did and never will."

"Those posters have been put up by some lovely towns-folk who wish I would run, but they are sadly mistaken. I may be the only name on the ballot, but I will never accept that position; there's not enough money in the world for me to do that and I have no desire to keep the peace around here."

"It sounds like that town needs someone to do just that," he brazenly suggested.

"Then why don't you take the fucking job?" Levi hissed and finished his first glass of beer.

"Actually, I'd be honored, but my employment takes me away from these parts ninety percent of the time."

"So, exactly when are you leaving?" Alex asked and smiled.

"Oh, my goodness. I came here to enjoy my little cabin on the lake, during the Fall season and I'm being asked to leave already?" So much for that New England hospitality."

"New Englander's are *not* hospitable and if you were truly from these neck of the woods, you would know that. Only the *transplants* are friendly, but that's only because they own and run all the business and tourist attractions here and pretend to be friendly, simply for the money they rake in," Levi said.

"Oh my God, will you all just stop this bickering!" ZenJa whispered.

"How are the onion rings, ZenJa?" Levi asked to change the subject. "I know they're your favorites."

"They are delicious and I do hope you save a few more for me," she replied and smiled, like a cat who swallowed the canary.

"So, tell me, gentlemen, what do you do for employment?" Brody asked.

"I used to be in the circus, but I recently sold my jack ass and bought a small parcel of land and hope to afford to build a little shack on it; I hope to get started on it before winter comes. I don't want to be sleeping in a snow bank, again this year," Levi said and glared at ZenJa.

"And you?" Brody asked Alex who was making every effort to keep from laughing.

"Oh, I'm still traveling with the circus, myself. I love the life on the open road."

"The circus life runs in the family, I take it?" Brody asked.

"Would you please let me out?" ZenJa asked Levi who was blocking her exit from the table.

"Are you not feeling well, my *dear*?" he asked but then noticed tears streaming down her cheeks.

"I have to go home," she said and quickly exited the café and sped down the highway.

"You want her half of the Club sandwich?" Alex callously asked Levi before pouring himself another beer.

"Sure! ZenJa and I always share with each other," Levi said and glared at Brody.

"May I have the bill, Miss and if you gentlemen will excuse me, I have another appointment this afternoon, but it was truly entertaining, meeting you," Brody said and offered his hand, but neither man, still sitting at the table, offered theirs in return.

"Thanks for the lunch," Alex said with his mouth full.

"Fucking hay-shakers," Brody whispered under his breath, but loud enough for Levi and Alex to hear his comment.

"Ya'll come back now, ya here!" Alex yelled to the man who paid the check and quickly left the café.

"What in God's name got into you two?" the waitress asked her best customers.

"Just having a little fun with that clown," Levi said and handed the waitress a large tip, on top of the one Mr. Black had given her.

"Let us know if he shows up here, again, okay?" Levi asked the young girl.

"Will do, Mr. Harris, and thank you," she added looking at the one hundred dollar bill that was placed in her hand.

"Where did that fucker go?" Alex asked, when the two men quickly left the café.

"There he is, he's riding a fucking bicycle!" Levi said and started to laugh.

"I wouldn't laugh, if I were you," Alex warned.

"Why not?"

"He seems to use modes of transportation that can not be easily identified. You know, the boat he arrived in, at ZenJa's and now this?" he cautioned.

"Hmmm! You're right."

"Let's see if we can follow him?" Alex suggested.

"This is a one way street and he's headed down the wrong way!" Levi yelled. "We'll never get him now, the traffic is too heavy and going the wrong way down the road."

"No, you mean the traffic is going down the right way, we would be going the wrong way." Alex reasoned. "Shit! He's gone!"

Brody Black placed the mountain bike in the back of his Cadillac Escalade, the same vehicle he had recently unhooked the boat trailer from. The man quickly left the parking lot, where he parked the vehicle, prior to biking to the café, and drove off into the darkening skies just before an evil storm descended upon the New Hampshire Lakes Region...or had the storm just recently arrived.

Brody Black arrived in the town of Guilford, on Lake Winnipesaukee, this first day of Fall, as ferocious as a hurricane; one the likes of which this area had never seen before.

Chapter 68

"Where are we going now?"

"I want to get to the Gilford Town Clerk's office before it closes," Levi said and maneuvered the black Camaro through the narrow, but crowded streets of the small town.

"Why?" Alex asked.

"I want to check on the property ZenJa bought, just to make sure she really is the owner and hasn't fallen victim to some sort of scam."

"Oh, God, that's a very distinct possibility, these days. She never did take your advice and go with the realtor you suggested, did she?"

"No, she didn't. She can, sometimes, be so full of herself, she doesn't listen to anyone else...just like me, I guess," Levi admitted and laughed.

Less than an hour before closing time, Levi and Alex rushed into the small, rustic town office building in search of the clerk.

Once they explained what they were looking for and the clerk checked the records she had on file, she said the only information she had was on the current owner. If they wanted more information about past property owners, they would have to visit the office of the Register of Deeds, in the next office.

"Wait!" the woman called just before the two men left the office.

"What?" Levi asked.

"Did you say the property owned by Mr. and Mrs. Black, on Sander's Bay?"

"Yes, what do you know about it?" Levi begged.

"You're referring to Mr. and Mrs. Brody Black?"

"Brody, appears to be the son's name," Levi replied.

"The Blacks did not or do not have any children, why, I don't know, but anyway, that's why the house went up for, foreclosure. There was no one around to settle the property matters."

"What the fuck?" Alex exclaimed to the startled elderly lady who found that language repulsive.

"How old were the Blacks, do you know?" Levi asked the woman.

"She was about twenty and he was thirty, I would say, the last time I saw either of them and that was when they bought the property."

"So they weren't elderly?"

"Oh, Heavens, no! They were a lovely, young couple, until..."

"Until what?"

"I shouldn't be gossiping," the woman said while she looked around the office to make sure no one else was listening.

"Tell us everything you know," Levi demanded.

"Mr. Black has been in prison, from what I heard for...I don't know, maybe ten years and Mrs. Black simply disappeared."

"Did she disappear before or after Black, allegedly, went to prison?" Levi asked.

"I believe it was after."

"So, no one was keeping up the payments or taxes on the house?"

"That appears to be the case," the clerk said.

"Thank you for your help, Miss," Alex said and ushered his shocked brother from the office and led him to the Registry of Deeds.

Within ten minutes, the men discovered the house had indeed been foreclosed on and ZenJa, thankfully, was the rightful owner.

Both men climbed into the Camaro and before starting the engine, Levi called ZenJa's number, but there was no answer.

"Where the fuck is she?" Levi yelled. "Keep trying her phone," he demanded and handed the phone to his brother.

"We better get over to her house and make sure she's all right," Alex said while the Caramo barreled through the narrow streets, once again, in the direction of Sander's Bay.

Fifteen minutes later, the Camaro came to a screeching halt in ZenJa's dooryard, but not before both men realized her car was not in the driveway and Levi ran to the garage, peaked inside, only to find that structure vacant of any car, either.

"Where in hell did she go?" Levi asked, climbing back inside the vehicle.

"You're probably getting all freaked out over nothing. She can take care of herself," Alex reminded his brother.

"I imagine she needs some time to cool down, after we humiliated her in front of that dashing, handsome man and don't tell me you're jealous?"

"Why would I be jealous? ZenJa's nothing to me," Levi retorted.

"No? She's just someone you *sleep* with now and then?"

"Sleep is not what we do, and if you're not man enough to use the word, sex, well, I guess you're a little naive, yourself."

"You simply have sex with her?" Alex, the usual callous one of the two brothers asked in surprise.

"Yes, that's it. Nothing more, nothing less."

"And here I thought I was the fucking bastard!"

"Some people are never lucky enough to meet the one person that is meant for them, in their entire lives, I did that once and know that will never happen again," Alex.

"Maybe ZenJa is looking for someone for purposes other than sex."

"Well, maybe she is and if Brody Black is the one for her, so be it. I really don't care, to be honest with you."

"I'm not sure who you're trying to convince, me or you," Alex mumbled.

"Come on back to my house and we can throw some steaks and corn-on-the-cob, on the grill and have a few more beers," Levi offered while he turned up the volume on his Bose stereo system and the song that fittingly was playing was *'Nomad'*, performed by Zakk Wylde and Black Label Society.

"That songs fits you to a tee," Alex said, with Levi nodding in agreement.

Chapter 69

"I'm glad you got the note I left on your door, ZenJa," Brody Black said and held the chair, she was about to sit in, at *'Le Crystal Lustre'*, an exquisite French restaurant, on the edge of Moulton's Cove, in Paugus Bay, not that far from her home.

"I knew it would be unwise for me to offer to pick you up at your residence, because you don't know me from Adam, but I wanted to try and make amends for the, shall we say, awkward lunch we had this afternoon. I realize there's more than a passing acquaintance, between you and Mr. Harris, and that is no business of mine, but I simply wanted to have dinner with a lovely lady, this evening and make amends."

"This is very kind Brody and what a lovely place this is. I've never been here before and no, I would not have accepted your offer to transport me here. I'm too independent for that."

"Only on the first date, I hope?" Brody said and laughed; a question ZenJa neglected to respond to.

Brody realized he had made an error in suggesting ZenJa's new home had been his parents in front of Alex and Levi. He quickly made the correct assumption they were not fools, so Brody felt this was the best way to change the web of lies he was weaving and cover his tracks.

"I hope you don't mind, but I have selected the menu, for tonight. As you may know many French Restaurants literally have twelve courses," he said and laughed.

"So, there really is such a thing as a twelve course meal?" ZenJa teased and blushed.

"Indeed, there is," he said when the Sommelier came to their table and brought a chilled bottle of Sauvignon Blanc and poured the wine, for the couple and after which the waiter brought a selection of tantalizing Hors d'oeuvres.

"This is a lovely restaurant, Brody; do you come here often?"

"Yes, this restaurant is a lovely place, *'Le Crystal Lustre'* or *Chandelie*r, if you might say in English. Those crystal pieces certainly are pieces of art, aren't they?" Brody asked and then he added, "this wine is delicate and aromatic, isn't it?"

"It is indeed," ZenJa replied and took another sip and tasted one of the dainty Hors d'oeuvres., but noticed the man never said if he dined there often.

"Let me know when you're ready for another course, ZenJa and I'll alert the waiter."

"Okay, I will," she said and selected another morsel to sample.

"Why I said that, is because we have a large menu to get through," he said and laughed. "But honestly, I have a confession to make and want to get the air cleared and as I'm dragging out this long boring story, I may forget about our meal."

"Maybe we should carry on to the Potage course?" she suggested and tried to be polite.

Brody nodded to the waiter and lovely bowls of Pumpkin Bisque were placed on their table and the waiter quickly disappeared, once again.

"I love this time of year and the apple and pumpkin items that abound," Brody began.

"This is delicious soup," ZenJa said and smiled and waited for what kind of bomb shell this man was about to drop on her.

After taking a deep breath, in an effort to get this story straight, Brody began to tell another version of the story he had told earlier in the day. Sadly, he had not been inside the house long enough to retrieve what he originally went there for.

"When I told you the house, that is now in your possession, belonged to my parents, I mislead you. It did not belong to my parents. It belonged to me and my wife. That is obviously why I had keys to it and let myself in.

"Were there any other details you mislead me about? I guess I should be thankful there weren't that many, so setting the record straight should be easy," she added sarcastically.

Before he responded the Sommelier came over to refill their wine glasses.

"May we have the next course, the Poisson, please?" Brody asked

"I will have your waiter bring it promptly," the young man said and scurried away.

"I selected a variety of shrimp and scallop masterpieces," Brody mentioned before he continued.

"No, to be honest with you, my owning the house was the only detail I mislead you about."

"So you have been out of the country for what...ten years?"

"Yes, I have."

"And was your wife there with you?"

"No, ZenJa...she was supposedly, at the house...what is now your house."

"When did you find out she was not at your...my house?"

"When I walked in the door and you and Alex came driving up," he lied.

"You actually walked into the house you honestly thought was still yours and your wife was going to be waiting for you with open arms?" she asked at the insanity of such a story while she sipped more wine and the couple both consumed some morsels of shrimp and scallops.

"I didn't...don't know where else to look for her," he replied sadly and continued to lie.

"When was the last time you heard from her or saw her?"

Brody continued to look down at his plate before responding. "It was three years ago."

"Just where have you been and if you hadn't heard from her in all that time, why didn't you come back sooner to find her?"

"I couldn't and I already told you, I was overseas."

"In the military?" ZenJa suggested.

"Something like that," he replied truthfully, this time.

"So, anyway, I simply wanted to clear up what I said about the house and why I was inside and yes, I was hoping my wife would be there waiting with open arms, but who knows, after all this time, I'm probably divorced...the reason being desertion, I assume."

"I won't keep on harping about this, because you obviously don't owe me any explanations and it's none of my business, but do you think she left willingly. In other words did she give up waiting for you, looking for you, began a new life, or might there be something more sinister about her leaving and did she even know where you were?"

"No, trust me there's nothing sinister about her leaving. I'm sure she left to make a new life for herself and I can't blame her. We married when she was twenty and I was thirty, so she's still very young and she deserves to enjoy life and not wait for me. She obviously left everything behind...the house and every other bad memory."

"So, now can we simply enjoy each other's company and the rest of our...what...eight courses?" Brody said and laughed.

"Okay, that sounds good and thank you, by the way, for telling me the truth. One thing I hate is a liar," she said with no hesitation.

The remainder of the evening the couple spent enjoying the cuisine and making small talk, no intense details about their past lives, but tales of childhood adventures, concerts they attended, movies, favorite music, books, and innocent conversation.

The meal was concluded, after the couple consumed coffee served in antique Demitasse cups and Brody paid the bill and walked ZenJa to her car.

"Which one is your car?" ZenJa asked, once seated inside her Charger.

"I walked. It does the body and soul good," he replied.

"Can I give you a lift?" she unwisely asked.

"No, thank you, ZenJa. You don't know me well enough to trust me, yet," he replied knowing how true that statement was.

Brody bend down and gently kissed the lady on her cheek, before bidding her a good night and then slowly walked to his Escalade that was parked two streets away.

Chapter 70

Not two minutes after ZenJa drove into her garage and entered her home, Levi sped into her driveway and simply stood at the door, without knocking.

Seconds later, ZenJa opened the front door and said, "You didn't knock."

"I knew you would be aware someone was coming up the driveway. I remember you have the motion sensor and I do hope you checked to see who it was before you opened the door," he added, still standing on the door step.

"I wasn't worried that it might be Brody Black, because I'm sure he probably still has a key," ZenJa replied realistically. "And another reason I doubt it was him, is because I just got home from having dinner with him!"

Levi looked like he had been, once again, slapped in the face and after a moment he said, "I tried calling you and guess I know where you were, then. The only reason I called you was because I wanted to make sure you were going to get these door locks changed, as a matter of fact."

"Yes, I have a locksmith coming over in the morning and I'm having deadbolts and other security measures added by a professional security company."

"Oh, well, that's good," Levi said and turned and walked toward his car.

"Levy, do you want to come inside?" ZenJa asked, knowing she was being a bitch.

"No, that's okay. I don't think there's room enough for three of us in your bed or in your life," he replied.

"I don't care how many people are in my bed or in my life, Levi. I only want one man to be in my heart," she said and turned to walk inside her home.

"ZenJa, I don't care who or what you do with your life and I certainly detest gossip, but I wanted you to be cautious when it comes to Brody Black."

"What makes you say that?"

"Alex and I went to the Town Clerk's office and Registry of Deeds. It appears your friend lied about his parents owning this home. Brody and his wife apparently owned it and you might be happy to know, you truly are the current owner."

"Brody already told me, tonight, that he lied about the ownership of this house," ZenJa said smugly.

"Well, that's good, but did he also tell you he has been in prison for ten years, and apparently, not working overseas for a government agency?" he retorted.

"Who told you that?" ZenJa hissed.

"The Town Clerk, as a matter of fact, though she couldn't swear that he had actually been in prison, but that is the rumor she heard and you might also be comforted to know, it appears his wife, left this house, *after*, he was either in prison or working at some bogus government agency."

"So, you're saying it appears Mr. Black did *not* murder his wife and bury her somewhere; so most likely he is *not* the person who may have aided Ivan in snatching my sister and the others from the face of the earth?" she screamed.

"At least he has one thing in his favor," Levy said and stormed back to his car and sped out of the driveway.

"Well, it appears Mr. Harris will be having sex by himself, tonight," Brody said and laughed and put his binoculars back in their case, walked through the woods and once again, climbed into his SUV and left the Sander's Bay area. While he headed back to his rental cottage his cell phone rang and immediately recognized the caller.

"Well?" was the only word spoken by the caller.

"I just had dinner with her," Brody responded.

"Get business taken care of," came the order and the call was disconnected.

Brody grabbed a beer and walked out onto the deck of his cottage and sat down to read the local newspaper that consisted of a small amount of news but mostly advertisements for the surrounding businesses for the benefit of the tourists and vendors tempting the visitors to open their wallets and go home with their credit cards maxed out.

Brody's eagle eyes spotted a column that mentioned recent property transfers in the local area and as expected, he noticed and was not surprised to discover the Black property having been sold to Miss ZenJa Beckwith; he already knew that, but what shocked him to the core was the fact The Beckwith Property, as it was called, had been recently been sold to an unknown buyer.

"Shit!" he yelled while he grabbed his cell phone and frightened two sea gulls from the deck railing.

"Lynx," was the simple response.

"We have a situation here."

"What is it?"

"I was just reading the local paper and The Beckwith Property was sold, recently, to an unknown buyer!" Brody whispered hoarsely.

"Well, she didn't waste any time unloading that did she? Must be she's money hungry."

"No, actually, that proves she's just the opposite. She, obviously, sold it to the first bidder," Brody reasoned.

"The fact she sold that property just saved her life, no doubt."

"We tried for the last ten years to get Beckwith to sell that property, damn it and then they're killed in a car wreck and the daughter sells it to the first slug to come along?" Lynx retorted.

"So that means we have more serious concerns now. We have to find out who bought that land. It borders *our* property."

"That's why you're cooling your heels in the Lakes Region, isn't it?"

"The good thing about that property is, there are over 300 some-odd acres and what's the chance anyone will stumble across an underground mine shaft that isn't even on their property?" Brody asked.

"None, but how are we going to hide huge cell towers if someone decides to develop that property? We have to find out who bought it and persuade them to sell!" Lynx replied before adding, "Fly in and out of there and when you check it out, in the next day or so, do not...I stress, do not drive there. We didn't make that landing pad there for nothing, you know and those dumb asses, the Sweeneys thought they were simply logging that parcel of land."

"That's not all they were doing with their logs."

"I love it when you talk dirty to me," Brody said and laughed.

"I know," was the response.

Chapter 71

AFT Agents Levi. Alex, and Brent, met with FBI Agent Emerson, back on the Sweeney property the first thing on Monday morning.

"Have the dogs even hinted that there might be cadavers buried here?" Levi asked. "Shit, they've been searching for a week and nothing!"

"I ordered more dogs to come in, today and here they are," Emerson said.

"Why more dogs?" Alex asked.

"These are your favorite kind of dogs...bomb and explosive sniffing dogs, fellas."

"Why? What makes you think they're needed?" Levi asked.

"We just got a report from the fire marshal, who investigated the log truck accident and fire that torched half the mountainside and it was determined there were explosives inside some of those logs!"

"No shit!" Levi said.

"That's why it burned so ferociously?" Brent asked.

"Yup, that appears to be a fact."

"Has anyone questioned Junior, lately?" Alex asked.

"He, of course is still in protective custody and in jail on transportation of weapons and drug charges, but he denies knowing anything about any explosives."

"Do you believe him?" Levi asked.

"Yes, as a matter of fact I do. His exact words were, "Do you think I'm fucking nuts? I would never have driven that truck up that mountain with the whole back end full of explosives!"

"Now, we're back to Ivan. What's he had to say for himself?" Brent asked.

"Nothing; absolutely nothing."

"Can anyone offer him a lighter sentence, than the death penalty, if he tells us where the girls are buried?" Levi asked.

"He claims he knows nothing about that."

"Why not admit to it, if he had any connection. He's charged with two counts of 1st degree murder, already, with the deaths of Lily and Wilbur," Brent mentioned.

"So we're at another dead end?" Levi asked.

"Looks that way," Emerson said as the bomb sniffing dogs scoured the area while a helicopter flew overhead.

"Who's that...the fucking media?" Emerson yelled.

"No, there's no logo on it," Alex said.

After a few minutes the aircraft disappeared toward the other end of town and was soon forgotten.

"Wonder what that's all about?" Brody asked out loud. "Looks like Feds, and why are they snooping around the Sweeney property?" he added nervously after spotting what appeared to be a search party and then noticed Alex's red Ford Mustang and Levi's black Chevy Camaro, and a Chevy Suburban with dark tinted windows, before he set down the helo in the small clearing designated as his landing zone, several miles away.

"I guess I'll have to find out more about Levi and Alex," Brody said aloud and moments later, another helicopter landed next to his and two men climbed from the cabin and approached him.

"When do we get started?" an Israeli soldier, named, Noam Krantz asked, in perfect English.

"We have a problem," Brody began.

"What's the problem?"

"The Beckwith property was just sold; to whom I don't know yet?"

"Why should that concern us?" another man, the Deputy Foreign Intelligence Officer of Israel, Daniel Rothschild a man who closely resembled the Prime Minister of Israel, Benjamin Netanyahu, asked.

"We have tried for the last ten years, as you know, to purchase that property to assure ourselves complete privacy for our mission, but we were comforted by the fact the family wasn't interested in selling it to anyone, but now it appears the owners were killed in a car accident, not so long ago, and the lone family member sold it; to whom I don't know, yet."

"If someone decides to develop that property into condominiums, a ski area or even worse, log that whole mountain side, we'll be screwed."

"Are you saying we should move this operation elsewhere?" Deputy Foreign Minister Daniel Rothschild suggested.

"This is the perfect spot; it's out in the middle of nowhere and the tests we've run on signals from the satellites are perfect." Brody began and we're about to embark on the next phase and lay the underground network and cables."

"The only other place that gives us the access we have from here is in

Maine," the Prime Minister look-alike confirmed.

"Well, what if the new owners of this property do decide to develop it? While they're busy expanding their land, we can simply go about our business of erecting our communications towers and who knows...those folks may be stupid enough to actually believe we are working for the power company and doing this for them!" Noam Krantz suggested.

"Actually, this might be a perfect *cover*," Rothchild surmised.

"And I want this operation to get started immediately!" the man continued. "The safety and security of my country is at stake and hell will freeze over before we will be annihilated!

"You, Mister Black, have been in Israel the last ten years, helping create a masterpiece of military defense for us and we expect you to do the same over here."

"It is my honor, Foreign Minister and I will die before I disappoint you." Brody responded.

"This is always something I wanted to ask you," the Foreign Minister asked.

"What's that?"

"Why did you decide to help us? No one simply does anything, these days, without a motive."

"My wife is of Israeli and Swedish decent and again, I will die before I let anything happen to her or her people!"

"Where did you meet her?"

"While I was on assignment, working for your government as a matter of fact."

"She is safe?"

"Yes, she is and I just spoke with her last night."

"When will you get to see her again?"

"If you tell me how long I'll be stationed here, I'll have a better idea."

"This operation will take years and simply keeping one step ahead of the enemy will drag this on forever, as well. But, the problem is we don't know how much time we have. We may be all dead tomorrow...we have no way to know."

"I need my wife with me here, then. She will be safer where I can keep an eye on her and she is vital to this project. She has proved that many times, over the last few years."

"I agree, Mr. Black. I believe we should all be around those we love at this terrible time in history. There may be no tomorrow," the man said.

"This is her contact number. She will tell you where she is," Brody replied.

"You're wife will be here tomorrow, at this same time and location. I will contact headquarters and see that her travel plans are made," the Israeli said before his team departed.

The duo left in their helicopter and Brody walked over toward the entrance to the underground mine, that was actually a secure storage facility that contained a supply of explosives that had been used, to clear the surrounding areas for the communications towers to be erected...when the time came.

Once his eyes grew accustomed to the darkness, he was horrified to discover a large portion of the explosives that included C-4 and dynamite were missing.

"What the fuck?" he exclaimed out loud. "That bastard Sweeney must have found this shit!" he said and with this discovery, it confirmed that Levi, Alex and the others at the Sweeney property were indeed Feds and now Brody realized why they had been snooping around the Sweeney property. Brody quickly secured the underground container and stormed over his mode of transportation.

Brody climbed back inside his helicopter, knew it was unwise to fly back over the Sweeney's place, in case the Feds were still there, so he decided while he was in the neighborhood, he would explore the layout of the Beckwith Property from the air. He also realized he had to gain access to the house, in an effort to assure himself, there was no paperwork or communication left behind. No traces of evidence left that would implicate himself and Beckwith with prior offers to purchase the property and he also had to, once again, gain access to ZenJa's new house to retrieve a briefcase, his wife had left behind, by mistake, when she fled in the middle of the night.

As Brody landed and darkness enveloped the vast acreage below him, he thought back to a question that was asked of him, earlier since he arrived on Lake Winnipesaukee; what job he held and he replied he was a government contractor, but he smiled when he realized he never said for *which* government.

Brody put his night vision goggles on and crept toward the Beckwith house, entered with a master key, and combed through the residence and inspected the contents of two, 4 drawer file cabinets and was able to retrieve a single folder that had notations Tony Beckwith had made of phone calls and monetary amounts Brody had offered over the years. Brody was then confident this was a very organized man and this was all there was to be found, but to take no chances, he left all the drawers to the file cabinets open, turned and set fire to the home. He knew no one lived there and never would, so it would save the new owner the trouble of burning it down, themselves.

Once Brody landed on the beach, near his lakeside cottage, he grabbed a beer, opened his laptop computer and as it appeared he was going to become a member of the community, again, he wanted to find out what had been going on, since he left.

He was well aware of Wilbur and Junior Sweeney and their logging operation, because he had hired them to clear some of the land, adjacent to the Beckwith property, and the men had completed almost the entire project, when suddenly he had no contact with the Sweeney's again, so that was one reason he had come back...to find out why he had no communication from them.

What Brody Black had no clue about and was mortified to learn was what other operations the Sweeney's had allegedly been in, after reading about the logging truck that exploded, barreling down a mountainside, and the fire that engulfed a ten square miles of forest. That confirmed what he had witnessed earlier; the search of the Sweeney property by the Feds.

Another article he noted was one he had known about, that he referred to as criminal activity to Levi, Alex and ZenJa while they had their lunch; about the missing and murdered girls that had plagued this area for more than ten years. But what he was haunted by was the fact that ZenJa Beckwith's sister was among the missing and the motor vehicle accident, her parents, allegedly had, was highly suspicious and murder charges were pending against a man by the name of Ivan Sweeney, in the murder of ZenJa's parents and possible connection with the disappearance and murders of local girls.

He also was stunned that two others, one the former police chief of Longberry, Bob Connors and a middle school assistant principal, Jackson Miller who had both, allegedly committed suicide in jail, had been charged, prior to their suicides, with the murder of at least two other girls from the area.

"Jesus, that town doesn't need a simple police chief, they need some serious kick ass Navy SEALS there," he said out loud.

One comforting thought, Black had was, he highly doubted those two men actually committed suicide in jail. He realized someone had eliminated them, and rightfully so, he concluded.

Chapter 72

"Well, come on guys, we've wasted enough time around here. It looks like there's nothing to find; Junior must have been right, there's nothing to be found on the property, so let's call it a night," Emerson said to those who had been searching the Sweeney property all day and into the evening.

"Where in hell did they get the explosives from, then?" Levi asked.

"I have no idea. We've checked with all the local construction sites and no one has reported any breeches to their stock piles..." Emerson said and drifted off.

"What the hell is that?" Levi asked of those on the property, who smelled smoke that drifted in from the East.

"Something's on fire?" Alex said while everyone climbed into their various vehicles and rushed onto the highway and headed in the direction the smoke was coming from.

Moments later, it was obvious, what once had been the Beckwith house was fully engulfed in flames and the fire depart was called to douse the flames before the whole property was destroyed.

"What the fuck started that fire?" Levi demanded, obviously to no one in particular.

"That property was just sold, wasn't it?" Brent Wyman asked while they watched the house collapse, to the ground.

"Yes, it was," Levi said knowing he, the lawyer, Alex, the Morrison family, from Virginia, and ZenJa were the only ones who were aware of who the actual owner was at this time.

"Was the power still on?" Alex asked.

"I doubt it," Levi replied, knowing it had indeed been turned off.

Without haste, Levi called ZenJa, on his cell phone and told her of the fire.

"I'll be there as soon as I can," she said and disconnected the call.

Levi watched the fire continue and realized this town was in need of a larger fire department, in light of these raging fires that seemed to plague this area more often. A simple house fire was one thing, but when these structures and events had the potential to consume a whole mountain or community, this small volunteer department they had in Longberry, was not adequate. That would be one of his top priorities if and when he developed this property for the rich and famous.

Less than a half an hour later, the fire was contained and ZenJa arrived on scene; the smoldering remains filling the air with smoke.

"How did this happen?" she asked and looked intently at Levi."

"I have no idea. We were over at the Sweeney place and smelled the smoke and came right over."

"I hope there was nothing inside that you still wanted," Levi said compassionately.

"It's your property now, Levi, not mine," she said and quickly realized she had just let the cat out of the bag, when he saw sparks fly from Levi's eyes; sparks that could easily have started another fire.

"This is your property?" Emerson and Wyman asked simultaneously.

"It was supposed to be a secret, but I guess it isn't any longer, now is it?" he asked and glared at ZenJa. "Last I knew only a few close friends knew about it."

"I'm sorry, Levi; I didn't mean to betray a confidence."

"No problem, I'm used to it," he said and walked off to talk with the fire chief about the fire.

"Any idea what started the fire?" Levi asked.

"Looks like arson. We can't get inside, yet, but because there was no power to the property, there's no other logical explanation. I mean it's not like it was struck by lightening, or anything."

"Well, can you let me know when you find out what it was; I'm the new owner of the property," Levi said and handed the man his business card. He realized it was not possible to keep this secret any longer.

Levy walked back over to where Emerson, Alex and Brent were standing, away from ZenJa and suggested, "Once this cools down, I want you to bring the cadaver dogs back, here."

"You think there might be bodies buried right here under or inside the house?" Emerson asked looking suspiciously at ZenJa.

"Nothing would surprise me, at this point," Levi said and glared at the woman while she slowly climbed back into her car and left the site.

"You think she might have set fire to the house?" Alex asked. "You still think she has something to do with this, don't you?"

"It makes me sick to my stomach to think so, but we're running out of suspects."

Chapter 73

The search team and dogs arrived at Levi's recently purchased property, early the next morning and, once again, the quest to solve the mystery of the missing girls continued.

While the search continued, Brody shut down the engine to his speed boat, after docking at ZenJa's house and knocked on her front door.

"Mr. Black, what are you doing here?" ZenJa asked nervously.

"I so enjoyed your company, for dinner, I wondered if you would like to have lunch with me, today and you know, I do wish you would give me your number, so I won't have to come sneaking over here in my boat," he said and laughed.

ZenJa was mesmerized by the tall, dark, handsome man and his easy, carefree laugh; he was so unlike Levi...not the tall, dark, and handsome features, Levi was blessed with, also, but Brody's manner was much more relaxed and kind.

"Let me get my card," ZenJa said, but neglected to invite Brody inside.

She came back after rummaging through her purse and found a card that simply had her name and cell number on it.

"I would invite you in, but I'm tearing the attic apart today, and I'm thinking of making an office out of it," she said and neglected to note the intense expression on Brody Black's face.

The attic is exactly where he had intended to ascend to, after setting foot inside this house in more than ten years, when he had his first encounter with ZenJa and Alex. What he was looking for was in that attic.

"I plan on spending about two hours upstairs and by then I bet I'll be famished, so, if you would like to meet back at The Opera House Café, that sounds like fun."

"I'll meet you then," Brody said and smiled and wondered how he was going to be in two places at once...the Café and inside her attic.

Less than two hours later, Brody parked his SUV in a strip mall parking lot and walked to The Opera House Café and waited for ZenJa to arrive.

Just as Brody walked in, the waitress who had waited on their table the last time, called Levi and told him Black was once, again at the Café.

"Thank you, sweetie," Levy responded and jumped inside his Camaro and sped to the café, himself.

A moment later, ZenJa walked in and Black's eyes focused on the large, leather brief case she carried with her.

"I'm glad you made it," Brody exclaimed, but didn't take his eyes off the briefcase for a second.

"I was tearing up the flooring, in one part of the attic and found this," she said and handed the leather object to Brody.

Brody simply stared into ZenJa's eyes, in an effort to discover how much investigating she had done, examining the contents of what was inside, before determining it belonged to him.

"You look like you've seen a ghost," ZenJa said, smiled and sat down.

"I never knew where that old thing ended up. I figured my wife took off with it."

"Why, what's inside," ZenJa asked innocently and Brody let out the air in his lungs he'd been holding.

"You mean you didn't look inside?" he asked, trying to be cool and calm.

"Of course not, I respect people's privacy and I noted the initials, in gold, I might add, on the outside, I assumed BB didn't stand for BB King!" she said and laughed and looked to her right and saw Levy standing right next to her.

"You respect people and their privacy?" Levi growled to her. "I find that hard to believe," he said and walked away.

"What was that all about?" Brody asked and smiled behind his menu.

"Well, everyone else in town probably knows by now, so I might as well tell you, too. There was a fire at what was once my parents property, last night and the house was burned down, and while we were all congregated there, I made the mistake of mentioning I was no longer the owner, but Levy had purchased it. That fact was only known by a few people and I opened my big mouth and spread the news, I'm afraid."

"That's it? He's all pissed off about something as stupid as that?" he asked and laughed.

"To him, that is a big deal. He has trust issues," she said and sadly watched him drive away.

"But, I guess we all know about that, now don't we?" Brody asked when the waitress came for their order.

"What would you like today, ZenJa?"

"It's kinda chilly, so I think I'll have a grilled ham and cheese with a bowl of Broccoli Cheddar soup."

"I'll have the same and what would you like to drink?"

"Just a large diet Coke," she said.

"I'll have the same, as well," he replied and looked at the waitress who appeared to glare at him, for no reason.

"What's her problem?" Brody asked.

"I have no idea, but enough about her...what did you mean when you said we all have trust issues?"

"Well, my wife apparently disappeared without letting me know or giving me a chance to keep my...our...house, so it didn't go on the auction block, so I have issues as well," he said and intently watched ZenJa's face.

While the couple waited for their meals Brody asked about the fire, that took place, the night before.

"What caused the fire at your parents...well, Levi's house last night?"

"The fire marshal is coming today to investigate, but it appears it was arson. There was no power supply to the house and no other flammable sources in or around the house."

"What, did Levi burn his own house down?" Brody asked and laughed. "I hope he's not one of those insurance fraud schemers."

"From what I understand he had no plans for the house, so it was going to be torn down anyway and I'm confident he's not into insurance fraud or arson, for that matter," she said in Levi's defense.

The waitress brought their meals and promptly left their table.

"Excellent choice, ZenJa. I can't remember when I had grilled ham and cheese," he said truthfully.

"And the soup is delicious, also," she added.

"If you forgive me for saying so, I get the impression you are very much in love with this Mr. Levi Harris?"

"Why would you say that?" ZenJa asked more calmly than Brody expected.

"There's a very thin line between love and hate, from what I've heard."

"From past experience?" ZenJa asked.

"No, actually, I can't say I've ever experienced the two emotions, with a single individual."

"You either love them or hate them?"

"Exactly!" was his reply.

"So, to get back to the briefcase, you know I didn't open, so can you tell me what I might have discovered, if I'd looked inside?" ZenJa asked wickedly and smiled. "I love a great mystery."

"You know, it's been more than a hundred years since I've looked inside, so let's take a look," he said and smirked.

"A hundred years?" ZenJa asked, fully aware this man was indeed one comical and entertaining individual, who she really had begun to like.

Brody placed the briefcase on a chair, he had pulled up beside himself, took out his key ring and found the key that would open the undamaged lock, he was thankful to notice. ZenJa obviously had *not* opened or examined its contents.

"I guess that truly is yours, if you have a key to it."

"Did you have any doubts?"

"No, not really."

Brody unlocked the brass lock, put his key ring back in his pocket, took another bite of his sandwich and another soup spoon of piping hot soup and then opened the case.

Brody noticed ZenJa sat up a little taller, in an effort to see what was inside, but he carefully placed his large hand over the top, before pulling out an old class picture and football and basketball awards, in the name of Brody Black, from the Penn State.

"You went to Penn State?" ZenJa asked.

"Yes, ma'am, I did," he said truthfully.

"Impressive," she said and looked over her glass at the man who sat at her table.

"Did you graduate from there?"

"No, actually, I graduated from TAU."

"TAU?" ZenJa asked.

"Tel Aviv University."

"Tel Aviv University?" ZenJa asked, obviously deeply impressed.

"You're not Jewish," she added without thinking?

"I"m not?" Brody asked and laughed so hard, he almost knocked his drink over. "Well, my mother lied to me then," he said and continued to laugh at ZenJa's expense.

"I'm sorry, I didn't mean..." she began.

"No, ZenJa, I'm just kidding with you! No, I'm not Jewish," he said and wiped a tear from his eye, that had slid down his cheek. "God, ZenJa! I haven't laughed this much in decades, I swear," Brody said. "You truly are a refreshing young woman and I can't tell you how much I enjoy spending time with you. You truly are delightful," he said honestly.

"So, if you don't mind-my asking, why were you studying in Israel and what did you study?"

"I went there to meet my wife." he said enjoying every minute he had to enhance the mystery of Brody Black, to this woman.

"She's from Israel, then?"

"No, actually she's a strikingly beautiful, tall blonde, with the biggest blue eyes you've ever seen," he said and smiled and thought about the woman he loved, but purposely avoided revealing her interesting heritage; being part Israeli and Swedish, but born and raised in France.

"And before you ask, no, I had no idea I was going to meet her there, when I arrived."

"Oh, so I see you were teasing me, when you said you went there to meet her."

"Yes, I was teasing you, but to answer the second part of the question, I majored in and have Masters Degrees in Security and Diplomacy, Crisis and Trauma, and Middle Eastern Studies."

"What an impressive education you, have, Brody. I'm truly impressed. Why go there to study?" ZenJa asked while the couple continued to eat their lunch.

"Several reasons, other than to meet my wife," he said and laughed "And for two other reasons; what better place in the world to learn, first hand about security, diplomacy, crisis and trauma and Middle Eastern affairs, than in Israel? I didn't want to simply sit in a classroom in Buffalo, New York and learn about the trials and tribulations that have effected that war torn country, one of the most beautiful places in the world, by the way, than right there?"

"And the other reason?" ZenJa asked.

"I have heard rumors that the Israeli's are God's chosen people and if I wanted to get on the good side of God and make my way into Heaven, when I die, I didn't want to take any chances," he whispered and laughed.

"You're laughing, but you truly believe that don't you!" ZenJa stated as a matter of fact.

"I do!" he replied.

"So, tell me a little about yourself," Brody suggested.

"There's not much to tell. I grew up in Longberry with my sister and parents.

"Oh, that's nice, where are they now?" he asked already knowing the truthful answer to that.

"Sometimes, things are very personal and certainly not something I discuss in a café," she said softly.

"Oh, I'm sorry, I never meant to intrude."

"It's okay, it's just hard to talk about."

"Okay, that's fine and I respect that. What do you say we finish up here and stroll around town and check out some of these lovely shops," he suggested in an effort to gain her trust, little by little.

"That sounds like fun," she agreed and shortly after Brody paid the bill and left a nice tip, in spite of the less than pleasant waitress.

"Don't forget your briefcase," ZenJa said before they got to the door.

"I have it right here," he said and smiled.

"Do you want to put it inside your car, so we don't have to drag it around on our afternoon adventure?" ZenJa asked.

Brody knew she was desperately trying to find out what mode of transportation he had, and as before, she was going to be sadly disappointed.

"I walked, so can we just lock it up in the trunk of your car?" he asked.

"Sure, no problem."

"Okay, now that's out of the way, where would you like to start?"

"You really want to go browsing in shops?" ZenJa asked like he had two heads. I don't know of any man who likes to do that," she added.

"I don't make a habit of it, but I don't see why not. Like Levi said, I want the shop owners to be nice to me; being I'm a flat-lander, and am going to spend my cash, though I'm not about to max out my credit cards," he added and laughed.

The duo spent the afternoon exploring every tourist trap and unique gift and designer stores and Brody carried the various shopping bags, from Armani, Gucci, The Monk's Candy Emporium, several book shops, and last but not least a jewelry store.

"You haven't bought anything," ZenJa commented, when they walked into The Quarry Treasure Chest.

"I told you I couldn't afford to max out my cards, but I do have something I have to buy, here," he said and the twosome went their own way, browsing through the outrageously expensive jewelry shop.

ZenJa was hoping this man was not about to buy her something expensive or anything for that matter. She had been single all her life and she was not about to fall for someone who was a smooth talker, polite and a gentlemen...someone so different than Levi, she thought and laughed. "God forbid," she said.

"God forbid what?" Brody asked when he carried his own small expensive shopping tote, along with ZenJa's other purchases, when they met at the front door.

"Oh, nothing, I was just thinking about something stupid," she said and blushed.

While the couple strolled along the sidewalk, heading back toward her parked car, Brody looked at his watch and realized he had an important meeting and was running late.

"Oh, I had no idea it was so late," he said and picked up the pace he was walking. "I really have to get going, but I want you to know what a lovely day I've had and thank you so much for finding and returning my brief case. There's so little left of my past, and I'm glad to have these few things back."

ZenJa opened the trunk of her car and removed the brief case while Brody carefully placed the shopping bags inside her car, all but the small item he had purchased at The Quarry, designer jewelry shop.

"Can I give you a lift?" ZenJa offered.

"Actually, you can, if you don't mind. I have a meeting with an old friend down the road a ways, if it's not too much trouble." Brody realized he had to make an effort to appear less mysterious, but only to a point.

Brody climbed in beside ZenJa and he directed her three streets over and climbed out of her car in front of a building that housed many different offices, so ZenJa would have no idea where he was going.

"Thank you for the ride, ZenJa and I hope we can have dinner again, soon," he said.

"Thank you for lunch and for going shopping with me; I really enjoyed myself today," she said honestly.

Brody waved and watched ZenJa drive away before he crossed the street and climbed inside his Escalade and headed back to his lake front cottage.

He immediately departed in his helicopter because he had a every import package to pick up...his wife, Lynx.

Chapter 74

ZenJa drove into her driveway and quickly notice Levi's Camaro parked near the garage.

At first, she didn't notice where he was, until he started walking from her dock toward the house.

"Fishing were you?" ZenJa asked snidely and grabbed some of the shopping bags from her trunk.

"As a matter of fact I think the fish are better on my part of the lake and I don't see any interesting *fish* here, today."

"Are you referring to Mr. Black?" she asked and struggled with her purchases and walked toward her door; Levi remaining in the drive way and smirked when ZenJa dropped one bag on the ground.

"I hope that wasn't a priceless antique you bought for me," he said and smiled.

"Buying anything for you, Mr. Harris, is the last thing I would do," she hissed and picked up the bag, that contained some books she purchased and opened her front door.

"What are you doing here?" she asked after placing the items inside the door.

"Actually, I stopped by to see if Brody and I could use his boat and go fishing," he lied.

"Why would Brody and his boat be here and what did you plan on using for an anchor, Brody, himself?" she retorted.

"I don't know, I simply figured he might be here; it being such a lovely Fall day and all and actually..." he said but never finished his sentence regarding the anchor.

"Again, what are you doing here and what do you want?"

"I heard from the fire marshal and he indicted, as we all assumed, the fire, last night, was arson."

"You couldn't call me and tell me that?" she snarled.

"No, actually, I wanted to know if you wanted to ride up there to check the place out, with me, but I guess I'll ask Alex to go; he has a better disposition than you do," he said and walked toward his car.

"Give me a minute...I'll be right there," she said and placed her bags on the breakfast nook, came back outside, locked the door and got inside the Camaro.

"You got the locks changed and security system in, today?" Levi asked.

"Yes, they were here first thing this morning and were all done before Brody..."

"Before Brody, what?" Levi encouraged.

"Before Brody and I had lunch and then went shopping!" she yelled.

"Brody's a shopper, huh?" Levi asked and laughed. "He likes all the little gift shops, does he?"

"And just what do you mean by that?"

"Nothing, I just thought he looked a little too rugged, like a bull in a China shop, if you get my drift. Personally, I can't picture him drinking out of a Demitasse cup, holding his pinkie out."

ZenJa chuckled, but refrained from mentioning that is exactly what Brody had done when they dined at '*Le Crystal Lustre*', though he did not extend his pinkie in any delicate fashion and she didn't bother to tell Levi what little fragments of Brody's past he had revealed to her, because she wasn't convinced he was telling her the truth, anyway.

Twenty miles later, Levi needlessly announced, "Well, here we are," and the couple exited the Camaro and were met with several volunteers who manned the fire truck, to extinguish any hot spots that may appear.

"Hello, Mr. Harris," one firefighter said. "We haven't seen any signs of flames or smoke in about an hour, so I think we're pretty much done here."

"Thank you so much for your assistance. I truly appreciate it."

"We weren't able to salvage anything," he added.

"I have what was most important," ZenJa said and walked toward the dwelling.

"Did the search dogs find anything, this morning?" the firefighter asked Levi.

"What search dogs?" ZenJa asked after she spun around and faced Levi, with her hands on her hips.

"We were here this morning with search dogs, looking for an accelerant that might have been used in this fire."

"Is that the only reason you had the dogs here?" she questioned.

"Why else?" Levi asked and looked into ZenJa's eyes.

"Nothing," she responded and let the subject drop before they got into another argument.

"Well, it's getting dark and there's nothing left to burn...the trees are too far away to catch fire, unless we have a hurricane pass through, so I guess we'll call it a night," the fire fighter said.

"Thanks again for coming to take care of this matter and is there any day of the week you guys all get together at the firehouse? I have a little something I want to run by you," Levi said mysteriously.

"Yes, we meet every Wednesday night. It give us a chance to get away from our wives, for a while," the man said and laughed until he looked at ZenJa, but continued to chuckle. Not to be outdone, by the comment, made in jest, Levi bent over with laughter and snorted through his nose.

"Don't worry, she's not my wife," Levi said and slapped the man on the back.

"We meet at 7 p.m. on Wednesdays," he continued and climbed into the tanker and left the couple standing by the Camaro.

"You know, ZenJa, I love it when you're mad," Levi said and reached out to pull her close to himself.

"You must be horny," ZenJa said and pulled away from him.

Levi felt like he had been punched in the stomach, but realized what she said must look that way to her.

"You're right, ZenJa. I had no right to do that. I apologize."

ZenJa was clearly shocked to hear him *admit* he wanted to take advantage of her, for his own selfish needs.

"Would you please take me home, now?" she asked.

"Sure, it's getting dark and there's nothing more to do here, tonight."

Chapter 75

Brody met the helicopter that approached him from the West and waited for the arrivals to depart the aircraft.

"You wife has safely been delivered," Noam Krant, the Israeli soldier declared, while he helped Lynx Black, make her exit and help her with her small duffle bag.

As far as Brody and his wife were concerned, not another person was living on earth at that moment. They were alone, had each other and nothing else mattered when she ran into her husband's waiting arms; having appeared to melt into one being. He savored the smell of her long blonde hair, gazed into her deep blue eyes and lifted the tall, slender woman into his embrace.

"Je t'aime et ont manque' plus que ce que vous ne le saurons jamais, Sweetheart," Brody whispered, in French, into his wife's ear.

"I love you and have missed you more than you will ever know, as well, Sweetheart," she echoed and kissed him and was enveloped into his strong arms.

"I will be off now," Noam said and bid the couple farewell.

"Thank you, my brother and safe travels. Until we meet again," Brody said and waved to the soldier.

"It's starting to rain, we better get in where it's warm and dry," Brody said; he and his wife holding hands, laughing like two teenagers, and ran toward the aircraft before he lifted his wife inside and placed her bag in the back.

"J 'ai cette douleur dans si longtemp. Plus que vous ne le saurons jamais," Brody said, again, in French and kissed his wife more passionately than before.

"No, it is I who has had a pain in my heart, for so long. Longer than you will ever know," she repeated what he had said while tears slipped down her cheeks.

"We are together, now and that's all that matters," Brody said and started up the aircraft's engine and began their short journey home.

Less than an hour later, the Blacks entered their present home, on Holt's Point, on Lake Winnipesaukee and once again, the couple embraced and kissed passionately and whispered words of endearment at the same time.

"Are you hungry or thirsty?" Brody asked.

"Do you have any bottled water? I'm only thirsty."

Brody went to get a bottle of iced water and a glass with ice and brought it into the living room, where Lynx was standing looking out the window, that led to the deck and the velvet blackness of the lake.

"This is a beautiful home," Lynx said and took the glass of water from her husband's hand while he drank the rest from the bottle.

"It needs a woman's touch, but I started working on it and now that I discover we will be here for what appears a long time, I know you will make this our home...our home."

Lynx suddenly noticed the old leather briefcase Brody had thrown on the sofa, before he flew to meet her. "You retrieved the briefcase," she said and breathed a sign of relief.

"Actually, the new owner of the house, brought it to me, today."

"She didn't look inside, did she?" the woman asked in distress.

For the next twenty minutes, Brody sat with his wife on the sofa and explained how he had been caught snooping in their former home and the details of the cat and mouse games he had been playing with ZenJa, Levi and Alex. And how he enjoyed every minute of it. He also mentioned having gone shopping with ZenJa and said he had made only one purchase.

"What did you buy?"

Brody reached in between the sofa cushions and handed the designer shopping bag and the gift that was inside to the woman he loved.

Lynx squealed in delight and peered in the bag and opened the stunning black velvet case at the same time Brody got down on his knees before her and said, again in French, "Je t'aime plus aujourd' hui que j'ai jamais eu dans le passe' et chaque jour, je vous aime plus."

" Brody, I love you more today than I ever have in the past and each day, I will love you more," she echoed what her husband had said to her, as well.

Brody took one of the rarest diamonds rings, a black, two and a half carat stone that was surrounded with smaller black diamonds in a platinum setting, and placed it on her ringer finger. He knew he could easily have afforded a much larger stone, but he realized with her small hands and slender body, anything larger would have looked fake. This new ring was to grace the presence of the ring that was now inside the briefcase on the coffee table, where it had been safely protected along with all the other important pieces of their lives.

Lynx fell into her husband's arms and clung to him, as if he were a life raft and he was...her life raft.

"Brody?" Lynx asked.

"Yes?" he replied.

"I want you in my arms tonight and never let go," she said while she placed her empty glass on the coffee table and the couple stumbled into the master bedroom, where they spent the next two days, other than eating, drinking, making love in their hot tub, and showering together; completely isolated from the rest of the world, in their own private Heaven on earth.

Sadly, the couple was brought back to reality, on the third day of their reunion, when they discovered they had run out of clean bedding and towels and food in the house, so they spent the next day getting household chores done and grocery shopping and arrived back home once the snow began to fall and the wind howled,

Brody lit a fire in the fireplace and turned on the Pellet stove and the lovers snuggled on their sofa to open the mysterious leather brief case and inspected the contents of which pretty much were the only pieces of their lives together, over the last ten years.

Brody unlocked the briefcase and reached into the bottom of the case and unwrapped their wedding bands, that they placed inside, before they went their separate ways, for the same purpose. Brody gently removed the striking black diamond ring from her finger and placed her wedding band back on, closest to her heart. After which he gently placed the diamond ring back over it and she took the wedding band from his hand and placed it back on his ring finger where it belonged, as well.

"We have a love like no other," Brody said and held his wife's hand. I have been away for ten years, sneaking back now and then to be with you and then you having to leave, for your own safety and again, only having fleeting moments and days to love you, but I have and never will love anyone but you and I have remained faithful to you since the day we were married."

"I have also loved no one but you, Brody and have never been unfaithful to you, either and never will," she declared and embraced her husband in a passionate, fiery kiss, one of many they had experienced in the last few days.

After a few minutes, Brody reached back inside the case and said, "When ZenJa brought me this briefcase, when we had lunch, I knew she was dying to know what was inside and the fact she hadn't taken it upon herself to snoop through it, I carefully selected a few items of interest to quell her curiosity."

"What did you show her?" Lynx asked and kissed her husband's neck.

"I wanted her to know what a rugged football and basketball player, I was, so I showed her these awards and she noticed they were from Penn State and of course she wanted to know if I graduated from there and I admitted I graduated, with several Masters Degrees, from TAU."

"And most likely she wanted to know why you would have gone to school there?" Lynx reasoned.

"Yes, and get this! She did ask why would I get my education there, because I am *not* Jewish!"

Both Lynx and Brody laughed before he added, "I looked at her, dumbfounded, of course and said, I'm *not*? That is something I'll have to discuss with my mother!" he added and the occupants on the sofa laughed, almost spilling their wine.

"I told her I went there to meet you and marry you and then she asked if you were Jewish and I said, no, you were a lovely slender, blonde, blue eyed vixen and only twenty years old, from Sweden!"

"You failed to tell her of my real heritage, thank goodness."

"Yes, actually, I divulged more than I intended to, but actually we had such a good time...she really is so funny and I hadn't laughed so hard in a long time. I know you'll love her, when you meet her."

"You know we have to keep our distance from people," Lynx warned.

"Is that because you want me all to yourself?" Brody teased.

"Yes, that's exactly what I want," she said and climbed onto his lap and began to kiss the man she loved, more than life itself.

"Now where were we?" Brody asked and removed copies of their birth certificates, identification cards, driver's licenses and passports...many copies in different names and bank books, as well. The amounts in the various banks, in America and overseas, amounted to many millions of dollars and as odd as this was, all the money had been accumulated legally. Working for the government paid very well...no matter what government that might be.

Chapter 76

Wednesday evening, as promised, Levi arrived at the Longberry Fire Department and was welcomed by the all volunteer fire fighters. John, Marcus, Chris, and Mike.

"Thanks for stopping by," John said and shook the men's hands.

"Well, I wanted to thank you, in person, for the great job you did in fighting the fire on my property and also for the valiant effort you guys exerted fighting the log truck/forest fire."

"Man, I never saw anything like that log truck fire, before," Marcus said. "I can't imagine seeing it when it unfolded."

"It certainly was a sight to see," Levi confessed, "But what I wanted to tell you, as you are all aware, by now, I recently purchased the Beckwith property and I plan on holding meetings with the folks in town, in the near future, who might be interested in what I have planned for that acreage."

Levi unrolled the blueprints for the area that would concern the fire department and the group gathered around.

"This is what I have planned for a new fire department building."

"Holy Smokes!" Chris said with everyone else in agreement.

"That's huge...I mean a six bay garage, offices and sleeping quarters?" Mike added.

"Why will we need something so massive?" Chris asked.

"Because, gentlemen, you are only the few people who know what this property will become, in time, of course," Levi said and placed a photograph of what the entire project would entail.

"Wow! My goodness, this blows my mind," Marcus said. "This certainly is a grandiose project," he added.

"Well, I'm open for comments and questions."

"I think I'm too stunned to even think of anything at this point, other than the fact where do you think the people will come to live here and work here?" Mike asked.

"These condos are going to be purchased by the rich and famous who want to escape to New England, in a secluded area to enjoy all the four seasons New Hampshire, the Lakes Region and White Mountains have to offer. The people who work here will be the members of our community who already reside here and others who will flock to the area to experience living like they do at Steam Boat Springs, Colorado or Stratton Mountain or Okemo, in

Vermont."

"Who else have you mentioned this project to," John asked.

"I ran it by Molly, my attorney, Jerry Johnson, Lanny and Carol Williams, and Jim Bacon and I have some other friends, from outside the area who are quite interested in relocating and expanding their own livelihoods, right here, in the area.

"This can be quite an elite community, but warm and friendly, with down the earth people living here. No snobs, allowed and the media will also, be off limits," Levi stressed. "Privacy and community will be the most important aspects."

"So there will be a strict application process for those purchasing condos?" Marcus asked.

"Indeed. I don't want the likes of the media magnets, who go out of their way to get their faces plastered on the front pages of the news by making asses out of themselves. I don't care how much money they have, they will not be welcome here."

"If the town is going to expand, as it appears to be, we certainly are going to need a bigger and better police force. We literally have none, now," Chris mentioned.

"I know and from what I understand, Miss Beckwith is *not* interested in the job, so we may have to advertise, from the outside, to get qualified and willing candidates."

"The best chance we may have to attract people who are qualified would be former military veterans," John said.

"Absolutely! I couldn't agree more," Levi agreed.

"Well, I've taken up enough of your time," Levi began and rolled the blueprints and sketches up and placed them back into the cardboard tube.

"Let us know when you plan on holding that town meeting," Marcus said.

"I will and I usually detest gossip, but if you gentlemen feel the need to discuss these plans, that are still in the infancy stages, please feel free to do so, among your family and friends," he added and walked toward the door.

"Thank you again for having faith in our little community and helping us move on, after...well, after the many painful years we have had here," Marcus said and bid Levi a good night.

Levi started the engine of his car, when his cell phone rang and he was startled to discover it was ZenJa calling him.

"Good evening, my dear, what can I do for you?" Levi asked and smirked. "Don't tell me you're calling to ask me if I'm still horny or are you calling to tell me you're the horny one?"

"Can you ever be serious?" she wailed.

"I am being very serious, actually and another bit of trivia you might be interested in, is...well, I was reading where every eight seconds, of every day, men are thinking about sex. Did you know that?" he asked and laughed out loud and turned up the volume on the stereo system and blasted the old Eric Clapton favorite, "*It's In The Way You Use it*", for ZenJa's listening pleasure.

"Nice song," ZenJa said.

"I always loved this one, too and I believe it's true, don't you?"

"Yes, actually, I do," she admitted and blushed though there was no one to see her.

Levi sat in his car, while it idled outside the fire station and continued his conversation with ZenJa.

"Do you like how I use mine?" he brazenly asked.

"I do," she whispered.

"Well, so let's admit we're both horny and do something about it?"

"Okay," she replied much to Levi's surprise.

"Where are you?"

"I'm at my house."

"I'll be over in a few minutes so take off all your clothes and wait for me, naked by the door, okay?" he said while the four fire fighters walked by to climb into the own vehicles and smiled.

"I was just talking to my dog," Levi said and howled with laughter, leaving the men in the dust, and sped toward ZenJa's house.

Levi arrived shortly after and discovered ZenJa's interior lights were out and he spotted her walking, slowly, from her dock.

"Fishing?" Levi asked sarcastically, as she had asked, previously when he was here last.

"I was just admiring the moon," she lied.

"It is very nice," he admitted.

"Would you like to come inside and have a beer?"

"I don't have to be drunk to have sex," he retorted and wondered what games she was playing.

"Is that all you came over for?" she asked.

"That's all you wanted me to come here for, wasn't it?" he asked, his eyes darkening and quickly scanning the area, thinking he was about to be ambushed.

"Levi, you're so funny," ZenJa replied and laughed, in an attempt to smooth Levi's ruffled feathers. "Come on," she added and the couple walked toward the back door.

"Oh, shit! I left my keys inside and this new security system freaks me out. I'm afraid if I try to enter without the key, the alarm will go off," she said, acting as innocent as a choir girl.

"So, this is the real reason you called me isn't it, ZenJa. You simply locked yourself out of your own house and wanted me to let you inside...am I right?" he hissed at her. "And it looks like you've been out here a while; there are no lights on inside your house. Am I right on that account, too?"

ZenJa simply stood beside Levi, but remained silent.

"Why didn't you call Brody or is he busy shopping?" Levi yelled.

"I don't have his number!"

"So, if you did have his number, you would have called him, instead of me, right?"

"Yes!" she screamed. "At least he wouldn't yell at me for being an ass. That's all you do, Levi, is yell at me!"

Levi simply walked to her door, used a master key he always had in his possession, turned on her lights and stood aside, while she walked inside and he turned to leave, but turned around and said, "You used me, ZenJa."

"Yes, and you've used me," she spat at him.

"I guess we're even, then, aren't we? Don't ever do that again," he warned so very softly, she almost didn't hear him.

"Don't ever use me again, either," she said and slammed the door shut.

Chapter 77

Alex Lyons and Brent Wyman left the lakes region before the holiday season approached, having been assigned to various AFT duties in Virginia.

Both ZenJa and Levi had retired from their jobs with the government and while ZenJa redecorated her new home and enjoyed the winter weather, Levi spent the winter in Virginia with his brother and friends, that included the Morrison family.

Levi, Alex, Brent and the Morrisons discussed their plans for expanding and developing the Beckwith property and Levi was more than happy to mention the excitement the fire fighters shared and the other town people he had met, at a town hall gathering, not long before he left for Virginia.

"I figured now was a good time to get away from New Hampshire. We can't start the ground breaking, wiring and God only knows what else we have to do first. This will give us time to plan a strategy"

"And it will give you time to be away from ZenJa," Alex mentioned in front of those gathered at the Morrison home for Christmas dinner.

"You got that right," Levi agreed and finished another beer while Darlene and Darcy brought the remaining holiday fixings to the overloaded dinning room table.

"You have outdone yourselves," Alex said and held Darcy's chair out for her to sit in.

"We've spent the last week cooking, baking and having a grand time," Darlene said.

"We helped, too," Rick said and his sister nodded in agreement.

"We made the Christmas cookies and put the marshmallows on top of the Jello," Betsy added.

"This is the best looking Jello, I have ever seen," Levi said and waited for everyone to be seated, before the children said Grace.

ZenJa waited for the roads to be plowed, on this Christmas Day, and drove to '*Le Crystal Lustre* ' to have her own Christmas dinner, alone. She had driven by Levi's home, on more than one occasion, and sadly realized he was obviously out of town and had been since before Thanksgiving. She hadn't heard from him since the night he unlocked her door and let her inside her own home and she had not seen or heard from Brody Black, either.

The Maitre d seated ZenJa at her reserved table and explained because it was Christmas, there was only one menu for the day and evening meals. "We wanted this Christmas Day to be special and all the courses are strictly of authentic French cuisine."

"That's fine," she said and smiled. "It will prevent me from having to make difficult choices."

"I also want to assure you, we have strict reservations for this mid-afternoon meal, so there is no need to hurry. No other patrons will be coming until dinner, that will be served at 8:00 p.m."

"Thank you."

"I will send the Sommelier with several wines, both red and white."

"Thank you, again," she said, while a tear slid down her cheek. Here she was, sitting at a exquisite French restaurant, on Christmas Day, all by herself.

A moment later she looked up and a nicely dressed man, who wore a dark blue suit, light blue turtleneck, with dark hair and eyes approached her table. She immediately noticed he was about fifty years old and reminded her of a college professor.

"Excuse me, Miss, but it appears we are the only dinners, here, who are alone. Would you mind if we shared a table, conversation and a delicious Christmas dinner?"

"Oh! That would be very nice," ZenJa said and blushed at this attractive man, who obviously noticed she was single, pathetic, and alone on Christmas.

The man reached for her hand and gently shook it while he introduced himself. "My name is Henri de Montesquiou," he said politely and kissed her fingertips.

"What a beautiful name," ZenJa said while the man seated himself across the table from her and the Sommelier and waiter came to place this man's place setting and wine glasses on this table and their first course, Chestnut Soup and a savory Tourtiere, which is a double crusted pork, beef and onion pie.

"I hope I am not making you uncomfortable?" Henri asked.

"Oh, no...forgive me, my name is ZenJa Beckwith," she replied and smiled.

"This is a delightful surprise, Miss Beckwith. I had visions of my celebrating Christmas Dinner, all by myself."

"To be honest with you, I almost decided to stay home today, but once the snow plow came by, I figured it would be safe to come outside for a little while. My car isn't the greatest in this winter weather."

"What kind of car do you have?" Henri asked and sampled more wine and the Beef Burgundy and Brandied Roast Goose that had been placed before them.

"More wine?" Henri asked.

"Please," ZenJa replied and also sampled more of her meal, before she told Henri that her mode of transportation was a Dodge Charger.

"Ahh, yes, a sports car. New England winters are no place for a sports car."

"I realize that and have been looking for something else, more suitable."

"Any idea what kind of vehicle you might feel safer driving?"

"I'm thinking of some sort of SUV."

"Most of those would be good choices, but the only thing with an SUV is, that some people have a false sense of security, driving those. I know as I've traveled back and forth, here and there, I see more of those SUV's off the road, in a snow bank or in a wreck, than any others," he said honestly.

"Those people believe nothing can stop them?"

"Exactly and driving on ice...doesn't matter what your driving, unless it's a tank," Henri said and laughed.

"I'm rather fond of my Volvo," Henri mentioned.

"Yes, I have heard that those are especially safe, as well as the Subaru."

"Anything with four-wheel drive is best in snow."

"But now, this conversation must be boring you to tears, tell me a little about yourself," Henri encouraged.

"I've decided I'm going to put my fiction writing skills to good use and write the equivalent of War and Peace," ZenJa said and laughed.

"You certainly are ambitious; there's no denying that."

"Oh my goodness, we are being served even more French delicacies," ZenJa said when the waiter brought Citrus Marinated Olives and Cauliflower Gratin and Braised Halibut,

"I guess it'll be time for me to start my diet, after New Year's Day," Henri stated and patted his rock hard stomach.

"You and me both," ZenJa replied and sat back and placed her hands in her lap.

More than two hours had passed, while the twosome chatted about everything from politics, to religion, and current events.

"So, tell me a little something about yourself," ZenJa encouraged the handsome man who sat across from her.

"I've decided to settle down in this area and I'm looking for some property to purchase. I'm in the process of opening my first bookstore in the Lakes Region and I will extend you this invitation to hold your first book signing at my store, when you've finished that masterpiece."

"Are you a writer as well?" ZenJa asked.

"I've dabbled a little in putting words on paper, now and then." he said and smiled.

"What are your creations about?"

"I write about family members."

"And would I know any of those family members?" ZenJa asked

"You may or may not," Henri replied coyly.

"Try me," ZenJa said.

"Oh, way back in the 1600's, one of my distant relatives was Charles d'Artagnan and other relative was the man I was named after, Henri Montesquiou. Henri was Charles' uncle."

"Charles d'Artagnan was actually, the fourth member of the Three Musketeers, was he not?" ZenJa asked.

"He was indeed, Miss Beckwith."

"The only reason I know about that is..." she began but stopped speaking.

"You were saying?" Henri asked as their plates and the table was cleared and Demitasse cups of a rich French coffee, a cheese and fruit platter was placed on their table, along with samples of Gingerbread Bombe and Buttered Rum Cheesecake.

"A friend and I were dining at a French restaurant in Boston, not that long ago and I recall my dinner date mentioned Charles d'Artagnan and the family who owned that very restaurant were decedents of his."

"Oh, just who may that date have been, if I may be so bold as to ask?"

"His name is Levi," she said without divulging his last name.

"Oh, I know Levi and ...," Henri said but stopped speaking.

"You know Levi and knew his wife, Isabella," ZenJa added to make her dinner date more comfortable.

"Yes, I did; Isabella was my cousin," Henri said soberly.

"I am sorry for her loss and I know Levi was and still is devastated by her death," ZenJa said.

"Yes, he is."

"May I ask you something?"

"Yes, of course."

"You're obviously married; you're wearing a wedding ring," one of the first things ZenJa noticed when the man sat at her table.

"Yes, I am," Henri admitted and smiled.

"Shouldn't you be spending Christmas Day with your wife?"

"I would, if I could, but her flight, from Paris was cancelled because of the weather and she's not expected to arrive until tomorrow."

"Oh, that explains it."

"Explains what?"

"Well, I almost thought, for a minute, Levi might have asked you to have Christmas dinner with me," she said and laughed.

"Who said he didn't?" Henri said and smiled.

"He did?"

"I didn't say that, one way or another now, did I?"

"No, you didn't," ZenJa admitted and sipped more of her coffee and sampled some fruit and cheese and the duo remained silent and savored the deserts and delightful ambiance that surround them, when other dinners began to depart.

After a few moments, ZenJa realized it was time to go home, in case it started to snow again.

"I can't thank you enough for your kindness and sharing your Christmas with me," she said and Henri stood to help her from her chair.

"It was my greatest pleasure and you certainly brightened up what would otherwise have been a dreadful holiday. I can't thank you enough," Henri added and held her hand and kissed her fingertips, once again. The duo walked toward the entrance, where they were met by the Maitre d who presented them both with holiday wrapped gift boxes of French Macaroons and Truffles.

"These are beautiful," ZenJa said and they each took the designer shopping bags filled with their Christmas treats.

"Your bills and very generous gratuities have been taken care of, sir," the man said and ushered the couple to the door and disappeared to assist more couples who were also, departing.

Henri walked ZenJa to her vehicle before he thanked her again, for a wonderful day, waved, and walked toward his own Volvo.

Before ZenJa and Henri left the parking lot, Brody and his wife arrived in his Escalade, for their evening dinning reservations, and he quickly spotted ZenJa in her Charger when she turned on her windshield wipers and waited for the car to warm up.

"That red haired, well auburn haired lady, in that black Charger is ZenJa!" Brody exclaimed to his wife, in surprise. I'm glad we made evening reservations," he added.

"Would it have mattered if she had seen us?" Lynx asked without a hint of suspicion.

"Well, no, but I did explain to her, about the house having been foreclosed, while I was away, and led her to believe you had simply given up hope of my ever coming home again, so being the young and beautiful woman that you are, you must have moved on the find a happier life and of course I had to open my big mouth and tell her you are a ravishing blonde, with the deepest blue eyes and from Sweden, as I already told you."

"You must have been beside yourself, but I do commend you, my love, you are quick witted and think fast, on your feet."

"I've had a lot of practice. I kept rehearsing this fable for three years. Three long years," he said and kissed his wife, again and saw a Volvo follow ZenJa from the parking lot, just as it started to snow, again.

"Wonder who that guy, in the Volvo was?" Brody asked when he and his wife entered '*Le Crystal Lustre* ' to celebrate their Christmas dinner.

ZenJa quickly, but safely drove home and put her car into the garage, before the snow would accumulate on it. She hated nothing more, than clearing her car off from mountains of snow, in order to drive anywhere.

Once she got inside her home and placed her Christmas treats on the counter, she lit her Christmas tree and tuned her Bose stereo system on and sat in front of the warmth of the fireplace, while she listened to Christmas carols and began to cry.

She missed Christmas with her family and knew there would never be any chance of finding her missing sister and the other girls or probably ever seeing Levi Harris again.

ZenJa curled up on the couch, covered herself with a heavy quilt and fell asleep until morning.

While ZenJa slept and the Blacks celebrated Christmas, Henri called Levi and wished him a Merry Christmas, as well.

"Merry Christmas, Levi!" Henri said.

"Merry Christmas to you, too Henri."

"What's all the noise in the background?"

"Oh, Alex and I are helping the kids play with their new Christmas presents."

"Helping them play and actually *allowing* them to play or have you got them tied to their chairs, while you *show* them how to play with them?"

"Alex, their Dad and I want to make sure they know how to play with them properly!" Levi said and laughed.

"Hey Levi, your race car just flew off the track and Tony Stewart just passed the leader!" Alex yelled in the background.

"A race car set?" Henri asked.

"Yes, you caught me red handed."

"So, not to keep you from all your fun and games, with the *other* kids, I wanted to thank you for allowing me to share a wonderful Christmas dinner with ZenJa and paying for it, I might add," Henri said and laughed.

"Did she have a good time?"

"Yes, she actually seemed to and once it was disclosed that I was a relative of Isabella's and her family, she immediately was suspicious of my intent and asked if you had anything to do with our *chance* meeting."

"What did you say?"

"I neither admitted it or denied it."

"How were you able to determine where she *might* have dinner?"

"I simply called around; nothing that time consuming."

"Thank you again, Henri, I appreciate you giving her a nice day and I hope the snow stops soon, so Margaux's flight lands in Boston tomorrow."

"I do, too! I miss her so much and speaking of missing someone, when are you going to come back up North? You know my wife and I want to be the first residents to occupy a condo at your resort and we want to see the plans you have so far."

"You know, of course, it will be a year or more until that happens. We don't even have the land all cleared, stumps removed or the underground cables for electricity, cable and natural gas laid, not to mention the sewer and I would like to have a half-way decent road system in, for the heavy equipment to use and not get swallowed up in the mud."

"It might be beneficial to have those stumps pulled from the ground during the winter, if they're not buried deeply in snow. The harder the ground, the easier it will be for those logging trucks to get in and out of there. I mean, the tires on those Skidders, I think they're called, are massive and are equipped with chains and what not."

"I never thought of that. That makes sense and I actually want to place an ad in some local and state-wide newspapers and on the Internet, requesting bids for contractors, to start with the underground work, first."

"It sounds like you have your work cut out for you, Levi."

"It's much easier than chasing gun runners and bad guys, all the time."

"Hey! Levi, they just hauled your race car to the garage, after it crashed into the wall, again!" Alex yelled from the Morrison living room.

"Your race car?" Henri asked and laughed.

"Yes, today I'm Kurt Busch and I bet Denny, put me in the wall, right?" Levi yelled in reply.

"How did you guess?" came the reply.

"Well, I'll let you go, Levi and I hope to see you up here soon and again, Merry Christmas."

"Merry Christmas to you and Margaux and thank you again for giving ZenJa a nice Christmas!"

Chapter 78

Over the weeks that followed Lynx and her husband were busy redecorating their new home and the married couple enjoyed spending every moment together. As before, they stayed close to home, spending time snowshoeing and cross country skiing in the wooded area on their property and enjoying nature, that included feeding the deer and birds that flocked to their home. On many evenings they took romantic strolls, in the moonlight, while flurries cascaded down, upon them and more than anything else, they made passionate love, every chance they had.

While the Blacks enjoyed the winter season, ZenJa was also busy decorating her new home and had purchased a new red Volvo, for her winter travels and she had also starting writing her first novel. A fictional tale about a French-Canadian couple who raised a family in the Green Mountains of Vermont, in the eighteen hundreds.

On Valentines Day, ZenJa heard her motion detector alarm sound and noticed a floral delivery truck stop in front of her door and the driver rang the door bell at the same time, ZenJa checked to make sure this man actually did have flowers to deliver.
"Good morning and Happy Valentines Day," the pleasant young man said. "I have a delivery for ZenJa Beckwith."
"Thank you so much," she said in shock. "I certainly wasn't expecting any flowers, today," she added and reached out to take the lovely bouquet of assorted colored roses, baby's breath, and other greenery, along with a card.
"Please wait here so I can give you a tip," she said and started to retrieve her purse from the desk.
"No, thank you, Miss; the bill and tip have all been taken care of ," he said and walked back toward his truck.
ZenJa carefully carried the delicate arrangement to her favorite *Cubby Chair,* she called it, which was simply an overstuffed club chair that she loved to nestle into, especially on cold days.
Her first reaction was to smell the dainty flowers that reminded her of her mother's garden and then reached for the card, almost dreading who had sent them. She wanted them to be from Levi and then yet again, she didn't.

Holding her breath, she opened the card and it simply said:

> ***Would you please meet me at***
> ***'Le Crystal Lustre',***
> ***this evening at 8?***

    This mysterious message gave no clue as to who had authored the note and she had no idea if it was Levi or Brody or someone else, all together. She had not seen or heard from either men since before Thanksgiving and now it was February, already and the last time she drove by Levi's home, there was no sign of life on the property and the driveway had not been plowed, all winter.

    The evening of Valentines Day arrived and the skies were clear and the temperature brisk. A line of cars entered the parking lot of *'Le Crystal Lustre'*, also known as *'Le Crystal Chandelier'*, shortly before 8:00 p.m.
    The first car to arrive was the red Volvo, followed closely behind by a black Lincoln Navigator and before either of these cars found parking places, a black Cadillac Escalade drove into another parking space, close by.
    The operator of the Navigator remained behind the wheel and watched ZenJa exit her car, scan the parking lot, and timidly walk toward the restaurant entrance. Once she got to the front door and looked back, once again, she walked inside and that was Levi's cue to leave his vehicle and follow her inside.
    From the Escalade, Brody and his wife, Lynx watched the duo walk inside and then exited their own mode of transportation and entered the luxury dining facility.
    "They came in separate cars?" Lynx asked.
    "Those two have a habit of rubbing each other the wrong way and I believe they spend the end of their dates, going home alone, to their own homes."
    "That's sad," Lynx admitted.
    "Well, they're both stubborn mules; so anyway this should be interesting," Brody said and laughed and escorted his wife across the parking lot, hugging her tightly not simply to keep Lynx warm, but to snuggle into the warmth of her full length fur coat, as well.

    "Good evening, Miss Beckwith the Maitre d said and helped ZenJa out of her mid-calf length, black, woolen cape and while he went to hang it up, Levi walked into the restaurant and kissed ZenJa on the back of the neck.

ZenJa spun around and was startled to see the most handsome man she had seen in a long time.

"Levi!" she said. "It was you, wasn't it?" she asked awkwardly.

"It was me, what?" he teased.

"You send me the lovely bouquet of roses and the invitation for dinner."

"I have no idea what you're talking about," he teased again. "I have another date, here, waiting for me." he said seriously, without laughing.

"And who might that date just be?" she asked and laughed.

"He's right over there," Levi said, "See, there's Alex, he's waving at me," he lied.

"You look ravishing!" Levi said and scanned ZenJa's lovely body that was dressed in a bright red, knee length, spaghetti strap dress, that was accented by a graceful, flippy skirt and her accessories included red high heels and a matching purse.

"You look rather dashing yourself," ZenJa said and noted Levi was dressed in black dress pants and black turtleneck sweater, along with his long leather coat.

At that moment the Maitre d came back and Levi said he was fine, keeping his leather coat on, and the man ushered the couple to an isolated table that shimmered with crystal, a white table and red napkins and roses in the center.

After ZenJa and Levi were seated, another Maitre d ushered the next couple, to their table at an equally sequestered area, a comfortable distance away from any other tables.

Brody seated his wife, with her back facing toward from the other couple's table, and looked over at ZenJa and Levi, simply smiled and nodded and Levi noticed Brody's smile was more like a smirk, but he dismissed it and simply nodded.

"Well, it seems as if we have an acquaintance dining here, this evening," Levi stated. "Valentines Day is such a romantic time of year, don't you think?"

"Why, who's here?"

"It seems as if Mr. Black and a very attractive young lady have the same idea, we do."

"What idea is that?" ZenJa asked and turned to look at the couple who were currently in a deep discussion, about something...most likely the menu.

"The idea to spent this romantic holiday with lovely women and fine dining," Levi simply replied.

"Oh, that's Brody, isn't it? Actually, I haven't seen hide nor hair of either of you," she admitted. "I thought you both fell off the face of the earth," she teased, but continued to look at the couple, in hopes of getting a better look at the lovely blonde he was sitting with.

"Would you like for us to go over and greet them?" Levi asked.

"No, that isn't necessary," ZenJa replied realizing that Levi clearly was offended that she was intently curious who the lady Brody had come to dinner with, was.

"She is lovely isn't she?" Levi offered.

"Yes, she is, but I'm actually more interested in what she's wearing," ZenJa lied.

"What would you describe her, as wearing?" Levi asked and smirked at the same time, the lovely blonde woman rose from her seat, while Brody moved her chair closer to his own...the couple would be nearly sitting in each other's laps, Levi and ZenJa both noticed.

"It looks like a designer outfit; a Chanel, I'd say. A black, long sleeved turtlenecked, figure hugging, three-quarter length dress and bright red knee high boots, with heels and a lovely red purse and wide belt; from what I can see. Her necklace and earrings appear to be pearl and I have no doubt, they are real and her hair is lovely, as well," ZenJa remarked.

"Her hair is lovely, as is yours. It seems you both had the same thing in mind...wearing your lovely hair piled on top of your heads."

"Well, thank you for the compliment, Levi. That is very sweet of you."

"Her dress certainly is figure hugging, now that you mention it," Levi said and gazed at the lovely woman before she was seated. "And what a lovely figure she has. I always love my women tall and slender with small breasts," Levi added. He figured if ZenJa could gawk at the woman, so could he.

"To get back to us..." ZenJa began while the Sommelier came to pour their wine.

"I'm glad you liked the flowers," Levi said and was surprised how nervous he was being around ZenJa, after all this time. He wondered if he had made a mistake to ask her to dinner, but realized it was only a dinner. It wasn't like they were going to get married anytime, soon; if ever.

"They truly are beautiful and I've had them right by my computer all day while I worked on my book. Thank you so much for them and for dinner. It really is nice to see you, after all this time," she blurted out, all at once.

"It is nice to see you, as well," Levi said and took a sip of wine while their first courses were brought to the table and Brody and his wife's courses were brought to their own table.

"Your first course, this evening includes pan seared Crab Cakes and Champagne Mustard Sicli," the waiters told their patrons, when the Sommelier came to refill their glasses with wine.

"Thank you," Levi replied; the couple sampling the delicious first course.

"These are magnificent," ZenJa said tasted the delicate treats before her.

"I was wondering where you had gone. I figured maybe you were basking in the sunshine in Hawaii, or something. I noticed your driveway hasn't been plowed, all winter," she said and wished she could have bitten her tongue off.

"So, you've drive by my house, have you?" he asked, not revealing where he had been spending the winter months, so far.

"I bought a new car...a winter car and I wanted to drive in on the snowy back roads to see how it handled in the inclement weather," she said defiantly.

"What kind of car did you get?"

"Henri, suggested I get a Volvo, so I did."

"Henri?" Levi asked and smiled.

"Yes, you know perfectly well who Henri is and thank you for making my Christmas very special."

Without commenting on her statement, Levi asked, "How is your house coming along? Have you got it all decorated, yet?"

"Yes, it is pretty much finished, but I'm still working on the attic. I want to make that my secret hiding place, to write."

"Why do you need a secret hiding place to write, may I ask? It's not like anyone will be snooping around, looking at your work in progress, will they?"

"It's kind of a spooky, but pleasant place to be. I know that sounds odd, but that area gives off a certain...how would you say...mysterious ambiance."

"Well, like I told you, Mr. Black apparently was in prison, somewhere and his wife was rumored to have disappeared, so maybe she'll be found in the recesses of the attic," Levi said and laughed.

"You really believe he was in prison and his wife disappeared?" ZenJa said and laughed.

"Stranger things have happened," Levi said without thinking.

"You're right, of course," ZenJa replied sadly.

"I didn't mean it like that, ZenJa. I was only teasing you."

"Well, if that woman is the missing Mrs. Black, the authorities would have searched high and low for her...she's one of the pretty ones," ZenJa acknowledged.

"Just in the nick of time; our second course has arrived," Levi said and breathed a sigh of relief.

"This evening we have a choice, for you of a Classic Caesar Salad with garlic toast points or a fresh Spring Salad with candied walnuts, Goat cheese, raisins and blood orange Vinaigrette," the waiter said.

"I think we will try one of each," Levi said. "They both sound so good, we can share each salad."

"Very good sir," the man said and left the two different salads on their table.

"So, back to the attic," ZenJa began and her eyes sparkled with delight.

"Pray tell, what did you find in the attic?"

"A leather briefcase, with the initials BB, etched in gold, on the clasp."

"Ahhh! That would be Brody Black's, I assume and do you think that was the reason he entered *your* house? In an effort to retrieve that briefcase?" Levi asked mysteriously?"

"Oh my God! I never gave that a thought!"

"Where is the brief case now?"

"I gave it back to him," she admitted sheepishly.

"Did you at least open it to see what was in it?" Levi asked as if he were speaking to a child.

"No, I didn't. The day I told you we met and had lunch was the day I gave it to him and he did open it, while we were at the table. He did have a key that unlocked it."

"Oh, that was the day you two had lunch and went *shopping*?" Levi asked and smirked.

"Yes, that was the same day, wise ass!"

"Well, so, what was inside?"

"He took out some football and basketball awards from Penn State and when I asked him if he graduated from there, he said no, that he has several Masters Degrees from TAU."

"TAU?" Levi asked.

"Tel Aviv University, in Israel."

"Why TAU? He's not Jewish," Levi said and looked over at the table where the other couple was deep in conversation, at their own table.

"That's exactly what I said!" ZenJa said and muffled her laughter.

"What did he say to that?" Levi asked with keen interest.

"He laughed and asked, I"m not? We both laughed and he went on to explain that he met his wife there."

"So she's Jewish?"

"That's what I assumed, as well and he said she is Swedish, actually."

"Do you think he was lying?"

"I don't see why he would, do you?"

"No I guess not and it appears that lovely woman, over there is the missing Mrs. Black, if I may be bold enough to assume that," Levi suggested. "She looks very Swedish to me."

"So anyway, what else did he drag out of the briefcase?"

"Nothing, actually. We were finished with lunch and we went shopping."

"Did he drag that leather case with him all afternoon or did he put it in his vehicle?"

"Now that you mention it he said he walked to the diner and asked if I would put it in the trunk of my car, until we were done."

"So, tell me this; have you ever seen Brody Black's vehicle?"

"No, I haven't," she admitted and frowned.

"Okay, so when you were finished shopping what did you two do?"

"We walked back to my car, I removed the briefcase from the trunk, handed it to Brody and he placed the shopping bags in the trunk, and he said he was running late and I offered to give him a lift."

"Did you give him a ride?"

"Yes, I took him about three or four streets over and he got out and waved, and I drove away."

"Where did you drop him off?" Levi asked as the waiter brought their next course.

"This evening we have Filet and Shrimp Oscar, grilled Asparagus, oven roasted potatoes and Truffle gravy."

"That sounds lovely," Levi said and wished the man would simply leave the dinners and get the hell back in the kitchen.

"So where were we?" ZenJa asked, after sampling the delicious dinner.

"Where did you drop him off?"

"On the corner of Main and Lakeside Avenue, in front of a line of offices, a bank, and several real estate offices."

"And of course he never took a step in any direction, until you were out of sight, did he?"

"No, he didn't."

"His vehicle could have been parked anywhere around there," Levi said angrily.

"What do you think he's up too?" ZenJa asked suspiciously and looked, once again, at the loving couple.

"I have no fucking idea," he whispered.

"Would you be okay, here by yourself, for a minute? I'm going to use the men's room and see if Brody follows."

"I'll be fine, but be careful," ZenJa warned.

"So you really do care about me," Levi said, rose, kissed her cheek, and left the table.

Levi stood at the sink, washing his hands and as expected, Brody Black walked in.

"Did you and your date ride your bikes here tonight or did you come by speed boat?" Levi asked without any other formalities.

Brody laughed out loud and his laughter was heard by the all restaurant patrons and staff.

"Oh my God, Levi, you have the same wonderful sense of humor as does ZenJa. I truly love a good laugh, now and then."

"So, I guess our lovely ZenJa has been filling you in on our various adventures?"

"Yes, she did mention you love to go shopping and are so thankful to get your leather briefcase back. All you had to do is ask, to get it back, you didn't have to break into her house."

"I did not break into her house, Levi. You know perfectly well, I used my keys," he added and smirked.

"I truly do admire her restraint and that she's a trusting soul and realizes people have a right to privacy."

"Sometimes, she's too trusting and naive."

"But, to answer your question, my date and I were going to arrive in my helicopter, but we were afraid we would have a difficult time finding a suitable parking place," Brody said and laughed again.

"You have a helicopter, as well?"

"I do indeed."

"So that was you flying over the Sweeney property, a few months ago?"

"I did, indeed."

"What were you doing there?"

"I was going to ask you the very same thing," Brody said; his eyes turned the color of rich, black, coal. "Why were you and the Feds exploring the property with search dogs?"

"We were looking for something."

"Did you find what you were looking for?"

"No, as a matter of fact we didn't and speaking of your flying over the Sweeney property, that was about the same time the house on my newly acquired property burned to the ground. Would you know anything about that?" Levy said, raising his voice to another level.

"Look, let's not spoil a perfectly romantic evening with this shit. I suggest we meet, tomorrow and lay all our cards out on the table, shall we?" Brody offered.

"I'll let you know right up front, I don't like liars and if you're going to bullshit me, don't bother to show up," Levi warned.

"I will expect the same honesty, as well."

"Where do you want to meet?" Brody asked.

"How about we meet at 1:00 p.m. at the new bookstore, that just opened on Main Street," Levi suggested, in an effort to be in familiar surroundings, where there was a known ally of his...Isabella's Uncle Henri.

"Oh, '*de Montesquiou Book Boutique ?*"

"Yes, that's the place."

"Sounds fine to me. Well, we better get back to our dates," Brody said and left the restroom, with Levi following.

"So what was that all about?" Lynx asked her husband when another course was brought to their table, that included Torteau Fromager, strawberry glaze, and Creme Fraiche, which the couple both knew to be a delicate cheese cake. And he also left a Townhouse Tiranisu; which is simply a sponge cake, soaked in coffee brandy, covered in powered chocolate and Mascarpone Cheese; the same deserts and coffee that was presented at Levi's table.

"I have a meeting with Mr. Harris tomorrow," Brody simply replied.

"Now what were we talking about before I departed?" Brody asked and kissed his wife's fingertips.

"We were talking about the two years I spent in Sweden, with my family and the last year I was in New York, with my mother, while you were out saving the world," Lynx said.

"I wish I had been able to see you more often, during those years, but, sadly, this war we fight is not easy and we all must make sacrifices," Brody said and sipped his coffee.

"I know and if you were not who you are and do what you do, I would never love you, as I do."

"So, as I was saying, once my mother and I went to her apartment in Manhattan, we went to all the shows, museums, local art fairs and of course we went to the new *Freedom Tower*, *The Memorial,* and *Museum*. My mother had connections, so we were able to visit after hours."

"What a tragic memorial that is...beautiful, but so sobering," she added.

"I know and you and your people are well aware of the evilness that encompasses the world and wickedness that lurks only a few feet away from each one of us. Your people have been living this nightmare since the beginning of time. We, in the United States have been sheltered from most of the brutality that has plagued the rest of the world, forever."

"That is another reason, I love you so much, Brody. You are the kindest, most compassionate man I have ever met. Deadly, but kind," she added and smiled.

"So, with that said, do you think Mr. Harris will sit and wait for us to leave?" Brody asked and smiled.

"Why would he do that?"

"He's dying to know what mode of transportation I'm using tonight!"

"Why would he care?"

"It's just a little game I've been playing with his crew."

"I have an idea," Lynx said and checked her cell phone.

"What are you doing?"

"I feel like going to a romantic sleigh ride," Lynx said and laughed.

"God, now I know why I love you more each day," he said and removed the phone from her hand and ordered a horse drawn sleigh to arrive at the front door in twenty minutes.

Both couples were finishing their meals, had paid their bills and Brody finally stood up to escort his wife to the door, when he saw the sleigh arrive out front, from their window seat.

While the lovely couple gathered their things and the Maitre d helped Mrs. Black on with her fur coat, they both walked by Levi and ZenJa's table. Brody simply nodded and ushered his wife outside.

Before Brody had placed the warm woolen blanket over their laps and the driver signaled the horses to continue on their journey, like clockwork, Levi and ZenJa came rushing out of the restaurant.

Brody looked at the couple; the expressions on their faces, priceless, and Brody laughed so loud, he frightened the horses, that took off like lightening across the parking lot, with the sleigh and occupants behind.

"Brody, you're so evil," Lynx said and snuggled close to the man she loved while they took a leisurely drive down the festive streets of this quaint town on Lake Winnipesaukee.

"What the fuck?" Levi swore and led ZenJa down the steps.

"It appears he outsmarted us once again," ZenJa said and laughed.

"Yeah, I guess I have to give it to him," he admitted while the couple walked toward ZenJa's car.

"So, this is the new vehicle you were telling me about?"

"You like it?"

"Yes, it is pretty snazzy, for a winter car and it does have excellent tires on it. I'm glad you decided to purchase a good set."

"Why?" ZenJa asked.

"I wouldn't want you to go off the road, while you're searching for me," he said arrogantly, but smiled.

"You *are* so full of yourself, aren't you?" ZenJa teased, making an effort to appear angry.

Levi opened her car door and once she settled inside and turned on the engine and car heater, he leaned inside and asked, "What, if anything, would you like to be full of, tonight? Would you like to be full of me, too?" he snickered.

"Are you simply asking me if I want to have sex with you?"

"Yeah, that pretty much sums it up or if you simply want to fuck, that's okay, too! I mean I don't want you to feel *used*, so if we simply fuck, neither of will be used, will we?" Levi growled at her.

"I feel the love," she hissed.

"If I loved you, ZenJa, you would know it," Levi said and walked toward his Navigator, started it up and left even with the windows fogged up and no heat inside the vehicle, yet.

ZenJa sat in her car, only two vehicles left in the parking lot, other than the kitchen workers and once again began to cry.

"Why in hell do you antagonize him like you, do?" she said aloud. "He's a man's man, not some candy ass, pussy, that can be led around by the nose...a man you would hate, to the core," she scolded herself.

Before ZenJa was able to put her car in gear, the horse drawn sleigh arrived back at the restaurant and Brody and his wife climbed out and had a few words with the older driver and he obviously paid the man and must have given him a handsome tip, some of which the elderly man tried to return.

Brody looked around and noticed Levi's Navigator was gone and but the red Volvo, ZenJa had arrived in, was still parked where it was when they came for dinner.

"Shit! That's Brody!" she cried, softly.

As the vehicle headed toward her car and the headlights focused on the red car, she ducked down in the seat, until it passed.

"Someone's in that car," Brody said and laughed.

"How can you tell?" Lynx asked and looked back.

"The windshield is all clear and exhaust is coming from the tail pipe and there's a woman crouched down...a woman with auburn hair and a black wrap, just as I predicted! Looks like the love birds had another quarrel and once again, Mr. Harris will be jerking himself off!" Brody said and laughed while his wife cuddled next to him.

"So now she knows what we have for a vehicle."

"That's okay my dear, I'm going to meet with Mr. Harris tomorrow and we're allegedly going to lay all the cards on the table and stop this cloak and dagger mystery shit and if everything goes well, we'll both come home, alive," he added seriously.

Chapter 79

A light dusting of snow was falling when Brody and his wife arrived at their home, after driving for an hour, to make sure they were not being followed.

"We're home!" Brody said cheerfully; the couple greeted by the smell of their wood stove and glistening lights, that reflected off the snow that was falling and what was already on the ground.

The couple rushed inside and stood in front of the wood stove for a few minutes, after removing their coats and shortly after, Brody added more wood to the stove and lit the fireplace.

"Can I get you anything from the kitchen?" Lynx asked, after removing her shoes and jewelry.

"I'm kinda thirsty, do we have any ginger ale?"

"Yes, I'll bring us both some. I think that wine made me thirsty, too."

"Oh, here's today's newspaper, I forgot to put it on your desk, this afternoon," Lynx said and handed her husband his drink and paper.

The couple cuddled on the sofa and they both scanned the contents of the local gossip sheet.

"Well, this is certainly interesting," Brody said and folded the paper in half.

"What is it?"

"There's a large ad in here for loggers, underground pipe layers and eventually construction workers in Longberry."

"Who has placed the ad?"

"Well, if the initials are any indication I would say it's the new owner of the former Beckwith Property."

"Levi Harris?" Lynx asked.

"Yes, my dear. It does appear so and with that said, I think we just struck gold!" Brody hollered. "God is truly blessing us," he added and hugged his wife. "I do believe the man is a little ahead of himself or purely egotistical, though."

"Why do you say that?"

Look at the design!" Brody said.

"That's the Loire Valley - The Garden of France - Chateau-de-Chaumont!" Lynx exclaimed.

"Must be Levi intends to build a replica of that majestic creation?"

WANTED

LOGGING CONTRACTORS
EXPLOSIVE EXPERTS
UNDERGROUND PIPE & CABLE TECHNICIANS
CELLULAR TOWER ERECTORS

These positions start immediately

****

CONSTRUCTION CONTRACTORS
WELL DRILLING FACILITATORS
ELECTRICAL, HEATING, PLUMBING
AND AIR CONDITIONING SPECIALISTS

These positions begin in April or May

****

MASONS
PAVING
LANDSCAPING
INTERIOR CONTRACTORS
INTERIOR DECORATORS

The dates for these jobs TBD

****

For further information contact
LH@@Lake.com
or leave message at
555-555-0098

Chapter 80

"Well, hello, ZenJa!" Molly greeted one of her favorite customers, who she had not seen in months.

"Hello, Molly," she replied and hugged the woman who sat down beside her at the counter.

"Where have you been, all this time. I thought for sure you and Levi had run off, gotten married, and had a family, by now," she said in jest.

"Oh, you have to be joking, right?"

"Why...why do you say that?"

"We simply don't get along; I think we're too much alike."

"What can I get you?" Molly asked and left her stool, at the counter.

"Just some coffee, thank you."

"Coming right up."

Less than a minute later, Molly placed the coffee on the counter and went back behind the counter.

"The reason I figured you and Levi would be married by now, is because on his way out of town, before Thanksgiving, he left this gift off for you and I assured him I would give it to you when you stopped by and of course, now we know you haven't been here, in months."

"He left this off here, for me?" ZenJa asked and opened the shopping bag, from the Quarry Treasure Chest, designer jewelry shop and took out a beautifully wrapped, shimmering silver paper box, that was embellished with a delicate silver, lace ribbon and a sprig of mistletoe and holly berries.

"Oh, my! This is so beautiful and I'm glad the box is wrapped to I can open it without pulverizing the wrapping," she said and laughed.

ZenJa carefully lifted off the lid to the package and was stunned to see what was inside. It was a platinum bracelet and matching necklace and hoop earring set. As she carefully lifted the half inch wide, necklace and bracelet from the box, she noted the message engraved on the inside:

Our First Christmas
LH

"Oh my God! I just had dinner with Levi last night and he probably wondered why I wasn't wearing these!" she exclaimed.

"Well, at least you spent Valentines Day with him."

"Yes, but our evening didn't end well. It ended like all our other times we spend together, for the most part; yelling and screaming, at each other."

"If that isn't a sure sign of love, I don't know what is," a customer said on his way by, to pay his bill.

"You're probably right," ZenJa agreed and laughed in spite of the remark from a total stranger.

"You're married, I gather?" ZenJa asked the middle aged man.

"Hell, no! I never found anyone I wanted to yell and scream at," he said and laughed and left the money for his bill on the counter and departed the café.

"I have got to call Levi and tell him why I wasn't wearing these last night. He must be so hurt and all I ever seem to do is wound him," she admitted. "Look, I have to go," ZenJa said and placed a five dollar bill on the counter and ran out of the café, herself.

She climbed inside her Volvo and quickly dialed Levi's cell phone number.

"What?" was the response she got.

"Levi, I owe you an apology," she began.

"You don't owe me anything," was his reply.

"Yes, I do. I stopped over to Molly's, this morning and hadn't been there since Thanksgiving and she gave me the lovely Christmas gift you had asked her to give me, when she saw me again and I haven't been there in months, to be honest with you! That's why I wasn't wearing these last night."

"What do you mean *these*?" he asked.

"The stunning necklace, bracelet and earrings. Why, what did you think I was referring to?" she asked in confusion.

"I must have gotten that gift mixed up with another I was giving out for Christmas. I didn't give you a three piece set of jewelry," he said, trying to hold onto what little dignity he had left, as far as she was concerned.

"What does the card say?" he asked with evil intent.

"There is no card, but the engraving on the necklace says, Our First Christmas and is signed LH.

"Well, that explains it," he continued to razz her further.

"Explains what?"

"That explains why you weren't wearing the kidney stone, I passed in November, and had placed in a plastic setting, just for you. The other jewelry items were for someone else."

"Levi, I am not going to hang up on you, as you expect, this time."

"I would if I were you. I mean, who wants someone else's kidney stone, though it was rather large, I have to admit."

"Levi, I want to come over to your house and apologize for my behavior and for being a bitch, all the time, but I want to ask you to forgive me, in person, not over the phone."

"That isn't necessary, ZenJa and I'm not home anyway. I'm on my way to a meeting."

"Can I see you later? Or can you come over to my house for dinner?"

"I don't think that's a good idea, ZenJa. I'm seeing someone else now," he lied.

"Oh, someone who doesn't mind being...?" she began.

"What were you going to say? Someone who doesn't mind being used...was that it?"

ZenJa disconnected the call and cried, sitting behind the wheel of her car before driving toward Sander's Bay.

Chapter 81

"Thank you for letting me hold a private meeting here in your magnificent book store, Henri," Levi said. "This truly is a wonderful place and I expect to spend a lot of time reading the books and magazines you have here...it's cheaper than purchasing them!" Levi said and laughed and hugged Isabella's uncle.

"I have missed your sense of humor more than I can tell you."

"Who said I was kidding?"

"Oh my goodness! It's my Levi!" Henri's wife, Margaux de Montesquiou said and hugged this handsome young man.

"I have missed you both more than you will ever know," Levi said truthfully.

"We have arranged this private sitting room for you and your guest," Margaux said and ushered Levi to a quiet, secluded area of the book store. "I also left a tray with coffee and some sweets to nibble on, if you like."

"That is very kind of you and I promise to be back, in a few days. There are some things I would like to discuss with you about my impending venture," he said and the trio heard the overhead door bell ring, when Brody walked inside.

Levi stood while Brody walked over to him and Henri closed the door behind the two men and went about his own business.

"Thank you for being prompt," Levi said sternly, getting right down to business.

"Let me begin by asking you what are the most important things in your life and the order in which they are of importance."

"My God, my wife, my country that I hold allegiance to and my honor."

"To cut to the chase, what country might that be?"

Brody looked Levi in the eye and without hesitation he replied, "Israel!"

That rather stunned Levi and Brody thought he noticed a slight change in facial expression, when he said it.

Levi stood up and helped himself to some coffee and offered Brody some, but he declined.

"You appear to be surprised."

"Frankly, I am," Levi admitted.

"Why so?"

"You said you worked as a contractor for a government agency and I assumed you meant the US government."

"And just what are your priories, if I may be so bold as to ask."

"God, country, my flag, honor and family. If I had a wife or children, I assume the order of those priorities would be shuffled around, to some extent."

"And you are referring to the US government, I assume?"

"Yes, no question about it."

"Were you in prison?" Levi asked.

"No, I was abroad in Israel for the last ten years, that I truthfully claimed when we first met, though I didn't mention where I was."

"That was your wife, with you last night?"

Brody smiled and from the expression of love on his face, he would not have had to reply, but he did. "Yes, that is my wife."

"She is lovely and I'm happy to see she has returned; I mean the story of the foreclosure was bogus, I assume?"

"No, actually, the foreclosure was honest. My wife, for her own safety, fled and forfeiting that home was the least of our concerns and I'm actually glad ZenJa was able to purchase it."

"And you're thankful she returned your mysterious leather brief case?"

"Indeed! It is rare, these days, to find anyone who is trustworthy," Brody said and watched for Levi's reaction.

"If she had opened it, what would she have found?"

"Inside that case are all my wife and I have of our lives together," he replied simply and offered no other explanation.

"If I may be so bold... who do you work for? I mean I saw you with the Feds browsing around the Sweeney property."

"I work for the US government," he replied and offered no other information.

"And your brother?"

"This conversation is about you and me, and no one else."

"That's fair."

"What are you doing around here?" Levi asked bluntly.

"I truly think God sent me here so we can help each other," Brody said mysteriously.

"How so?"

Brody stood and removed his leather coat, placing in on a adjacent cushioned seat, but only after removing the advertisement Levi had place in the local paper in recent days and laid it on the table.

"This is your ad, I assume?"

Levi looked at the paper, knowing exactly what it was and had no reason to deny it.

"It is," he said.

"This is now where we start to get down to the nitty gritty," Brody began.

"I have many things to disclose, under the threat of the death by our enemies. And as of this moment, I will put you on notice, you fuck me or my wife over or my government, I will personally kill you, do you understand!" Brody said as calmly as if he were saying good night to a child.

Levi returned the stare, without batting an eye and simply nodded.

"I assume you would do the same!"

"That goes without saying," Levi assured him.

"I think what we have to discuss will have to continue at another location and I think you know where that is," Brody stood up, grabbed the advertisement and left the book store, with Levi close behind him.

Less than an hour later, the two men climbed out of there vehicles and stood in front of the Beckwith home that still remained nothing more than a pile of burned timber.

"I decided not to ride my bike," Brody said and laughed to ease some of the tension.

"I was just going to ask you if you just stole this vehicle, for this occasion."

"First, let me explain about the fire," Brody said and pointed toward the ruins.

"I set fire to the house, only to cover up what *might* have been left behind."

"What do you mean, what might have been left behind?" Levi shot back.

"My country had been trying to persuade Mr. Beckwith to sell this property for a project we had orchestrated; a plan that I had spend the last ten years working on, in Israel. I simply wanted to make sure there was no communication linking me or my country to this attempt to encourage him to sell."

Levi shook his head, appearing to clear the cobwebs from his brain.

"You appear to be confused," Brody noted.

"This doesn't have anything to do with missing girls or buried bodies?"

"What?" Brody exclaimed in shock. "Fuck no!"

"You are aware of the missing girls, as you already mentioned that in another conversation we had, not so long ago, from the newspapers your *parents* sent you?" Levi said sarcastically.

"Yes, and I just recently did some more research on that and discovered ZenJa's sister is one of the missing and I am truly, truly sorry about that."

"That probably explains why Beckwith never wanted to sell the property. In his heart he always felt Zippy would return or her body may have actually been buried on this property," Levi reasoned.

"You may very well be right!"

"Is that why you were searching the Sweeney property? Do you have reason to believe they may have been, somehow, involved?"

"Yes, especially after our number one living suspect, Ivan Sweeney, is related to Wilbur and Lily Sweeney and actually murdered them before our very eyes."

"Oh shit!" Brody said and was honestly stunned.

"Did you have any luck, while searching the property?"

"No, we didn't and we were not only looking for the bodies, but we had dogs searching for explosives, on the property."

"Did you find any?" Brody asked, shifting his eyes nervously.

"Only small fragments and nothing of any significance."

"Why would you think there would be explosives, other than for blowing up stumps; they being in the logging business?" Brody asked.

"I guess, if you read the local papers, you might have stumbled upon the log truck, with it's cargo, going over the mountainside and exploding and nearly burning the entire mountain, right?"

"Yes, I did read that."

"The Fire Marshal told us it was obvious there were more than logs and fuel in the truck, to burn that hot and fast."

"Why would the Sweeney's be involved with transportation of explosives," Brody asked nervously.

"To be honest with you, we don't think they even knew it. We think Ivan was involved and that's why he had to silence his aunt and uncle. They had come to us and wanted to get out of the business."

"The logging business?"

"No, the transportation of illegal weapons that the dear police chief of Longberry had been giving them access to."

"Holy shit! This story is bizarre. I mean you can't make this shit up."

Brody and Levi were getting cold. The North wind had picked up and darkness was falling.

"So, you think Ivan Sweeney, whoever he is, was behind the theft of the explosives?"

"Not only that, but he is involved with the missing and murdered girls and the deaths of ZenJa's parents."

"They were killed in a car accident, I remember reading," Brody said honestly.

"Yes, but with a little effort and tracking his one odd tire, on his truck, it has been determined someone made a bogus call to alert ZenJa's parents that ZenJa had been in a car accident, on this dreadful fogging, rainy night. As expected Ivan knew the direction her parents would be coming from and he basically ran them off the road. They died on Blackberry Road."

Brody was deeply moved by these events and was unable to hide his sorrow.

"This is too much for me to absorb," Brody said honestly.

"It's damn cold out here, but we still have a lot to talk about," Levi said. He was suddenly intrigued as he watched Brody's expressions change and it was clear he knew more than he was saying and trying to connect the dots, but did not appear to be a part of these events, directly, anyway.

"Why don't you come to my house, I assume you know where it is?" Levi asked.

"No, to be honest with you, I don't."

"What do you drink?"

"Beer is fine," Brody replied.

"Give me time to grab some steaks from the butcher, some beer and salad stuff and I'll meet you at my house in about two hours."

"I would like to bring my wife, if I may?" Brody asked.

"I would be delighted to meet her," Levi said honestly.

"Oh, I suppose I have to ask ZenJa to come, too?" Levi asked and cringed.

"You two are really madly in love aren't you?" Brody asked and laughed.

"I don't know…everyone else seems to think so, but I sure as hell don't get that warm and fuzzy feeling one gets when they're in love," he admitted and howled with laughter.

"You will, give it time," Brody said when Levi gave him his card that had his address on it.

"See you in a couple of hours," Levi said; both men driving to the highway.

What bothered Brody most about the conversation he and Levi had just had was the carnage, that man, Ivan Sweeney had caused so many people in this once peaceful town. He had no idea who Ivan Sweeney was, but he now knew who had stolen the explosives from his stock pile, on the adjacent property...his property and if Ivan thought he had ever seen a hurricane or tornado come through, town, he was sadly mistaken and in for a big surprise.

Chapter 82

Brody called his wife from his cell phone and gave her a quick update on the status of the meeting he and Levi had and she was as shocked at the details he relayed to her, as he had been.

"Our lives have been intertwined for a reason," Lynx said honestly.

"I couldn't agree more. I just wish this could have been under better circumstances."

"We're going to continue this meeting at Levi's house and he has invited us for dinner, that will include steak, so if you would be so kind, will you select a bottle of wine, we can bring?"

"I can't believe we're actually going to meet with another couple! It's always been just the two of us," Lynx said.

"We have to trust someone, sometime, sweetheart. We can't keep doing this all on our own and these secrets are too hard to keep to ourselves. We need help."

"You trust him?"

"I do...I do and this is the first time I can remember saying that, other than about family."

"Of course you threatened to kill him if you double crossed us?"

"You know me better than that, Lynx," Brody said and laughed.

"See you soon," his wife replied.

Levi drove in his driveway and low and behold, ZenJa was parked in his driveway, blocking the entrance to his garage.

He exited his car, grabbed the three paper bags full of groceries and walked up to ZenJa, but didn't say a word.

"Levi, please hear me out!" she begged. "I am so sorry for the way I've treated you. I don't know what the hell's the matter with me. I have never treated anyone like I treat you," she admitted.

Levi stood silently and looked into ZenJa's tear filled eyes for a moment and finally said, "Maybe you've never been in love before," and walked past her to open the door and turned back and saw her simply stand there, her brain trying to decipher what Levi had just said. She was so used to him and his snide remarks, she actually thought he told her she must be in love with him.

Levi walked into his kitchen, having left the door open and placed the bags on the counter, when ZenJa stepped inside the door.

"I'm not heating the whole outdoors, am I?" he asked coarsely, his defensive *Mode of Operandi*."

ZenJa quietly shut the door and removed her boots and placed them on the mat, to dry.

"I'm glad you stopped by."

"You are?" ZenJa asked but stood where she was.

"I'm having guests for dinner and thought you might like to have a steak and salad with us."

"Who's coming over?"

"We don't have time for idle chatter; I have a grill to fire up and if you would like, you can wash the veggies and prepare the salad, but if you don't want to, that's fine, I had planned on doing it myself, anyway. He was not about to admit he had already planned to invite her, but having her arrive on his doorstep saved him what little ego he had left and hadn't had to actually invite her.

Before ZenJa prepared the garden salad, she placed the exquisite silver box on the counter. "I brought this back so you can give it to the rightful owner," she said softly.

Levi stepped back inside, from the deck, after lighting the charcoals and closed the sliding door.

"Oh, thank you, I never thought I would see those again," he said dryly.

"You can punish me all you want, Levi. I'm not going to argue with you. You've been right all along."

"Right about what? " he asked and stood next to her and the counter, but not touching her.

"I've been such a bitch and I have no excuse for it. You're the sweetest, kindest man I have ever known and I know I can only ask you to forgive me, but I don't expect you to. The only explanation I have and it may not even be true, but I think I was so hurt, having lost my sister, I was never going allow my heart to be broken, ever again. I know I should have sought therapy but I was too stubborn and I think if I searched for help, that would have been an admission, that I had given up on ever finding Zippy, again."

Levi reached for the box, opened it and removed the necklace from the package and gently placed it around ZenJa's neck. He tenderly kissed her before she turned around and looked Levi in his eyes.

"I love you, Levi," she said and kissed and held him as if she were drowning.

"I love you, too, ZenJa and I always have," he said.

Just then, the motion sensor, at the end of his driveway sounded and the couple gained control of themselves before their guests arrived.

"You have one, too?" ZenJa said and laughed.

"Of course. I wanted to know when you might be trying to sneak up on me, while I was in bed," he teased.

"Would you have let me in?"

"Only if you told me you loved me," he said and opened the door to welcome Brody and his stunning wife, Lynx, into his home.

"Okay, I love you, so let us in!" Brody said and laughed, having heard the couple's last two sentences, through the door.

Lynx stood at the door, held her hands as if in prayer, looked up at Heaven and simply said, "Oh God, help us!" and laughed.

"This is such a delightful pleasure," Levi said and took both Brody's and Lynx's coats and hung them up.

"This is Levi Harris and his friend, ZenJa Beckwith, my dear, and may I introduce my wife, Lynx."

"It is very nice to finally meet you," Levi and ZenJa both said and shook hands with their guests.

Please come inside," Levi said and ushered the guests into his warm and inviting living room that was accented with a massive stone fireplace and cathedral ceilings and windows that surrounded the lower floor and outside deck.

"Is that lovely bottle of wine for us or are you going to save it for later, in an effort to force us to talk?" Levi asked and smirked.

"Is that what it's going to take?" Brody asked and handed the wine to Levi.

"It may," ZenJa said.

"What a lovely home you have, Levi," Lynx said. "We've never been in one place long enough to call anywhere home and certainly not long enough to have a beautiful place such as this," Lynx admitted.

"We're going to have to do something about that, now aren't we?" Levi asked and immediately thought about the prospects of having this couple be the second residents of his new development, after Henri and his wife.

"I have to go out and turn the steaks; how do you folks like yours?"

"I'll help you," Brody said as the two men went out onto the deck and closed the sliding glass door behind them.

"Would you like me to help set the table?" Lynx asked ZenJa.

"Thank you, I guess we can find what we're looking for," she replied.

"You don't live here?" Lynx asked.

"No, I live in your old house."

"Oh, that's right. I've had so much going on lately and Brody has been trying to update me on all the activities; so please forgive me."

"Thank you, by the way, for returning the briefcase to my husband, unopened. Every meaningful thing we have is in there," she admitted and placed the plates and silverware on the table that ZenJa had found.

"That sounds like such a lonely life, if you don't mind my saying so."

"Sometimes, duty comes before ourselves," Lynx said mysteriously, but sincerely.

ZenJa looked at the young, beautiful blonde woman who moved around the dining room table with the grace of an actual Lynx before turning to the counter to prepare the salad and put the garlic bread in the oven.

"What do you actually want to discuss, tonight, over dinner, Levi?" Brody asked, while the homeowner turned the steaks.

"I mean should we simply continue where we left off, or start from the beginning, once again. I have no idea what ZenJa knows, obviously or how much you trust her or what she even wants to know."

"What does your wife know?"

"To be honest with you, I learned a great deal...things I had no idea about, myself, until this afternoon."

"Like what?"

"About the Sweeney's, Ivan, and really never thought much about the missing girls. My focus is connected with yours, but for different reasons and I sense this connection goes much deeper than we could imagine."

"Let's save time and simply continue where we left off and in our own time and way, we can update and connect the dots of what we've already discovered to our lady friends. They will remind us, I'm sure, of any details we inadvertently omit."

"I want to get all the facts, as best as we can and sort this out and to be honest with you, my head is swimming," Levy admitted.

"Well, I think we better get inside. It looks like the ladies are telling stories about us," Levi said and was happy to see the women laughing over something and appeared to enjoy each other's company.

"Mrs. Black, I do hope you don't believe anything ZenJa said about me, because I know, whatever it was, it's not the truth," Levi said, when the two men walked inside with the steaks.

"Well, with that said, I guess you're not a handsome and compassionate man and by the way my name is Lynx," she said and smiled.

"Actually, ZenJa was just showing me her belated Christmas gift and explained how these jewelry pieces, she is wearing, were meant for someone else and you meant to give her one of your large kidney stones, you passed and had mounted in what once had been a plastic carrying case for a six pack of beer," Lynx said as the foursome laughed.

"I asked you not to tell anyone about that, ZenJa. Some treasured gifts are meant to be kept secret. And I can also assure you that passing a kidney stone was much more painful than it was to pay for those jewels."

"And with that said, our meal is all ready to eat if you folks will be seated. Have we decided what beverages we would all like. We have everything, soda, beer, iced water and of course the wine should be chilled by now, if you would like that," Levi said.

"Everything looks lovely," Lynx said.

"It's not *'Le Crystal Lustre'*, but we can kick our shoes off and relax," Levi said. "And before we discuss business, I hope we can simply enjoy our meal and make small talk and over coffee and brandy; and then we can then get down to brass tacks," Levy seriously.

"That sounds wonderful and if I may, I would like to say grace before we begin," Brody announced.

"Please do," Levi said.

"Louez notre seigneur pour nos nouveaux amis et cette conjointe mous sommes sur le point d'entreprendre. Amen."

Lynx, opened her eyes and nodded and smiled to her husband.

"What my husband said, is Praise our Lord for our new friends and this joint venture we are about to embark on. Amen."

Levi and ZenJa simply sat there for a moment and let the words sink into their souls and suddenly there was a calming, almost serene, presence in the house. Almost mystical, was how ZenJa would describe it to Levi, later that evening.

"That was very nice, thank you," Levi said.

The foursome ate their meal and discussed this house that had once belonged to his father and how Alex was related; simply having the same mother; which explained the different last names.

"ZenJa remained fairly quiet and enjoyed listening to Lynx speak about having lived in Sweden and her latest period of time she had spent with her mother in Manhattan and having gone to school in Israel.

"You two should really travel there, one day," Brody suggested. "You will come home with a totally different outlook on life. The thousand years of history engulfs your very soul and you will find a peace you never knew existed," he reassured them.

"That does sound wonderful. I think we can all use a little peace," Levi said and looked at ZenJa who nodded in agreement.

The foursome finished their meals that include homemade apple pie with cheddar cheese and coffee before settling themselves on two comfortable couches, facing each other, at the same time huddled near the fireplace, with glasses of Cognac.

"Brody and I decided not to rehash what we already discussed today. It appears both you ladies are already aware of most of the details, though your husband will fill you in on the details he had no clue about, when we first met, today to speak."

ZenJa looked puzzled and Levi went on to give a rough draft of what Brody had been clueless about, for the most part, or at least the connections they had, now.

"About Zippy, having been your sister and the other missing girls, the Sweeneys, Miller, Connors and Ivan," he briefly stated.

"I am deeply sorry for the unknown status of your sister and her friend, I truly am," Brody said at the same time Lynx nodded, having been informed about these developments on the ride to the house, that evening.

"So, where were we, as we froze our butts off?" "Levi began. "Oh, yes, I remember, you were telling me you burned my house down," he added and laughed.

"What?" ZenJa asked.

"It will all come togther, ZenJa and what other questions you have that we don't answer, I'll answer later."

"I'll simply mention that I've been trying to buy your parents property for ten years or so," Brody offered and I simply wanted to make sure there was no trace of any communication we might have had, over the years, left in the house and I knew it was vacant and had been sold," he offered.

"Why were you attempting to buy my parents property?"

"We will get to that in a minute, but first where we left off, our conversation, this afternoon, Levy was...we were discussing the Sweeneys and their having access to explosives, were we not?"

"Yes, we were."

"I can answer that question for you."

"You can?" Levi and ZenJa said at the same time.

"Yes...that bastard stole them from me...from my stash."

"Your stash?" Levi asked as if he had a hearing problem.

"This is where our stories and lives become intertwined, so it seems," Brody began, but stopped and took a deep breath before continuing and deciding where to start, but chose to keep the conversation current.

"My people wanted to purchase your parents property for one reason and one reason only.

"Which was?"

"Your property aligns, perfectly, with an overhead satellite, my government has launched."

'What the fuck?" Levi asked, not believing what he was hearing.

"You mean to tell me this is much bigger than something on our local level...that we have been caught up in, all these years...finding our missing girls?"

"Not to minimize the disappearance of your loved ones, one iota, but yes," Lynx confirmed.

"Okay, before we go any further, I want to know exactly what country you are loyal to," Levi demanded.

"I have been totally truthful with you, Levi. It is Israel."

"We certainly hope that is not a problem for either of you?" Lynx asked.

"Oh, of course not! I always said I want to love the Jewish people as they are God's chosen ones and if I ever plan to get to Heaven, I want them on my side," Levi said and laughed to break the tension.

"That's exactly what Brody told me, when we went shopping," Zena said and laughed.

"Good, so now I won't have to kill you," Brody said, his eyes did not show any signs of merriment.

"Before we go any further, what did you mean about Ivan allegedly stealing your stash of explosives?"

"Our people have purchased the property, next to the Beckwith property, as you call it, and that's where I have an underground facility, so to speak and that's where I have housed the explosives we need to clear the land for our mission."

"I noticed that's where Sweeney had been logging, at the adjacent property to ZenJa's parents," Levi acknowledged.

"Yes, we hired him to clear a wide swath of trees."

"So you think Wilbur or Junior Sweeney found your stash?"

"No, from what you said, I think Ivan was the one who found them and planted them in amongst the logs."

"That makes sense because I questioned Junior about the explosives and he completely denied any knowledge of them and I truly believe him. Like he said, if he had known there was C-4 in that wood pile, he was hauling, he sure as hell wouldn't have driven that truck up that steep mountain."

"And before we get off the topic of Ivan, I want you to arrange a meeting with he and I," Brody said without hesitation.

"He's in jail," ZenJa said.

"I know," was Brody's response. "I have a score to settle with him."

"For stealing your stash?" Levi asked.

"No!" Brody replied without a hint of doubt. "There are just certain people who don't deserve to live."

"If you weren't married, I think I would fall in love with you," Levi said; the foursome chuckled at that outrageous statement. "You're a man after my own heart."

"Anyone want more Cognac?" ZenJa asked.

"No, but I would like to use the ladies room," Lynx said.

"Oh, well, I'm afraid, in this house, we only have a men's room, so you'll have to go down to the local garage," he said and once again howled at his own joke.

"I'll show you were it is," ZenJa said and simply shook her head at Levi.

"ZenJa and Lynx went into the huge bathroom that also had a seating room and while Lynx attended to her business, ZenJa sat in a chair.

"Forgive Levi. He's always cracking jokes. I think it's his way of dealing with stress and never realized it, myself until today."

"Levi is a delight! He truly is a wonderful man. I picked up good vibrations from him, the first time our paths crossed at the restaurant and mentioned it to Brody."

"He really is delightful, serious and dedicated to his work and I've been the fool, for so long. I've made every effort to keep him at a distance, even though I am madly in love with him."

"Life is too short to waste," Lynx said and washed her hands.

While the ladies were using the bathroom, Brody looked out the window and noticed it was snowing quite heavily.

"I think we better call it a night, sweetheart. I don't want to get stuck in a snow bank somewhere?"

"I meant to ask you, when you first arrived, what was your mode of transportation this time, your bicycles?" Levi asked and laughed.

"Actually, I plan to bring them to the garage, tomorrow and have snow tires put on them," Brody responded without replying to the question.

"We want to thank you for a lovely dinner and exceptional company, this evening," Lynx said at the same time Levi handed the couple their coats.

"This is quite the place you have here, on Governor's Island," Brody said.

"Well, there are no connections with the Beckwith's and your negotiations here, so you won't have to burn it down!" Levi said and laughed, but was completely serious.

"There aren't at this moment, but when we finish our discussions, there will be," Brody said soberly, without a hint of a smile.

"What will there be here, tying us to discussions?" ZenJa asked.

"The connections will be the four of us," Brody said and showed his wife out the door.

"Have a good night, folks and thank you again for a lovely evening. I hope we can get together tomorrow and continue with our discussion and if you will bring the blue prints and designs you have, with you. We have a great deal to discuss," Brody said and waved as he helped his wife into their Escalade and then drove away, into the night.

Chapter 83

Levi went out onto the deck and noticed there was nearly a foot of new snow on the ground and suggested ZenJa spend the night at his house; for her own safety, of course.

"Thank you for asking me to stay, I really don't want to venture out in this weather, especially in the dark," she said.

"Would you like more Cognac or something else?" Levi asked from the kitchen.

"No, thank you, I'm all set, but can we just sit here by the fire and discuss all we have heard in the last few hours? My head is swimming with facts and innuendoes, Brody mentioned, but didn't fully explain."

For the next hour, Levi explained all he had learned from Brody, at the former Beckwith house and discussion they had at *'de Montesquiou Book Boutique'* and assured ZenJa of the fact that it appeared Brody had not been in prison, but working for the Israeli government.

"Why do you think he wants to inspect the blueprints and plans you have for the property?"

"He obviously wanted to buy that property from your parents, for years and I have to assume he told the truth when he said it was because of the close proximity and alignment with an Israeli space satellite overhead."

"I don't understand what that would have to do with that property."

"The only thing that I can think of is he wants to erect communication towers!" Levi said as if a lightbulb had suddenly gone off in his head. "And that makes perfect sense, because he wants to see the plans I have and he brought the ad, I had placed in the local and state newspapers, looking for construction help, in the hear future."

"He must see this to be a perfect opportunity to erect what he wants and intermingle with our development...no one the wiser!" ZenJa intelligently surmised, at the prospect.

"I have no doubt you're right, ZenJa! But, now the question is who's side is he really on? He might even be working against the Israeli government, for all we know!"

"Not to mention against the US, and with that said, how are we going to find out?"

"He must realize we aren't simply going to take *his* word for it. I mean he *is* going to have to come across with some proof."

"I guess we better call it a night, turn on the dishwasher and get some sleep," Levi said and walked into the kitchen and turned the appliance on.

"The spare bedroom is all made up for you, ZenJa,"

"I'm rather chilly, do you mind if I sleep with you tonight?" she asked timidly.

Levi turned around and looked at ZenJa; his expression was neutral; a perfect poker face that clearly gave nothing away.

"Are you sure?" he finally asked.

"Yes, I'm sure. I love you Levi and I know I've made so many mistakes, where we're concerned and..." she began and before she could finish what she has to say, she fell into Levi's welcoming arms and for more than ten minutes, the couple simply stood there embracing and passionately expressing their love, without words, to each other.

"Were you just saying something about being chilly?" Levi asked, leading ZenJa to his bedroom.

"I don't think I will be for long," she whispered.

The couple snuggled in the king size bed where they spent the remainder of that cold winter's night wrapped in each other's embrace.

Chapter 84

The next morning, Brody called Levi on his cell phone and made arrangements for another meeting, that day and asked if it would be possible to meet at the book boutique, once again.

"I'll arrange it and I would like ZenJa in on this and your wife, as well. I'm going to involve Alex in on this, but not right now."

"What time would you like us to meet you there?" Brody asked.

"Let's say 1:00 p.m.?"

"We'll be there," Brody said and disconnected the call.

Three hours later, the foursome entered the cozy, private reading room at Henri's and Margaux's book boutique and once again a fresh pot of coffee and sweets were made available.

"Thank you for coming and again thank you for dinner, last night. We had a very enjoyable evening," Lynx said and smiled while she sat down, next to her husband who had gathered around a large table, that had the blue prints for the resort spread out, along with the ad from the newspaper.

"Before we get started, I would like to ask you a few more questions about the communications satellites and towers you are speaking about," Levi said seriously. "I want to know *exactly* what they are going to be used for, by whom, and why?"

"Of course," Brody said without batting an eye. "I'll begin with what I've been doing for the last ten years and what that has been, will be exactly what we will do here and for the same reasons."

"We are all aware of the satellites that have filled outer space like yesterday's accumulated trash; that goes without saying. Satellites are used for many things; to track the weather, other satellites and most importantly, in our case, counter terrorism and spying."

"The good stuff," ZenJa replied.

"Yes! We in Israel," Brody began, "Are not concerned so much about weather or having access to televised sporting events or the latest talent shows, from all over the world. We're simply determined to keep our country safe, as safe as we can and know what's going to happen, before it does."

"And if there's an impending attack, we'll be able to respond in a timely fashion and eliminate a catastrophic event from taking place in our small country," Lynx added.

"Not to beat a dead horse, Brody, but you keep calling Israel, your country," Levi said.

"I was born in the US, but I am loyal to Israel and I consider it my country."

"Let me play the devil's advocate, for a minute. How do we know you're not planning strategies against Israel?" Levi asked.

"Thank you for considering that and I'm happy to see you'd think of that as a distinct possibility. Under the circumstances, I would be just as suspicious as you are, so in an effort to ease your mind, I have taken the liberty of inviting you to a residence, near here on Lake Winnipesaukee, this evening for a meeting."

"Your house?" ZenJa asked.

"No, but let me ask you; have you ever wondered who the highest government officials and world leaders are who come to meet here, every summer, in New Hampshire?"

"You mean like presidential candidates, presidents, kings, and other dignitaries from around the world?" ZenJa asked.

"Yes, as has every other resident of New Hampshire," Levi added.

"There is a residence here, much like Camp David, and I can assure you there is more security there than there is at the White House," Brody said.

"Is that where we will be meeting?" ZenJa asked, her eyes as wide as saucers.

"Yes, it will be," Lynx replied.

"No shit!" Levi said, nearly falling out of his chair.

"So, I assume you must realize, by this time, we are on the same side of things?" Brody asked.

"So, this has already been cleared by the US government; I mean this project you're working on?" Levi asked.

"Absolutely not!" Brody said more loudly than he intended.

"But you said this Camp David-like residence hosts world leaders." ZenJa said.

"Yes, but I did not say this residence is under control of the US government. It's a completely separate entity, not controlled by any government. This residence is directed by those *above* any single government," Brody added mysteriously.

"I remember reading where it was rumored the decedents of Christ are among us," Levi stated.

Brody looked at Lynx, but did not respond, they simply smiled.

"Holy shit!" Levi said and stood up and began to pace the floor.

"We're not saying these people are or are not. We have no more idea than you do."

"Oh, my gosh. What does one wear to meet...well, possibly meet decedents of Christ?" ZenJa asked and laughed.

"Let's say we leave the men to continue this meeting and we go shopping?" Lynx suggested.

"Yes, it's obvious you have been to this residence before, so you'll know what to wear," ZenJa cried with excitement.

"Probably a simple white robe and sandals?" Levy offered. "I think I have white sheets, back at the house!"

ZenJa, once again, rolled her eyes; the foursome laughed and the ladies left to spend some money.

"It appears the ladies have hit it off," Levi said and watched them begin by exploring the book boutique.

"Ah, yes! That was all Lynx spoke about, last night. She has never or rarely, had the opportunity to become friendly with anyone, much less another woman to actually call a friend. Our lives have been one big, deep, dark secret and speaking of deep dark secrets, Lynx and I'll pick you up at your house, tonight at 7:00 and take you to our destination."

"You have sacrificed a lot," Levi admitted.

"Yes, we have, but if not us, who will?"

Levi sat for a minute and didn't respond. He had never met anyone who was so devoted to their country than these two, unless it were some US Navy SEALS or other Special Ops. forces.

Levy and Brody grabbed cups of coffee and sat back down at the table.

"Using this drawing you have of the Beckwith property and what you can see of mine, this is what I had the Sweeney's doing. They were clearing out this whole, what I called a divide. It was going to be, when it was finished, just wide enough for the towers and lines. It was not meant to be an eyesore or to be seen, actually. It's tricky and we had to use the dips and rises in the mountainside in an effort to conceal as much of what would be, once the towers were to be erected."

Levi studied the landscape and realized his, future resort would be perfect in many ways; that Brody had already surmised.

"By creating my masterpiece, this will give you a cover for what you're going to do."

"Exactly! That is exactly what I thought when I saw your ad in the newspaper. It was like a gift from God and, after we have this meeting tonight and probably several more, down the road, I can almost assure you that we can accommodate all your power needs from those same towers and as we have to run underground electric cables, the earth will be torn up and your cables and whatever other lines you plan to lay can be done at the same time."

"We will have electric lines, sewer, water, television and computer cables. I can't believe this stroke of luck and it's not about my saving money, because that's not an issue, but it's simply a way of saving time.

"I can also save you the task of finding reliable help to dig your tunnels and erect our towers," Brody said mysteriously.

"How so?"

"I have a crew that has spent the last ten years creating this exact masterpiece in Israel and they have learned all the lessons and made all the mistakes one usually encounters, the initial time an endeavor like this is attempted."

"It's not going to take ten years is it?"

"Oh, no, it won't take long at all. Our tunnels and towers have been built all over our country, not simply on one mountain or two."

"I have to admit, I'm simply blown away by all this," Levi admitted.

"You'll not only be helping Israel, but you'll be helping the US to stay safe as well."

"Safe from whom, may I ask?" Levi asked cautiously.

"Safe from all enemies, *domestic* and foreign," Brody said, emphasizing the word domestic. "We live in very scary times, Levi and there are many wolves in sheep's clothing, all around us."

"Yeah, I know," he said and thought about those he feared were presently attempting to destroy the US, from within.

"We have discussed enough for now and you will be filled in more tonight," Brody assured Levi.

"Well, I suppose we better track down the ladies before they max out their credit cards," Levi said and laughed.

"The one good thing about living *underground,* for the most part, is one earns a fabulous amount of money, but has no chance to spend it," Brody said and laughed, again.

Chapter 85

Promptly at 7:00 p.m., Brody and Lynx arrived and simply waited in the Escalade for the couple to climb into the vehicle and hastily sped off into the darkness of the night.

"How long should it take us to arrive?" ZenJa asked. She was more than curious where this mysterious place was. She had lived in the area all her life and like everyone else, had heard the rumors of this mystifying residence, but never knew where it was.

Brody stopped the vehicle at a deserted intersection of the highway and Lynx reached into a designer shopping bag and removed two oversized scarves from inside.

"I hate to ask you to do this, but if we are to continue our journey, we must ask that you place these over your eyes." she said and handed each of their guests a scarf.

"Oh boy! Here's were we get shot!" Levi said nervously.

"If it makes you feel better, I will let you hold my weapon," Brody said.

"Oh, yeah, so it has my finger prints on it?"

"Levi, you really need to stop watching so many cops and robbers on television," Lynx said and laughed, while handing Levi, Brody's Glock after the couple both tied the scarves around the heads.

"I'm confident that trust is a big concern of yours?" Brody asked at the same time Levi took the weapon.

"Yes, if there is no trust, there is nothing."

"I agree, so I trust neither of you can see through those scarves and if you can, please adjust them so you can't," Brody said and noticed neither made an effort or needed to fix their blindfolds.

"We're all set," Levy said and ZenJa agreed and the Escalade sped down the highway toward it's destination.

"These are the scarves you bought this afternoon, aren't they," ZenJa asked and laughed.

"I wanted you to select the ones you liked the best," Lynx said and laughed.

"Oh, good, we get to keep these?" Levi joked, but still remained nervous. "I do hope they match my robe and sandals," he added for good measure.

"You look fine," ZenJa said and held his hand.

An hour later, after driving around in circles, much of the time, as a diversion, the Escalade and it's passengers arrived at it's destination and a helicopter could be heard, landing near by.

"He's right on time," Brody said to his wife at the same time the Escalade was allowed to enter the secure site, before traveling another mile down a paved driveway.

"Please allow us to usher you inside and then you will be able to remove your blindfolds," Lynx said and with the help of her husband, they led the couple inside the vault like entrance of a monestrous estate and entered into something right out of a movie set; a stunning castle from the French countryside.

"Good evening Mr, and Mrs, Black, Miss Beckwith and Mr. Harris," a distinguished man, obviously a butler or door man, said.

"Good evening, sir," Brody replied and Levi noticed he never said the man's name and smiled to himself. Brody Black had done this many times before, it was obvious.

"Please follow me," the handsomely dressed, distinguished silver-haired man said and led the foursome down a long, wide richly furnished, thickly carpeted, hallway that ZenJa and Levi had only seen in theaters.

"I will leave you here," the man said and if you wish to freshen up please be our guests. The power rooms are here," he added and waved his hand to the right.

"Thank you, sir and Lynx and I will take it from here," Brody said.

Neither man needed to use the rest room, so they sat on a lovely antique Queen Ann style sofa, from years long since past.

"Shit! I hope we don't break this," Levi said and once again, laughed nervously. "It does appear to be delicate."

"Let me reassure you, if this does collapse underneath us, I know where there's a duplicate, in the next room, so we can swap them out," Brody said. Both men's laughter filling the massive structure, from one end to the other.

The ladies reentered the hallway and ZenJa asked, "What in Heaven's name are you two laughing at, now?"

"You don't want to know," Brody replied in an effort to keep ZenJa wondering.

"I love nothing more than to hear cheerful laughter in these halls," a male voice was heard from the doorway, at the end of the corridor that led to a massive room that contained a piano, three fireplaces, enough room for a major symphony to be seated comfortably and several more Queen Anne sofas, sporadically placed in group settings.

The handsome, elderly man said, "These are more sturdy than they appear and none of these have ever broken before," he added and looked at Levi.

"I guess you could hear my big mouth all over these great walls, huh?"

"It takes one a while to get used to the echoes in here and as most of the conversations that are held within these great walls, as you call them, are of the strictest confidence, one does learn very quickly how to whisper," the man said and laughed.

"He's only pulling your leg, Levi," Brody assured his friend.

"Please make yourselves comfortable; our other guest is a little behind schedule, but I will have someone bring you some refreshments," the man said and left the room.

"Does anyone have a name, here?" ZenJa asked.

"No!" Both Brody and Lynx replied simultaneously.

"So that was Old Man One and this one was Old Man Two?" Levi whispered

"Yes!" Came the second duplicate response from their hosts.

Shortly after, a tiny elderly lady wheeled in a cart that had an assortment of French Pastries, and bottles of Cognac and wine and a steaming pot of hot coffee and appropriate glassware and antique plates.

The foursome thanked the lady and rose to help themselves to some refreshments and without missing a beat, Brody said, "Yes, that is Old Lady One."

"They have code names like all the president's men," Levi teased.

"I haven't decided what code name I'm going to give you," ZenJa said and chuckled.

"I have an idea."

"Let's simply save that for another time," ZenJa teased.

The couples sat down on two sofas facing each other, savoring the warmth of the fireplace and gazed at the architecture, moldings and paintings.

From the rear of the room, a door opened and two men approached the foursome, who stood to greet their hosts.

"I hope you have made yourselves comfortable and are warm enough?" Noam Krantz, the Israeli soldier who, along with the Deputy Foreign Minister, Daniel Rothschild, had previously met with Brody at the helicopter landing site.

"Yes, thank you," the foursome replied and greeted their hosts.

"My name is Krantz and his gentleman is Rothschild," Krantz simply said, without offering an explanation as to who either of them were, but it was obvious, at least Krantz was Israeli, by his accent.

"It is my deepest pleasure to meet you," Rothschild said, also in an Israeli accent.

"Our main guest has been delayed in New York, but is expected to arrive any moment now," Rothschild said while and Krantz sat down on another sofa, facing their guests.

"I am pleased, with these latest developments and the cooperation you have bestowed on the Blacks and are willing to help save both of our countries, Miss Beckwith and Mr. Harris," Rothschild began. "I won't get ahead of ourselves, but will let our next guest give thanks when he arrives," he added and the sound of a Black Hawk helicopter was heard, through the thickness of the estate walls, that shook the windows, as well.

"While we await his arrival, I imagine you have many questions about this castle-like fortress that is located in New Hampshire."

"We have always heard rumors about such a fortress, and of course, we have wondered where it is and why it is located here?" Levi asked.

"This is essentially an Embassy, of sorts and is used by world wide dignitaries and of course those of the United States for meetings such as this." Rothschild continued.

"So, it is common knowledge, by many people where this site is?" ZenJa asked.

"No, actually that is not a correct assumption," Krantz added.

"There are only five pilots in the world, who have security clearance to bring associates here."

"And the staff you have working here?" ZenJa asked.

"The staff, as you say, actually own this estate," Rothschild said and simply smiled. "They have known where this fortress has been located for hundreds if not thousands of years!"

Levi and ZenJa looked at each other, their eyes nearly bulging from their eye sockets.

"So it is true?" Levi asked, meaning there most likely were decedents of

Christ still alive, but dared not ask.

Brody and Lynx simply remained seated and smiled at each other, thrilled to see the reaction they had from their guests.

"Oh, just in the nick of time," Krantz announced when the door, at the rear of the stately room opened and another gentleman walked toward those already in the room; who immediately clamored to their feet.

"Oh my God!" ZenJa whispered, but her statement echoed within the walls that surrounded them.

"May I present Israeli Prime Minister Benjamin Netanyahu," Rothschild said with a wave of his hand.

"I am not God, but we are pretty good friends," the Prime Minister said and laughed.

"Oh, my, I am delighted to meet you, sir," ZenJa said and stepped forward to shake this man's hand, before Levy, who was also astonished, by this introduction of one of the world's most powerful leaders.

"Prime Minister, this is one of the greatest honors I have ever had," Levi finally was able to say.

Lynx and Brody both stepped forward and hugged and kissed both cheeks of this great man; being the usual custom of Israelis.

"Brody, Lynx, it is so wonderful to see you again," Netanyahu said and was seated before the others.

Shortly after, Old Lady One reentered the vast room and wheeled another cart around and offered more refreshments to everyone who had been seated.

She smiled and walked past ZenJa and Levi...it was not uncommon for people to stare at her, after it being suggested she may be a decedent of Christ. Everyone who was informed of this possibility always searched her face for some likeness to the Holy Father, but then everyone realized no one knew what Christ had actually looked like.

"Again, thank you all for coming, tonight and because I was already in New York on business matters, I felt it wasn't that difficult to alter my plans and meet some new soldiers in our war."

"I'm going to get to the chase and not add more mystery or intrigue to this, than is actually warranted," he continued. "I know Brody has mentioned the towers and underground cables to you, Mr. Harris and I will explain exactly what those towers are going to be used for, other than to power your future development."

"We all know, there are hundreds of satellites in orbit. Some are used for weather related issues, simple internet connections, around the world and the most lethal and frightening modules are those used to hack into banking and financial institutions, power and military grids, and other nations security systems. Others are more dangerous and are used to steal nation's intelligence and hard earned research and development from the military, your Pentagon, National Security Administration, and Department of Defense, much like the agencies we have in Israel."

"The towers we are going to build are only going to be used for means of peace and protecting Israel, and actually the United States, as well. I know it doesn't appear...well, let me say, I know it appears to many Israelis that the United States has drifted away from being one of our strongest allies, and I admit, I have to agree with that. We are in hopes that will change, in the next elections you hold...if we can wait that long."

Both ZenJa and Levi nodded their heads and agreed, much to all the other attendees relief. This couple was so deeply entrenched in the details of the conversation, they were oblivious to the fact, their every move and facial expression was being monitored, much like a laser, targeting a Bradley Tank.

Levi, finally found his voice and said, "This is astounding!"

"To make this as simple as possible," the Prime Minister continued. "These towers and the transmissions they pick up, from the sources programmed into them, from the air, will be transmitted to our towers in Israel. We will be able to detect hackers, into the US systems and our own, on all levels, from banking to military and it will also alert us to all threats of missile attacks about to or that will be taking place anywhere around the world and they are especially designed to detect and destroy any nuclear or dirty bombs that are in flight and heading to a city near you or us," he said truthfully.

"That pretty much sums it up," the man said and rose to get more coffee.

Brody stood up and got himself more coffee and continued, "We are not simply facing threats of terrorism, from radical fundamentalists, in a self-proclaimed *religious* war and I truly believe this is being used as smoke and mirrors for a much larger battle, one of which we are fully aware of, but sometimes seems to get lost in all the chaos that has been, *deliberately*, created, from what I see."

"It's so we miss the bigger picture?" Levi asked.

"Absolutely," Netanyahu confirmed. "I, in no way, wish to minimize the slaughter of thousands of innocent Christians, or any people of religious faith, whatever that might be, or the terror of 9-11, subway and bus bombings all around the world, but those tragedies and now the Ebola scare is claiming more of the headlines, we are forgetting that Iran is building nuclear weapons and our other enemies, like North Korea, China and Russia, all have those weapons that could completely destroy the earth, as we know it!"

"We must be prepared for the worst," Lynx added.

ZenJa and Levi simply sat on the sofa, stunned by the conversation they had listened to, in the last few minutes.

'We can help you make a difference?" Levi asked.

"You can absolutely make a difference, Mr. Harris," the Prime Minister replied.

"You see," the man continued and returned to his seat. "We have no use for your technology, I hate to admit it, but I think we are technologically more advanced than the US and we certainly don't need to hack into the credit card you may have from Home Depot or Macy's or the meager funds US citizens have in their bank accounts," he added and laughed.

"You see, Miss Beckwith, we were unable to explain the real purpose of our deep interest in purchasing that three hundred some-odd acreage from your parents. Your parents were adamant about not selling that land and it was much to risky for us to divulge what we had planned for that area."

"Your parents would have been billionaires," Netanyahu stated.

"There were only two reasons why my parents would never have sold that property. There wasn't enough money in the whole world for them to sell."

"Why was that?" the man asked.

"They feared my sister, her friend and two other missing girls were buried on that property, somewhere and the other reason was, in their hearts they hoped and prayed my sister was alive and would one day come back home. They *never* would have left that property...alive, that is."

The Prime Minister actually wiped a tear from his eye and said, "I would have done the exact same thing and I am sorry for your loss and the fact you have never had any answers. I am so sorry."

"Sir, your helicopter is all refueled and ready to leave, whenever you are," Old Man One, announced from the doorway, at the rear of the room.

Everyone in the room stood up and hugged this brave man thanked him for his time.

"We have much more to discuss and most of that being financial, but I can assure you, the staff you will need for all the ground work, above and below will be covered by our government and that includes whatever underground work you need done for your resort and by the way, you can be assured that all the manual labor needed for this part of your project will be done by our own contractors, from Israel, who are specialists in this type of work. They will simply need accommodations, rental vehicles, for their personal use and help in securing the appropriate equipment to get the job done and as I stated before all these expenses will be covered."

"About how many contractors do you expect to arrive?" Levi asked.

"Not less than twenty," Brody replied.

"Molly is going to be busy," Levi said.

"Molly?" Rothschild asked.

"Molly, is the owner of the best diner in that area and I assure you, she will treat them all, like family. She always does."

"I also know where we can begin to secure logging trucks and skidders," Levi added.

"The Sweeneys?" Brody asked and laughed.

"Yes, Junior nor Ivan won't be in any need of that equipment for a long time."

"What if we used that as a base of the operation, for the contractors?" Brody asked.

"The Sweeney property?" ZenJa asked.

"Why not? There's plenty of room in that farm house and the two guest cottages they have and if need be, we can simply add some more rooms onto the house," Levi suggested.

"Don't we have to purchase that property before we embark on a venture such as that?" ZenJa asked, logically.

"We could do that, or simply put a Federal lien on the property and hold it for as long as we're in need of it," Levy said and laughed.

"This has been a wonderful pleasure, to meet you and I know we'll be in touch. I will forward a secure internet and phone connection, through Brody, where you can reach me at anytime, day or night," the man said to Levi and ZenJa.

"It has been our deepest pleasure to meet you, sir and you gentlemen, as well," Levi said nodding in the direction of Krantz and Rothschild.

"Well, I do have to leave now, but I am pleased with the progress we have made in such a short period of time," Netanyahu said and exited the room.

Krantz, Rothschild and the four guests, two of who were, again, blindfolded, left shortly after the Prime Minister made his exit and climbed into the vehicles they had each arrived in.

Brody turned the engine of the Escalade on and allowed it to warm up for a few minutes before they departed.

"Does the Prime Minister have to wear a blind fold when he arrives and departs," Levi asked and laughed.

"No, I think he has proven he can be trusted, but you, two, on the other hand..." Lynx began.

"I know this was a lot to absorb, all at once, so we'll let it sink in and we can continue with this project in another day or two. I don't want to overwhelm you with all of this. I mean, we're only focusing on the towers and underground, work, you, on the other hand, Levi, have to focus on your resort, so I am hoping by having our crew come on board, that will relieve you of some of those problems," Brody said.

"I can assign Alex to take care of the necessary work that needs to be done on the Sweeney residence, get the proper Federal liens in place, and he can see that the equipment is brought to the site and see what needs to be done to house twenty or more contractors." Levi offered.

"That sounds fine," Brody said.

"I just want to let you know, some of these young contractors are married and their wives will also be with them, not only as wives, but as contractors as well. Our women, as you know, are in our military and are no one to mess with," Brody added as a warning.

"That will help with the housing situation. We all know what happens when men are left to their own devices."

"Just what exactly do you mean by that?" Levi asked.

"I simply mean, the house won't be trashed like it's a college fraternity," she relied sternly.

"Oh, I knew that's what you meant," Levi responded and Brody and Lynx looked at each other and laughed.

After driving around for more than an hour, in a continued effort to confuse their passengers, Brody and Lynx left their guests off at Levi's house and they all retired for the night.

Chapter 86

First thing the next morning, after ZenJa and Levi showered and were sitting down to breakfast, Levi called Alex and asked him to come to the house for an important meeting.

Once Alex arrived and helped himself to left over pancakes, sausage, juice and coffee, Levi and ZenJa give him the complete low-down on the mysterious Blacks, what their plans were and how they had met the Prime Minister of Israel, the previous evening and the operation they were planning, such as it was, at this time.

"You went to the mysterious mansion in New Hampshire?" was Alex's first question.

"Yes, and we were blindfolded, so we have no idea where it's located, I hate to tell you." ZenJa replied.

"So you met Bibi, too?"

"Yes, and what a delightful man he is. It's a shame I admire him more than I do..." Levi began but never bothered to finish his statement.

"So, I'm in charge of the Sweeney aspect of all this?"

"You mean to tell me you're not mesmerized by this plan...this cloak and dagger plot?" Levi asked his brother.

"Oh, indeed, it is brilliant and I'm honored to be trusted to be included in this endeavor. I just don't think the gravity of it has sunk in, yet."

"I'm going to have to contact the FBI, Edward Emerson, about having a federal lien put on the property. Do you know long it will take?"

"The team that are arriving to complete this task are pros and my first guess would be less than a year and I think it will be a lot less than that. I'd just give Emerson, the high end of the spectrum, in case we run into problems."

"Who much information do you want me to divulge to him?"

"Nothing! Absolutely nothing!" Levi warned.

"He isn't going to buy having a lien placed on that property without an explanation," Alex reasoned.

"Let me check something," ZenJa said and ran to retrieve her laptop computer.

"Why what's up?" Levi asked and smiled at ZenJa who knew what had been up, but wouldn't be for a while, anyway.

"I remember when I was looking for foreclosed property, the Sweeney property was about to go into foreclosure, too!" she said cheerfully.

"So where are you going to get the extra cash to buy that place?" Alex asked his brother.

"I omitted to tell you that the Israeli government is paying all the costs for the contractors, towers and underground systems, so that should save us a few cool millions," Levi reasoned.

"I'm going to call my lawyer, Jerry Johnson, and have him see what he can find out about the property and when the sale may be coming up," ZenJa said and went into the living room to make her call.

She came back into the kitchen and sat down before explaining the lawyer would call her back when he had something to report.

While the trio anxiously waited for the phone to ring, they discussed more about the evening's adventures they shared with the Blacks and the others.

Not more than twenty minutes passed and ZenJa's cell phone rang.

"I have good news, ZenJa," Jerry said.

"What is it?"

"The property is going on the auction block this very afternoon, so I suggest I meet you and your other investors by 2:00, this afternoon, so we can take a tour. The auction starts at four."

"Is there any indication of who many others are interested in the property?"

"I know of at least one other party."

"Shit!" ZenJa said.

"If you're interested, I have the name of the inquiring party," he said.

"Who is it?" she cried.

"A man by the last name of Black, that's all I know," the attorney replied.

"You aren't representing him are you?" she asked while Levi and Alex were curious where this conversation was leading.

"No, of course not. I wouldn't be able to represent you and Mr. Black, at the same time."

"Okay, we'll meet you there at two."

"Goodbye ZenJa and see you then."

"So, I assume the property goes up for auction today?" Levi asked.

"Yes, but guess who the other interested party is?"

"Oh, I don't know, Molly?"

"No, a man by the last name of Black!"

"I wonder why he didn't mention anything about it last night?" Levi asked

"I don't know, but I guess we can wait a few more hours to find out," Alex said.

"So why we're waiting, let's go out for lunch and this time I'm paying," Alex offered.

"We just ate," Levi replied.

"I know, so the bill shouldn't be that costly, now should it?"

"You always were a cheap son of a bitch."

"I know and that's why you love me."

"Love isn't the term I would use, but..."

"So are we all taking one vehicle or should we all drive over there?" ZenJa asked.

"Let's each take our own rides. God only knows where the rest of the day will lead us, all."

"Not stuck in the mud, I hope. I can't believe how much the snow has melted and the ground must be free of frost by now," Alex mentioned.

"I know and I was hoping to get started with the logging aspect of this, before now, when the ground was still fairly hard. What a mess this will be now, with those skidders and equipment buried up to their axles, in mud."

"They can handle it," Alex assured his brother with more confidence than he felt, himself.

After a quick lunch at a local café, the trio arrived, followed behind by Jerry Johnson, the attorney and two other vehicles.

"I expected to see the Escalade, but who's in the other car?" Levi asked.

"You were expecting Mr. Black?" Jerry asked.

"I had a suspicion he might show up."

"Well, I will strongly suggest to him this property isn't worth the risk of purchasing it," Jerry said.

Black exited his vehicle and the others, who were unaware of who this second man was, were introduced.

"May I introduce to you Mr. Daniel Rothschild and you know Levi and ZenJa, sir, and this man is Levi's brother Alex Lyons and this is...?"

"This is our attorney, Jerry Johnson," Levi said.

"Glad to meet you all," Rothschild said, not explaining who he was.

"Levi, ZenJa, and Alex, we're surprised to see you here. After our conversation last night, I wasn't aware you knew about this property is being foreclosed on."

"I wasn't until this morning, when ZenJa remembered seeing something about it when she checked other foreclosed properties in the area," Levi said and noticed the corner of Brody's lip raise with a hint of a smile on his face.

"Well, this should be easy," Brody said and laughed.

'Well, the asking price is two million dollars and of course that includes all the property, buildings, and equipment," Jerry mentioned in an effort to discourage this person from buying this property and his losing his commission on it.

"You are the realtor and attorney representing this estate?" Brody asked. "Isn't that a conflict of interests?" he added giving the man a hard time and enjoying every minute of it.

"I have been designated and entrusted with the sale of this property under the terms of the Sweeney's Will and my firm is also representing Junior Sweeney for his legal defense and strictly on a pro bono basis."

"I do trust no one has a problem with that?" he asked.

"No, absolutely not, Levi responded with Brody Black nodding.

"May I have a word with you, Mr. Black?" Levi asked and ushered him away from the onlookers.

"What are you going to do with that property, after we get what we need from it?"

"Like I said, I had no idea you would be here for one thing and Rothschild and I decided it would be cheaper to buy this right out and not involve the Feds."

"I have no problem with that; you obviously have more money at your disposal that I do," Levi said honestly.

"I think the only thing worrying Jerry is his commission." Brody suggested. "He probably thinks Rothschild is my attorney."

"But Jerry is the appointed seller, so he would get the commission no matter who buys it," Levi mentioned.

"So, what do you say?"

"Go ahead and buy it, if you want, Brody. I have enough property of my own to develop, without adding a farm," he said and laughed.

The two men walked back over to the others and Levi said, "Come on folks, Mr. Black has decided he needs this more than we do, so I will leave you with our trusted attorney, Jerry Johnson to seal the deal."

"Thank you Levi and ZenJa," Jerry said and wondered what had just happened. He had never sold a property in less than ten minutes, before.

Chapter 87

Within a week, the contractors, including those who's wives were also contractors, arrived in a caravan of rented mini vans and descended upon the nearly purchased Sweeney Property and Alex began his role, in this part of the project with earnest. He had recently put in for a leave of absence from the ATF.

The first two days, after the contractors arrived, Alex and the group toured the site, adjacent to the Beckwith property, where the majority of the logging had already taken place, by the Sweeney's.

Seth Cohen, the Israeli foreman was impressed with the tree removal that had been underway, when the Sweeney's met their untimely fate and gave Alex an estimated date to complete clearing the lumber and remaining stubs of about two weeks.

"As we finish each portion of the excavation, our other crews can begin digging the trenches that will house the underground piping and wiring," Seth said.

"You're going to dig the tunnels and *then* erect the towers?" Alex asked.

"Yes, it's easier to dig straight through the earth rather than dig around objects," he stated, logically. "And in case we run into trouble, like massive boulders, we can simply blow them out of the way, rather than remove them by blowing up our towers," he added and laughed.

"I can see why you're the expert," Alex said and laughed.

"It's takes years of practice to become good at any task," Seth replied humbly.

"This afternoon, I want to head over to the Sweeney property," Alex began. "And start to bring over the equipment to get started."

"Can you give me a general idea of what's over there?

"There are two skidders, three log trucks...there would have been four, but one had a minor accident," Alex said and laughed before explaining about the truck's demise, over the guard rails and bursting into flames. He omitted the facts of what led up to the accident, though.

"There are also several pieces of earthmoving equipment, including three bulldozers and four backhoes, that I remember."

"That sounds adequate for what little is left to be done; concerning the lumber and hauling it away.

"The majority of the work will then be digging the trenches, laying the piping and threading the various cables and wires."

"How do you thread the pipes? As you go along or all at once?"

"We start from the top and line up the various spools of cable and wiring, above the trenches and as we lay the pipes, we thread the wiring through, as we go along. We make gravity work in our favor."

"I hope those spools are secure!" Alex said and laughed.

"They're lined up on a flatbed trailer, several steel rods running through the center and securely fastened to both ends of the trailer. If that trailer does, fail, well, we'll already have our graves dug," Seth said and howled with laughter.

"I can see you and my brother will get along just fine."

"Why's that?"

"He has a sick sense of humor, just like you do," Alex said and patted the man on the back.

"So what kind of piping do you use? I mean this is New England and the ground shifts all the time, with frost and we even have minor earthquakes around here."

"We use a specially designed plastic pipe that is made in Israel. I don't think Americans or the world, for that matter, gives us enough credit for being industrious. I think the world simply feels all we do is fight."

"You, know, I have to admit it, I would be included in that percentage of clueless people."

"Another safety mechanism that is added to each tower, is a sensor, that alerts the main computer if a wire has been severed or the casing around it has been breeched and exactly where it is, so finding and replacing that section of pipe will be easy."

"Where is that main computer going to be located?" Alex asked out of curiosity

"I can't tell you that," Seth said and simply smiled. "But I can assure you there will be more than one computer system monitoring this project."

"One, I assume one will be several thousand miles from here?" Alex bravely asked.

"One would think so," Seth said and howled with laughter once again.

"Can you tell me where the focus of these towers will be centered around?"

"They are strictly going to be targeting a satellite above us."

"They can see us now?" Alex asked and looked up.

"One never knows, these days," Seth replied coyly.

"Smile for the camera," Alex said and waved toward the cloudless sky overhead.

"It's almost lunch time, I want to take you all out for lunch, at the best café around," Alex offered. "You might as well get to know who two of our great friends are. One is the owner and the other is a hell of a good cook, too."

"Seth blew a whistle and all the contractors came to their meeting point.

"Neat idea!" Alex said and marveled at the simple tools, of yesteryear that were so useful today.

"We're all equipped with whistles, for safety reasons, primarily, and we have certain codes for certain alerts."

"Like an SOS code?"

"Yes, indeed. It makes more sense for us to use a whistle than try to reach in a pocket to grab a cell phone, in case of an emergency. One might not be able to reach their pocket, if they're buried in four feet of dirt," Seth said laughed once again.

"Has that ever happened before?" Alex asked in alarm.

"Only once!" Seth said and howled again, as did all the others who had congregated around them.

The caravan of vehicles drove into Molly's Café just after the normal lunch crowd had departed, so the dining facility was at their disposal."

"It's so good to see you, again Alex!" Molly yelled and ran to greet her customer. "I have a new name for you," she added.

"What just might that me?"

"Nomad! I never see you any more," she wailed.

"I know, but you'll be seeing more of my ugly face than you want, in the next few weeks or years, I'm afraid."

"Why's that?"

"We are starting to develop the former Beckwith property into our dream-come-true town."

"Oh my God! This is wonderful!"

"And these fine people are here to get things started, so I wanted them to feel welcomed and know where the best place to eat, in the area is."

Molly was startled to see twenty people walking inside the café, many of whom appeared to be couples and took seats at the counter.

"These are our new friends and they are here, learning the art of logging and building as guests of the United States," Alex said and looked at Seth who merely smirked and even Alex had to laugh at this insane statement knowing the Israelis have been digging tunnels and building since before Christ.

"Welcome to my café," she greeted them. "We run a very loose ship around here. If you run out of coffee and we're busy, please simply come back here and help yourselves and make yourselves comfortable in the kitchen, too. I sometimes forget to put butter patties with the rolls or Catsup on the tables," she admitted.

"Thank you for your warm greeting," Seth said, speaking for all his crew.

"You're Israeli?" Molly asked.

"Yes, ma'am, we are."

"Welcome to America," she added and placed menus in front of the group and Molly began to fill glasses with iced cold water and place them on trays.

"May we help you with that," Seth's wife, Eliora asked, while she and another woman took a tray and began to serve the water.

"You're a God sent," Molly said.

"That pretty much sums up the meaning of my name, Eliora," the young lady said.

"It is a beautiful name," Molly said and hugged her.

"I won't introduce you to everyone, right now, but my name is Seth and Eliora is my wife. You will get to know everyone, soon," he assured the proprietor.

"What would you folks like?" Molly asked.

"Why don't you simply prepare the day's specials and other assorted items for us all to sample," Seth suggested. "I can assure you, there won't be so many of us barging in on you, all at once, in the future," he said and laughed.

Oscar and Molly disappeared into the kitchen and Eliora and several other ladies went behind the counter and poured more coffee, tea, sodas and milk for the crew while they waited for their meals.

Less than half an hour later, Molly and Oscar brought out several platters that contained nearly every item on the menu and place them strategically along the counter with piles of clean dishes and silverware.

"These meals look delightful," several of the crew said and thanked their hosts.

Molly sat beside Alex, while the customers ate their meals and chatted among themselves.

"I think I'm going to have to hire more help and add on to this building, don't you?"

"I do, now that things will be booming, soon and with all the construction crews who'll be in the area for years to come, no doubt, you'll want to add onto the café. This's what Levi had dreamed of for this town."

"I think I know who I might ask to be a new employee," Molly said.

"Who?" Alex asked.

"Lanny's wife, Carol and actually, their two sons might be old enough to help in the kitchen with dishes, as well."

"Sounds like you have your work cut out for you, too," Alex said and laughed.

"I know and to have this be a cheerful and happy place to live again, will be wonderful. I never thought we could find peace and happiness here after..." she began but neglected to finish.

"I do not mean to overhear your conversation, but I couldn't help it," Seth said, being seated on the stool, on the other side of Alex. "If I may be so bold to ask why there is no happiness or peace in this town?"

Alex went on to describe the events that had destroyed the town over the decades and concluded with, "Levi's girlfriend, ZenJa, who you have yet to meet, is the sister of one of those missing girls."

"Oh my! I am so sorry and will extend our deepest condolences, when we have a chance to meet," Seth said and Eliora nodded.

"Do you think there's a possibility the remains might be buried right there on the Beckwith property or the property, next door, that we will be excavating?" Seth asked. "Sometimes evidence is buried right in front of our own eyes."

Alex knew everyone had suspected the possibility of that being the case but wondered if anyone was brave enough to actually discover the truth and face the reality of that truthfulness.

"We all suspected that, I think, but no one wanted to admit it and I especially think, to this day, ZenJa is hoping she will find her sister, alive."

"Of course, that's completely understandable. She wouldn't be human, if she felt any other way," Eliora assured Alex.

"I'll instruct our crew to treat the sites we're working on, as if we're excavating a possible burial ground. I will only suggest there may have been a cemetery around here at one time. No one needs to know about the mystery that surrounds this town," Seth assured Alex and Molly.

"I know the folks in town and especially ZenJa, will appreciate this." Molly said.

After Alex paid the bill and left a tip he and the crew spent the rest of the afternoon transporting the equipment from the former Sweeney property and locating it were they were about to begin their work, the next day, on the acreage next to Levi's newly acquired land.

Chapter 88

While the excavation was progressing on schedule next door, Levi had several mobile office trailers delivered to the former Beckwith property so he could meet with the architects and road crews who were going to build basic roads for the building contractors to traverse the building site, without being buried in mud, until the ground surface became firm, once spring turned into summer.

And on this day Levi asked Brody, Lynx, ZenJa, Alex and all the other contractors from Israel to celebrate with him. The first important item on the agenda was the Christening of the massive granite stonewall, that enhanced the entrance to the majestic colony, soon to be called home to so many. This rock formation had been laid by several local masons and the evening before this commencement was to take place, a local woodworking craftsman had finished layering the final coats of urethane on the immense solid oak sign, that was highlighted with gold leaf lettering. This was the first completed piece of this enormous project Levi had taken on and with his help, the craftsman mounted the sign and covered it with an enormous velvet covering.

"I'm so glad you all could come for this very special event. You're the people who have and will make my dream come true," Levi began.

"So without further delay, I present to you *'Le Château Napoléon Condominiums & Resort',"* he said and ceremoniously removed the red velvet covering to the delight of everyone standing by for this special occasion. The applause and cheers could have been heard for miles around, if one were in the area to testify.

ZenJa hugged Levi tightly while the thunderous applause continued for several more minutes.

"Congratulations! Everyone shouted and the attendees, walked closer to the stone and oak structure to inspect the detail of the work that had been done.

"This was the easy part," Levi said and took a big sigh of relief. "I guess you know where you'll be able to find me, for the next year or two...right there in those mobile offices," he said and pointed to the right.

"Oh, by the way, you just received a message from the Prime Minister," Brody said and smiled and handed Levi his cell phone.

"How did he know about this? It was a secret."

"I just sent him a picture of this ceremony and he wanted to be the first to congratulate you."

Levi opened the video that had just been sent and turned up the volume so everyone could hear.

"Congratulation, Mr. Harris and all of you who are making this project special in so many ways! God bless you and I wish you much continued success!"

"How cool is that?" Levi asked.

"That is very cool!" Alex said and smiled.

"Okay, if you will excuse us, we have a lot of work to get done today and a schedule to keep," Seth said and smiled.

"Thank you, again, for coming," Levi said.

"While the rest of you are still here, I just wanted to let you know we have received all the necessary permits to begin to build *'Le Château'."*

"I think a celebration is order," Brody announced.

"What do you have in mind?" Levi asked.

"I suggest we have a business luncheon and if you bring the plans and other blue prints we can continue to discuss priorities and get a sense of order with this endeavor. I also suggest you appoint who is in charge of what. I know you have chosen Alex to take are of business over there," he said pointing to the acreage that would house the communication towers.

"Okay, that sounds reasonable," Levy agreed. "And just so we make this perfectly clear, whoever does what and is assigned to whatever, will be on the payroll. We have to get the first priority which is to keep track of every cent we spend and to get every damn tax deduction we can get!" he said and laughed.

"Everyone will have a authorized credit card and trust me, every transaction will be closely monitored and recorded, as I said, for tax purposes and because this will be a business meeting, today, this will be our first business deduction!" Levi said cheerfully.

"I hope we have many such business meetings," Alex replied.

"Where shall we go for lunch?" Levi asked.

"I think we should head over to Molly's and discuss with her, the addition she's going to need for her café and I think, if we assist her, financially, with the renovations, we can at least require a private meeting room, so we don't have to hang out in one of the those trailers, for the next two years," ZenJa suggested and cringed.

"I have to agree with that. I think having a constant supply of food, bathrooms, and running water, and office space will be more than we can ask for until we get our own offices in *'Le Château'*," Levi said and laughed once again.

Brody, Lynx, Alex, ZenJa and Levi arrived at Molly's in the middle of the afternoon, during a lull in the business and the asked Molly to sit with them, as they had their lunches, and discuss plans for her café and their shared office space.

"This is such a wonderful and generous offer," Molly said. "But, I have more than enough money to make the renovations you're talking about. I've been in this business for over forty years and never spent a dime of my profits, so I'm good to go, on my own."

"You're not interested in a partnership, I gather?" Levi asked.

"If I wanted to be in a partnership, Levi, I'd have gotten married, again," she said and howled with laugher.

"Now, before you folks get all involved with...what are you calling your resort?"

"*Le Château Napoléon*," Levi replied.

"Okay, so I'm guessing you would like what few structures we have in Longberry, to compliment a small French town?" Molly asked.

"Exactly!" Levi replied and shoved another onion ring in his mouth.

"It'll almost be like a fairy land," Lynx added, her eyes sparkling at the many ideas she had running through her head.

"And before I forget it, Lanny's wife, Carol and their two sons will start work this weekend," Molly said cheerfully.

"Wonderful!" ZenJa said.

"I'm going to have to hire at least one more cook, I mean chef, to help poor Oscar. He's been running ragged, lately."

ZenJa watched Levi's face and she swore she could see the wheels turning inside his head.

"Don't do anything hasty," Levi said mysteriously. "I may have a temporary solution to this problem."

"Isabella's family?" ZenJa asked and smiled.

"Who better to learn from, than the best?"

"Would you want to ask them to leave Boston to come here?"

"I wouldn't ask them to leave, but you simply have no idea how many cousins, nephews, aunts and uncles Pierre d'Artagnan and Adrianna Vaccarelli have, my dear."

"d'Artagnan?" Lynx asked.

"Yes, the fourth of the Three Musketeers; relatives of course and I can assure you all, that those relatives were born wearing chef's hats and aprons!"

"Would you like me to have my architect draw up some plans, for you to look over and perhaps chose from?" Levi asked Molly.

"That would be wonderful. I don't have time to go running around doing all that and run this café," she admitted.

"I'm thinking, though, of keeping the small time café feel to this place, but adding on a larger dining room to accommodate large functions and parties."

"That sounds like a wonderful start and what about having a large patio for summer functions?" ZenJa suggested. "Nothing better than ribs and corn on the cob from the grill."

"This is exciting," Molly said and rose to wait on several customers who entered the café.

"I'll have the architect stop by when it's convenient for you," Levi hollered.

"Okay, so let's get down to our own business here," Levi said while ZenJa refreshed everyone's beverages and brought over some homemade apple pie.

Levi, once again, spread out the drawings of the structures that were to be built.

"This does look like a French town from yesteryear, and this, the castle, I assume, are the main offices?" Alex asked.

"The castle, as you call it, is appropriately named and yes, a small section of that structure will be our offices, but the majority of this complex will be a grand hotel and dining facility."

"The condos will encompass the rest of the property, in a circular design, much like a fort, so all the condos face the mountains and also have views of the extensive botanical gardens, pools and other sitting areas, from each unit."

"And as you can see, here, there will be a golf course, that will also be visible from each condo and hotel room. The eighteen holes surrounds the exterior of the resort.

"You have given thought to security, I assume?" Brody asked.

"No, I haven't given it much thought," Levi admitted.

"Why not let me take care of that?" Brody offered.

"Okay...that sounds like a great idea. You, obviously have the background for that."

"I'll get right on it and I'll check out plans, we have in Israel, to keep the diplomats and their dwellings secure. I know a great deal of that is done from the towers, electronically, of course and would be manned 24/7 by cameras and actual security on the ground. Trust me they will blend in, so no one is the wiser," he added, before Levi was about to voice is opinion about that.

"Are you interested in becoming a partner, in this business?" Levi asked Lynx.

"I would love to, but not a financial partner and neither Brody or I will be seeking an income for our services, for now anyway. And if I may be so bold, I would love to oversee the interior designs and decorating. I have a fairly good idea of what should be inside this castle and adjacent areas and I know where to find the treasures that should be used and I can get them at a steal," she added and smiled.

"Who's house are you going to pilfer though," Levi laughed.

"It's not a house, but rather a castle or two," she said and chuckled.

"Okay, I think the less we know about your plans, the better off we'll be, Lynx," Alex said for everyone else who was thinking the same thing.

"I do have one question," ZenJa began and looked at Brody and Lynx.

"You appear to be independently wealthy, and that's all well and good, but why was your house foreclosed on...you know, the house I now own?"

"I didn't have time to fuss with any details about the house and it was only a dwelling to reside in, for the time being. I had important issues to take care of," she said without continuing any further with the conversation.

She and Brody were the only ones who knew how close to being kidnaped she had been. Some of Israeli enemies discovered she was an undercover Israeli spy for Mossad, their equivalent, to our CIA, and had been hiding out on Lake Winnipesaukee, the three years before her disappearance.

"Okay, so with that said, my position will be the person who writes the checks and what would you like to do, ZenJa?" Levi asked.

"I would like to be your secretary and accountant and work with the CPA."

"Okay that sounds great and I know I'll need a lot of help with the finances. I do not want any bill to be paid late, but I also will not pay for something I have not purchased or authorized to be purchased. I know you will scan those bills with a fine tooth comb, ZenJa," he added with confidence.

"How are we going to manage deliveries and bills of lading and inventory?" ZenJa asked.

"I think each of us, in our own department, will have to take care of that. I authorize Alex to take care of the shit from his area that will include wiring, fuel for the rigs, and the steel for the towers, once that is delivered, and cement and God only knows what else will be needed and I imagine having Seth help you, also will be a good thing. It's not like you're going to be available for every truck load of shit that gets delivered, but I do insist, I get copies from any delivery at the end of each work day. If not in my hand, I will have a secure drop box for that. And that goes for everyone. All delivery slips must be turned in each day and any credit card receipts, as well."

Chapter 89

The next morning, when Levi stopped by ZenJa's house for breakfast, he told her he had been in contact with Keith, Darlene and his family, that included Darcy and asked them if they had made a decision about moving this business up north.

"What did he say?" ZenJa asked and placed a plate of bacon, eggs, toast and butter in front of Levi and poured them both cups of coffee and orange juice.

"He said his business, in Virginia hadn't worked out, like he hoped and Darlene was still working at the donut shop and of course that meant Darcy has to babysit for the children."

"So, if they had some financial help, for moving expenses, they would be willing to pull up stakes and relocate?"

"I think so. Of course he never suggested needing any help to move."

"How difficult do you think it will be for him to sell his garage and their house?" ZenJa asked.

"Actually, he said someone approached him, the other day and wanted to buy him out and some other nearby property for a strip mall. And he actually said he was being offered twice what he paid for the property, three years ago."

"That's awesome!"

"I stopped by Jim Bacon's garage, the other day, also and he said he would welcome more qualified mechanics to help him out and he also suggested he was thinking of retiring, so maybe Keith can buy him out and expand,' Levi said. "And I also made another call, this morning."

"Who did you call?"

"You remember, my personal nurse, Abby Patten and her firefighter husband, Owen and children, Rick and Dominic?"

"Yes, I remember," ZenJa said and was unable to hide the fact she had been jealous of that woman, at one time.

"I told him how we need more members of the fire department, here in Longberry and how I hoped to make them full time positions with pay and benefits and not simply volunteer. So he said he would be willing to check out our plans and at least volunteer until he decided if he wanted to make a permanent change and it's not like they live that far away and won't have to relocate."

"That's sounds wonderful. You're now going to be the chairman of the

Chamber of Commerce and Welcome Wagon?" ZenJa asked and laughed.

"We need to start bringing in more population to what will be a peaceful, but friendly community. We need trusted people to live here in our growing community. We'll need people in the service industry, store keepers, medical facilities, a Post Office, I suppose, bigger schools...well you get my drift!"

"We still don't have a police chief or any officers," ZenJa reminded him.

"I know and I've been thinking about asking Brian Miller to come back. Now that the town isn't going to be some rinky dink, off the map location, any longer, maybe we can convince him to come home."

"Why would he want to quit working for your agency?" ZenJa asked in hopes of tricking Levi to tell her what agency he actually worked for. After all this time, she still didn't know he and Alex worked for the ATF.

"ZenJa, my dear, Miller works for the FBI, if I'm not mistaken, that was *your* agency," Levi said and laughed and got up from the table and put his dishes in the sink.

"Are you ever going to tell me who you work for?"

"Do you have any reason to know who I *worked* for?" he corrected her.

"Will you ever tell me?"

"If and when we get married, maybe."

Later that afternoon Levi did call Brian and much to his surprise, the former Police Chief of Longberry, said he was disillusioned with the inner workings of the FBI and actually disliked taking orders, so he agreed to meet with Levi and the town fathers the following day, when he was in town on some personal business. That business included putting his mother's house up for sale with a local realtor.

.

Bright and early the next day, Brian, Levi and several town fathers and selectmen met in hopes of convincing Brian to, once again, be the police chief of their fine town.

"If you do accept this offer, Brian, are you sure you want to sell your mother's property right now?" one of the officials asked.

"Why not?"

"Because, I know this may sound like insider trading, but I think that property will be worth a lot more than it is today, in another year or two because of '*Le Château Napoléan*.'"

"And if you're coming back here to live, Brian, you're going to need a place to live," another selectman reminded him.

"You all have certainly made good arguments, I do agree," Brian said and stood up and paced the floor.

"What do you say?" Levi asked with his fingers crossed.

"Okay! I accept your offer," Brian said and shook hands, all around.

"We haven't discussed money or getting you more help," Levi said.

"I was happy with what I earned before."

"Yes, but you're going to be charge of a whole new world out there. This place will be booming in no time!" Levi reminded him.

"Well, let's not go overboard here," one of the town fathers said.

"Let's say, I put you on our payroll, until we start getting some tax revue from the rich and famous," Levi offered. "Every employee I have on my rolls, is another tax deduction for me," he added and laughed. "You can have the same insurance all our other employees have, as well."

"You drive a hard bargain," Brian said and laughed knowing that was the farthest thing from the truth.

"Okay, so let's drive over to my new development and I'll show you around," Levi said.

"I'll be right behind you," Brian said, and both men climbed into the separate vehicles.

Chapter 90

"I'll take you to the adjacent property, after I give you a tour of what we've done so far, here," Levi told Brian.

"I love the granite stone wall and sign. It's very, how do you say, ritzy?" Brian asked using a pitiful French accent.

"I guess that describes it, okay."

"So the structure and surrounding land will be raised, off from the main road?"

"As most of this property is already steep, we figured it best to simply decrease the upper mountainside, to about half it's present height and use that earth and stone to fill in the lower portion of the property and level this whole thing off. All we'll need is a long winding road, from the main highway to access our own Heaven on earth. It will appear to be secluded from the rest of the world."

"I have an idea those words will be part of your advertising campaign and strategy Brian asked.

"Indeed, it will be."

"Over here we're planning..." Levi began and before he could continue, these two men heard several loud whistles off in the distance.

"Shit!" Levi yelled.

"What's that?" Brian asked.

"Get in your car and follow me," Levi ordered while the two men raced toward the communication and cell towers, being erected, farther down the highway.

Both vehicles sped into the dusty roadway and climbed out of their vehicles where the Israeli construction workers had all assembled and Alex, his face ashen, the color of ice cold clay, slowly walked toward them.

"What the fuck's wrong?" Levi demanded. He had been unable to determine why there appeared to be this emergency and his brother looked like he was about to vomit, but walked slowly toward them.

"I think we may have found...Zippy and Olive. The other girls, Ashley Winters and Rose-Ann Olsen, may very well be buried here, too!" Alex said.

"Oh, fuck me!" Levi said.

"If I may, please step back, everyone. I'm Police Chief Brian Miller and I will take over," he said without a moments hesitation.

The Israeli crew quietly stood back while Brian, Levi and Alex returned to the area where at least two skeletal remains had just been unearthed.

While Alex wiped the tears from his face he quietly dismissed the crew for the next day or so.

"If my crew and I can be of any help, please let us know," Seth said. "We've dug up more burial sites than we care to remember."

"Thank you and I know this goes without saying, but this is a personal matter, no doubt, and please ask the crew not to discuss this, except amongst themselves," Alex said.

"I'll call you later, Seth."

The Israeli's left for the day while Alex, Levi, and Brian examined what was visible, from above ground; not touching anything.

"Are we going to have to notify, Emerson and the FBI?" Alex asked.

"I have no friggin idea who has jurisdiction, at this point," Levi admitted.

"I think out of respect, after all the work they did, involving these missing girls, he should be notified," Brian said.

"While he's here, you can tell him you're the new Police Chief of Longberry," Levi said without smiling.

"I will," Brian said soberly.

Levi walked closer to the burial pit and made a mental note of what articles, other than skeletal remains were obvious from that vantage point.

While Brian was on his cell phone with Emerson, Levi said, barely loud enough to be heard, "I don't remember if ZenJa ever said what Zippy was wearing the last day...anyone saw her."

"I actually saw both Zippy and Olive, if you remember. I was giving them shit about how pretty they would be, one day," Alex recalled.

"Yeah, like Bob Connors said, "They only look for the pretty ones."

"Of course they went missing a day or two after I saw them, but oh, shit!"

"What?" Levi asked.

"That backpack is the one Zippy was lugging with her. I remember it like it was yesterday," he replied much like a wounded animal might.

"There's another purse or something, over there,' Levi said.

"That was the purse Olive opened to swipe some napkins, from the container, on the counter, after they finished mixing the sugar with the salt."

"We have to tell ZenJa and the Pickerings," Alex said.

"We should wait until these bodies have been positively identified, I think," Levi said.

"You don't want to tell ZenJa the bad news, do you?" Alex asked.

"No I don't. I'd do anything not to have to tell her."

After making his phone call, Brian took a large white sheet from the trunk of his car and covered the opening in the earth that held secrets from so many, long years ago.

Five minutes later, Brody drove up and wondered what all the commotion was.

"I just passed the crew and they were heading home. What's up"

"I think we found at least two bodies, buried here," Levi said.

"Shit! The missing girls?"

"I think so. God only knows, there may be more, if not here, around here somewhere. Seth and his crew just found the skeletal remains," Levy added.

"You think one of these remains may be of ZenJa's sister?"

"I think so, from what we could see of a backpack that Alex said he remembered seeing her carrying two days before she went missing."

"The FBI are on their way," Brian said after he was introduced to Brody and informed the man that he was the current Police Chief of Longberry.

The only information Brian was given, regarding the identity of Brody Black, was that he was in charge of security of this property, that would house the communication towers and *'The Château Napoléan'*.

"Do you want me to have Lynx call ZenJa and pick her up, to bring her here?" Brody asked.

"If you wouldn't mind. I think she'd be a big comfort to her. I know they've become steadfast friends."

"Do you want me to call Lynx first?"

"Yes, I guess you better, but have Lynx call you, when she gets a mile or two away from my house. That's where ZenJa is and I don't want her to have enough time to climb in her car and drive over here, by herself. I'll call her after Lynx calls you."

"I'm on it," Brody said.

Lynx and ZenJa arrived at the site at the same time a helicopter landed with FBI Agent Emerson, two special agents, and Deidre Roberts, on board.

Ms. Roberts, was the FBI forensic pathologist who previously investigated the accident scene where Tony and Ann Beckwith crashed and found the remains of Constance O'Leary and Morgan Childress on Blackberry

Road. Deidre offered her assistance when Emerson told her of the events that had just unfolded. She was familiar with the surrounding area, and the details that had haunted that town for so many years. To her, this was similar to an unfinished book that needed to have a final chapter written and she hoped to be the one to do it.

ZenJa slowly walked toward Levi in a zombie-like state and simply asked to have the white sheet removed.

Brian carefully withdrew the covering and ZenJa looked down and without any emotion, she quickly identified the yellow and black plaid backpack and matching plaid jacket that laid on top of the skeleton.

"Those are Zippy's and I don't know who's purse that is. It is not hers," she said and walked away with Levi supporting her.

"I need to get out of here!" ZenJa cried and climbed inside the Camaro.

Levi got behind the wheel and the couple simply sped away with no destination in mind.

"I am so sorry, ZenJa. I truly am," Levi said and handed her his handkerchief.

"I can't explain it, but as sick as this sounds, I feel relief to know she isn't suffering and hasn't been all this time. There's nothing worse than not knowing where a loved one is. You want them to be alive, but you don't want them to be living if they're being beaten and tortured, so you'd rather know they are at peace."

"That makes complete sense," Levi reasoned.

"Can we go visit your childhood favorite place, in the White Mountains?" ZenJa asked. "I want that to be our favorite place, now."

"Your wish is my command, Miss," Levi said and the couple traveled a majority of the way in silence, each grappling with their own thoughts.

"Once the remains are identified, do you want to go with Brian to let Olive's parents know...if she is indeed one of the victims there."

"Yes, I would and do you have any idea how many victims may be there?"

"At least two. I'm not sure if there are more or not, yet."

"I hope we also find Ashley and Rose-Ann and let this nightmare end, once and for all," ZenJa said.

Chapter 91

A week after the remains had been removed from the property, adjacent to *'Le Château Napoléan'*; the medical examiner, in Concord, New Hampshire positively identified the remains belonging to Zippy, Olive, Rose-Ann and her friend Ashley.

This completed the investigation into any reported disappearances in the area and Police Chief Brian Miller, Levi, and ZenJa were those who notified the parents. This inquest had been done under the radar and no media outlets were aware the DNA tests were being conducted or that the remains had been found. It had been unnecessary to get DNA samples from the families involved; those samples had been obtained years ago.

Funerals were held and the families decided to bury their loved ones, side by side. They have been together for more than five years and Rose-Ann and Ashley had been buried together for more than fourteen years.

After the towns-folk gathered for the funeral, they congregated at one of the larger church reception halls, that was needed to accommodate everyone who wanted to pay their respects.

Two days after the funerals Brody reminded Levi he wanted to meet Ivan Sweeney.

"Why do you want to meet him?" Levi asked. "He'll be going on trial in another month or so."

"Are you sure the authorities have enough solid evidence against him?"

"What makes you think they don't?" Levi asked with great interest.

"Oh! I'm not, I just wanted to let you know, if there's any doubt, we in Israel, have methods that make people admit to their wrong doings," Brody said and laughed.

"What do you have in mind?"

"Just simple psychological warfare; nothing torturous," he added and laughed even louder.

"Does Ivan know the remains have been found?" Brody asked.

"No! Absolutely not!"

"Well, that's perfect."

"For what?"

"I'm going to convince Ivan I'm going to help him escape and he'll actually be free for a short period of time. Simply long enough to lead me to the burial site."

"But the burial site no longer exists."

"Yes, but you just said Ivan doesn't know that and I'm going to convince him you folks are digging around on that property, which we are, and have him lead to the site and assure him I'll help him dig up the skeletal remains before they're found."

"How do you know he'll take the bait?"

"I'm going to assure him of safe passage to Israel, to work for our intelligence over there. I will actually have a fake passport with his name and picture on it, drivers licenses and all the other necessary papers he'd need, but in another name."

"Who's ID's will he be using?" Levi asked and smiled.

"Some of my old ones, I have lurking around."

"In the brief case?"

"Yes, in the brief case."

"I'm not going to be the one who can introduce you, though. He knows I...well, he must know I had something to do with the demise of the former Police Chief Bob Connors while he was in jail," Levi admitted.

"What if I pretend to be a new guard at the jail?"

"How long do you think it would take to gain his confidence?" Levi asked. "I mean, you have to have some sort of motive for helping him."

"What if I told him I have purchased the Sweeney property, which I have...well, our government has, and tell him I found a million dollars in the wall boards, or something and am willing to give it to him to make his get away?"

"Just being the devil's advocate here, but why would you give him the money?"

"Because I know it's drug money and I don't deal with that shit...after the death of my beloved wife, by the drug cartel...or some such shit! He might buy that story line."

"But if you're a jail guard, you obviously couldn't afford to purchased the Sweeney Property...think about it." Levy replied logically.

"Okay, well, I'll just be the purchaser of the property, a rich dude and gain his trust that way. What does he have to lose? If he's found guilty he'll never see the light of day again, anyway."

"Okay, I have connections in the jail and you and I'll get you inside to meet the bastard and I'll be watching from a two way mirror."

"When do you want to get started?"

"Visiting days are tomorrow and Friday."

"Let's make a date for tomorrow, then. No time to waste. I won't approach him with the escape plan yet, but after a few meetings, we can get down the business." Brody said.

"Why are you taking such an interest in this?" Levi asked.

"I have a thing about young girls and boys, for that matter, being murdered. My wife and I have seen too many in our careers."

"Seeing Ivan tomorrow, will give me some time to decide what route to take with that bastard. Lynx and I can come up with something," Brody assured Levi. "I'll play it by ear."

Chapter 92

"We're here to see Ivan Sweeney," Levi said and both he and Brody produced their identification, after they entered the Center Street Jail.

"Only one visitor is allowed at a time," the guard said.

"I'll go first, then," Brody said and received his seating number card and was ushered into the enclosed visiting area.

Levi made his way toward the next room where there was a two way mirror to get a visual on Ivan. As promised, the door was unlocked and Levi quickly entered and closed the door behind him.

Five minutes later, Ivan was ushered behind the bulletproof glass and removed the telephone, like Brody had done, on his side of the partition.

"Who are you?" Ivan asked. "You're not on my visitors list!" he snarled.

"I'm the man who recently bought Wilbur and Lily's property," he said truthfully.

"So, what's that got to do with me?" Ivan retorted.

Brody knew he had promised to go slow with this creature, but Brody had found out Ivan's trial date of coming up soon, and once that happened, his lawyer would have to be given the results of the autopsies and the cat would be out of the bag and Ivan would simply deny any involvement.

"Well, there are several things that concern you," Brody continued, his eyes, dark like pieces of coal.

"Like what?" he barked.

"Do you want the good news first or the bad?" Brody asked, toying with the psyche of the inmate.

"The good news!" Ivan replied and his face brightening into a smile.

"While I was tearing apart the attic, I found a whole lot of cash buried in the walls and floorboards. It appears your aunt and uncle had been holding out on you," he added to rile this man up even more.

"Those, no good..." Ivan began, but abruptly stopped speaking and added, "I have no idea what you're talking about."

"Oh, okay," Brody said and started to stand, from his seated position on the metal stool.

"Wait!" Ivan yelled.

"How much money are you talking about?" Ivan whispered.

"There's over one million dollars there."

"Why aren't you keeping it?' Ivan asked, as Brody expected.

"I know what you and your family were into, and a little bit more, if you get my drift and I don't need or want any dirty drug money."

"Why not turn it over to the Feds?"

"Because I want something from you."

"Like what?" Ivan asked suspiciously.

"Not so fast," Brody replied, adding to the inmate's stress level.

"Before I tell you what kind of deal I have for you, I must alert you to the fact that the Beckwith Property has recently been sold and the new owner is going to develop it in a luxury resort and condominium complex."

"So, what's that to me?"

"The adjacent acreage was also sold and I bought that property and my crew has begun excavating it and we're going to erect communication towers on that site."

"Again, so what that's to me?" Ivan asked, but his eyes were flickering back and forth, Brody quickly noticed. This Israeli intelligence operator had interviewed many degenerates in his lifetime and knew the signs...he was getting to this man and it wasn't going to be long before he broke him.

The guard came to the visiting area and announced visiting hours were over.

"Well, I guess we're all done," Brody said and stood, still holding the telephone in his hand.

"Visiting hours are again on Friday, can you come back?" Ivan pleaded.

"I have to be out of town," Brody replied jerking this depraved individual around, for the sake of his own warped sense of humor.

"Please, I need to talk to you," he said and the guard removed the phone from Ivan's hand and led him away.

Levi and Brody met at the front door and while they walked away the, guard hollered after them, "See you Friday!"

When the duo sped from the parking lot, driving towards the nearest bar, Levi said, "You're one hot shit!"

Once the men were seated in a quiet corner of a local bar, Levi said, "You know that this is going to amount to entrapment, don't you?"

"Official authorities are the only law enforcement folks who can be accused of entrapment. You and I are merely civilians, at the point and we're not investigating these crimes."

"I was at one time," Levi admitted.

"Lynx and I were studying your laws and it strictly says any person who is *not* a vehicle of the government or law enforcement, can not be charged with entrapment. At this time neither you, Alex or I are investigating this matter and the law also states that the person who will claim the defense of entrapment, which he will, can only be free of those charges if the alleged criminal would not be predisposed to committing that crime, all on his own, given the means to do so."

"So you're saying if Ivan were given the opportunity to have a million dollars in his greedy bloody hands, he'd run the risk of escape?"

"Wouldn't you, knowing you'd never see the light of day, again?" Brody asked needlessly.

"So this plan *we* have, no one is the wiser?" Levi asked.

"Nope...just you and me and Lynx, of course."

"If we get him to escape and lead us to the now empty grave site, how can we get the authorities there to arrest him, before he takes off? I mean we want the authorities there to witness his disclosing the site, don't we, and by informing the cops to come to that certain place, at a certain time, that will be considered entrapment!"

"You're really concerned about that entrapment thing, aren't you?" Brody asked.

"Hell yes, I don't want that bastard to walk on some technicality."

"So what do you suggest?" Brody asked.

"The only other way we can get him to tell us where the burial site is, is verbally, while he's still incarcerated," Levi said thoughtfully. "As crazy as this sounds, I really don't want the bastard to be charged with escaping."

"You Americans are really so soft hearted," Brody said and smiled and that's why I like you."

"Were you just testing me?" Levi asked angrily.

"Let's have another round," Brody simply said without replying to the question.

Chapter 93

The clouds broke and a beautiful spring day surrounded the entire state of New Hampshire.

Levi and Brody, once again, walked into the Center City Jail, identified themselves and as before, Levi went into an adjoining room, to observe the exchange between Brody and Ivan.

"I didn't think you were coming!" Ivan nervously.

"I told you, on my last visit, I had things to do on Friday, last week. I didn't say I had anything to do, this Friday," he added and laughed after which Brody simply sat on the stool and held the phone up to his ear, but remained silent.

Brody and Lynx spent the last two days wrestling with how to proceed, volleying ideas off each other, but Brody still wasn't sure how he wanted to handle this.

"What's the matter?" Ivan asked after several more moments of silence.

"I'm trying to decide whether to be an honest man, for once in my life," Brody began.

Levi listened and grew nervous and wondered what was about to take place and he didn't like it one bit. "What the fuck are you doing?" he yelled inside the soundproof room.

After another pause, Brody began to speak. "You do know you're going to be convicted of the kidnaping and murders of Zippy, Olive, Rose-Ann and Ashley, don't you?" he asked point blank.

The shock on Ivan's face was indescribable. No one had ever come right out and told him he was going to be convicted of those crimes, which he knew he had committed.

"You're crazy. I had nothing to do with those...girls!" he screamed.

"I told you we were excavating the property adjacent to the Beckwith Estate, didn't I?"

"Yes, but...!"

"You do remember, the last time you saw, Zippy, she was wearing a yellow and black plaid jacket and matching back pack, don't you?" Brody said stared, like the devil, into the eyes of this horrendous piece of flesh who sat before him.

"I don't know any such thing," Ivan said, his eyes darting all over the room, appearing to be seeking a means of escape.

"Ivan make it easy on yourself. Give it up. Aren't you hoping to get a good night's sleep sometime in your life?"

"I don't know what you're talking about," he said and looked down.

Brody assumed he had just wet himself, but continued. "I know it was you," Brody whispered, in a hoarse whisper only liken to the devil himself.

"How could you know it was me?" Ivan said; tears forming in his eyes.

"How do I know it was you?" Brody, again whispered.

"Because Zippy had a handful of your fucking hair in her hands when you buried her, you mother fucking bastard!" he yelled so loudly the alarms sounded.

Ivan vomited all over the table and phone that he still had in his hands, at the same time Brody stood up and walked away.

Levi left the adjacent room and sat down on a bench and held his head in his hands and cried like he had when his wife had died.

Brody sat down beside him, while a wrestling match ensued from the confines of the jail. Ivan Sweeney, being combative as he was, was soon forced back into his cell, still wearing his filthy clothes.

"You ought to smell really good by tomorrow!" one guard yelled and laughed.

On the way out of the Center Street Jail, the attending guard gave the two gentlemen the thumbs up sign and watched them leave the parking lot, once again.

Levi climbed into the Escalade, Brody had driven them in, to the jail and said, "There was no hair in Zippy's hands."

"He doesn't know that, now does he and what am I going to be charged with, lying to a criminal?" Brody replied and laughed.

Ivan's trial only lasted one week. He pled guilty to kidnaping and 1st degree murder of the four young girls, but he only did so with the guarantee that the death penalty would be off the table.

Other than the fact he made the mistake of believing his hair had been found in the hands of one of his victims, the prosecutor mentioned one other thing to Ivan, during his trial.

"Mr. Sweeney," the prosecutor began, using extremely unethical tactics to unnerve the defendant. "You were led to believe a weapon and some of your DNA was found along with the skeletal remains of four of our victims, is that correct?"

Ivan was stunned by the question. He had never heard about any weapon being found with the bodies.

"That's a lie! There was no gun buried there...I hid it...!" he began and realized he had signed his own sentence to prison, most likely for the rest of his life.

"Objection!" the defense cried.

"The prosecutor is lying to my client. That is a bold face lie!"

"Oh, I am sorry. You are correct. It appears there is a typo in this report. The weapon was *not* at the grave site, but if you would please continue with your reply...where *did* you hide it? Come on, Mr. Sweeney, we all know where you hid it, now don't we?"

"I don't know what you're talking about!" he lied.

"You broke into the Beckwith home, removed a picture of a horse, from Zippy Beckwith's wall, removed some of the plaster, and hid it in the wall, and then replaced the picture, didn't you. And not only that, your high school ring, with your initials and DNA on it was also found behind that wall!" the prosecutor screamed at the defendant.

"This weapon and ring were placed inside that wall, after the girls were buried. These pieces of evidence might not have been found, if you had been a little more tidy and cleaned up the pieces of plaster you left on the floor!" he continued to growl, while the court room erupted in chaos by the families of those who had their children taken away from them, by this animal and two other murderers.

With the testimony, given by Junior, against Ivan Sweeney, Junior was only sentenced to five years in prison for his actions in connection with the weapons running scheme and would be released early, for good behavior.

After more than ten years of heart ache and pain for the families of the victims and the residents of Longberry, this case was solved and all the perpetrators had either paid the price, with their lives, or as in Ivan's case, he would spend the rest of his life behind bars.

To the relief of all the families and residents of Longberry, their town was now going to be able to move on and heal.

The day after the trial was over, the Blacks, ZenJa and Levi walked back to the site where the bodies had been found.

"I don't know how you feel about having these communication towers placed over this site, especially this one tower," Brody said and touched the structure that had been placed over the actual burial place."

"As odd as this may sound, I feel comforted to know this spot is being protected from Heaven and the satellites above and there is a connection with this spot to Israel and the people of God," ZenJa said and began to cry.

"Your sister and her friends couldn't have a bigger and more honorable structure dedicated to them, than this," Brody said. "We and our small group of trusted comrades are the only ones who know the true significance of this site."

"Thank you, God, for this," was all ZenJa could say and touched the tower and placed a simple rose underneath it.

Epilogue

Two years had passed since the first shovel of dirt had been moved on *'Le Château Napoléan'* resort complex and condominiums, that were bordered by an exclusive golf course, tennis courts and several Olympic-sized pools, and nature paths.

Henri and his wife Margaux de Montesquiou were the first couple to reside in this luxury castle, of sorts.

The second owners of lavish accommodations were Brody and Lynx Black, who had found the secure hideaway they had been seeking for years.

Though Brody's continued assignments, for the Israeli government, took him away from home for months at a time, he was relieved not to have to be concerned about his wife's safety and she and ZenJa had bonded closer than friends, more like the sisters, they needed in their lives.

The communication towers had long since been completed and were operating with no failures in the slightest, and the Israeli crew were working on another project and as usual, in another part of the world and again no one was privileged to that information.

After the towers had been functioning for more than six months, one of the first guests to arrive and spend more than a week, vacationing at *'Le Château Napoléan'*, was the Israeli Prime Minister Benjamin (Bibi) Netanyahu and his lovely wife, to inspect the work that had been done and accounting for the money their government had spent on this project.

They were given a grand tour and a demonstration of the operation from the towers through the bowels of *'Le Château'* and with confidence the signals were beaming to and from the Heavens above and beyond.

Their evenings were spent dining and dancing in the company of Levi, ZenJa, Brody, Lynx, and Alex and his new wife, Darcy Harris.

On their last day in New Hampshire, the Prime Minister and his wife were going to join the NASCAR Nation at New Hampshire Motor Speedway for the September race in a deluxe suite above the start/finish line.

"Did you see the looks those pilots and team owners just gave us?" Alex asked, like a kid in a candy store.

"We just blew their helicopters off the tarmac," Brody said and laughed, after the Israeli piloted Black Hawk landed and the occupants were quickly escorted from the landing zone and were ushered into a deluxe suite high above the racetrack.

"This sure beats sitting in traffic for five hours, doesn't it?" Darcy asked.

"Now, this is what I'm talking about!" Alex cheered and entered the suite that was complete with two chefs and a full wait staff.

"What, this isn't as good as the first time you took us here?" Levi asked.

"Not by a long shot!" he said and described their first outing, to the newbies to NASCAR Racing, and how naive Levi and ZenJa had been. "They didn't even have racing tee shirts or ball caps!" he informed the Israeli Prime Minister and his wife.

"My wife and I don't have any either," Bibi said and laughed.

"Oh, yes you do," Levi said and handed the couple Tony Stewart and Dale Junior outfits.

"Who said they like Tony and Junior?" Alex asked and laughed.

"We do!" ZenJa said and helped the couple into their shirts and hats.

"We're new to this, too, so don't feel alone," Brody said to Bibi, speaking of himself and his wife.

"And we have tee shirts and hats for you, as well," ZenJa began.

"Oh, no you don't!" Alex retorted.

"What are you complaining about? We haven't even shown you what we picked out for them, yet!" ZenJa said.

"What are they?" Darcy asked accusingly.

"We chose Jeff Gordon and Jimmie Johnson, if that makes you happy!"

"Oh. okay," Alex conceited.

"Are you happy now?" Levi asked and laughed.

"Well, the race isn't going to start for another hour, so let's all grab something to eat!" Alex said, not replying to Levi's question.

The next morning, the Israeli couple were whisked away from the helipad, that was located on the south lawn of the resort, again in the Black Hawk helicopter, but only after tearful farewells and promises to visit each other's countries whenever possible, the allies bid each other goodbye and God's blessings.

Keith and his family came north, after the resort was finished, for

Darcy and Alex's impending wedding and never left.

Keith and his family had moved into the house ZenJa once owned when she arrived on Lake Winnipesaukee. She and Levi stopped fighting and arguing long enough to move into his house, together.

Keith and Jim Bacon joined a partnership and were building a whole new six bay garage /service center and gas station in the center of Longerry and with a little financial help from friends, Darlene was able to stay home and take care of her children, when the garage started making a profit, which it did, in no time.

Alex was now in charge of the security team at the communications site and the resort with a team who had been specially trained by Brody and Alex, themselves.

After the simple wedding ceremony, six months after the resort opened, the newly weds, Alex and Darcy, decided to wait and have children and not rush into parenthood so they could enjoy traveling, when time allowed, to as many NASCAR races as they could, during the long season; the longest of any sport.

Molly's Café had expanded, thanks to some local architects and builders who designed the interior and patio in a French theme, with quaint coach lanterns at each heavy oak booth and tables that had throne-like seating for each customer.

The theme of the patio was of a sidewalk café on the streets of Paris, complete with a miniature version of the Eiffel Tower in the center.

As promised, Isabella's grandmother, Adrianna Vaccarelli and Isabella's father, Pierre d'Artagnan 'volunteered' the services of many cousins, nieces and nephews to help train Oscar and several new chefs to make Molly's a dining experience this town had never seen before.

And when the cousins and other relatives were not helping at Molly's they were full time employees of the luxurious dinning establishment, inside *'Le Château Napoléan'*, which was named *Le D'Artagnan de la Gascorgne Restaurant,* after the famous Musketeer, Charles de Batz-Castlemore d'Artagnan of Gascony, France.

The six bay fire station, complete with full kitchen and sleeping quarters had been built and Owen Patten had been elected fire chief and the remaining fire fighters, John, Marcus, Chris, and Mike were also made full time associates of the department. Wednesday evenings were the highlight of the department when weekly games of Bingo were played, to raise funds for *The Santa Claus Club* and on many other occasions the department held turkey and ham raffles and along with summer balloon festivals, with local charity organizations, being the beneficiaries.

    Two new schools were built, adjacent to the new River View Gymnasium that had been built after the former Police Chief Bob Connors actions demolished the existing one, years before. The town voted to combine the middle school and high school onto one campus and that new facility was named *The Beckwith Charter Memorial School* and the other was named *The Musketeers Elementary School*. This community now had a solid foundation to build on and everyone was united and would have each other's backs, as did the Musketeers of ages long past.

    These schools were built like fortresses to assimilate French castles, to blend in with the theme of the town, but in reality they were as secure as Fort Knox and intended that way, for the safety of the children and teachers.

    Neither Levi or ZenJa had intentions of getting married, any time soon; they both agreed, they loved each other, but admitted they were so much alike, they had no desire to press the issue, with legal documents, that forced them to stay together.

    If and when the subject of marriage ever arose, by either party, the other would simply play the Ted Nugent song, '*Stranglehold*' and that cleared the air, for the time being with things settling back to normal and common sense.

    Two lingering questions ZenJa had and Levi never answered were what federal agency he had worked for and what the real story behind Levi's and Alex's mother's death had been.

    "I know you'll never tell me who you worked for, in the government, but are you ever going to tell me about how Alex's and your mother really died?

    "Those are deep family secrets and even Darcy doesn't know and she's married to Alex, so I guess until we're married and even, then, I doubt it," Levi said harshly.

    Levi noticed the hurt expression on ZenJa's face and decided to add, "

Let me put it to you this way. If you want to know what happened to our mother, you'll have to ask Alex. If he tells you, that's his business!"

"So, you're saying he knows more about her death than you do or was responsible, in some way?" she continued to badger Levi.

Levi simply walked out the door of his lovely home, without responding and almost knocked Alex, to the ground.

Alex entered Levy's home and asked abruptly, "I overheard your conversation with my brother and understand you have some question about our mother's death?"

"I'm sorry and I know it's none of my business," ZenJa said and brought a fresh cup of coffee to the breakfast bar, for Alex.

"You're correct; it is none of your business, but if you want the truth and my brother is the person I most respect, in the world, and he has kept my confidence for all these years; oddly as it seems, I have no problem telling you about it, because, frankly I don't care who knows about it, but I do suggest you keep this to yourself, or..."

"Or?" ZenJa asked nervously. "Is that some kind of threat?"

"Yes, as a matter of fact it is!"

"I murdered my mother and made it look like a suicide; hence the callous title Levy used, in his fictitious book, *'Swinging From The Rafters'!*"

"What in God's name did you do that for?" ZenJa cried.

"Because she was about to murder Levi and his father!"

"Why in hell would she do that?"

"Maybe a little thing called money!"

"She had more money than anyone would ever need!" ZenJa reasoned.

"She was broke, when she died, as odd as that may seem. She was being blackmailed about me and my father...you remember the handy man? If you recall whenever she had a book tour and signing, she boasted about the wonderful husband and son, Levi, and her impeccable heritage she had and all that shit?"

"Who was blackmailing her?"

"My father...you know, the handy man?" he repeated.

"How was she going to murder them?"

"Levi and his father, as you know, spent many wonderful times on their boat, cruising around the lake. Well, she hired a hit man, to kill them in their boat and that person was simply going to shoot them and let them drown, after they fell overboard."

"How do you know she was actually going to do that?" ZenJa asked.

"Because she hired me to do it!" Alex shouted.

"You're not serious!"

"Yes, I am. Why would I lie?"

"So how do you know she really meant it?"

"Because I told her I had taken care of matters and she actually watched, using binoculars, to see that I had done the dirty deed."

"Obviously, you didn't kill his father or Levi, for that matter."

"No, but she didn't know that. The whole event was staged and both Levi and his father were willing participants."

"The duo climbed back on board their boat, after I got back to the house and assured my mother they were dead and do you know what she wanted to do first?"

"No, I can't imagine!"

"She wanted to take me out to lunch! There was not a tear in her eye, no sudden change of heart...nothing...her heart was as cold as marble."

"So...?"

"So, that's where the story ends. You don't need to know anything more and I suggest, like I said before, keep your mouth shut! I will inform Levi that you know the story and will *not* be mentioning it again."

"That's what he meant when he said there are some family secrets that need to remain that, secret and loyalty and trust is his top priority, isn't it?"

"You finally figured that out, did you?"

"You saved Levi and his father's life and I admire you more, now than I ever did. Thank you for telling me about his, Alex; I now have a new perspective on the true meaning of family loyalty."

"Thanks for the coffee, but I guess I'll head over to Levi's office. I assume that's where he went when he almost knocked me down," Alex said and left the residence.

Levi grabbed some breakfast before he entered his office, to find peace and quiet at *'Le Château Napoléan'*. Upon entering and closing the door behind him, his cell phone rang and Alex was on the line.

"So, just before you almost plowed me be down, I overheard ZenJa asking you about our beloved mother's demise," Alex said and laughed.

"Yeah, I figured you did. What did you tell her?"

"I told her an elaborate tale about Mommy Dearest contracting me to '*hit*' both you and your father and how I had to end her sorry life for her."

"Do you think she bought it?" Levi asked and laughed.

"Hook, line, and sinker!"

"Well, at least now I'll know if I can truly trust her, down the road, won't I?" Levi sincerely stated.

"That's pretty rough, wouldn't you say?"

"I've always found it best not to trust anyone, then there are no surprises and you really didn't lie, all that much. You did say she was hung from the rafters, but she did it herself, so you simply added a little color to the story, right?" Levi added solidifying the secret of their mother's demise between themselves.

Alex remained silent, a smirk on his face, and failed to respond with the confidence that they were the only people who truly knew how their mother had died. And he planned to keep it that way, when another call came in on Levi's cell phone.

"I have to go; I have another call. Talk to you later," Levi said and took the next call that was an urgent message from Israeli Prime Minister Benjamin Netanyahu, concerning Brody Black, the man who had arrived like a hurricane, on Lake Winnipesaukee much the same way he left.

The Prime Minister informed Levi that Brody had missed a scheduled meeting he and his security team were to have, that morning and it appeared he had been kidnaped...or worse and Netanyahu needed Levi's help.

"I know, he boarded his flight at Manchester-Boston International Airport because ZenJa and I left him off late last night. Do you actually know if Brody ever arrived in Israel?" was the first question Levi asked.

"It *appears* he boarded the flight in Manchester, New Hampshire, from what we have determined. It made an emergency landing in Boston and it *appears* the flight left two hours later and continued to Paris and then Israel," the Prime Minister replied.

"What was the reason for the emergency landing?"

"Smoke in the cockpit, but nothing suspicious, from what we have gathered."

"Did the passengers disembark, in Boston and board another plane?"

"I just received word, the passengers did exit that flight and board another plane. I didn't know that until this moment."

"Any word if he was on the flight to Paris and disembarked in Israel?" Levi asked.

"No, there's no confirmation one way or another if he got on *any* plane, and there has been no report of any missing aircraft, as of yet!"

"Let me know if there's anything I can do from here or if you need me, there," Levi said and without hesitation, he was on his way to Israel and would arrive in less than twenty four hours.

THE END

For more adventures in the lives of Levi Harris and Brody Black read the next book, written by J. Cherbonneau entitled:

'RICOCHET'

Nestled among the beauty of the White Mountains and Lake Winnipeaski, in New Hampshire, is the tiny hamlet of Longberry where many missing girls and deep, dark secrets have been hidden for decades.

The reason many of those mysterious disappearances remained so long, without answers, was due to the fact that most of the girls, were not rich or famous, and certainly not beautiful. Their stories never grabbed the national media spotlight or nightly news.

No one in Longberry was above suspicion, even Zenja Beckwith, whose sister disappeared and undercover ATF agents, from around the area, were not to be ruled out, as suspects, either.

It would take outsiders, from the country of Israel to help end the mystery and bring closure to the families and people of that town.

Those children, from that small hometown, may have been found sooner, if they were

'ONLY THE PRETTY ONES'

J Cherbonneau has been writing novels, novellas, poetry, and children's books for over thirty five years. Included in these creations of fiction are trilogies and longer series about rogue Harley biker, DEA agents who are on missions to end corruption within the Administration and government.

Two published works she has to her credit are 'A Mortally Wounded Heart' and 'Vanish Into Thin Air', available on Amazon.com. The first creation encompasses a Vietnam War veteran's life and the woman who had an impact on his entire future.

'Vanish Into Thin Air' is a fictional novel concerning a Navy SEAL sniper who must decide whether to surrender is heart and soul to keep his family together or leave it all behind to honor God and country. Was he going to simply fade into the sunset and regret every breath he took or simply 'Vanish Into Thin Air'?

J Cherbonneau has also written other works about military veterans and documented veterans experiences for the Veteran's History Project, in conjunction with the Library of Congress.

J Cherbonneau lives in New Hampshire near her two children and five grandchildren.

Made in the USA
Middletown, DE
08 June 2016